"Welcome to 21st century Atlanta.

During your stay, depending on your tastes, you can cruise gay Midtown (I hear that the Inquisition Health Club has introduced manacles and chains to the aerobics class) or check out Reverend-Senator Stonewall's headquarters at Freedom Plaza (watch out for the Christian Militia guarding it, though) or attend a sky-clad Wiccan sabbat (by invitation only).

Avoid the courthouse, where the Cheyenne have turned out in full war-paint to renegotiate a nineteenth century land deal.

Also stay away from all cemeteries, at least until the police find out why someone is disinterring and crucifying corpses.

As you can tell, this is a lively novel, full of intricate plotting and engaging, off-beat characters. Among the latter are a gay detective, a Wiccan family, an ambitious televangelist with an eye on the White House, an artist whose medium is flesh and blood, a Cheyenne drag queen—and then there's poor Benji, who would just like to make it to his fifteenth birthday, assuming the MIBS don't get him first or his Baptist parents don't ground him for life because his new girlfriend is a witch.

Oh yes, I enjoyed this novel. Very much. It's a deft, unusual combination of mystery, social commentary, fantasy, and humor. I couldn't have told you where it was going until the last chapter, but I kept reading faster and faster to find out."

—P. C. Hodgell

# Praise for Keith Hartman's debut novel!

"*The Gumshoe, the Witch, and the Virtual Corpse* is a genuine original. Keith Hartman has written a merry mayhem with horror at its heart. Witty, inventive, and endlessly entertaining, Hartman's debut novel seamlessly weaves the plausible and the outrageous, the hilarious and the fearful. Where else can you find a murder mystery peopled by hackers and Baptists, detectives and witches, Cherokees and cross-dressers, cops and artists? This is an amazing book."
—Nancy Kress

"*The Gumshoe, the Witch, and the Virtual Corpse* is very well-written, tightly plotted, and contains a surprisingly large dose of humor as well. Liked his hero, loved his plot, and envied his style."
—Mike Resnick

"Keith Hartman's *The Gumshoe, the Witch, and the Virtual Corpse* kept me up half the night. It's robust, exhilarating, intense, bursting with satiric *wake-up-America* social commentary, and steamy enough to top the milk of human kindness with a heavy dose of foam. Literary cappuccino!"—Leslie What

"Keith Hartman's first novel, *The Gumshoe, the Witch, and the Virtual Corpse*, is a fantastic thrill ride through several meshed worlds: police work, the underside of art, Cherokee shamanism, Wicca, detection, high school, and more, all packed into a near-future Atlanta full of wild but plausible reality shifts. Hartman's characters are smart; his worldbuilding is broad, convincing, and exciting; his choice of detail is exquisite. Compelling and engrossing, this book grabbed me and didn't let go until long after the end."
—Nina Kiriki Hoffman

"Good mysteries need good writing to get up to speed, and Keith Hartman manages to floor the gas pedal in a sleek, next-century coupe while still keeping an eye on the rear-view mirror for all the Chandlers and Hammetts who've been down the same road before. His first novel is a fun ride with some darkly intriguing blind alleys along the way—read it with your seat belt on, and enjoy."—
K. W. Jeter, author of *Noir* and *Dr. Adder*

"This novel breaks some prime rules drummed into beginning writers—limit the number of main characters, limit the number of viewpoint characters—but Keith Hartman has taken a complex structure with a myriad of characters and a different viewpoint in every chapter and miraculously made it work. Chapter headings help the reader keep the well-drawn characters and their situations straight as the multiple story lines weave together into an engrossing novel with a logical and satisfying ending. Particularly fascinating is how Hartman mixes high tech and magic in a world where disparate belief systems exist in segregated parallels, but with all taken for granted, even when one group wants to destroy another. This is wonderful first novel by an exciting new author. I look forward to seeing more of his work."—Lee Killough

"I loved it. I love a book that breaks down the walls between genres, that just tells a story, the author trusting himself and the story enough to let it go wherever it leads him. I had a lot of fun with the novel. It made me think, made me smile, kept me on the edge of my chair—all the good things we look for in a book."—Charles de Lint

"Eleven points of view. Eight interwoven plot lines. Six days. One mystery, and a positive fifty-seven varieties of tone! Hartman has borrowed generously from both other genres and his own fertile imagination and thrown everything in by the double handful, producing an irresistibly entertaining book. The satirical take on the futures of various subcultures is particularly good."—Roland Green

"Keith Hartman has written more than a good science fiction novel with noir trappings. At a time when both gay and straight politics have hit a new low, we need more thoughtful books like this one; books that make us rethink issues of individual sovereignty in an ever more collectivist world. Hartman writes with a passion that can never be understood through something as limited as sexual politics. This novel is about integrity as the only hope for the human race."—Brad Linaweaver Author of *Moon of Ice*

# The Gumshoe,
# the Witch,
# and the Virtual Corpse

by

# Keith Hartman

*Keith Hartman*

THE GUMSHOE, THE WITCH, AND THE VIRTUAL CORPSE

An MM Publishing Book
Published by Meisha Merlin Publishing, Inc.
PO Box 7
Decatur, GA   30031

Editing & interior layout by Stephen Pagel
Copyediting & proofreading by Teddi Stransky
Cover art by Stephen Daniele
Cover design by Teddi Stransky

ISBN: 1-892065-05-3

http://www.angelfire.com/biz/MeishaMerlin

First MM Publishing edition: April 1999

Printed in the United States of America
0 9 8 7 6 5 4 3 2 1

## Dedication

For my parents, who gave me a love of books, a good education, and a surprising amount of understanding when I dropped out of my PhD program to become a starving writer.

## Acknowledgements

Thanks to my publisher, Stephe Pagel, my agent Eleanor Wood, and all the folks who critiqued the manuscript and gave me advice on rewrites, in particular: Jim Gilkeson, Thomas Fuller, Brad Linaweaver, Bill Ritch, Donny Moore, Mickey Desai, and The Dark River Writers.

Also, special thanks to Georgia Volunteer Lawyers for the Arts and Mary Anne Walser, Esquire, who really came through for me last summer.

# Chapter 1: The Gumshoe
## Sunday the Eighth, 8:21 PM

I set my drink down on the polished black table. It chimed politely, and a message lit up next to my empty glass.

"**Want another?** Yes / No / New Order"

I touched the spot that said "**Yes**" and ran my cash card through the slot on the side of the table. Mentally, I deducted another nine dollars from my rapidly dwindling bank balance.

The hotel waiter came over with another glass of iced mocha.

"Sure I can't get you a glass of wine, maybe a beer or something?" he asked, smiling.

"Not just now," I said.

"Clean living, huh?" he said, still smiling. He had wavy black hair, slightly pronounced canines, and brilliant green eyes. Of course, so did half the other kids his age. It was the clone look among the tragically hip that year.

Usually, I hated it.

"Uh. Yeah. Sort of." I mumbled, grinning stupidly. I have an annoyingly trigger happy blush reflex. My ex used to think it was cute.

"Well, my name's Gregor," the waiter said, leaning over, "Let me know if there's anything else you need."

We exchanged a glance that went on a little too long to be entirely proper, and then he left. Well, I am a sucker for friendly service. I slipped my cash card back into the table and was punching up his tip when I saw *her*.

Oh great. Like I needed this kind of trouble.

My client had just walked in through the hotel's big front doors. She was wearing a trench coat and dark sunglasses, a look that practically screamed "PLEASE! I am trying not to be recognized!" The ensemble was capped off by a huge floppy hat, which did succeed in covering half of her face but was so damn enormous that it called even more attention to her. Apparently her mother had never taught her how to properly accessorize for a stakeout.

I had chosen my table because it had a clear view of both the main entrance and the elevators, without being too close to either. I stood up and waved to her. The lobby of the DC Hilton is huge, so it took her a few seconds to spot me. When she did, she walked over, briskly.

"How nice to see you, Ms. Churchill," I lied, keeping my voice bland and conversational. "Why the Hell are you here?"

"I would appreciate you not using that word in jest."

"My apologies, ma'am." I had forgotten how uptight Southern Baptists can be about the H-word. "Why the *heck* are you here?"

She took the seat next to mine. The table chimed and asked if she would like to order, but she ignored it.

"I've decided to watch," she said.

Ms. Churchill was in her late thirties, tall for a woman, and always spoke in the confident manner of someone who expects to be taken seriously. Not the sort of woman that anyone would ever call "cute". Possibly "striking". Maybe even "attractive," if she were smiling at them. But I wouldn't know. She had never smiled at me.

"No." I said firmly.

"No, what?" she asked.

"No, this was not a part of the deal. No, you are not going to stay here. No, we are not going to run the risk that he will walk in the door, spot you, and blow our whole operation. Go back to your hotel. I'll bring you a full report and pictures when it's done."

She raised an eyebrow, then responded without bothering to look directly at me.

"I believe that *I* am the one paying for *your* services, Mr. Parker. I will go where I please."

"Then go find yourself another detective."

That got her attention. She paused, trying to decide if I was bluffing. I needed the money, badly. She needed me. No breeder PI could handle a case like this one. And no other queer detective would go anywhere near it.

Finally, she spoke. "What's the problem? So I watch it for myself. Afraid I might see something that you wouldn't have included in your report?"

Ms. Churchill had no tact. It was the one thing I liked about her.

"No. But this is not the way that things are done," I explained.

When my partner Jen had joined my firm a few years back, I had drilled three rules into her head. The first of them was: Never take a client on a stakeout. No matter how much they plead, no matter how quiet they promise to be, no matter how much money they offer. You don't do it. I had broken that rule once, back in 2019. It had nearly gotten both me and the client killed.

We sat there for a minute or two, neither of us willing to blink.

"Pictures are not good enough," she said slowly.

"Why not?"

"Because they're too easy to fake. Because I have to be *sure*."

She took off her glasses and tried to stare me down. We sat there looking at each other for almost a minute. Her eyes were brown. Not brilliant green, not vivid blue, not stunning violet, not lustrous gold. None of the designer colors. Brown. She was the first to look away. And when she finally spoke, her voice had lost its assertive bite.

"I don't know how it is with...your kind," she began, and then stopped. She was staring down at her purse, clutching it like it was some sort of talisman. I wondered what was so special about it. Had he bought it for her? Or was it something inside? A picture of them together? A love note? It didn't matter. I needed to make her go.

"Joseph and I, we..." she started to say, and then trailed off again.

I waited for her to go on, but she never did. I didn't know what to say, either, so we sat there in silence. When this was all over, she would go back to her Christian neighborhood in North Georgia, back to Baptist News Network and *Revelations* magazine. I would go back to the gay ghetto of Midtown Atlanta, back to Queer-TV and hanging out in coffee shops. The only thing we had in common was that we didn't like each other.

But she was right about one thing: *I* would never trust a picture on something as important as this. Images are too easy to play with. An overlay here, a deletion there, and voilá, you can make an incriminating photo of anyone. I know more than a few private detectives who have found it cheaper to invest in a good graphics program than in good legwork.

This was all wrong. I should make her leave. Or get up and leave myself. Just get up and walk away from this lousy case and back to my office. I would just have to tell Jen that she'd have to sell her other kidney to pay our bills this month.

Ms. Churchill doesn't like homosexuals, and I'm not much keener on Southern Baptists. Probably because I was raised by a pair of them. But then, my client and I had never pretended to like each other. And I guess even honest hatred is at least an honest connection between two people. I studied her face, trying to figure out what was going on behind her eyes.

We sat in silence for a few more minutes. Finally, she looked away from me, out into the lobby. Scanning the crowd, she did a momentary double take, and then stared intently at a kid in his early twenties who was hanging out by the glass elevators.

"That's Daniel, isn't it?" she said, pointing.

"Yes" I answered, gently taking her outstretched hand and placing it back on the table. I was surprised that she could recognize him. The last time she'd seen Daniel had been in my office, a week ago. He'd had curly black hair then, and dark eyes and beautiful bronze skin. I never did find out what sort of gig that was all for; somebody wanting a Mediterranean look, I guess. Greek slave boy or some such thing. Now Daniel was back to blond hair and blue eyes, which makes him look even more like a kid. I don't know if those are his real colors or not, but it was the way he'd looked when I first met him. And blond suits him. Like a collie. Cute and playful and...and *God damn it he was smiling at me again.*

I frowned, hoping he would take the hint and buzz off. He didn't. He had been playing this game with me all afternoon, and it was beginning to wear thin. Thompson, the guy we were going after, was both smart and perceptive, and any little thing might tip him off that he was being set up. So I did not need my temporary operative making faces at me from across the lobby. Still not making eye contact with Daniel, I mouthed the words "KNOCK IT OFF!" The bastard winked at me. Finally, I glared at him, trying to shake him off without drawing any more attention to the two of us. Daniel feigned a hurt look and went back to watching the glass elevators go up and down. I prayed that no one had been watching our little melodrama.

That matter settled, I turned back to my client. Ms. Churchill was staring at Daniel, a mixture of contempt and curiosity on her face.

"You shouldn't look directly at him." I said. "It calls attention to both of you." The hat gave her some cover, but it was still damn risky having her here. If Thompson spotted her, the whole operation would go up in smoke.

"Why in the world is he wearing that shirt?" she asked, ignoring my advice about staring. Daniel was wearing his usual work clothes, ripped jeans and a white tank top printed with a disturbingly realistic crucifix. Christ's final agonies, captured in vivid color and full anatomic detail, over the slogan "And You Think *You've* Had a Rough Day?"

She continued staring. "Isn't that a bit...?"

"Trust me," I said, "Daniel's a pro, and he knows exactly what signals he's sending. The crucifix is part of his advertising."

"*Advertising?*"

"Yeah. If he were older, he'd probably wear a rainbow flag or a pink triangle on his T-shirt. But since most of the gay men under 23 are Roman Catholic, the kids have all adopted Catholic regalia as a sort of uniform."

"Roman Catholic?" She looked at me skeptically, as if I were making the whole thing up just to test her gullibility. "Why on earth would they be converting to that?"

I was kind of surprised that she didn't know. But then, I guess outsiders don't follow demographic trends in the gay community too closely.

"They don't convert," I said. "They're just born that way. It's one of the side effects of the test." She continued to stare at me as if I was out of my mind. Well, at least she wasn't staring at Daniel anymore.

"Think of it this way," I said. "What will you do if the test comes back saying that your child is gay?"

She looked down at her belly. She wasn't showing yet, and it would be another month before they could do amniocentesis safely. She didn't say anything, but we both knew what would happen if the genetic test came back positive. The Southern Baptist Convention doesn't like abortions. But it *really* doesn't like homosexuals.

"That's why there haven't been a lot of gay Baptists born in the last 23 years," I said, "or Methodists. Or Mormons. Or Lutherans. You all make a lot of noise about being pro-life, but in the clinch, you make…'exceptions'. Not the Catholics, though. You gotta love the Pope. She may be a reactionary old cow, but at least she's consistent."

Ms. Churchill turned her cold stare back to Daniel. I don't know why I kept baiting her like that. I hated the case, but that wasn't her fault.

"He's practically a child," she said. "How do you know that he's even Joseph's type?"

"I know because I did my job," I said flatly. For the past two weeks I had been shadowing Joseph Thompson, and I knew things about him that no straight detective would ever have picked up on. I knew which people got that second glance when he passed them in the street. I knew which people he talked to when he shared an elevator ride with them. I even knew which waiters he over-tipped at his favorite restaurants.

I had also been into his financial records, and knew that Thompson was in the habit of withdrawing several hundred dollars in cash every few weeks, usually right before one of his business trips. No one uses cash anymore. Not unless they're trying to hide something. Like hiring a private detective. Or a hustler. I had a feeling that Thompson knew exactly what boys like Daniel were for.

I felt Ms. Churchill stiffen next to me. Speak of the Devil. Thompson had just come in through the Hilton's big revolving doors. He was still dressed for his job: tailored jacket, bright tie, expensive shoes. He worked for a Southern Baptist advertising firm, doing PR work for one of their senators. He was 34, the same age as me, a little too attractive, and not married. I bet the gossip around the office was already becoming a problem.

Of course, I could be wrong about Thompson. Maybe he was really was just a thirty-four-year-old man who had decided it was time to settle down and start a family. Maybe he was getting married for all the right reasons. He did trip my *Gadar*, but that doesn't necessarily mean anything; evangelicals have been known to scramble my sixth sense about men. It's just that they do all the same things as a guy who's trying to pick you up. They stand too close. They smile too much. They look into your eyes with feigned sincerity and pretend to hang on your every word. All getting you ready for the sales pitch.

Daniel intercepted Thompson while the man was waiting for an elevator. I wasn't close enough to make out their conversation, but Thompson looked at his watch, so I guess Daniel must have asked him the time. I watched Thompson's eyes drift from his watch to Daniel's shoes, up Daniel's rather pleasant physique, and finally come to rest on the saint medallion around Daniel's neck. I could tell from Thompson's smile that he knew what it meant.

In adopting the Catholic roster of Saints, the gay subculture has added a few of its own. There's Saint Marilyn, patron of blonds and the blond at heart. Saint Judy, the patron of drag queens and twelve-step programs. Saint Liz, patron of marriage and other hopeless causes. Saint Dolly, patron of big dreams and silicone. Daniel was wearing a medallion depicting the Madonna—not the holy virgin, but the like-a-virgin. She who is the patron saint and protector of all sex workers.

Beside me, Ms. Churchill was staring straight at them. Fortunately, Thompson's attention seemed to be completely focused on Daniel, with none left over to notice us. I looked at my client. There were a lot of good reasons for her to be any place but here right now. Even if Thompson didn't spot her, there was always the risk that she would snap and blow everything. I tried to read her expression. How much of what she was seeing did she understand? Could she read the body language of the transaction that was taking place? The way that Thompson stepped into Daniel's space, so close that they were almost touching. The way that Daniel laughed a little too hard at some joke of Thompson's, and steadied himself on Thompson's shoulder. Soon, Daniel would ask some inane question about the man's family. Ask to see a picture of his sister, or something else that would give Thompson an excuse to pull out his wallet. An excuse to show that he was carrying cash.

When my client spoke it startled me. "Doesn't it bother you to exploit Daniel like this?" She had not taken her eyes off them.

"Daniel is a twenty-two-year-old with a public high school education." I told her. "He's bright, so he taught himself to read, a little at least. What exactly do you expect him to do for a living? Become a journalist? How about a computer programmer?

A quantum physicist? Daniel does what Daniel has to. And who's really exploiting Daniel, anyway? The guy who is willing to pay him $300 an hour for sex, or the guy who'll pay him $9.75 an hour for flipping burgers?"

I should have stopped there. I didn't. "And if I were in your shoes right now, I would not complain about *other people* exploiting Daniel."

She turned. The look she shot at me would have made a cobra curl up and whimper. I admitted defeat and looked away.

Ms. Churchill had never pretended to like me, but she did need me. For now, at least. My firm has three listings in the yellow pages. There's the number for "Fortress Security", which we use to solicit corporate clients. Then there's "Jennifer Gray, licensed psychic detective", which Jen uses to pull in the new age crowd. Ms. Churchill had known what skills this particular job required. She had called our third line, the one for "Drew Parker, PI—proudly serving the gay and lesbian community."

When I turned back to Ms. Churchill, she was staring at Daniel and Thompson again, looking as though she could control the situation through sheer force of will.

"You don't have to be here." I said quietly. "I will tell you what happens. I have no reason to lie to you."

"No," she answered, her voice surprisingly soft. "I have to be sure."

Right on schedule, Thompson pulled out his wallet and showed a picture to Daniel. I could feel the tension building in my client. Screw the bonus.

"Forget this," I told her. "Go home. Ask him to get a blood test before the wedding. It's a little embarrassing, but other people have done it."

She turned to me, her eyes flashing. For a second I thought she was going to scream at me, but when she spoke it was very slowly, as if she was picking each word with care.

"Mr. Parker, you may not understand this, but I am very much in love with Joseph, and I wouldn't care even if he did test positive. So what if he has the gay gene? We all have a propensity to some form of evil. Our own demon. But not all of us act on it. I don't care what's in Joseph's DNA. I care about what is in his heart. I have to know if he loves me, or if he's just using me."

I knew I shouldn't say it. But I did. "With men, it's always a little of both."

We looked back in time to see Daniel and Thompson get on an elevator together. The doors closed. I watched Ms. Churchill's expression slowly crumble. Her mouth go slack. Her lips tremble. Her eyes grow damp.

When she snatched up her purse and started for the elevator, I grabbed her arm. She shook it free, angry.

"Look," I said, "if you've seen enough, go home. I'll make a full report. You'll have your answer. But if we do this, we do this right. No unresolved questions. No doubts. No ambiguous situations that he can talk his way out of. And that means we give them a head start. Fifteen minutes. To let things...develop."

For a moment, I thought she might actually take my advice and leave. Go to the airport. Fly home. Wait for my call. Instead, she gave me an icy *"Fine"* and flopped back down on a bench.

While she sat there thinking about...no. Skip it. I don't even want to guess at what she was thinking about. I sat down a few feet away and flipped on the throat mike under my tie. I had some final preparations to make.

"Sherwin." I said, under my breath.

There was a slight buzz as the speaker in my left ear came to life, and then Sherwin's sullen voice.

"Yeah boss, what is it this time?"

The company that I purchased Sherwin from claims that the program is supposed to adapt its word choice and inflection to suit its user. I am not sure what it says about me, but my particular copy seems to be evolving into an insolent manic-depressive.

I took the palm display out of my jacket pocket.

"Sherwin, pull up the photos I shot this morning."

"Yeah, whatever."

Sherwin displayed the first shot: a hotel maid about to clean a room. The angle wasn't right.

"Next."

Sherwin obliged and produced an image I had shot a couple seconds later. Still not the one I was looking for.

"Next."

Sherwin pulled up a third.

Bingo. I touched a spot on the display and said, "Enlarge on this."

Sherwin zeroed in on the maid's pass key. I pulled a piece of cardboard and a hole punch out of my pocket and went to work on a duplicate. I glanced at Ms. Churchill, but I couldn't read her expression at all. Whatever was going on behind those eyes would stay a mystery to me.

I checked my watch. Five minutes. Upstairs, it would be starting. Daniel and Thompson. A first kiss. Daniel would taste like that wintergreen gum he's always chewing. Thompson would run his fingers through Daniel's curls. Clothed bodies moving against each other.

I had never even seen Thompson until two weeks ago. He had never crossed me. Never hurt me. Never given me any reason to hate him. But I was about to destroy his life. Oh, he would probably get over losing Ms. Churchill. But his secret would be out. He'd be finished at his job. They'd never let him in a Southern Baptist church again. He'd lose his friends, his family. Maybe he'd be able to start over again. Get a job in a gay firm, move into the gay subculture, build a new life. It might even turn out good for him. But I wasn't giving him a choice.

Eight minutes. Daniel would be loosening the man's tie. Thompson would be lifting Daniel's tank top, sliding a hand over the muscles of Daniel's stomach. Daniel's arms around his waist. Daniel's jeans pressed up against Thompson's khakis.

I had not wanted to take this case. When Ms. Churchill called, I had turned her down. Then I turned her down again. And again. But she had been relentless. She just kept saying it over and over again: "I have a right to know." Then she'd told me what Thompson does for a living, and who he does it for. The Reverend Senator Zachariah Stonewall. Just the sort of asshole that my father used to listened to. And probably still does, for all I know.

Ten minutes. Their clothing would be in piles on the floor, thrown over the backs of chairs, lying on the bed. They would be learning each other's secrets. Does Thompson like to kiss, or to be kissed? Does Daniel like to have his ears nibbled on? His neck? His fingers?

I hoped that Thompson was a jerk. I hoped that this woman beside me meant nothing to him, that she was just a convenient bit of camouflage he had acquired so that he could go on working at his wonderful job and fucking his beautiful men. I didn't want it to be anything more complicated.

But then, I would never know. I would never know what he really felt for her. On bad days, did he think of her and smile? Were there special things he had never told to anyone else in the world but her? Moments they had shared? Did he daydream about the children they would have? Kicking a soccer ball with their daughter? Telling a bedtime story to their son?

Twelve minutes. By now they would know each other's private sounds. The little gasps, or moans, or growls a man makes when he forgets himself in sex. His intimate sounds, as unique as fingerprints. I wonder if the FBI keeps a file of them. They seem to know everything else about us.

"I have a right to know." She had said that over and over again. And damn it, she was right.

Fifteen minutes. I stood up. Ms. Churchill grabbed her purse and followed me into an elevator. I pressed the button for the 47th floor. She leaned her face against the glass, watching the lobby drop away beneath us.

"Have you ever been in love, Mr. Parker?"

The question surprised me. She had not looked up. The trees in the lobby grew smaller in the distance.

"Yes." I said.

"With Daniel?"

I laughed. "Lord no. Whatever gave you that idea?"

"I've seen the way he acts around you."

Maybe she understood more than I had given her credit for.

"I just pulled him out of a bar fight once, and he's been following me around ever since."

"Are you two sleeping together?"

Ah. I could see where this was going now. She was hurt, and looking for some way to get under my skin.

"No. Daniel's too...cheerful. I mean, *all the time*. It would be like having sex with a cocker spaniel."

She thought about that answer for awhile.

"Don't you worry about him?"

"Daniel's a smart boy. He carries a taser when he works."

"That's not what I meant."

Another elevator passed us going down. A man and a woman, dressed for a party. Our own glass cage raced silently upward.

"You two aren't...?"

"No," I said again. For the first time since we got on the elevator, she looked at me.

"Why not?"

I almost took the easy way out and said that Daniel was too young for me. But that wasn't quite it. The truth was complicated, and I didn't know how to make her understand it. Hell, I couldn't even make Daniel understand it. Daniel is just too...innocent? No, that's not right. Daniel has slept with more men than Mata Hari. And yet, somehow Daniel has never managed to fall in love.

And I don't want to be the first. I don't want to be the one who ruins the fantasy for him. I don't want to be the one who can't live up to all his impossible twenty-two-year-old expectations of love.

In his overly dramatic way, Daniel had once told me that while his body might have racked up the mileage, his heart was still virgin territory. But I don't want a virgin. I want someone who has been through the whole show before. Someone who has been hurt, and stepped on, and had every last illusion shattered. Someone who comes to me cautiously, knowing that falling in love is easy and staying in love is hard, that passion dies and most relationships are doomed before they start. Someone I can love as an equal, not a student. Someone...like Ms. Churchill, actually. Maybe that's why I had taken the case.

The elevator stopped at the forty-seventh floor. We stepped off and walked down the hall to 4717, the room in which Thompson was staying. I got the fiber optic snake out of my pocket, unlooped it, and slid a strand under the door.

"What's that?" asked Ms. Churchill.

"It's a camera on a fiber-optic cable," I explained as I plugged the free end into my palm display. Then I whispered, "Sherwin, record."

She grabbed my wrist. "I told you. With *my eyes*. I have to see it with my eyes."

I looked into those eyes and wanted to say something, but anything I could say would be stupid. So I just shrugged, and then I glanced down at the image on my palm display anyway: I don't go into a room blind. She was certainly going to get an eyeful. I put the palm display down on the floor and slid my duplicate pass key into the lock. The indicator light flashed from red to green.

The door opened quietly. Well, quietly enough. Daniel and Thompson were making more than enough noise to cover our movements. From the doorway, I could see a pair of feet hanging over the edge of the bed. I stepped forward into the room and saw the whole picture. Daniel, on his back, a look of ecstasy on his face. Thompson, his back to us, his face buried in Daniel's neck, his hips grinding into Daniel. I stood there, looking at them, reminding myself that I am not a jealous person. Looking at Daniel's beautiful muscles, tensing and relaxing in time to Thompson's hips. Looking at the expression on Daniel's face, how it changed with every twinge of pleasure. How he bites his lip, how he opens his mouth, how he arches his neck. I wondered if it was an act, or if he really enjoyed his work this much. I must have stared at Daniel a little too long, because when I glanced back at Ms. Churchill, she already had the gun out.

## Chapter 2: The Artist
## Sunday the Eighth, 8:32 PM

The applause died and the crowd broke up into pockets of conversation. Foy Kucu finished toweling off. She grabbed a glass of wine from a waiter and made her way over. Wiping a last bit of vanilla frosting out of her belly button, she addressed me.

"So James, what did *you* think?"

Foy had been born Francis Desoto, but had had her name legally changed when she began doing performance art. Her current appellation is a rather transparent anagram for "Fuck You." A fact which I think elegantly sums up her artistic career to date.

"Foy! What can I say? It was...finger licking good."

Foy noted my simple evasion and frowned. I have to play her just right. Foy loves praise as much as the next person, but she doesn't respect it. The trick is to take her down a notch without getting her too mad. Later, when we're alone, I'll risk a more detailed critique.

Not that I really need to stay on Foy's good side. She's not on the grant review board or anything. But she does have powerful friends. This is the fourth year in a row that she's won an NEA grant, and the second year she's been asked to perform at the awards ceremony.

For this year's piece, "Bodies Impolitic," Foy had stripped naked and smeared her body with vanilla frosting. For the next forty-five minutes she had rolled various parts of her anatomy in chocolate sprinkles while screaming "Nigger!", "Honkie!", "Jungle Bunny!", and a slew of other racial epithets at the audience. It would have been funny if Foy didn't take herself so damn seriously.

"How did you come up with the idea for that piece?" I asked. I half expected Foy to come clean and admit that she had been cleaning her pantry and decided to use some items before they hit their expiration dates. Instead, she launched into some thesis on how foodstuffs have historically been used as symbols of racial oppression.

"Like, have you noticed how the *white* cake is *angel food*, but the *black* cake is *devil's food*?"

Fortunately, I was spared further lecture on the social relevance of baked goods by the timely arrival of Green Davidsdaughter and ¥. Green was wearing something shapeless made of undyed wool. Knowing her, the wool probably came from free-range sheep who had signed documents of informed consent before being sheared. ¥ was wearing a kilt, bobby socks, plaid beret, and a leather harness. Going for the Catholic school girl in bondage look, I guess.

"Hello...?" I started to greet the man, then realized I had no idea how to pronounce ¥. I turned to his companion.

"Hello, Green." Green was actually the Christian name her parents had chosen for her, and she had kept it. However, she found their surname, "Davidson," to be hopelessly sexist, and had changed that.

"Hello, James," she said, a little too formally. I couldn't decide whether she had come over to network with Foy or with me. We both have good contacts on the board.

"James," said Green, "I don't believe you two have met before." She motioned to ¥.

"No," I admitted. I had, however, seen his most recent play. It was an adaptation of *Romeo and Juliet*, performed completely without the use of nouns. "Naming, speaking, cataloging, indexing, identifying and for what? For what to name? To bloom by any other would be as sweet."

"James, this is..." said Green, holding up a palm display which was flashing the ¥ character. I had been wondering how she would handle introductions.

"Pleased to meet you," I said.

She turned to ¥. "And this is James Calerant."

¥ looked me over.

"Calerant. Odd name. French?"

How anyone calling himself ¥ could call my name odd was beyond me.

"Actually, it's an acronym. C.A.L.E.R.A.N.T."

¥ waited for me to explain what the initials stood for. I let him go on waiting.

My legal name is James Coleman-Abernathy—LeBrock-Ericson—RuSan-Angleson—Newberg-Tang. While I can understand my ancestors' desire to keep their names intact after marriage, I do wish that someone had thought about the consequences before one Susan Coleman-Abernathy—LeBrock-Ericson had married one Paul RuSan-Angleson—Newberg-Tang and created me. Although I wish to honor my forbearers, there is simply no way to fit a name like that in the corner of a painting, so I took the initials and started signing my work CALERANT. My ancestors will just have to settle for one letter apiece.

There was an awkward silence, as my fellow artists realized that I was not going to offer further explanation. Finally, Foy broke the silence.

"So, what did you think of my piece?" she asked, indifferently. Green jumped right in. "Shocking!"

"*Wonderfully* shocking," agreed ¥, his face beaming.

Foy stared at me, making my continued silence conspicuous.

"Yeah right," I mumbled. "Shocking."

Foy glared at me, then shrugged it off. I had not crossed the line—yet.

Four thousand years of civilization, of art, and it all finally boils down to the pursuit of...shock value. It's a stupid game, but it is the only one in town. And I can't win if I don't play.

As if reading my mind, Green turned to me. "Speaking of performances, shouldn't you be getting into costume, James?"

"I *am* in costume for my piece," I told her, gesturing at my tuxedo. "And I intend to go on drinking this free booze right up until the moment they drag me up on stage and pry the glass out of my hand."

Green laughed politely. ¥ smiled. Foy looked at me suspiciously.

"Just what are you doing tonight?"

"Something special," I said. "I think it will make quite an impression on you." That is, if *anything* can impress these people. They are all so jaded that nothing can hold their attention for long. Their art isn't about life, or passion, or even ideas. It's about ennui. I would love to shatter their complacency. I would love to pull out some of my old material, one of the paintings I did before prison, just to show these three horsemen of the avant-garde what real art is all about. But they wouldn't understand it. You have to have a soul for that.

While I was musing, my companions had started in on their list of "other artists we hate." Currently, they were sharing insights on the work of choreographer Ermegarde Van-Gelder, a.k.a. the one-step-wonder. I considered joining in, but frankly, Ermegarde is just too easy a target. She's built her entire career on one step, a sort of nauseating spin. At her first performance, she went out and did that one step over and over again for an hour and a half. Then the NEA gave her a grant, which allowed her to hire a troop of dancers—who went out and each did that same damn step for an hour and a half. Then the National Endowment for the Arts gave her a really big grant, which had allowed her to hire an orchestra and costumes and an even bigger troop of dancers...who still go out on stage and do that same damn step over and over again.

While the three of them dissected Ermegarde's latest work, I noticed a couple of my men moving into position. I grimaced. They were not blending in as well as I would have liked. I made a mental note: Next time I hire security, I'm going to insist on seeing what they look like in a tuxedo, first. Even dressed up, these two looked like they belonged in some beer bar throwing out drunk patrons. Oh, well, at least no one seemed to have noticed them yet.

I glanced over at Cynthia, who was coordinating my hired help for this little performance. Cynthia *was* being noticed, but for all the right reasons: black dress, auburn hair, crimson lips, ebony spiked heels, brilliant green eyes, and a face as exquisitely painted as the Sistine Chapel. It is such a pleasure to work with a professional. Cynthia made eye contact briefly and flashed me the OK sign. Excellent.

The chatter around me fell silent as Theresa Sanchez joined our group. Her vivid red dress screamed "I want to be the center of attention," while her manner indicated that she was clearly not comfortable with the role.

"Hello," she said, trying to sound more confident than she was. Green pretended not to notice her, while Foy affected a sneer. Theresa Sanchez was sleeping with one of the members of the grant board, and nobody liked her.

"Such an *interesting* piece," said ¥, motioning across the room to where one of Theresa's paintings was hanging. His inflection on the word "interesting" was unmistakably patronizing. He looked at me, as if to say "the ball is in your court."

I smiled at Theresa and said, "Actually, I think it's brilliant."

¥ blinked in surprise. Green's jaw dropped. Foy looked at me as if I had gone out of my mind.

"I think there is more real painting in that one empty eye socket than in all the other paintings done since 1950 put together."

Theresa was a bit surprised herself, not sure how to accept such a gushing fountain of praise. I took her arm and lead her over to her painting, all the while expounding on her composition, her choice of subject matter, her breathtaking use of light, the eerie texture she had created for the rotting flesh of the corpse. I found it surprisingly easy, since I actually believed what I was saying. Theresa has a certain spark, a way of getting passion onto canvas that I haven't seen in a long time.

In a very small way, she reminds me of Alicia. Alicia had the sort of gift that comes along once in a generation or so. She had been able to crawl into people's heads and catch what she found there in colored pigments. Not abstract. If anything, her paintings were more real than the real thing. Looking at one of her portraits, it was like seeing the subject's naked soul. It was almost voyeuristic. Alicia had brought out the best in me. Oh, I had better technique, but she was the flash of insight in all the art we made together. I did my best work with her. And I will never be that good again.

Theresa's painting didn't come close. It was juvenile and over-studied. But still, it had that glimmer of something great. It gave me hope. Hope that bits of Alicia's gift might still be floating around in the gene pool, to arise some day in another artist. Theresa would never make it, of course. Sleeping with that board member had been a stupid opening gambit. It had gotten her work shown, but it had also alienated all the other board members and every artist in town. True, as long as her patron stayed happy with her, the grant money would keep flowing. But when things went sour between them, she would be left out in the cold. And things always go sour, eventually.

In the meantime, though, Theresa Sanchez had that one useful connection, and I was making quite an impression on her. That night, she would go home to her patron, bubbling with enthusiasm for me, telling him what a brilliant and insightful person I am. The human mind is a funny thing. Her patron would cling to that first impression of me long after he has discarded the woman who said it.

From out of the corner of my eye I caught sight of Letticia Washington, the newest appointee to the grant review board. I did not yet have an in with her. She was standing behind us, inspecting the Sanchez painting. I continued my critique of the piece.

"And I am particularly drawn to the starkness of the shapes," I said, gesturing to opposing corners of the painting. "The skull and broken glass here, the amputated breast and nursing child here. The way they relate to each other across the empty center is almost, well...dare I say it? Duchampian."

"Really?" said Ms. Washington, speaking up. "What makes you say that?"

"Oh," I said, feigning a start. "Well, let me think of a good example. Hm. Are you familiar with Duchamp's multi-media work *The Bride Laid Barren by her Bachelors, Even?*"

"Why yes!" she said, her face betraying her excitement. "In fact, I did my masters' thesis on it!"

"Really!" I said. "What a coincidence." Yes, quite a coincidence. Almost as if her thesis were easily accessible to anyone who bothered to go hunting for it at Harvard's web site.

"You know," I said, "I've always wondered about those cracks in the painting's glass."

"Yes, yes!" she agreed, "Those are by far the most interesting thing about *The Bride.*"

"Yes," I responded. "They almost seem..." However, before I could fully spring the trap, the lights dimmed.

"I'm sorry, it's time for my number. Perhaps we could discuss this later? Maybe lunch next week?"

"Yes," said Ms. Washington. "Let us do that."

I took my leave of her, and made my way though the crowd. The performance space wasn't much, just a raised platform in the middle of the gallery. Elegant people politely jockeyed for the best place from which to view it. I reached the platform and climbed the few steps. Cynthia winked at me as I passed. Four of my men had taken up positions near the corners of the stage, while Cynthia and two more were standing by the steps.

I looked out at the crowd, waiting for them to quiet down. A few seconds later the lights came up on me, and I was rewarded with the most delicious silence. So silent you could hear the anticipation. "What is he going to do this year?" I was the final act of the night, and I had my reputation to live up to. They were waiting for the moment, the moment when I would do something more shocking than anything they had ever seen before. More shocking than Foy's naked, screaming frosting show. More shocking than Larry slitting his own wrist on stage. More shocking than Youssef relieving himself and then whipping his posterior with pages from the Koran. Something new. I smiled. These people had no idea what they were in for.

The stage was bare, except for a large easel draped with canvas. I stood perfectly still for 15 seconds, just to let the suspense build. Then I walked over and slowly unveiled it.

The painting was huge, 8' x 6', like something you'd expect to find in the DeMedici's summer home.

It was a Dutch family dinner scene. The mother, scolding a child. Two sons kicking each other under the table. Father, very proper, reaching for another plate of food. And in the lower left hand corner there was a girl who was turned around in her chair, staring straight out of the painting. It was as if she knew the painter, and had turned around to look at him while he worked. She was the only figure in the painting who wasn't doing anything, and yet she was what the painting was all about.

I could feel the audience's confusion. This painting was supposed to be shocking?

"This year," I announced, "I have used my grant money to purchase this painting. It was completed in 1787 by Thomas Allen Bruce, a British expatriate living in the Netherlands."

The audience's confusion grew into a quiet murmur, almost too soft to hear. But I knew what they were saying "That's it? He bought a painting?"

I continued. "Bruce has never attained much fame. He was a competent craftsman, but this seems to be the only time that he ever achieved real brilliance. Why? Why in this one painting? Never before, and never again. Was it this woman in the corner? Did she mean something special to him? Were they lovers? Or friends? Or did she just have some special fire that impressed him, that sparked something in his soul? We will never know. Since Bruce was not a major artist, no one ever recorded the details of his life and his associations."

The murmur grew louder, past the threshold of audibility. "Has he lost his mind? All he did was buy some stupid painting that no one has ever heard of?"

"I purchased the painting from the Wake museum, which recently had to liquidate a portion of its collection for financial reasons. It was last exhibited fifty years ago, and has been sitting in the museum's basement ever since."

The voices grew louder, to the soft hiss of a hundred whispers. "He's lost it. His edge is gone." I tried not to smile at how well things were going.

"Think about that. Never shown once in all that time. Sitting in the dark for fifty years. Cared for. Preserved. But unseen. Something beautiful. Something that had once had meaning. Consigned to slowly be forgotten. But I won't allow that to happen."

The whispers became the clamor of distinct voices. Coughs. People clearing their throats. The sounds of a crowd that is losing interest. I saw Foy start to turn away. Then she did a double take and looked back. She must have seen the flash of gold, and realized what was in my hand.

A.S.C. It has her initials on it. Strange that it should be the one thing of Alicia's that I've kept. I spent most of our relationship trying to get her to quit. But then, I guess she was right about that, after all. It certainly wasn't cigarettes that killed her.

I flipped the lighter open and struck it. On cue, the stage lights dimmed. The tiny flame glowed bright and steady, throwing eerie shadows across my face. I knew from rehearsals how disturbing my features would appear. I held the flame under the lower right corner of the painting.

The whispering stopped dead. So silent I could hear the popping of the frame as it heated. I turned back to look at the audience. They were looking at each other, not sure how they were supposed to react. The frame caught with a sudden crackling.

There was movement in the audience. Someone took a step forward. Indecisive.

The canvas of the right corner caught. The painter's name illuminated for a moment by the flame. Then gone.

Someone else started for the stage, stopped short. A voice in the audience shouted "He's crazy!"

The flames danced upward. The younger brothers vanished in a rush of orange. The mother turned slowly brown. Someone else yelled "Stop him!" More movement. Hesitant. Restrained. Ineffectual.

The mother grew blacker, blacker, blacker. Gone. The father, still reaching for the potatoes, darkened beneath a flickering orange curtain.

Suddenly it broke. Three different people bolting from audience and trying to rush the stage. My security caught and held them. This was where things would get dicey. If these people had more guts than I gave them credit for, this wouldn't work. If more than five tried to rush the stage, they would make it.

My security pinned the three with gumption up against the stage. I watched the audience, waiting for the sign. Finally, it came. One of them broke and charged the stage, but no one followed her. I looked in amazement. It was Foy! I had never guessed she had it in her.

Cynthia caught her at the steps and wrestled her into an arm lock. I motioned for her to bring Foy up to me.

Squirming, Foy glared at me.

"This isn't funny, Jim."

The father vanished. Gone. The flames licked at the curls of the girl. *Who had she been?*

"It's not supposed to be."

Cynthia muscled Foy forward. The girl's hair went from blond to brunette, to black. Her face stared out from behind the flames.

I grabbed Foy's hair, pulling her head up, making her watch.

"Look at it. It's making you feel something. Loss. Pain. When was the last time you ever felt anything, Foy? When was the last time a piece of art made you cry? Now it has meaning again."

I watched her eyes. Scanning the burning wreckage. Trying to catch every detail before the flames destroyed them forever.

There was nothing left now but the girl. She had been at the furthest, lowermost corner from the point of ignition. I had planned it that way.

"That's it. Look at her. Memorize every detail. Those lips. That expression. Those eyes."

But even as we looked, the eyes vanished into the flames, and there was only an empty hole where she had been.

"Now it's done." I said. I moved my lips to Foy's ear. "For the rest of your life, you're going to remember that face. And it will always be something special. Something beautiful that you lost. Isn't that better than having it lie forgotten in a basement?"

The frame collapsed in on itself, falling off the easel into a burning pile on the stage. There was not a sound from the audience. Cynthia released Foy, who continued to stare at the fragments. I walked off stage, down the steps.

The audience parted in front of me, still too stunned to make a sound. I walked out the big double doors of the gallery, and heard the first odd solitary clap. Then a few more picked it up, and it built to a roar. They want to be shocked, to remember that they are alive, if only for a moment. Give the people what they want.

I'll have to call Foy in a couple of days, after she's had a chance to calm down. She really surprised me tonight. There is passion in her after all. And in the end she had understood.

Sometimes you can only save a thing by destroying it.

## Chapter 3: The Gumshoe
## Sunday the Eighth, 8:47 PM

It was a 9mm. A small gun, the sort of thing that would fit in a lady's handbag, but still quite capable of punching a nice size hole in someone. At the moment, this particular 9mm was about to blow a nice size hole in the back of Mr. Thompson. And from the angle she was shooting at, it stood a good chance of blowing a nice size hole in Daniel as well. I lunged.

The gun went off and then I knocked her arm back. Or maybe I knocked her arm back and then the gun went off. My brain wasn't working quite fast enough to tell which had happened first. She hadn't been ready for the gun's recoil, and my shove had put her further off balance. Ms. Churchill caught herself on the wall and looked up at me, her eyes like cold fire. For once, I had no trouble reading her expression. She brought the gun back around toward me.

I caught her full in the jaw with an uppercut. It didn't knock her out, but it did take her mind off shooting me for a few seconds. While she was disoriented, I risked a quick glance at the bed. Just in time to see Thompson barreling up at me.

I grabbed his arm and tried to roll him into one of those fancy aikido throws that would have sent him flying across the room and smashing into the wall. You know, it's a real shame that I never had a chance to finish those aikido lessons. I keep meaning to, but something always comes up. Anyway, my feet got tangled and I wound up flat on my back with a hundred and eighty pounds of fully aroused, naked Baptist on top of me with his hands around my neck. It might have been fun under better circumstances.

"What the Hell are you doing here!?" he screamed at me, slamming my head into the floor for emphasis.

Even if I'd had a good explanation, I couldn't have said it while he was throttling me. So when he lifted me up for another slam I settled for a good head-butt to his face. There was a satisfying crunch as my forehead impacted his nose. Unfortunately, all it made him do was grunt and start strangling me even harder.

I have got to start charging more for cases like this.

There was no room to throw a punch, and it felt like Thompson was going to rip my head off my shoulders by brute strength. I tried to get my hands at his face, but the blood from his nose was dripping into my eyes and I couldn't see what I was doing. He smashed my head into the floor again, and the world exploded into reds and yellows.

I heard the shot and felt his weight shift. This time my brain was working fast enough to pick up the small delay between the two events. It even knew what the delay meant, Thompson hadn't been hit; he was only turning to look in the direction of the shot. It wasn't much, but it did give me an opening.

While Thompson was off balance, I braced an arm under his ribcage and managed to roll him off me. I still couldn't see anything, and my head felt like a piñata after a birthday party. I scrambled in the opposite direction until I found a wall. Steadying myself against it with one hand, I tried to wipe the blood out of my eyes with the other. Standing up I saw...

The Last Supper. I knew it was the Last Supper because it was just like the painting. You know, Leonardo Da Vinci and all. Except Jesus was a girl, and Judas and Matthew were fighting over the bill. And everything had a red tint to it, as if the painting itself was on fire. Then St. Peter stood up and walked over to me, and smiled. Then he decked me.

Great. There's a loaded gun and at least two crazy people in the room, and my mind has decided to fly south for the winter. Well I may be crazy, but I'm not stupid. When I saw St. Peter lining up a haymaker, I ducked. There was a sound of breaking plaster, and when I looked back up it was Thompson, cursing, his fist stuck in the wall. He looked at me and screamed something incomprehensible.

I grinned back at him. I hit him once in the solar plexus, which kind of took the fight out of him. A second blow to the nerve center in the small of his back pretty much stopped his misbehaving. I should have hit him once more, just to make sure, but my heart wasn't in it anymore.

Turning to take in the rest of the room, I noticed that Ms. Churchill seemed to be suffering the after-effects of a taser dart. Daniel had relieved her of the 9mm, which must have gone off when he zapped her. He looked indecently pleased with himself.

"Gee," he said with a grin, "and you complain about my line of work being dangerous."

I ignored him and picked my client up in a fireman's carry. Daniel grabbed his clothes in one hand and my optical cable in the other and caught up with us as I was loading Ms. Churchill into one of the glass elevators. We started down. A couple floors up from the lobby I pressed the emergency stop button to give her a few more minutes to come around. I could have just carried her through the lobby and out to a cab, but I did not feel like trying to explain the whole situation to the hotel's concierge.

A group of women in an ascending elevator passed us. A couple of them pointed at Daniel and started giggling. He smiled back, flexing his arms in a muscle-man pose.

I frowned at him. "Put on your clothes and stop flirting." Daniel pouted as he got dressed. He has raised pouting to an art form.

"You fucking bastard!"

My client had regained consciousness.

"How nice to see you again, Ms. Churchill," I said. "I believe our business together has been successfully completed." I handed her the bill. "Payment of the agreed upon bonus may be wired to this account number or delivered in cash to my place of business no later than…"

She tore up the bill and screamed at me some more. Something generic about damnation and burning in Hell.

"People often have that reaction to my fees. Sherwin, another copy of the bill, please."

While my wallet printed out another copy of the document, I held the palm display in front of her.

"Before you tear up this copy, you might want to take a look at the video feed from the snake. Sherwin, play the last recording."

She stared at the tiny screen, watching the whole affair played out again. The camera's position wasn't very good, and even with a wide angle lens it had missed some of the action. Still, there was enough there to warrant a couple charges of attempted murder. And the whole situation would take a long, long time to explain to her friends and family. She glared at me when I handed her the second bill. But she didn't tear it up.

I started the elevator again, and Daniel and I left her in the lobby. On the cab ride to the train station I tried calling Jen, just to let her know that the case had been resolved, and we would be able to pay the office rent this month. Strangely, she wasn't answering her phone. Normally Jen carries it everywhere, even the shower. Well, we had a morning court appointment tomorrow to testify in a divorce suit, and I'd tell her about it then.

A couple hours later, Daniel and I caught the evening train back to Atlanta. He sat next to me, and fell asleep within five minutes of leaving the station. I watched him as the train raced silently through the night, gliding over its single rail, with only the sound of the wind to remind you that you've moving at a hundred fifty miles an hour. Daniel sleeps so easily.

Life is strange. You do all the right things. You expose the villain. You save the damsel in distress. You beat up the bad guy, and you take some knocks doing it. And somehow, when the day is over, you still can't sleep.

## Chapter 4:  The Singer
## Sunday the Eighth, 9:03 PM

"You've got about twenty minutes, Mr. Weir." a voice behind me said.

I turned around to see who it was, but the young woman  had already set off on some other errand.

Technicians amaze me.  There were ten of them running around backstage.  Mumbling into headsets.  Reading out of notebooks. Stringing cable.  Adjusting lights.  Fetching props.  And not a one of them looking where they were going.  I kept expecting a collision, but it never happened.  It was like they had all developed some telepathic communications system, so that they always knew when Joe was coming up behind them with a ladder or Susan was about to come running around a corner with a coil of cable.  For awhile I just sat there and watched the patterns as they wove in and out among each other, always on the edge of a crash, always just avoiding it.  It was sort of like watching God juggle.

Live video broadcasts.  I can't believe people still do this.  It really is madness.  A million things have to come together correctly for every show.  A million little disasters just waiting to happen.  But somehow they always pull it off.

I couldn't see the stage from where I was standing, so I had been watching the show on one of the backstage monitors.  At the moment, the cast were finishing up the news analysis.  I'd managed to follow the early part of the show when they were talking about the riots in Jerusalem.  But now they had gone on to some trade deal that was being approved with the South American Union, and my attention had wandered.  The guy who sits in the right hand chair (you know, the one who does all the scriptural analysis, I can't remember his name) had just finished explaining how the rise of the South American trading block had been prophesied in *Revelations*, and how it was a sign of the end times.

The blond girl on the left (her name is Sandy something) chimed in with one of her usual leading questions.

"But that doesn't seem fair!  Why would the Senate agree to that?"

Sandy's job on the show is to prime the pump.  She throws out the questions that let the man in the middle vent about whatever is on his mind.  So far tonight she'd had such immortal lines as "Boy, that doesn't seem right!", "But how can that be?", and "Wow, you mean they can do that?"

The man in the middle, of course, was the right honorable Reverend Senator Zachariah Stonewall, leader of the Christian Alliance Party and host of the show. The Reverend Senator was in good form tonight, off on some tear about how the Democrats and Republicans were selling out the country to foreign powers. Stonewall's role on the show is to vent. But oh! How well he does it! Zachary does not whine. Zachary does not complain. No. Zachary orates.

Since I wasn't trying to follow the words anymore, I could appreciate his speech for the pure music of it. His phrasing is stately and measured, the tones alone revealing his indignation, the rhythm and the volume building and building toward the big crescendo of outrage, the wrath of the righteous descending on a world of the wicked. The voice of justice lashing out at those who would hold down and oppress the true people of God. Zachariah Stonewall is a force to be reckoned with when he gets riled. I was not looking forward to getting him riled at me.

Having suitably laid low his enemies, the Reverend Senator finished off his speech, and then asked for the audience's indulgence while he took a short break for an important commercial message. I braced myself for the sudden shift of volume.

"DIET SECRETS OF THE BIBLE REVEALED!" boomed the announcer's voice. "Did you know that the Bible tells you exactly what foods to eat in order to stay slim and fit? Dr. Wolfgang Peterson of the Bible Studies Institute has prepared this informative guide, which translates the Scripture into easily understood, modern English! Now you too can understand God's plan for your diet!"

The commercial plugged on for the remainder of its allotted thirty seconds, and then an ad for a Christian singles chat line came on. Lots of wholesome, extremely attractive young people talking about how they had met their spouses through the service.

I walked to the side of the stage and looked out at the studio audience. The network had a good crowd tonight. Over in the sound and light booth my assistant Linda was riding herd on a couple of the techies and getting things ready for my number that was coming up. She had her notebook out and jacked into their board, ostensibly to download a sound filter or something like that. The techies didn't look too happy about having her there, but they weren't stupid enough to argue with her. Few people are. When I first met Linda, she was working as the bouncer at a whore house in Nevada. Not that I was there to…oh skip it. It's a long story.

Anyway, tech is a whole lot easier on taped shows. They can play around with the sound and the images for hours until they get everything just the way they want it. Looking a little pale? No problem, we'll add a little tan to you. Bags under your eyes? We can edit those out too. Forget to shave? We'll erase that five o'clock shadow.

Live shows are a whole different ballgame, though. They've gotta catch everything on the fly, and rely on preprogrammed filters a lot more. Fortunately, the Lord saw fit to give me a nice enough face, and I'd just as soon stick with it. Just make sure I don't wind up looking green under the lights, and I'm happy. As for the Reverend-Senator, well they do a little more work on him. They run a program that takes some of the lines off his face, roseys up his cheeks just a bit, and even adds a twinkle to his eye that isn't there in real life. I'm just waiting for the day when they start painting in a halo over the guy.

One of the sound techies stood up and started counting down to the end of the commercial.

"And we're back in five, four, three..."

He counted off the last two numbers silently on his fingers. During the commercial the scripture guy and the primer girl had left the set, leaving the Reverend Senator alone at his desk.

"Hello and welcome back." he said, sounding stern and determined. "You parents with young children may want to take them out of the room for the next part of the show. For those of you who haven't seen our show before, this is the segment where I issue my weekly challenge to the forces of darkness. You see, I spend all week in Washington, dealing with Democrats and Republicans and other Satanist dupes. Folks who are either too blind or too narrow-minded to see the truth of the scriptures: that the end times are upon us. That the Beast is rising in the world, and the armies of Satan are gathering.

"Well, I get a little tired of arguing with dupes. I want to see the face of my enemy. So every week I make this public challenge to the forces of Satan. Are you out there watching, keeping an eye on us? You think you're strong? You think you're powerful? Well then, why don't you go on and call the number at the bottom of the screen and face *me*. For I have the authority of the believer on my side, and Satan and all his works cannot stand against that!"

Zachary glanced up at the tech booth, and the show's producer flashed him a thumbs up. He looked pleased.

"Well, it looks like we already have our first caller. Let's put him through."

"Reverend Stonewall..." the voice spoke in a sinister whisper, which was a little too high-pitched. Like some kid trying to sound scary.

"That's me. And who..."

"You are a joke, Stonewall! I've seen the *real* power! You are nothing before Satan! I know! I've seen him! Lord Satan is coming! He will have your soul before he is done. He will rip open your weak old body and feast on your heart!"

They never show the faces on these calls. I guess satanists don't use video conferencing. Zach was a model of calm all the way through the boy's tirade. Finally the kid ran out of breath, and the Rev-Sen was able to get a word in.

"What's your name, son?"

"Ha! My parents call me Jim, but they don't know my real name, my secret name, my magic name. Lord Satan has told me my magic name, and I..."

"Tell me something, Jimmy: Does Satan love you?"

"YES! Because I am strong like him. He hates the weak and the meek, but I revel in his power and his glory! I am filled with it! I am mighty and magical, fearsome and..."

"Are you really, Jimmy? Are you really strong? Or are you really just a scared little boy?"

"No!"

"You want to know something, Jimmy? I love you."

"Ha!" shot back the voice on the phone. But underneath the arrogance, there was now a hint of doubt. "*You*? Love *me*? You don't even know me, old man!"

"Yes Jimmy, I think I do. I know that you're hurting a lot right now. I know that you're not very popular at school, that you don't have many friends, that nobody seems to care what happens to you. I know that the world doesn't seem like a very fair place right now."

Zachary's voice was soft, and his delivery sincere.

"So, Jimmy, how did you come to join Satan's service?"

"Well...I...I..." The kid's voice was starting to break now. "I had a friend who got me started playing this game."

"And what game was it, Jimmy?"

"It was this magic game, where we rolled dice and pretended to be vampires and cast spells."

"But it wasn't just a game, was it Jimmy?"

"No! I mean...it started out just fun. Then she said that we could cast the spells for real. She had some friends who were magicians."

Zachary kept picking away at the kid. Zach's voice was like a bassoon, low and soft, but always probing. After a couple minutes, the kid was starting to cry.

"...Then, oh God, they had this baby. This little baby! And they gave me this black knife. And they told me that if I didn't do it, then I'd have to take its place! And I didn't want to, but...oh God, how it screamed! Then..."

"Yes Jimmy. What did you do then?"

"They made me...I mean we had to...drink...the blood..."

There was nothing but sobbing on the other end of the phone line.

"Jimmy? Jimmy, you don't have to be a part of this anymore."

"It's too late! It's too late! He's got me! I belong to him now."

"No Jimmy. It's not too late for you. I want you to repeat after me. I believe in Jesus Christ, my Lord and Savior."

"I...believe...in Jesus Christ...my..."

Zachary lead the kid through the whole catechism. Zachary sounding confident and strong. The kid struggling with the words, trying to find hope. I found myself tearing up, even though the kid's conversion seemed a little rushed. I remember ten years ago, when Zach used to spend an entire half hour program leading just one Satanist back to redemption. When I was a kid, I used to watch that part of the show every single week. It always got to me. The idea that one man's voice could save a soul so far gone. I loved those old shows. But I guess modern audiences just don't have the patience for that sort of thing anymore. Now Zach squeezes in three conversions during the space between two sets of commercials.

The next caller was a little more low-key, to give the audience a chance to catch their breath. This one claimed she was a Unitarian, and that she was furious with the Reverend Senator for saying that her church was a part of the Satanic Conspiracy. Zach primed her with a few easy questions, then tricked her into admitting that she had pagans in her congregation, and that they used the church for secret rituals at midnight. Zachary kept winding her up tighter and tighter, until she eventually wound up defending animal sacrifice as just another way of celebrating communion. Once she was beaten, Zach motioned the producer to cut her off. The camera zoomed in for one of his monologues.

"I was talking about dupes earlier. You see, Satan was cast out of Heaven for challenging God's authority. Satan wants to be God. He wants to be worshipped like God, which is why he has led so many of our brethren astray. Oh, they may still go to church and say the words, but the moral fire has gone out of their congregations. We've lost whole denominations that way. And some of their members don't even know it! There are people, people who are convinced that they are good Christians, who belong to churches that are firmly in the grip of Satan: churches that advocate abortion, premarital sex, homosexuality, and all manner of perversions. And that is why we who remain must always be on our guard, watching for Satan no matter what form he comes in."

How true, Zachary. We must always be on our guard. For Satan will paint himself as an angel, and charm the world with a seeming holiness.

"OK. And we seem to have another caller."

The third caller was a teenage girl, who was phoning in to say that she was a witch, but that she didn't worship Satan, she worshipped nature. She said her name was Shawna. Zachary lured her in with a few easy questions, pretending some interest in her religion. Then he started turning up the heat.

"So tell me, Shawna...Have you done a lot of rituals?"

"Oh yeah."

"Hm. That's interesting. Have you ever done one where you summoned up...the Horned Man?"

There was a little gasp from the other end of the phone.

"How...how did you know about him?"

"Oh, I know a lot of things about the so-called 'Church of Wicca' that I'm not supposed to. So what happened when you called him?"

"He...came. Cold. And dark. It was like a nightmare. I wanted to run, but I couldn't make my legs work. Then the others took my arms and held me. Then he...he..."

"Yes Shawna. What did he do when you called him?"

"He...took me!" she screamed, bursting into sobs. "It was horrible. I'd been saving myself for...well, for...and then he was inside me, cold as ice. So cold he burned. And I was bleeding. Oh God, I was bleeding!"

He let her cry for a few seconds without saying anything, her scream hanging in the silence of the studio.

"So once you knew what the coven was all about, why didn't you leave?"

"I wanted to. But they wouldn't let me."

"Who wouldn't let you, Shawna?"

"The other witches. They'll kill me if I try to get away. You don't know what they can do!"

"Yes, Shawna, I do. And I also know what they can't do. And I tell you, if you accept Jesus Christ into your heart, then their black magic will have no power over you! Do you accept Jesus Christ as your Lord and Savior?"

"I...yes, I do."

"Then say it."

"I accept Jesus as my Lord and Savior."

Looked like things were winding down with this caller. I glanced at the studio clock. Less than a minute till the next commercial break.

"That's good Shawna. That's the first step. Now I want you to come into a church. A *real* church, and get baptized. After that, you'll be safe."

"I will. I will! But it's not just the magic. What if they come after me? What if they try to hurt me..."

"Now don't you worry, Shawna. That's why we have the Christian Militia, to protect people from the forces of the Conspiracy. You just come on back to the fold, and we'll see to it that nobody hurts you."

"I will. Goodbye. God bless you!"

I glanced at the clock again. Twenty seconds left. You've got to admire his timing.

"Brethren, I know that you can see why the Militia is so important. We're going to take a short break right now, while these fine people explain what you can do to help the Militia protect our families and our children. If you can't donate your time, please consider donating your money. Afterward, we'll be back with something a little lighter: one of my favorite singers, musical guest Justin Weir."

One of his favorite singers? Oh please. The only thing Zachary likes about me is my demographics. He needs a boost in the 15 to 25 age range.

Well, time for me to take the stage. I gave my palm display one last look; still no message from Jen. Well, she had said that it might take awhile to find the information I needed. Still, I'd been hoping that somehow she would manage it before I went on tonight. It would be nice to know that at least one part of our plan had succeeded before I sailed past the point of no return. I picked up my guitar.

The commercial was playing on the monitor as I walked past it. Fresh-faced teenagers and young adults camping, reading scripture, and learning to shoot. It all looked frighteningly normal. Like boyscouts. Well, boyscouts with assault rifles and body armor.

The network had a stool and a microphone set up for me. I sat down and rested my guitar on my lap. I hate performing for television. It always throws me, even when I don't have this much at stake. Live audiences are great—they laugh, they applaud, they do all sort of little things to let you know if they're enjoying the show. And that makes it fun. With television though, you get nothin' back. There could be a half million people out there watching you and hating your guts and you'd never even know it.

For a moment, I thought about doing another song. Something safe that wouldn't get anybody riled. There was still time to back out of this. Once I started, though...

On the monitor, the happy campers were using rifles to blow apart silhouettes of people with horns and tails.

At some point, we must all take a risk for what we believe in. I looked up at Linda in the control booth. She was still barking orders to one of the techies, but she must have sensed that I needed her. She looked up from the control screens and caught my gaze.

I shot her a worried look. She smiled and gave me the thumbs up. Thank God. At least her part of the plan had gone smoothly.

A techie on the edge of the stage was holding up a hand.

"And we're back in five, four, three..."

He counted off two and one silently on his fingers.

Zachary had left the set for a drink of water or something. Sandy the primer girl handled my intro.

"Hey Folks! Thanks for joining us once again on the Baptist News Network for Zachariah Stonewall's Hour of Deliverance! As most of you probably know, the Christian Music Awards were held last night. Here with us tonight is the winner for best male vocalist, Justin Weir!"

I smiled and tried to look natural as the "Active" sign lit up atop the camera in front of me.

"Hi y'all." I said, and instantly regretted it. I hate it when this happens. Normally I have no accent at all. But the minute I get nervous my mother's southern drawl comes creeping in out of nowhere. And tonight, I was very nervous.

"Well, this is a song that wasn't on my last album. It's a little somethin' that I've been playin' 'round with the last couple a days. I hope you like it."

I looked down at my guitar.

Don't think about the camera pointing in your face.

Don't think about how stupid you just sounded.

Don't think about what's gonna happen when this song is over. Just focus.

I closed my eyes and tried to make the world go away. My fingers found the first guitar string.

It still seems like magic to me. That you can pluck one string and get such a pure, beautiful sound. My fingers built up the melody, and I forgot myself in the act of playing.

To forget oneself. To lose oneself in something else. The Bible talks about losing oneself in God. Maybe that's why I've never been able to picture God as a person, with a human face and all that. You can't lose yourself in a person. And besides, God just isn't there the way a person is, standing in right in front of you. No, God is more like music. Music playing so faintly that you can't really hear it, but you can just kind of feel it. And sometimes, you *can* get lost in it.

I opened myself, and the words came pouring out.

When I was young, my parents taught me
The things I owe the one who wrought me.
"Be kind and honest, just and true,
And love the Lord, as is his due."

"Of all your duties, that's the greatest,
To Love the Lord, the one who made us.
To Love the Lord, and live for ever,
With the Father and Son and the Ghost together."

It's easy to say "I love You," but do I feel it?
Until I come to know You, it can't be real.
It is only an empty word, an actors's part,
For how can I love You, till I know You and Your heart?

So I read the Bible through and through,
Hoping to catch some glimpse of You.
Now I'm not the brightest fella, but still and all I read
All 'bout those guys in ancient times and all the things they said,

'Bout plagues and locusts and family trees,
And begattings and beginnings and prophecies,
And a whale and some fish and when I was done,
I was even more confused than when I'd begun.

Why do You hide from us, why don't You visit?
Is there a reason why, and just what is it?
You're the All Mighty One, You make the rules.
Are You off on vacation, or just tired of fools?

So I went to college, for I had heard
It could help me understand the meaning of Your word,
So I learned to read in Latin and in ancient Greek,
And a couple other languages that no one ever speaks.

I learned the length of a rod and the value of a sheckle,
And eleven dirty words that Jews would use when they would heckle,
And I learned about the Hittites and the Pharisees of history,
But as to what it all means—well that's still a mystery.

Is this some game You play, to mock our guesses?
Why don't You just tell us what Your address is?
Or pick up the phone, and say it clearly,
We would obey Thee, if only we could hear Thee.

So I sought out those who claimed they understood,
The ministers and priests and the monks in hoods,
And I asked them for the secret that would let me see Your heart,
And I asked them why the Father and His children live apart.

And sure enough they told me, but not one of them agreed
On a solitary fact or a solitary creed.
They argued over water, and they argued over wine,
And they fought among themselves until they'd struck each other blind.

You could appear before us, if only You desired.
Have You gone to sleep, or are You only tired?
Nations go to war, and in Your name they kill.
Are you too lazy to correct them, or is this as You will?

And finally I left them, and in a field I wept,
And cried until my voice gave out, and then at last I slept.
And awoke past hope or thought, to a night of perfect still.
And in that stillness heard You, knew Your heart, and knew Your will.

It was You who gave us life, and some spark of You remains,
In all your children's children, in their laughter and their pain.
And if You let us stumble, on our own path to the true,
Still, by looking at each other's hearts, we catch a glimpse of You.

And so I learned to love my Lord, by loving first Your children,
Though we pray to You by different names,
I think one day we will then
All find the common truth, in the parts of You we see,
For drawing close to one another draws us closer still to Thee.

My fingers played the last few notes, and they hung there, dying in the still air. For one uncertain moment there was silence. Then the room erupted into noise as the audience cheered and applauded. Not that I wasn't expecting them to. After all, there was a big sign behind me telling them to.

I nodded in polite appreciation while the applause went on, and then they finally cut away to some commercial about a 1-900 prayer line, and the camera in front of me went dead. The techie who had been operating it leaned out to get a look at me. She gave me a look that seemed to ask, "Do you know what you just did?"

Zachary was back on the set. We were supposed to do an interview after the song, so I started walking over to the empty chair next to him. He shot me a look that felt like someone pouring ice water into my veins.

"Mr. Weir," he said, "could I have a word with you backstage?" His tone was coldly civil. I felt like I was thirteen years old again and facing the principal.

"Certainly, Reverend-Senator, but aren't we supposed to..."

A techie popped up in front of us.

"And we're back from commercial in five, four, three..."

"RUN ANOTHER ONE." growled Stonewall.

For a second I thought that the techie really had suffered a stroke. Then she stopped twitching and started shouting something into her headset as she frantically waved to the other techies in the control booth.

Stonewall grabbed Sandy the primer girl by the shoulder and shoved her in front of a camera. "Cover for me." Then he strode back stage, and I followed.

As soon as we had passed through one of the soundproof doors leading off the set, he turned around and grabbed my collar.

"JUST WHAT THE HELL WAS THAT CRAP!"

"I...uh...I..." I stammered. The surprised expression on my face was an act. The look of mind-numbing fear was not. "What did I..."

"You know *exactly* what you did."

Of course I knew. I had done the unforgivable, deliberately, with malice and forethought. I had spoken out against Stonewall's teachings, and I had used his own show to do it. I had made an enemy of the most powerful man in the Christian Alliance.

"Boy, do you have *any* idea what I can do to you?"

Actually, I knew all too well what he could do, but he went ahead and elaborated on it in some detail while I played dumb. It's not much of a stretch for me.

"You can just forget about our studio ever doing another one of your records. I do believe there is a morals clause in your contract..."

I'm not a rocket scientist. I'm just a guy who can see trouble when it's barreling down the road at me going 90 miles an hour.

"...Hell, maybe we should do a nice special on corruption in the music industry, starring Justin Weir?"

Left alone, the Reverend-Senator will lead us into civil war. He will have Christians killing each other in the name of God.

"Do you know how fast I could sink your career? All I have to do is go out there and denounce you as an instrument of Satan, and they'll rip you to..."

So someone has to make sure that he isn't left alone. And unfortunately, that someone is going to have to be me.

"...and don't think it will stop at this network. I've got friends who work for every media company in..."

Like it or not, I have a following. Like it or not, the Lord saw fit to endow me with a certain amount of charisma. Granted I don't have much going in the way of IQ. But sometimes that can be an advantage.

"...and that's before I even bring my lawyers in! They'll..."

For the past year, I'd been carefully cultivating a reputation in certain circles for being just a little slow and a little naive. The whispering had started. "He's a bit innocent, poor dear. His manager Linda is the one with all the business sense. She manipulates him completely...and so could we." Currently, I had six of the major power brokers in the Christian Alliance each convinced that I was wrapped around his little finger.

"...if that wasn't a fucking breach of contract I don't know what is..."

The powerbrokers will not be as angry about the song. They do not all agree with Stonewall. Some of them are jealous of his power. They will not be upset to see him taken down a notch. "It was an innocent mistake," they will say, "by a naive young man."

"Do you get it, you half-whit? You're finished!"

Stonewall is at the center of the party. He pulls all the strings. But what would happen if some unfavorable information suddenly came to light about him? The party would have to choose a new leader. It would have to be someone who had not been tainted by his fall. Someone who wasn't too close to him. Maybe even an enemy. Someone popular, that could serve as a figure head to hold the party together in that time of crisis. And preferably someone that the power brokers think they can control.

"No Christian station will broadcast your music."

It will take years to pull the party back from the brink.

"No Christian magazine will mention you."

Maybe decades. To turn it back from the armed monstrosity it has become, toward one that fulfills the mission Christ set for his disciples.

"No studio will touch you."

Feed the hungry. Clothe the poor. Lead by example, not intimidation.

"You'll wind up playing two-buck beer halls and bar mitzvahs!"

The door burst open and Linda walked into the hallway. Stonewall didn't even pause in his tirade, but Linda wasn't going to let that stop her.

"REVEREND SENATOR STONEWALL!" she shouted over him. "Am I to take it that you have a problem with my client's performance?"

"You whore! You know damn well what I'm mad about!"

Ooh. Such colorful language. Of course, everyone who has worked at the station knows about Zach's rages. But he's always been careful to keep them off camera and out of his public persona.

"No sir, I don't." she said, "All that song said was that every person has a link to God. Which is, I believe, standard Baptist Theology. Or do I need to remind you of the Doctrine of the Priesthood of the Believer?"

That really sent him over the edge. His face turned purple, and for a second I thought his head was actually going to pop like a balloon. I hoped that the camera in Linda's brooch was able to get that color right. It really was impressive.

When Zachary finally did burst, he let loose with a rush of profanities concerning Linda's sex life, my parents, and the exact state of things in Hell before I would ever cut another record. I'm so glad that Linda had thought of recording all this.

"Oh, don't even try that with me, Zach." she said with a laugh. "You are not the only media company around. Time-Warner-Sony would love to get their hands on him for their Christian Music label."

The video clip of Stonewall shouting would make a nice addition to our file, which already had some interesting material. During the call in part of the show, Linda had been jacked into the network's board, and had obtained proof that the "satanic" calls were originating in another studio.

"They wouldn't dare," he shot back. "They know how much trouble I can make for them in Washington. They are not going to tick off a senator over some lousy musician."

Of course, proving that he has a bad temper and fakes the calls into his show won't necessarily finish him. I suspect that most of the thinking members of the CA have already figured out that the show is fixed. I mean really, it's about as obvious as professional wrestling. The rest will probably believe him when he says that it's all a Satanic plot to discredit him.

"Yeah," said Linda, "and they also know damn well that you're not going to waste political capital going after them, either. They've got a few senators of their own, Zach, and you're not going to mess with them over this. So don't even try to bluff me."

I've accumulated a lot of dirt on Zachary. Several shady business deals, some dubious campaign contributions. But no smoking gun. Nothing that would guarantee his downfall. I was counting on Jen for that. She'd told me that she was getting close to something. But I hadn't heard from her in two days now. If she couldn't deliver...well, this was gonna get real ugly.

Zach was off on another tear, threatening to declare me a member of the Conspiracy.

"...one word from me, and they'll rip him apart!"

"Yeah," admitted Linda, "they would. But you're not going to do it. And you know why Zach? Demographics. You declare him a Satanist, and you alienate every one of his fans. And you can't afford to take that hit in the under 25 age group."

Sometimes I try to figure Zachary out. He's leading us down a dark path, and I wonder why he's doing it. Religious wars are always the most brutal. Does he think that they'll make him a king when the fighting's all over? Is he just too blind to see the river of blood that he's marching us into? Does he really believe that this is what God wants? Or is he just truly evil?

Linda's last rebuttal had left him gasping and directionless. "I'll...I'll..."

"Of course you will, Zachary," she continued, "but not in public. Oh, you'll exclude Justin from any participation in your network or media companies, and you'll make whatever trouble for him that you can behind the scenes. But there is a limit to that.

"Come, Justin. I believe that it is time we were going."

Linda held the door for me and we left.

You did have one thing right, Zachariah. I am just a two buck musician with no ambition. I never wanted your job.

But we all make certain sacrifices.

## Chapter 5: The Witch
## Sunday the Eighth, 9:03 PM

It is dark in the clearing. The razor crescent of the new moon hangs low over the tree line, and the Milky Way stretches out above us. In the woods, I can see the flickering of candles as the others make their way to us. A warm breeze blows, full of honeysuckle. It smells like summer nights when I was a child, playing capture the flag in the vacant lot behind our house. It is a night full of magick.

But I am not thinking about magick. I'm thinking about the fact that my phone is back in the car. Which is where I want it—after all, I still remember that incident last year when Tina Ostfield's phone started ringing just as we were raising the cone of power on Mid-Summer's Eve. But what if something happens to one of the kids or there's an emergency and the sitter has to get in touch with us? I know, I know. It's not the most spiritual frame of mind I could be in. But it's where I am.

One by one, the others emerge from the woods, the dark blue robes concealing their identities. One by one, they take their place in the circle. One by one, they set their candles down and face the center, where the old oak stump waits. Upon it rests a copper cauldron, filled with new earth and new possibilities. And the sacred dagger.

Eleven members join the circle. Next to me is one of the four flat stones that mark the cardinal directions. It is the west stone, where Jen should be. But she isn't, and there is a hole in our circle. We wait. The night is full of sound, crickets and frogs and a nearby owl. We wait. But Jen never comes. The place next to me remains empty. Then we can wait no more.

A single figure in a white robe comes. Walking confidently through the dark woods with no candle to guide her. Raven, the seer. She walks to the center of our circle and takes up the antame. The polished black blade flashes in the candlelight. It is a relic of the coven, forged from the metal of a meteorite, and handed down from high priestess to high priestess.

Raven walks out of our midst. She raises the antame, and slowly begins to trace the circle. As she passes the first rock, a figure in a blue robe steps forward. The figure pulls back the hood to reveal her long red hair, and the infinity symbol tattooed on her forehead. It is Shard. She unties the cord at her waist, and the blue robe slips off her tall, slender form. Then, naked before the Goddess, Shard leaps to the top of the rock. She raises her arms and shouts:

"Hail to the Guardians of the Watchtowers of the East, Keepers of the Air, of intellect and of storm. We invoke thee! We invoke thee! WE INVOKE THEE!"

The breeze shifts, and the honeysuckle is replaced by the stronger smell of cedar. Raven continues casting the circle. As she passes each member, they step out of their sandals and let the robes fall from their bodies. Raven reaches the second rock. The short white hair of Margaret emerges from beneath a hood, and her squat, tattooed body emerges from the robes. Margaret steps onto the second rock, and shouts in her husky voice:

"Hail to the Guardians of the Watchtowers of the South! Keepers of the Inner Flame, of intuition, and of poetry! We invoke thee! We invoke thee! WE INVOKE THEE!"

The treetops dance in a sudden rush of wind, but here on the ground there is only the slow breeze. Slower now, warmer now. Raven continues to trace the circle. Next to me, my husband emerges from beneath his robes, his jet black eyes flashing in the candlelight, his familiar body strange and magick in the dancing shadows. Raven comes to me, and I shed my garment as well, revealing myself to the Goddess. The breeze washes over my naked body, sending electric tingles everywhere. Then, because Jen is not here, I take her place atop the rock and raise my voice.

"Hail to the Guardians of the Watchtowers of the West, Keepers of the Dark Waters, of the hidden depths and the unknown mysteries. We invoke thee! We invoke thee! WE INVOKE THEE!"

The wind continues to roar in the treetops, but down here the breeze has died. All is still. Waiting. Like a storm about to break. Raven continues around the circle, finally reaching the fourth rock, where the bear-like form of Ivan emerges from a robe. He stands upon the fourth rock and booms in his huge bass voice:

"Hail to the Guardians of the Watchtowers of the North, Keepers of the Earth, of fertility and the life force. We invoke thee! We invoke thee! WE INVOKE THEE!"

The hair on my forearms is standing on end, and I can feel the circle close like a circuit. The air is still, and full of the damp smell of old leaves on the forest floor. The sound of the wind seems far away. Raven walks to the stump and sheds her robe. She is short, wrinkled, and her long silver hair flows down over her breasts. But her voice is as pure and musical as windchimes.

"The circle is complete," she says, sheathing the antame back in the fresh earth of the cauldron. "We are between the worlds. On the edge of reality where the mundane and the fantastic embrace each other, and magick may be worked."

And there is a new smell, there in the quiet air. A smell that tugs at my memory, like something from a childhood dream that I can't quite remember, but have never forgotten.

Raven stands on the stump, her feet to either side of the small copper cauldron. She has a leather pouch around her neck, from which she removes something small and precious. I can't see it in the dim candlelight, but I know that it's an acorn.

"Tonight is the first night of the new moon," she says. "The time of new beginnings. When ideas may be planted, so that their power may one day fill both the worlds."

Raven cups the acorn in her hands. "Tonight we plant harmony. That which brings together competing forces and creates something new and better from their union."

Harmony? An interesting choice. I wonder if Raven had any two particular coven members in mind when she chose that ideal. We'll see.

Raven raises her cupped hands, and it begins. We raise the cone of power. Twelve people, joining their wills to a common objective. The joint power of the coven focused on a single seed. The coven grows closer. Our breathing falls into synch. The energy within the circle is like a lighting bolt waiting to strike. Then suddenly, it does.

There is no outward sign, but somehow, we all know that it is over. The energy is gone, but something has awakened within the seed. Raven withdraws the antame from the cauldron and drops the acorn into the waiting earth.

Each month we plant a new seed, dedicated to an ideal. If all goes well, and the seed germinates, we tend the tree here in our sacred wood for the first seven years of its life. Then we take the tree and plant it somewhere where it will do some good. We have planted trees dedicated to imagination and hope around our children's school. We have planted trees of rebirth and protection in the national forests. And we have planted trees of peace and understanding in the downtown parks.

Raven steps down from the stump. My husband Alex steps forward, carrying the silver bowl. He holds it before Raven, who dips the antame into the water, consecrating it. She withdraws the blade, and then she and Alex look into the water. It is on this, the darkest of nights, that one can see the faintest of stars. They stare into the water and hope to glimpse a reflection of the future.

For a second, I am sure that something has gone wrong. Raven's face betrays a moment of shock. Alex has his back to me, but I can see his posture suddenly tense. I look for some clue, wondering what is happening. But the moment passes. Alex relaxes, and Raven takes the bowl from him. She sprinkles the holy water on our new seed, blessing it.

"It is done." she says. "The seed of Harmony is planted. By our thoughts and our actions let us nurture it in the coming month. Blessed be."

"Blessed be!" comes the chorus from the coven. Then the sound of friendly chatter wells up, and we break into small groups, with the circle of candles left to mark the boundaries between the worlds. I see Alex and Raven talking, and I go to join them.

Shard beats me there. She comes striding across the circle like a shopper in the last five minutes of a Macy's sale. She steps in right between Alex and Raven, corners the high priestess, and starts talking her ear off. I catch a bit of her monologue as I approach.

"...and the fact of the matter is that we just don't have the funds for a full-time soccer coach. We've got to have somebody on the board who is willing to stand up to the sports parents and say that academics has got to take..."

Surprisingly, Shard stops her campaign speech to acknowledge my presence. "Oh, Holly. You did a nice job filling in for Jen tonight."

"Thanks," I say, even though I know that the comment was not directed toward my ears.

"Speaking of Jen," Shard continues, "what did happen to her?"

Raven rolls here eyes. We both know what's going on here. Shard could care less where Jen is right now. She just wants to keep pointing out that Jen isn't here.

"I don't know," I admit, "but we're supposed to have lunch tomorrow. I'm sure I'll find out then.

"Please do," insists Shard. "We need everybody here for a new moon ceremony. And she didn't even warn us that she would be absent. I just hope it doesn't affect the magick. I mean, what if..."

"You know," says Raven, "I had no idea that the coven had appointed a truancy officer. Did you all take a vote on it before I got here this evening?"

Shard's self-confident expression collapses. I try not to smile.

"No Ma'am," Shard replies.

"Oh?" says Raven, her voice full of maternal understanding. "Well then, while I appreciate your enthusiasm in jumping in to fill the post, I do think it would be best if you waited for us to create the position, first."

"Yes ma'am," says Shard. Then she goes off to seek other company. Raven and I are both trying to hold in our laughter, and neither of us is doing a very good job of it. Alex has been thinking about something, and seems to have missed the entire exchange.

"By the Goddess," says Raven with a chuckle, "this is going to be an interesting election. Which one are you going to vote for?"

Our coven gets to elect one of the board members for the local Wiccan high school. My husband Alex has held the position for the last three years, but his term is up in a month. Both Shard and Jen have expressed an interest in the post.

"I really haven't made up my mind yet."

"Neither have I," says Raven. "Of course, even if I had, I would never admit to it. The minute I express support for either one of them, they'll go running around the coven claiming to have my official endorsement. I can't believe how silly those two are being about this."

"What did you expect?" I ask. "They're both warriors."

Of the three kinds of witches, warriors are the most aggressive. They are the ones who want things, and that is both their great strength and their great weakness. Warriors are the dreamers, the planners, the builders. They are the ones who can't sit still and wait for a problem to resolve itself, the ones who have to act, the ones who plunge in headfirst. Unfortunately, this makes it really difficult for warrior witches to cooperate with each other. And when two of them set their sights on the same thing, it can get ugly.

Me, I'm a healer witch. We're the ones who support, who respond, who wait to see how things will play out before we make our move. We're also the ones who pick up the pieces when the warriors screw up. The warriors may be the ones who do the spectacular magick, who take the big chances and make the great advances, but it's the healers who hold our society together and keep it running.

Raven is a seer. So is my husband. They are the rarest kind of witch. You have to be very still to be a seer. To neither act nor react. But to just sit and listen. To let go of what you want to see, so that you can see what is really there. Alex explained it to me once. "Any idiot can talk to a tree," he said, "but there aren't many with the patience to listen to one."

A burst of laughter comes from a group over by the east rock. I listen to them for awhile. They're playing a poetry game, where each member improvises the next line. A couple of others are over by the north rock, trying to do some sort of minor magick with a sprig of mistletoe. The rest of the coven is clustered together by the stump, singing. Our newest member, Stacy, is playing the harmonica. Shard has her arms around her and is singing along. They've been dating for about a year. Rumor has it that they're thinking of moving in together.

I hope they do. Stacy has been good for Shard. She takes a little of the assertive edge off her. And I think she's going to be good for the coven as well. Stacy hasn't chosen her path yet, but I'm betting that she'll turn out to be a seer. We could use another one. I'm not sure why I'm so sure she is one. It's something about her personality that makes me think she's always been a little of an outsider. All seers are…well, different. Like they've never quite fit in. I guess it's because you can't really see something when you're a part of it.

Alex is still lost in his own thoughts. He does that sometimes. I guess it's a good thing he's a mathematician and not an air traffic controller. I walk up behind him and put my arms around him.

"What 'cha thinkin'?"

He strokes my arms, but says nothing. I hold him for awhile, then go off to sing with the others. This is always my favorite time with the coven, and it's all too short. A half-hour later we have donned our robes and sandals, and once gain take up our positions before the candles. Raven stands beside the stump. She raises the antame above her head, and intones the parting words.

"The circle is open, but not broken. Though we may be far apart in the coming month, none the less we are always together. Go now, and nurture the seed that we have planted here tonight."

Then we pull the hoods over our heads, take up our candles, and make our separate ways back through the dark woods. Alex and I walk in silence back to the road where our station wagon is parked. We get our clothes out of the back and change out of the robes.

Alex gets behind the wheel, and we start the drive home. He still hasn't said anything. He can do this for hours sometimes, when he wraps his brain around a problem. I give him another five minutes before I say anything.

"OK, what's the matter?"

Alex keeps his eyes locked on the road, and makes no indication that he's heard me. A couple minutes later, he finally says.

"Something happened tonight that worries me."

"What? Jen? It's probably nothing. You know her job. She probably got called away on a case or…"

"No. Not that. I felt like…"

I wait for him to find a word, but nothing comes.

"…like we were being watched?" I prompt. We'd been having trouble with some local yokels sneaking out into the woods to watch our ceremonies. You'd think they'd never seen naked people before.

"No," says Alex, "not that either. I think Raven saw something when we blessed the water. But she wouldn't tell me what it was."

"But you didn't see anything?"

"No, I looked, but I only saw reflected stars. But I *felt* it."

"Well what did it feel like?"

Alex screws his face up in concentration, and doesn't say anything for five or six minutes.

"I don't have good words for it. It's like...It's like...It's like standing underneath a dam that's about to break."

"Well, that's cheery."

"I'm sorry," he says. "I wish I had better words. It's complicated."

I put my head on his shoulder. "Well, try to put it out of your head for awhile. Let your subconscious kick it around overnight, and see what comes to you in the morning."

Alex pulls the car into the driveway, and parks. We get out. The lights in the bushes come on, illuminating the footpath around to our front door. I put my hand on the knob, say "it's me," and feel the reassuring click of the door unlocking.

We step into the familiar smells of the house. Mint, Thai basil, and some rosemary that I grow in window boxes. The house is quiet, but there's a light on at the end of the hall, in the family room.

That's where I find my two darling children, sprawled out on the carpet, wearing their visors and thoroughly zombified on the latest shows. Urvashi, our orange tabby cat, is sleeping on the floor between them. She stretches and looks up as we enter the room.

Crystal, our baby sitter, is sitting on the couch, absentmindedly drawing something on a sketch pad with a magenta crayon. As near as I can tell, she's redesigned a Burger King outlet to include battlements, a moat, and a small hoard of vegetarian barbarians intent on burning the whole thing to the ground. I touch her on the shoulder.

"Hi, Crystal."

She looks up suddenly. "Oh, hi Ms. Jacobs, Mr. Flint. I didn't hear you come in. Wow, you're back early."

"No, Crystal, we're not." I say, showing her my watch. "Shouldn't the girls be in bed by now?"

"What? Oh come on, it's only eight thir..." She glances at her own watch and does a double take. "But, I just checked it a minute ago...I...how...I mean, I sat down, and Winter handed me one of her crayons, and...Oh."

She glares at my youngest daughter, Winter. "She did it to me again, didn't she?"

"Sure looks that way." I say.

"Don't worry about it." Alex says. "It's not your fault. Her teachers at school are having the same problem."

Winter is a bit of a prodigy. She was conceived seven years ago during the coven's celebration of the Great Rite of the Spring Equinox, when the Horned Man, lord of the winter and the hunt, yields himself to the Earth Mother, and the world is born anew. Alex and I were playing the lead roles in the ceremony that year. To this day, I still smile when I think about him wearing those antlers.

Crystal continues to apologize while she gets out her wallet, Alex gets out his cash card, and the two of them go through the mechanics of punching up her night's pay. In the meantime, I decide to check up on what our daughters are watching. I grab my visor off the counter and set it for Winter's channel. I slip it on and flip down the ear flaps.

*A high school gym, decked out with balloons and streamers for a dance. Panning shot of the crowd. Closeup on a couple as they enter beneath a sign that says "Homecoming 2024". Some guy in a varsity jacket looking nervously around. The girl on his arm is a blond with way too much hair.*

*"Oh Steve," she says. "I'm so glad you finally decided to ask me out. You're just lucky I was available on such short notice."*

*"Yeah, " says the jock, still looking around. "You don't think Xarena and Bolt are gonna come, do you?"*

*The blond is not happy about this question. "Will you just forget about that ditzy little cheerleader! Look, she's the one who cheated on you, not the other way around, remember! Don't you think its about time you moved on?"*

*A girl's face suddenly appears, floating inside one of the balloons behind them.*

And I suddenly realize what I'm watching. No, not this. Not "Xarena the Cheerleader Witch."

*"So that's what's going on!" says the disembodied head of Xarena. "I was wondering who set me up. And with Bolt, too! As if I'd ever!"*

*The camera cuts back to the couple, who are now standing over by the punch bowl. The jock is still looking around. The blond is pouring herself a glass of green punch.*

*"You know," she says, "nobody wanted to say anything while you two were dating, but we were all wondering why you were going out with that dumpy little thing."*

*The camera zooms in on the punch bowl, where Xarena's face appears. "Dumpy, huh!" She crosses her eyes and blinks.*

*Closeup on the glass of punch, which glows briefly.*

*"You know," says the blond, "my father has a house up by the lake. I was thinking..."*

*She takes a sip of the punch. It leaves a glowing green mustache on her upper lip. When she opens her mouth, her teeth are also glowing green.*

*"...that we could head up after school on Friday and...why are you looking at me funny?"*

*The jock has a horrified look on his face.*

*"Um. You've got something on your lip."*

*Canned laughter. The blond tries to wipe her lip, but it won't come off and everything she wipes it with turns a glowing green. She gets more frantic, and more and more people at the dance come over to stare at her.*

I take off the visor. I can only handle so much of this show at once. I've told Winter that I don't approve of it, but so far I haven't taken the step of actually blocking her access to it. I don't know what the writers on this show think they're doing, but I don't want them doing it to my daughter. The lead character on the show throws around insanely powerful magick with no thought of the consequences. Real witches have to be more careful. You can only harm someone if by so doing you teach them a lesson. And the threefold law hangs over all our heads. Do good with your powers, and the blessings will come back to your threefold. But do harm...

Winter and I are going to have a talk tomorrow. In the meantime, I put the visor back on and flip over to the channel used by Summer, my older daughter.

*"Well sir, I couldn't have done it without Lois. If she hadn't figured out the location of Dr. Doom's hideaway, I might still be caught in that Kryptonite death trap. And if it hadn't been for Jimmy buying us time with that diversion...Which reminds me, Jimmy. 'Avon calling'? You couldn't think of something more subtle?"*

*"Hey, I had to get their attention off those monitors fast, and it was the first thing that popped into my head."*

*"All right," says the guy in blue with the big 'S' on his chest, "but next time could you think of something a little less obvious?"*

*"**You** are calling **me** obvious?!" protests Jimmy, "You're the one who flies around in those spandex tights. Tell me, are all the guys on Krypton uncircumsized, or are you just..."*

*"Oh," says Superman, "I don't think we want to go there, Jimmy..."*

*The camera cuts away to Lois Lane and her publisher, who are watching the pair bicker.*

*"Those two," says Lois. "Do you think they're ever going to figure it out?"*

*Her boss laughs and points. "I think they just did."*

*The camera cuts back to Jimmy and Superman in a major clinch. As they kiss, they rise into the air, and then bits of clothing start falling back to earth.*

Wow. That's some aerial sex scene. I wonder how the actors can get into those positions without falling over. I'll bet they shot the whole thing underwater and then bluescreened it onto a back-drop of Metropolis.

Funny, I don't remember Jimmy Olsen being quite so buff. But then, I'd never watched this particular cut of the show before. For Summer's fourteenth birthday, Alex and I had taken the lock off her media agent. The deal is that she can set her preferences anyway she wants, but she has to talk to us about what she's watching. Of course, the first thing she did was set the sex and violence content controls to ten.

As we'd expected, she'd gotten tired of that after a few days. At those settings, everything you watch winds up looking like a James Bond film—they have to cut out all the plot and character development to make room for the chase scenes and extra skin. She'd been edging the violence controls down all week, and now they were set at six

Sex is taking a little longer to lose its fascination. She still has the sexual content control jacked up to ten, but now she's playing around with some of the other parameters. First, she'd told her agent to include the versions of scenes written for aggressive women and passive men. Then she'd set her preference for passive women and aggressive men. Then for lesbians. And now...well, judging by the way that Superman and Jimmy Olsen were going at it, she'd gotten curious about gay sex.

I take off my visor. Alex and Crystal are chatting about her schoolwork as he shows her to the door. I say a quick goodnight to her, then plop down on the floor next to my two children.

"Hello, family!" I shout, making sure that I'm loud enough to be heard over the headphones.

"Pause," my two daughters say in unison before removing their visors.

"Oh. Hi, mom," says Summer.

"Hi, Mommy!" says Winter, standing up to give me a hug.

"How were services?" asks Summer.

"Just fine." I say. It's out of my mouth before I realize that it's a lie. Well, oops. "Now, don't you think it's time the two of you were heading off to bed? It is a school night."

"Aww Mom!" my offspring screech together, hitting a particularly nasty harmonic. I wonder if they'd been rehearsing it.

Summer goes on the offensive.

"Mom, I am *fourteen*. Jenny Brooks is the same age as me, and her mother let's her stay up 'til..."

Kids. They act as if their shows won't still be there for them when they come home from school tomorrow. While Summer whines on, I begin to concentrate. I summon my magick, focus it with a hand gesture, inhale...and then release a wave of soothing, calming energy at my children.

Summer stops her tirade long enough to yawn.

"But I...*yawn*...should be allowed...*yawn*...to...oh, forget it. I'm beat."

One of these days Summer is going to find out about that spell, and then I'm going to be in trouble. Hopefully though, no one will teach it to her until she has children of her own.

Summer starts up to bed. Winter, though, is still a stubborn little bundle of energy. My magick never seems to work on her.

"Honey bunch, why don't you go up to bed with your sister?"

"Because I DON'T WANT TO!"

Hm. Well, that was pretty definitive. I probed for an opening.

"Don't you want me to tuck you in, sweetie? Aren't you tired?"

"No, Mommy. But if you're tired you can go up to bed. I'll come up as soon as my show is over. I'm a big girl now. I can tuck myself in."

I yawn. That does seem like a good idea. It's been a full day. I'm just turning to go upstairs when Alex taps me on the shoulder.

"She's doing it to you again."

Oh.

You know, I'm sure that one day Winter will use her magick in a profound way that will change the very nature of the world. But right now she's a *real handful*. It's a shame that Dr. Spock never wrote any books on the raising of magically adept children. I wonder if Merlin's parents had these problems.

Alex and I turn back to deal with our youngest. Oh, she's a powerful little witch, all right. But she's never been able to zap both of us at the same time. Well, not yet, anyway.

"Honey," says Alex, "It's time for you to go to bed. Do you want me to carry you up?"

"NO!" says Winter. Then she changes tactics. She smiles, and her face lights up like an angel. Like the most pure and innocent child the world has ever known. "But Daddy, if you let me stay up tonight, I promise I'll be good all day tomorrow!"

"No you won't." says Alex. "If you don't get sleep tonight, you'll be a grouchy little sourpuss all day tomorrow, and no one will want to be around you. And by the way, you can drop the glamour, sweetie, Daddy's not buying it."

Winter abandons her minor illusion, and her face goes dark and sullen again. While she and Alex continue to duel back and forth, I try going around for a flank attack. I shoot a look at Urvashi, our cat. Well, actually, she's Winter's cat.

Urvashi had turned up on our back porch a few weeks after Winter was conceived. Just this skinny little orange kitten, no more than a few weeks old. She used to follow me around the house and crawl into my lap whenever I sat down. I had thought that she would be my familiar. My mistake.

Urvashi's attention shifted the moment that Winter was born. She stopped hanging out with me and started sleeping by Winter's crib. She's even tried to follow Winter to school a couple of times. But even if she is closer to my daughter, there's still some special connection between us. Now I try to open that connection.

Urvashi roles over on her back and stretches. She stares up at me, blinking slowly. I hold eye contact, forming a mental picture of Urvashi going up to bed and Winter following her.

Urvashi stops blinking. She rolls over on her stomach. She licks a paw, and then looks back up at me. Something in her expression clearly conveys a message.

"What's in it for me?"

I shoot her back a look that says, as clearly as I can, "Who do you think buys the tuna in this household, huh?"

Urvashi considers this for a moment, then gets up and walks over to Winter. Alex and Winter seem to be dueling to a standstill. Urvashi wraps her tail around Winter's leg. She saunters down the hall a few feet, and then begins mewing.

"Honey Bunch," I say, "it looks like Urvashi wants to go up to bed. Shouldn't you go up to tuck her in?"

"OK, Mommy. Come on, Urvashi!"

Winter and the cat start off down the hall. Alex wrinkles up his forehead.

"What's wrong now?" I ask.

"She's up to something." he says. His eyes narrow as he looks at our departing daughter. "I think she's got another glamour up."

I apprehend our youngest before she can make it to the stairs. Alex and I stare at her for a good two minutes before I realize that she's still got her visor with her. She probably would have sat up in bed all night watching dreck. I go put it back on the family room shelf while Alex carries Winter and Urvashi up to bed.

While Alex dresses our youngest for bed, I go around and knock on Summer's bathroom door. She opens it.

"Huh?" she asks, without taking the toothbrush out of her mouth.

"Hey dear, I just wanted to talk for a minute."

"Oh. OK. Shoot Mom."

"Look, we both know your sister is special, but she's still only a seven year old. And seven year olds need their sleep. Now, I've got to be able to count on you to help me out. If you're going to let your sister go around zapping baby sitters like that just because you want to stay up late, then I'm not going to be able..."

"Mom, what do you expect me to do about it? The brat must have zapped me too, because I didn't even notice the time until..."

I reach out and gently take hold of the silver chain around Summer's neck.

"Oh, really?" I say. "You know, it's strange. But I've noticed that for almost a week now, Winter hasn't been able to talk you into doing her chores or giving up your dessert. That's about the same time that you started wearing this."

I pull on the chain and fish out the charm she's been wearing underneath her shirt. An interesting little talisman, woven out of brown hair. An extremely familiar shade of brown hair.

"Let me guess, you went in and cut it off while she was sleeping. Nasty trick to play on your sister."

"Mom, come on. Do you have any idea what it's like growing up with the uber-witch for your little sister? This is simple self-defense."

"I never said it wasn't. I just said it was a nasty trick, to go around cutting your sister's hair in her sleep. Unnecessary, too. She's got a barber's appointment on Saturday. That's when I'm getting the trimmings for the one I'm making."

Summer looks at me with an unaccustomed respect.

"You're making one, too? You're sneaky mom."

"Well, I want to be able to give the next babysitter a fighting chance. By the way, where did you learn to make one of these? I haven't shown you that spell yet."

"Oh, I found it on the Web. You're the one who is always telling me to read more."

I kiss her on the forehead.

"Goodnight, dear."

"Goodnight, mom."

I go into our bathroom and wash up. I'm already changed into my nightgown and crawled underneath the covers by the time that Alex finishes tucking in Winter and comes to bed. He's still tense. I rub his back for awhile, trying to calm him, and then cuddle with him as he falls asleep. What had he and Raven seen?

Well, I do have lunch with Jen tomorrow. Maybe she can help me make sense of all this.

## CHAPTER 6: The Police
## Monday Morning, the 9th

I glanced at my watch as I dashed into the station house. 9:07 am. Jan Torcelli was running the security checkpoint at the front door.

"Me-gan, you're la-ate," she chimed, in her annoyingly cute soprano.

I passed her my gun, and walked through the metal detector.

"I kno-ow," I responded, in my completely uncute alto.

She passed me back my gun and I started across the lobby. I saw an elevator door starting to close and sprinted for it. I managed to catch it, but the darn thing was packed with circus clowns. 9:08 I turned for the stairs and ran.

I only had two flights to climb, but they seemed to go on and on forever. I hit the landing for the third floor and slammed open the door to the detective squad room. 9:11. I forced myself to slow down to a walk. No point in attracting attention. If I could just make it to my desk before the Squad Commander noticed I was...

I turned into my cubicle and found him sitting on my desk.

"Lieutenant Strand, how nice of you to fit us into your busy morning schedule."

"Sorry, Captain," I said, preparing to launch into the pro-forma groveling that the situation required, "I was just..." I was just what? Wait a minute, I'm *never* late. What was going on here?

"Skip it." said the Captain. "Much as I'd love to listen to the product of your inventive imagination, I have work to do."

He tossed me a note card with a case file number on it.

"They started on this one last night. See what you can make of it."

I flipped on my computer to call up the case file. I was just starting to read when I heard a squishing noise behind me.

I turned around to see Drew in a soaking wet gorilla suit, with the head tucked under his arm.

"Parker? What the Hell happened to you? Rough undercover assignment?"

Drew glared at me.

"Don't even start with me today." he growled, and sloshed on. I was about to get back to work when he poked his head over the partition between our cubicles.

"By the way, hate the new makeup."

That seemed like an odd thing for him to say. Particularly since I don't wear makeup on the job. I pulled a mirror out of my desk. My skin was vivid blue. Well, I knew that wasn't right. I blinked. Now I was green. I blinked again, and my skin returned to its usual caramel-brown. Good. I'd just have to remember not to blink anymore today, and I'd be fine.

I was putting the mirror away and finally getting down to work when a voice said, "Good Mornin, Megan." It was a deep, masculine voice, with soft Southern drawl.

I looked up to see Tony Browning come walking over to my desk. He was wearing a big cowboy hat, a pair of white boots with fringe, and...nothing in between. OK, OK. I should have known that something was going on right then. I mean, Tony and Drew don't work for the same precinct. In fact, it seemed to me that Drew had left the force a few years back. Still, I was a little too distracted to worry about that right now.

"Um, hi Tony," I said. "Uh...new uniform?"

"We're workin' a drug bust over at one of the gay strip clubs. Undercover work."

"Oh," I said.

Tony is tall, and blond, with blue eyes and the sort of square chin that makes you think he should be a comic book superhero. I bet he was doing well on tips.

With that thought, I suddenly found my wallet in my hand.

"Um...where do they...?"

"Oh," said Tony, flashing that electric smile of his, "there's a card reader built right into the side of the boot. See?"

He put his right boot up on the arm of my chair. My computer started beeping, but I was too distracted to deal with it. Tony leaned over me. The beeping of my computer became a painful buzz. He lowered his face to mine. The buzz became a deafening whine. Windows shattered. The computer screen exploded outward. His lips touched mine. And the booming exploded through my body.

Then suddenly Tony dissolved, and I was alone in the dark.

What the heck was going on here?

BEEP!

Oh. The alarm.

I sat up and tried to find it in the dark. Wait a minute. The dark? Why was it still dark outside?

BEEP!

I found the clock and looked at the time. 5:27 am? What the Hell? I hit the off button. OK. Back to sleep.

BEEP!

I propped myself back up, hit the off button again, and collapsed back into the bed. Sleep now.

BEEP!

I rolled back over, grabbed the alarm, and gave it a good sharp tug. I felt the plug come out of the wall socket.

Good. Now, sleep.

BEEP!

Huh? It can't still be the alarm.

BEEP!

Oh. Phone.

BEEP!

I got up and stepped on something sharp. Limping across the room in the dark, I made my way toward the sound of my phone.

BEEP!

Wait a minute, it can't be the phone. My voicemail picks up calls automatically between midnight and eight in the morning.

BEEP!

Unless someone was using the emergency code. I tried to think of everyone that I had given that code to, but my brain wasn't working yet.

BEEP!

I found the pants I had been wearing the day before and fished the phone out of the pocket.

"Hello?" I mumbled.

"Strand?"

"Yeah." I answered as I tried to coax my brain into identifying the voice. "Commander Davison?"

"You awake Strand?"

"Um..."

"Get there. We've got a mess on our hands. Get dressed. There will be a squad car by to pick you up in fifteen minutes."

"Um, Commander, it's 5:30 in the morning."

"And I've already approved your overtime for coming in early. Now throw on some clothes. I've flagged the relevant case number with your agent. You can read the file on your way to the graveyard."

"Graveyard?"

"WAKE UP, STRAND! I don't have time for this! When the press finds out about this one it's going to get real ugly, real quick. Now I want..."

"Wait a minute, Commander. What's going on? Why are you even in the office this time of day?"

"I came in early to catch up on some paperwork."

"At 5:30 in the morning?" I had long suspected that my 'Watch Commander at the Special Investigations Bureau was a tireless alien cyborg. Now I was sure. "And why aren't night shift detectives working this?"

"They *are* working on this. I've got three of 'em on it already, crunching the data as fast as it comes in. We should have a rough crime scene simulation up and running by the time you get there. But I want you working point on this."

"Oh...OK."

"Do you remember a precinct cop named Browning? Your file says you worked together a few times when you were out at the Fourth Precinct."

"Yeah. Browning. I remember him." In fact, hadn't I just been having a dream about him? Now what had that dream been about...

"Strand? STRAND? YOU'RE DRIFTING, STRAND! Listen, Browning is the precinct detective who started the investigation. We're working off his initial reports right now. I want you to be the one who goes out there and takes over from him. You can keep him on the case if you want to, but keep him away from reporters. OK?"

"Huh?"

"I said, 'OK?'"

"OK."

"Good. Call me as soon as you've got a handle on the crime scene. I want to wrap this one up fast."

He hung up. I walked a couple of steps in the dark, before I realized that I was heading back to my bed. I managed to turn myself around and escape from its gravitational pull. I stumbled over to the light switch.

Ack. Bright light. I blinked back the glare and found my watch. 5:36 am. I made my way to the bathroom and set a North American land speed record for showering and personal hygiene—not including hair. That was a lost cause. I had picked up a brush, looked in the mirror, and knew exactly how Don Quixote must have felt when he picked up his lance and squared off against that windmill. My mother has that rich dark hair that black women are sometimes blessed with, the kind that always curls in just the right places. My dad had straight red hair that was always getting in his face, but in an endearing sort of way. Put 'em together and you get mine—a kinky mess that defies any conventional management technique. Anyway, like I said, lost cause. I went back to my bedroom and threw on a shirt and some pants.

Someone knocked at my door. 5:47. They were four minutes early.

I opened the front door to a beat cop. She looked like she'd been on duty most of the night, and should be nearing the end of her shift. Behind her, the sky was turning pink.

"Good morning, Lieutenant," she said, "I'm..."

"You're Konig," I interrupted. "It says so on your badge."

"Yes, well, if you'll just come..."

"I hope you have coffee." I said.

"Coffee? Well, I..."

"And I don't drink instant."

Konig swallowed. I'm not pretty when I don't get my beauty sleep.

"Um, look, Lieutenant," she said, "my orders are to take you straight to Forest Green Cem..."

I stared at her. She swallowed again.

"...etary. But I think there may be a Dunkin' Donuts with a drive-thru window on the way."

I smiled. She looked relieved.

"Then why don't we get started," I said.

We got in the car, and she started driving. Since my headset was currently sitting in my desk drawer at HQ, I opened the glove compartment and took out her spare. I put it on and flipped on the mike.

"This is Strand, badge number 334057. You there Mindy?"

"Well of course I am, sugar!" the voice came back in the earphone. "You were thinking I might have gone out for a stroll? My, but we are up *early* this mornin'!"

Groan. Ever since I busted that fourteen-year-old hacker last year, my agent program has been speaking with a cornball Texas accent. I've deleted it and reinstalled it four times, but every new copy gets infected within a few hours. I've crawled from one end of the Atlanta Police IntraNet to the other, but I still haven't figured out where he's hidden that damn virus.

"Mindy, Davison was supposed to have flagged a case file for me. Have you got it?"

"Well of course I do, darlin'."

Darlin'? Oh, please. I could almost get used to the accent. It's the preternatural perkiness that really works my nerves. Boy that kid had figured out how to get under my skin.

"Mindy, just shut up and give me the file on visual."

"Ooh, somebody got up on the wrong side of the bed this morning. I'll bet you..."

I flipped off the earphones, pulled out my palm display, and started reading the file. I glanced at the case number.

What the Hell? The first character of the case number was *V*, the code letter for a vandalism case. The commander had gotten me out of bed two hours early for a vandalism case? I tried to think of something I might have done to tick him off. I was scanning the third paragraph of the report when Konig handed me a cup of coffee. Just the smell put me in a better mood.

"Thank you," I said, taking a gulp.

"You're welcome," she answered, as she pulled us away from the donut shop.

"Look, I'm sorry. I'm not much of a morning person."

"I noticed. Don't sweat it, Lieutenant."

"My friends call me Megan."

She took her eyes off the road long enough to shoot me a look that said, "Oh? You *have* friends?" After a moment, she said, "I'm Wendy. Skip the Peter Pan jokes and we'll get along fine."

I skimmed some more of the file while she drove. Beat cop responds to complaint from a household...funny sounds coming from the cemetery... beat cop goes over to check it out...

I couldn't believe that the Commander had gotten me out of bed for this. So help me, if this turned out to be nothing more than a bunch of kids knocking over tombstones, I was going to...

Then I saw the first of the visuals that the beat cop had sent back. My God. I scanned through the rest of the pictures, ignoring the text. No wonder the Commander was freaking about this. The public would go nuts when they saw this.

We hit a bump as the car turned into the cemetery's private road. 6:04. The sun was just poking up over the horizon. We passed a couple of women in jogging shorts.

"People jog at this time of day?" I asked.

"Some people actually like the dawn," said Konig.

"But in a graveyard?"

"Hey, it's open, it's green, and you don't have to dodge traffic. Great way to greet the day. Starts you off with a smile on your face. *You* should try it sometime."

Konig pulled us up behind a crime tech van and an unmarked sedan. 6:07. Up ahead, they had parked a squad car lengthwise across the road as a barricade. It wasn't really blocking much of anything, but it gave the spectators a clear indication of how close they were allowed to get. There were already several joggers gathered to watch the proceedings. Five women, two men. One of the men had a phone with him and was talking into it.

The beat cop who should have been watching the crowd was looking at something on the far side of the car. I couldn't see what it was from this angle, but I assumed it was the crime techs working the scene.

"Thanks for the ride, Wendy."

"Don't mention it."

"Say, Wendy, you've worked a major crime scene before, haven't you?"

"Yeah. A few shootings."

"Hm. What do you think of our friend leaning on the car over there?"

She studied him for a second.

"Clueless."

"Yeah, that's what I thought. How much longer you on duty?"

"Couple more hours."

"You ever been assigned to Special Investigations?" I asked.

"No."

"You want to be?"

It was a loaded question. Special Investigations is supposed to tackle cases which attract substantial media interest and worry the general public. All the precinct cops hate us because we get all the flashy, high profile cases. Of course, they all want to work with us because...we get all the flashy, high profile cases.

Wendy was trying to play it cool.

"Sure."

"Good." I flipped the headset back on. "Mindy, tell Commander Davison that I want to hang on to Officer Konig for awhile. Get her assigned to us."

Wendy was impressed. "That all it takes? You just ask?"

"Normally, no. On a day that the Commander is waking me up to come in two hours early? You betcha."

"OK. What do you want me to do?"

"Well for starters, I want some pictures on the bystanders. Be discreet, but get me some good face shots. After that, take down their names and phone numbers. If anybody says they saw anything, separate them from the rest of the crowd, I don't want them comparing stories and getting each other confused."

"Got it." Wendy unbuckled her seat belt and opened the door.

"Oh, and if anybody turns up *not* dressed for jogging, you're to call me immediately."

"You think the perps are going to come back to watch the excitement?"

"Maybe," I said. "They were clearly going for shock value with this one."

We got out of the car, and Wendy went around to the trunk to get out the camera. Police headsets all have optical pick-ups built in, but they're small, and the depth of focus isn't too good. And since they track where your head points, not your eyes, they don't always see everything you do. Bottom line, if you want to be *sure* you got the shot, you still use a Kodak.

I stretched and took a deep breath. Wendy was right. It was nice out here, this time of day. The sun was just clearing the horizon.

There was a fresh breeze, full of the warm summer smell of cut grass. Yep, I could definitely get to like this dawn thing. If they would just reschedule it for about two in the afternoon.

I walked up to the uniform who was supposed to be monitoring the crowd and tapped him on the shoulder. His badge said "Jefferson". I showed him my ID and he waved me on. I walked past him and around the front of the squad car. That's when I got my first good look at it.

The body was hung upside-down from one of the taller stone monuments. It looked like the perps had used piano wire or something like it to tie him up by his feet. They'd used more wire to suspend the arms out from the sides of the body so the whole corpse formed an inverted cross.

He was nude, and there was a hole cut from his crotch down to his solar plexus. Parts of his intestines were still hanging from the opening, but most of them had fallen in a pile beneath his head. A pile that was attracting a lot of flies.

He was in an uneven, but fairly advanced, state of decay. Some parts of the body were still recognizable—probably where the embalming had been more thorough—but others had rotted away completely. There was enough of the chest and genitalia left to clearly identify the body as male. An exposed bone showed through one of the forearms. But the thing that really bothered me was the face. His tongue was hanging out of his mouth, and his eyes were open. One was completely rotted out. But the other was only half decomposed, and still had this expression of horror in it. Like there was still somebody trapped in that thing.

I was feeling dizzy, and I could taste that damn cup of coffee trying to come back up. I wanted to sit down and put my head between my legs, but it's real hard to give orders from that position. I forced myself to focus and keep walking toward the crime scene. Then the breeze shifted, and I got my first good smell of it.

I'll spare you the description of what a weeks-old rotting corpse smells like on a warm August morning. Something turned over in my stomach. I was trying to catch my breath, but every gasp just brought in more of that smell. I felt my knees going, and I was sure I was going to pass out. I tottered, and then someone put his hand on my shoulder and stopped me from falling.

## Chapter 7: The Police
## Monday the Ninth, 6:11 AM

"You OK?" The voice was male, and had a familiar, soft southern drawl.

I nodded assent, but I was doubled over and hyperventilating and couldn't get enough breath to answer. God, this was embarrassing. I've seen dead bodies before, but something about this one had caught me off guard. Then it occurred to me that my headset was still feeding video into the case log. Great. Somewhere back at headquarters, the image of my thighs was being permanently burned into crystal memory.

I managed to get my balance and straighten up. I found myself looking into the deep blue eyes of Tony Browning. A single blond curl was hanging down over his forehead. God, he really was the Aryan love god from Hell.

"Oh, Megan. I wasn't spectin' them to send you."

There was something odd about the way he said it. Like it was a surprise to see me. And not a good surprise.

"Tony. Good to see you. They told me you were still with the Fourth." It was a stupid observation, and we both knew it. Tony was a good detective, and if he wanted he could move up to Special Investigations, or Homicide, or even Organized Crime. But that would mean leaving the Fourth Precinct, and Tony was never going to leave the Fourth.

"Yeah, well, you know what they say. Birds of a feather. You ever miss the ole gang, now that you're workin up in SIB?"

To tell the truth, I did. I appreciate a well run outfit, and the Fourth is the tightest ship in the department. The precinct runs through the north end of town, up in Cobb County, where the Baptists run things. I'm a Quaker, which means that even though I didn't quite fit the mold, I could get along with powers that be. But Tony, he was born and bred for that precinct.

"Sometimes," I admitted.

Tony was looking at me skeptically. "You sure you're OK?" he asked. "If you need some fresh air, we can..."

"No." I knew from experience how to deal with situations like this. If you keep walking out of the smell for fresh air, then you never get used to it. But if you can force yourself to stay in it for about five minutes, your sense of smell will just give up and shut down.

Tony's hand was still on my shoulder. I lifted it off gently. I couldn't help but notice that there was still no wedding band on it. "Really, Tony, I'm OK now. Thanks for the catch, though."

"No problem. Dang thing freaked me out when I first saw it, too."

There was still that odd tension in his voice. Maybe it was just that we hadn't seen each other in two years. And even before, things had always been a little strange between us. It's like we should have dated when we first met, had a wild passionate affair, realized that we were all wrong for each other, and then broken up on good terms. The problem is that we're both way too sensible for that and had skipped right to the "realizing we're all wrong for each other" part. So it's kind of weird between Tony and me— even though we never dated, it still feels like he's my ex.

"Tell you what, Tony, how about you walk me through what we've got so far."

"Sure thing."

I followed Tony as he walked across the crime scene and stopped next to an open grave.

"As you see, we have a recently excavated hole, with an empty coffin at the bottom. Judgin' by how the top is torn up, it looks like the perps used an axe of some sort. Your crime techs have photographed the tool marks and are gonna try to get a decent impression of the blade from the wood."

He was putting an odd emphasis on the word "your." *"Your* crime techs." Not "the crime techs" or "our crime techs," but *"your* crime techs."

A patch of earth next to the grave had been marked off with little red flags. Tony knelt down next to it and continued.

"We've also got some dandy prints in the soft earth that the perps dug up. These here have been photographed, and your crime techs will be makin' plaster casts as soon as they're done with the body."

There was that "your" again. Something was eating at Tony. Did he think I was going to get him bumped off this case or some-thing? Admittedly, we were taking over the case from his pre-cinct, but the SIB usually asks for the original investigating detec-tive to be assigned to us for the duration of the case. And usually, the precinct detectives are happy to get a chance to work with us and steal a little of the spotlight. So what was Tony's problem?

I knelt down to get a good look at the prints. They belonged to a pair of men's shoes. Loafers or something of that sort. There was an irregularity in the print near the ball of the foot, a thin raised line that could have been from a nick or a cut in the sole of the shoe.

"Any other prints?" I asked.

"Several other partials, no complete sets. Some of the partials don't match up with these, so we're lookin' at more than one perp. They've been photographed, and your folks back at SIB are runnin' comparisons on the images to get some notion of just how many feet we're lookin' at."

Tony stood up and walked around the grave, toward the body and the occult paraphenalia surrounding it.

"If you look here, you'll see that the lines of the pentagram run over some of the loose dirt, so it must have been laid down aftah they dug up the body."

I bent down to take a look at the lines.

"Do you know what this white stuff is yet? Chalk?"

"Naw. Turns out to be lime. Your crime techs say they can run a mass-spectroscopy on it to pin down the maker, but they don't know that it's worth the trouble. Stuff's pretty common. People buy it for their lawns and such. Y'all may have more luck with the candles. They look homemade. If they're wax, we can pin down the manufacturer and canvas the local craft shops. But that's assumin' that they are made out of wax."

"What else would they be made of?"

Tony looked at me like I was stupid, then continued.

"As for the rooster—well, your crime techs say that whatever the perps used to decapitate it was very sharp. No usable tool marks on the animal or the stone it's on. Still, they say they might be able to find some microscopic metal fragments embedded in the flesh. That would at least tell us what the knife was made of. Oh, and I told 'em to go ahead and run a DNA profile on it. Since livestock genes are copyrighted, that might give us some idea what farm it came from."

I was beginning to remember why I liked working with Tony so much. He's thorough, and he thinks of odd things like that. I wouldn't be surprised if he made squad commander in the next five years.

"The plastic bowl next to the rooster," he continued, "is a common brand. No help there. Your crime techs ran a laser over it and didn't spot any prints. We're guessin' the black stuff in the bottom of the bowl is dried chicken blood, but no one has tested or typed it yet. I should point out that what's in the bowl, and the small stain on this here stone, are the only signs of blood in the area. Now, I haven't consulted a vet yet, but I'm guessin' that rooster probably pumped out at least a pint before it expired. Since there's a lot less than that here, the perps must have either put the blood in a container and taken it with them, or..."

"Or they drank it." I said.

Tony looked at me as if I had pulled the thought out of his head. And for just a second, it seemed like old times.

"Yeah, right. We also haven't found any clothin'. So unless this corpse was buried in the nude, the perps must have taken his clothes with them. Which brings us to the ole boy himself."

Tony walked over to the corpse, which was still hanging upside-down. A crime tech was going over the body with a laser. I could see the base of a red pony tail that she'd tucked into the back of her shirt.

"Any luck yet?" I asked her. I noticed that Tony had not spoken to her as we approached. In fact, he seemed to be going out of his way to avoid even looking at her. What was eating him?

"Nothing yet." she answered, turning around. She had an infinity symbol tattooed on her forehead.

"Hi Shard," I said. "Have you met Lieutenant Browning, from the Fourth? Tony, this is Shard Lewis, head of our..."

"Yeah," Tony said. "We all did the meet and greet when she got here."

"Oh." I turned back to Shard. "Think you'll be able to get anything off this guy?" I continued.

"Well," she said, "I've never tried to lift prints off anything this long dead before. Still, there are some good smooth, porous surfaces on him that should hold a print. If there's anything there, I should be able to get it. If I can't find something with the laser, I'll try soft tissue x-ray—that's what we use for lifting prints off live flesh, for rape cases and such. But that will have to wait till we get this guy back to the lab. Oh, there is one interesting thing I did find, though."

Lewis pointed to a spot on the man's chest, near the shoulder. Tony and I knelt down to get a look at it.

"I don't see anything," said Tony. "Just what am I supposed to be lookin' at?"

"Oh, here," said the tech as she swung the laser around. "You can only see it when the light hits it just right. I wouldn't have seen it myself if I hadn't been using the laser."

She moved the beam around, and suddenly I saw it. A faint impression in the flesh. An X, surrounded by a circle.

"What is that?" I asked.

"I think it's a ring." said Lewis. "Maybe an initial ring, or a Malcolm X ring. One of the perps must have banged the back of his hand into the corpse while they were moving it. I've got the impression photographed, and we'll try to protect it when we package this guy for transport."

The crime tech went back to her work. I was about to stand up, but Tony put a hand on my shoulder.

"As long we're down here, I want you to take a look at this." He was pointing toward the corpse's mouth. The tongue had been pulled out and split down the middle like a snake's. I looked closer, and realized that the lips had been sewn shut around it with black thread.

"This is going to be a weird one," I said.

"Oh, it gets even stranger."

We stood up, and Tony pointed toward the triangular incision in the corpse's abdomen. A big chunk of flesh had been removed.

"I checked the name on the grave marker," said Tony, "and pulled up the death certificate. There's no mention of any wound like this. Does the shape remind you of anything?"

I looked at the wound. Tony was right. The shape and the location were too suggestive to be ignored.

"It's a womb," I said. "They cut a *womb* into this guy?"

"That's what it looks like to me."

"What the Hell is going on here?"

Tony opened his mouth and started to say something, but stopped himself.

"Well?" I said. "Tony?"

He still wasn't saying anything.

"Lieutenant Browning, do you have an opinion you would like to voice?"

Tony glanced nervously at Lewis, who was trying to work around us. I followed his gaze to the infinity symbol on her forehead.

All right, I'd had about enough of this nonsense. I turned to Tony.

"You know, I think I do need a breath of fresh air after all. How about you walk with me."

We walked away from the corpse. I waited till we were outside the crime scene and out of earshot of any other cops. I turned and looked at Tony. He stared back. We stood there on the grass, awkwardly watching each other for about a minute. Finally I broke the silence.

"Well, no point in wasting batteries," I said, flipping off my headset and removing it. Everything that goes out over the headsets gets burned into crystal memory back at HQ. No way to delete it. It has to be that way, or some defense attorney could accuse us of altering or planting evidence.

Tony took the hint.

"'Course. Waste not, want not," he said, and removed his headset.

I waited, hoping he would tell me what was going on. When he didn't, I jumped in.

"OK Tony, spill it."

"Spill what?"

"Don't play the dumb blond with *me*, Tony. You've been holding out on me ever since I got here. What gives?"

Tony looked up at the sky.

"Megan, why are you here?"

"You know Tony, that sounded suspiciously like a question," I said in my best no-nonsense voice. "You were not supposed to ask me a question, you were supposed to give me an answer. In case you'd forgotten, *I* am in charge of this investigation, and I will pull your ass off this case if you don't level with me. Now what is going on?"

"Why don't you tell me, Megan? I'm sent out here to investigate a crime scene that reeks to high heaven of black magic and Satan worship. And I'm just startin' to get down to work on it when all of a sudden Special Investigations turns up and throws a net over the whole thing, and tells me to back off while they send in a *witch* to head up the crime tech work. Do I have to spell it out for you? What's going on is that the Conspiracy is covering its tracks. And I have to wonder why it sent you out here to do it."

The Conspiracy. So that's what this was all about. The Baptists and their damn Conspiracy Theory. I'd read a couple of their books on it, back when I was with the Fourth. I'd found the literature to be long on preaching and short on proof, but it pays to keep an open mind. And even when you don't agree with your boss, it pays to know where he's coming from. Basically, the Baptists are convinced that the country is going to pot, and that there must be a secret Organization of Satanists behind all of it: missing children, bad music, teenagers with attitude, role playing games, the rise of Wicca and other New Age religions, drug abuse, the teaching of evolution in public schools, same-sex marriage, the trade deficit, and even cattle mutilations.

So what was I gonna do with Tony? I knew better than to try and explain that my Wiccan crime tech was actually worshipping a pre-Christian nature Goddess. Nope, arguments like that don't fly. As far as the Baptists are concerned, Witches are Satanists, end of story. Hell, the Baptists think that even some of the other *Christian* denominations are satanic.

I looked Tony square in the eye.

"Tony, you and I go way back. You really think I'm a Satanist?"

"Naw," Tony admitted, a little reluctantly.

"Oh, so you just think I'm a dupe."

"I did not say that."

"Yeah, Tony, basically you just did. Come on, you've worked with me before. You think anybody's going to slip *anything* past me?"

Tony looked at his shoes.

"Naw."

"Good. I'm glad we agree on something."

Over Tony's shoulder, I could see one of the uniforms waving at us and tapping his ear. Something must have happened while I was off line.

"Look Tony. You got your way of looking at things, and that's fine. Maybe it even helps you see some things that I don't. But we deal in proof. And you better have a lot more than a tattoo and some religious bigotry to go on before you accuse another cop of being dirty. I'd love to have you on this case, but if you can't buckle down and start dealing in hard evidence, then I don't need you. I'm going to go do my job now. Let me know if you're up to doing yours."

I stormed off, heading back to the crime scene. I was worrying that I might have played that confrontation a little too dramatic. Well, maybe. But at least now I knew why the Commander had been so hot to get me out here. If he left this case with the Fourth, and they went on a witch-hunting crusade, then the Wiccans would scream bloody murder. On the other hand, if SIB sent in someone that the Fourth didn't trust, and the investigation turned up anything other than witches, then the Baptists would be screaming about a cover up. I was the only politically feasible choice.

I put my headset back on and activated it.

"Sugar, where have you been?" said Mindy's irritating little saccharine voice. "Konig has been trying to reach you for the past two minutes."

"Put her through."

"Lieutenant Strand?"

"Yeah, it's me. What you got for me, Konig?"

"Bad news. I was photographing the crowd when I overheard a guy on a cell phone talking to the Baptist News Network."

"Oh great."

"Yeah," she said, "I thought you'd want to know."

"Thanks, Wendy."

Well, I knew the press was going to get ahold of this sooner or later. But I'd been hoping for later.

I took another look at the crime scene. The body, the pentagram, the headless rooster. I thought about what would happen when pictures of those hit the news.

I'd read a book once on rumor panics and how they propagate. Usually they're set off by something small. Somebody vandalizes a church, some kids paint 666 on a tomb stone, a bunch of teenagers start wearing black. And before you know it, people are telling crazy stories about mysterious cultists who are going to kidnap a blond virgin for sacrifice on Friday the 13th. There's never any evidence to back up the rumor, but because people hear the same story repeated over and over again, they start to believe it. They organize vigilante groups, and keep their children home from school, and...

Oh no. Wait a minute. Today was Monday the ninth. Tuesday the tenth. Wednesday the eleventh. Thursday the twelfth. Friday the Thirteenth. Oh, just great.

I looked at the corpse, which was still hanging upside-down from the monument. Rumor panics usually only happen in small towns, where everybody knows everybody else. Big cities like Atlanta are generally immune. But then, generally there isn't something this graphic to set them off. Even Tony, who was a pretty level-headed guy, was freaked by this one. When this story hit the news, there were going to be a lot of scared people screaming for answers. And I didn't have a thing to give them. Yet.

OK, Megan. You know the problem, now how are you going to deal with it? You're stuck with an outdoor crime scene, so there's a limit to how well you can keep this thing under wraps. Even if you bring in twenty uniforms to cordon off the whole area, the news service will just bring in a helicopter and shoot footage from the air.

I glanced at my watch. 6:32. Konig was still waiting for my orders.

"OK, Wendy. Pass your camera off to one of the other uniforms and have him finish photographing the bystanders. Take your car and block the cemetery entrance. Call me the minute any news vans turn up."

"Uh...I can do that, but I don't think it will help much. The cemetary wall is only about two feet high. They'll just step over it and keep going."

"Yeah," I agreed. "But at least then they'll be on foot, and there's a fair amount of ground to cover between here and the entrance. That should buy us at least a five minute warning after your call."

"OK, I'm on it."

I walked over to Lewis. She was stowing the laser back in its carrying case.

"How close are your techs to being done with this thing?"

She thought for a moment.

"Well, we've finished photography and the latent print search. We've got some plaster casts to make, and we have to get everything bagged and tagged. Maybe another hour, to do it right."

We didn't have an hour.

"What if you concentrated on the body and made it priority one," I said. "How soon could you have this thing shipped off to the lab?"

"Well, I'd like to do at least a rough pass for hair and fibers, and we're going to have to be careful how we pack him. At least fifteen minutes."

"Get started on it. Take the time you need, but I want this thing out of sight as soon as possible."

"Yeah," she said, "I can see why."

"Oh, and is there enough skin left on this guy's fingers to take his prints?"

Shard looked at the corpse's fingers, which were badly deteriorated.

"Uh...maybe. I don't think there's much left to work with on the surface, but I can try peeling back the skin and lifting the prints from the underside. What do you want them for, anyway?"

"I want to run them through the national database and see if we can get a definite ID on this guy."

She laughed.

"Don't you think the name on the tombstone is a safe bet?"

"Not the way this case is looking. It's a weird one, and I'm not assuming anything about that corpse until somebody makes a positive ID."

"Well," Shard said, "if I can't get the prints, I can always make a dental X-ray. Assuming that the guy buried in this hole ever went to a dentist, we should be able to match them up with his records. Of course, if he's not a match, I don't know how we'll ever track this guy's name down. Dentists don't turn their records over to any central database."

"We'll deal with that problem if it comes up. Have you pinned down what time this all took place?"

"Not yet. I think we're guessing sometime between sundown and 4:56 am, which is when the first patrolman found all this."

"In that case," I said, "I'll want an autopsy to determine the time of death."

Lewis looked at me like I was out of my mind.

"Um, Lieutenant, this body has been dead for at least a couple months. We're not..."

"No," I said, "not him. I mean the rooster."

The crime tech was still staring at me.

"You want me to do an autopsy on a *chicken?*"

I had a feeling that I was never going to hear the end of this one.

"Well, I can guess the cause of death. All I need from you is the time. Can you do it?"

She though for a moment.

"Well, I can take a liver temperature, but I have no idea how fast a chicken cools off after it dies. I don't even know where to find a table on something like that. It's smaller than a human, so it must cool off faster, but...Or I guess I could try gauging the level of rigor-mortis."

"Can you do it?" I pressed.

"...Yeah. I'll find some way to make it happen."

Just what I like to hear. I turned away and saw that Tony was still standing where I'd left him. I walked over. He had his headset on and was running something on his palm display. I tapped him on the shoulder.

"What you working on?"

Tony looked up.

"I was runnin' a search through the case files, looking for crime scenes with similar imagery." Then Tony straightened up, and with mock formality said, "Ma'am, I do apologize for insinuating that you are, or ever have been, a Satanist dupe."

"Apology accepted, Lieutenant," I said. "Nice to have you onboard, Tony."

"Thanks. Can I ask you somethin', Megan?"

"Shoot."

"Well, I'm worried about you. We're walking into a real mess here, and it's hard to be on guard against something you don't believe in. And you don't believe in the Conspiracy, do you?"

"No, Tony, I don't. I know you guys in the Fourth all buy into it, but I'm a show-me-the-facts kind of girl. And so far I've never seen a scrap of proof that this thing even exists."

"No proof? What do ya call all those survivors that testify on television? They're not proof enough for ya?"

Oh, yeah. The Survivors. People who go into psychotherapy with Christian counselors and come out saying that their parents were Satanists who forced them to drink blood, eat feces, and have sex with demons—and then made them forget all about it.

"Tony, you never wonder why only people who go to Christian counselors turn out to have repressed memories of Satanic rites? How come nobody every goes to a secular psychotherapist and comes out remembering these things?"

"Because the Christian therapists know what to look for. The witches use spells to make their children forget the rites, 'least 'til there old enough to be inducted into the church of Satan. Secular counselors don't know how to get around that."

You know, Tony and I are both bright people, but we really do inhabit different worlds.

"Tell you what, Tony, I don't think we're going to get anywhere arguing the big issues. How about we concentrate on the case. You come at it your way, I'll come at it mine, and maybe together we can make some sense out of it."

"All right. How you wanna run this?"

"Well, we know what happened. Now maybe if we can figure out why, it will give us a lead on who."

"OK. You got any ideas?"

"Well," I said, "let's start with the simplest explanation. Vandals are usually social outsiders. They feel helpless, so they destroy things to show that they have power. Graveyard vandalism is usually the work of teenagers on vision quests. A clique of outsider kids who do something scary and forbidden to build group cohesion..."

Tony cut in. "I don't see it. For one thing, that body took a lot of work to dig up. I don't see a bunch of drunk teenagers going to all the trouble."

"Yeah," I admitted. "And the rooster bothers me. It doesn't seem like something a drunk teenager could get on the spur of the moment. I mean, it would be one thing if we were out in the country, near a farm. But we're in the middle of the suburbs here. Getting ahold of that bird must have taken some planning."

"Then there's that dang smell," said Tony. "Maybe I could buy some kids diggin' up the coffin and breaking it open. But once they got a whiff o' that, you think they're gonna hang around in the smell long enough to do all this occult mumbo-jumbo?"

"Good point," I conceded. Then I thought of something. "Say, did they find any vomit on the scene?"

"No. Well, not unless you count a little accident we had with one of the beat cops."

"Right," I said. "A bunch of drunk teenagers break open the coffin and get a nose full of *that*, and not one of them hurls? I had nothing but a cup of coffee in my stomach and I nearly threw up."

"All right," said Tony, "we agree that it's not just a bunch of kids. Who then?"

"Well," I said, "the imagery reminds me of some the weird shit I've seen serial killers leave behind. And there have been cases of psychopaths who start off mutilating corpses and then work their way up to live victims."

"Yeah," said Tony, "I've read about cases like that too. But serial killers almost always work alone. Very rarely you'll see a pair of them workin' together. And we've got at least three sets of footprints here, maybe more."

"You're right. Which raises the question of how these perps knew each other. I mean, it's not like they could advertise. 'Psychopath, into cutting up corpses, seeking like-minded individuals.' No, the perps had to have some previous connection."

Tony didn't say anything, but he had his "I told you so" look on his face.

"All right," I said. "The obvious answer is that they all belong to some sort of occult organization."

Tony grinned.

"I was wonderin' when you'd get around to the obvious."

"Now hold on, cowboy," I said. "I'm not quite ready to buy the whole Conspiracy story yet. I mean, you guys have been trying to sell this theory for a long time, and so far the most conspicuous feature of the Conspiracy has been the complete lack of hard evidence on it."

"They cover their tracks well."

"Damn well," I said. "So far all you've had on them is some dubious testimony from mental patients, a bunch of dead cows, and some crop circles. You ever seen them do anything this blatant before?"

"Naw," admitted Tony. "I ran a search through every police database in the U.S., and the FBI's occult crime section. Found a lot of sick stuff, but nothin' like this."

"OK. So suddenly this vast secret organization has screwed up and left something like *this* lying around?"

Tony wrinkled up his face, trying to think his way out of that one. "You got a point. The Conspiracy is too smart to leave something like this out in plain sight."

"OK. So where does that leave us? A small group with occult ties of some sort. And some seriously anti-social tendencies."

"Agreed," said Tony.

"Which brings us back to the question of 'why?'. They had to have some reason for doing this ritual. What do you think they were trying to accomplish?"

"Hm." Tony rubbed the back of his head while he thought. "Tell me this Megan. What's the one thing about this whole thing that really grabs your attention?"

"The corpse."

"Yeah, but more specific."

I looked at it again.

"The womb they cut out of him."

"Yeah, that's the thing that I noticed, too. I'm bettin' that they were tryin' to give birth to somethin'. Somethin' that could only spring from a dead man. An imp, or a demon, or somethin' else blasphemous."

"OK," I said, "that seems like a reasonable hypothesis." Then an ugly thought occurred to me. "If they were trying to give birth to something, they might actually have tried to impregnate the body. We should probably have the crime techs check the corpse for signs of semen."

Tony grimaced. "Yuck. You got a nasty imagination there. But you're right. I'll make a note of it."

"Thanks. Now what about the rest of the image? The split tongue and the sewn-up mouth. They don't seem to quite jive with this birthing theory."

"Well, 'forked tongue' is a common expression for a liar," said Tony.

"Right, and the lips sewn shut would seem to be symbolic of trying to silence someone. Like they didn't want this guy talking about something."

"So, what did they think he was gonna say?"

"I don't know," I admitted, "unless...Why do you think they chose this guy to dig up?"

"What do ya mean?"

"Well this grave is a couple months old. It would have been easier for them to dig up a fresher grave, because the soil would be looser. It's also not in the most isolated spot in the cemetery, so they probably didn't choose it for privacy. But it's also not near an edge of the graveyard, so it couldn't have been the first grave they came to. So either they chose this one completely at random..."

Tony caught on. "...Or they knew this guy." He cast another glance at the body. "And from the look of it, they had quite a grudge to settle."

"And that," I responded, "just might give us a short list of suspects. We should have a talk with this guy's family, see if he had any enemies."

"Yeah, I'll get right on..." his voice trailed off as he thought about something. "Wait a minute," he continued. "I've got another question. Why do it now? I mean, this guy's been in the ground for a couple of months. If somebody had a score to settle with him, then why didn't they dig him up before now?"

"Hm. That is an interesting question. Well, you know more about this occult stuff than I do. Was last night of any special significance on the astrological calendar?"

"Let me check." Tony pulled out his palm display and mumbled something into his mouthpiece. "Well, it was a new moon, but not much else. Not the equinox, not one of the annual meteor showers, not one of the pagan holidays. Can't think of anything else to look for. 'Course, there are some other people I can ask."

"Do that. In the meantime, I want us to..."

A voice spoke up in my headset.

"Lieutenant Strand?"

"Here," I responded.

"It's Konig. They've turned up. A Baptist News Network crew. They're coming at you on foot. You got four, maybe five minutes."

I checked my watch. 6:41.

"Oh, great. I hadn't expected them so soon."

"It gets better. There's a Microsoft Information Service van just parking now. They won't be more than a minute behind the BNN. "

"OK. Thanks Wendy. Hang out there and give me a heads up as the other networks arrive."

I turned to Tony.

"The news crews have started to arrive. I want to try to keep the body off-camera."

"Hm. That's not gonna be easy with this setup."

We turned and walked back over to the site. Two of the crime techs were lifting fibers from the body. A third was packaging their finds in small plastic bags and labeling them.

"How's it coming?" I asked.

Shard looked up.

"Well, I need another 7 or 8 minutes to do it right. Any faster than that and..."

"You've got it. But then get this thing in the bag and out of here. We've got media coming down on us."

"Gotcha," said Shard.

I looked around the perimeter. We had six uniforms on hand. I had to leave at least three working crime scene isolation. That left me three to run interference. I picked out the three largest.

"You, you, and...you. Over here."

Three beefy uniforms came over at a jog.

"OK guys, here's the situation. We've got two news crews coming in, and I don't want pictures of that corpse going out on the net. You're going to buy us a few minutes to get that body packaged and out of here. Go out and greet those camera crews. Be polite. Be friendly. Be helpful. But be in the way.

"Now, if they try to get you to say something on camera, just come back at them with some stupid questions. You probably know the drill. 'What network are you guys with? What kind of camera is that? Is my mom going to see...'"

My eyes had strayed down to the right hand of one of the beat cops. There was something about it that caught my attention. Something that tickled the back of my brain, warning me that I was about to miss something important. I stared at his hand for a few more seonds, and then finally realized what I was seeing.

"Excuse me..." I read the name off his badge. "...Wilson. Have you come into contact with the corpse at all?"

"No, ma'am."

"You're absolutely sure?"

"Yes, ma'am."

"What's up?" asked Tony.

I took Wilson's right hand and held it up for Tony to see.

"Look familiar?"

Tony scrunched up his forehead, like he always does when he can't quite remember something. Then his face lit up.

"Yeah. The impression on the body."

Not an X surrounded by a circle. A cross. A silver cross surrounded by a gold circle with some sort of inscription. I looked closely and read it.

"One Nation Under God."

## Chapter 8:  The Lunatic
## Monday the Ninth, 8:22 AM

It was a beautiful August morning, and the drive in from the country had been splendid.  I'd passed most of the ride in meditation, dreaming of a poem that hadn't been written yet.

"And why is it we envy so
The mysteries that children know
Of faerie forts and haunted wood
Of cowboys, knights, and Robin Hood?

And why do we presume to teach
Who've place our dreams so out of reach.
And why must children learn *our* truth:
The bitter aftertaste of youth?"

The limousine turned a corner and I caught a glimpse of a street sign.  Courtland.  That meant we were only a few minutes away from the Atlanta courthouse.

Across from me, Broken Arrow opened his pistol to check the magazine.  He seemed satisfied with it and put the gun back in his shoulder holster.  Beneath the blue war paint, his face was a study of calm concentration.  The other men in my detail always took their cues off him.  He was the model, the way a warrior is supposed to behave under pressure.  Of course, for me the effect was ruined by his totem, a cartoon woodpecker that circled his head, giggling maniacally and drilling his temples.

My other body guard, Last Mouse, was staring out the window.  He had been born 19 years before, on the day that the Kangaroo Rat became extinct.  I sometimes wish his parents had not named him so hastily.  He is always trying to live down the name, and appear tougher than he is.  But he can't mask his gentleness from me.  When it comes down to the wire, and he is faced with the need to kill, he will hesitate.  And he will die.  But that day is many years off, and I will be dead by the end of the week.  And in the meantime, I enjoy his company.

Between them, my apprentice, Forgets-to-Smile, sat jotting something down in a notebook.  Her totem, a cat, appeared every few seconds to bat at her pencil.  She wrote on without seeing it. I watched the two of them, and hoped they were ready for the test that was coming. This was the day that would see my successor chosen. I desperately wanted it to be her. But it was not my choice to make.

The limo hit a bump, and Laughing Bear, who had been sitting next to me, used it as an excuse to fall into my lap.

"Oops!" he said with a grin.

"Is that a revolver in your loincloth," I responded, "or are you just glad to see me?"

He answered by leaning up to kiss me, then settled his head back into my lap. Actually, he wasn't even wearing a loincloth, just traditional deerskin breeches and a quill breastplate that left his arms and shoulders bare. A bit hokey, but he looks damn good in it. I have never stopped wondering how a crazy old woman like me wound up with such a hunky young husband. But then, Laughing Bear is a member of the Bowstring Warrior Society, and they're supposed to do everything backwards: laugh in battle, weep at jokes. Maybe marrying an ugly old woman is just another part of their game. No matter. He's made me very happy.

I heard the shouting, and then something bounced off the roof of the limo. We were only a few blocks away from the courthouse now, and the sidewalk was thick with people. We passed a group of Christians who were waving Bibles and U.S. flags and screaming bloody murder. One of them had a ten-foot tall cross outlined in gold tinsel with a liquid crystal display on the crossbar. I watched its flashing words:

"...*One* Nation under *God*!..."

"...Give Satan an Acre..."

"...And he'll take the world!..."

Next to the guy with the cross stood a kid who couldn't have been more than fifteen. He wasn't shouting anything, he was just holding up a hand painted sign that said, "Satin get out of Georgia." And he had the sweetest smile on his face. He looked so innocent that I just wanted to walk over and inform him that he was making a fashion statement rather than a political one. His totem was a monkey that sat on his shoulders with his hands over the boy's ears.

On the other side of the street were the Cherokee: Purebloods in jeans and T-shirts, Returnees in buckskins and crazy feathered head dresses. Even a few white New Agers with wooden staffs and crystal pendants.

In front of the courthouse, a policeman stopped us while he checked the limo's license plate number against the approved list. Then he came around to the side of the car and knocked on the window. Broken Arrow rolled it down and handed over our identification. The noise from the crowd was deafening. The policeman looked over our ID cards, checking our faces against the pictures, and then motioned for Broken Arrow to get out of the car. I saw the two of them talk for a moment as the cop pointed to the courthouse entrance, the lines of protesters flanking it, and the police holding them at bay. From the look of it, the police had even managed to keep the Cherokee and Baptists more or less separated, on opposite sides of the corridor.

Broken Arrow stuck his head back in the limo and began giving orders. He and Last Mouse took up positions on the right, trying to screen my apprentice and me from any rifles on the Baptist side of the corridor. Laughing Bear walked to our left, in case there were any guns hiding among the Cherokee. We started for the entrance.

It was only fifty feet. Just across the street, over the sidewalk, and up the steps. But there was a world of trouble between us and that front door. Oh, the police were keeping the protesters separated, but their spirits were in full battle over the courthouse steps.

Most of the Christian's totems were manifesting as angels. I saw a couple of plump cherubim in camo with AK-47's go flitting past to engage a mountain lion that was slashing back at them with its claws. Another angel with a cowboy hat, sixshooters, and a serious John Wayne wannabe complex was going after a thunder hawk. And some Baptist had a totem that looked like a basset hound with wings and a halo. It was getting into a rumble with a coyote.

There were also a bunch of spirits that I couldn't classify. I mean, one guy's totem was manifesting as the Professor from Gilligan's Island. Whose side was he on? Or what about the four spirits that all turned up looking like Bugs Bunny? Or the big crystal thing that was slowly spinning and shooting out rays of light? It took me a minute to figure out where I'd seen that one before. Clearly somebody in this mob has been watching *way* too much *Star Trek*.

We made it halfway up the steps before any of the spirits challenged us directly. Joan of Arc dropped down out of the sky and leveled a flamethrower at us.

"And just where do you think you're going, little Witch-Doctor?"

"Buzz off, sister, I don't scare easy."

She laughed. It was a particularly nasty laugh. "Then maybe I should teach you what to be afraid of," she said.

I don't know what trick she had up her sleeve, but I wasn't in a mood to play. I unleashed my own totem. A twenty foot snake sprang up, hissing and rattling and dripping venom from its fangs. Joan looked at it and knew she was outclassed.

"Just kidding," she said with a nervous giggle. Then took off. The last I saw of her, she was opening fire on some totem that had turned up as Batman.

I've often thought that life must have been a lot easier for Shamans before the advent of television. You saw talking animals. OK, it was a little odd, but you could get used to it. And maybe you saw an angel if you ran across a Christian, or a twenty-armed demon if you happened across a Hindu, but mostly you just saw animals. I'm not sure why all the new manifestations have turned up. There was a panel discussion on it at a cross-tribal shamanic conference in Alaska a few years back. We decided that one possibility was that people were subconsciously choosing new forms for their totem spirits based on what they were seeing on TV. The more disturbing possibility is that the spirits themselves had started watching TV, and were choosing these new forms on their own.

We reached the entrance, where my husband, my apprentice, and I passed through the metal detector and into the courthouse. Broken Arrow and Last Mouse, who were packing the real weapons, headed back to the car to wait for our departure. Theoretically, I would be safe as long as I stayed in the controlled environment of the courthouse. And if that theory broke down in practice, I still had Laughing Bear to protect me. He might giggle in battle, but he was one Hell of a hand-to-hand fighter.

In the lobby we were met by First Robin, one of the junior law clerks on the case.

"Ice-in-Summer'" she said, extending her hand to me. "It's an honor to meet you again. I don't know if you remember me, but..."

"Of course I do. And I told you the last time we met to call me Grandma. Everybody else does."

(OK. I admit it's a bit odd to have an entire tribe calling me their Grandmother. But none of the alternatives worked. "Your Eminence"? Please, way too formal. "Holy Woman"? You ever tried getting a date with a title like that? "Cranky old lady who sees things and rambles on and on but we all put up with her because she's older than Methuselah and just might say something important"? Close to my job description, but a real mouthful. And isn't "Grandma" so much more succinct?)

Robin's face brightened. "All right then, Grandmother." She took my hand in hers and lead us across the lobby to the elevators. On the way she whispered in my ear. "It's not going well."

That surprised me.

"I thought they had settled on a legal strategy weeks ago. What's gone wrong?"

"Roaring Grizzly is here."

Oh, just great. Of all the people I wanted to deal with today, Roaring Grizzly was at the bottom of the list. Roaring Grizzly is the Cherokee Shaman who proved that televangelism is not an exclusively Christian phenomenon. His show airs five times a week on our cable channel. And in the Nation's spiritual life, he is second only to me. Ironically, it is my isolation that has made me the more potent force. Put a person on TV, and he becomes familiar. But hide her away, and she becomes mythic.

I suppose he had to be here. After all, it was Roaring Grizzly who organized the Ghost Dance. Roaring Grizzly who led his followers out into that National Forest to perform it. Roaring Grizzly who sought to drive the white man from the lands of our ancestors by magic ritual. Did he really think the Christians would sit back and let him try it? It didn't take the Baptists long to conclude that he was trying to summon Satan himself. I don't know if that fundamentalist minister knew how much trouble he was starting when he set out to disrupt the ceremony. Did he really think he could control a bunch of his good old boys with guns? Or that we didn't have guns of our own? We're lucky it was only seven Cherokee and four Baptists that died in that shootout.

Maybe it's not fair to blame Roaring Grizzly for the whole mess. But then, it's not like I need another reason to hate him, anyway. He's slick and he's self-centered and he never thinks about the consequences of what he starts. But the real kicker is that *he's got the sight*. He may be a buffoon and a showman, but he's also the real McCoy. And that makes him dangerous. I would rather that he was nowhere near the place of testing.

We boarded an elevator, and Last Robin punched the button for the seventh floor. I noted the sour expression that still lingered on her face.

"I take it you don't like Roaring Grizzly," I said.

"He's a crazy Returnee," she said, matter-of-factly.

I sighed. It is an understandable prejudice. Last Robin was one of the Purebloods, those whose ancestors had stayed on the reservation and learned how to play the white man's game. How to make money from casino gambling, and how to turn that money into political clout. How to live in the modern world. The Returnees, on the other hand, were part Cherokee who mostly came back to the tribe because they were rejecting the modern world. They tended to be extreme environmentalists or crystal-worshiping New Agers who wanted to go back to the land and forget about everything since the development of fire. New Returnees in particular have an annoying habit of trying to out-Cherokee the Cherokee. They wear traditional dress everywhere, spend weeks learning to hunt with a bow and arrow, and in some particularly annoying cases, give up the use of soap and deodorant. Usually they mellow out after a few years, though. And for all the trouble they cause, the

Nation desperately needs the manpower the returnees provide. After seven generations where the rate of outbreeding topped 70%, there aren't many Purebloods left.

I took Last Robin's hand and pressed it to my face. The brick red of her skin against the wrinkled pale white of mine. She caught her breath and lowered her eyes.

"I'm sorry Grandmother. I forgot. But you're not like the other Returnees."

No, that was true enough. My return to the nation had nothing to do with green politics or a fascination with crystal magic. I had been quite happy living in the white world, vaguely aware that one of my grandparents had been Cherokee. I had a swell apartment, a good income, and a great job as a graphic designer for a software firm. And sure, sometimes I saw things that hadn't happened yet, but everybody gets *déjà vu*. And if I dreamed of a poet who hadn't been born yet, and poems that hadn't been written, at least I couldn't remember much of them when I woke up.

Then, on my 35th birthday, I got blindsided by a drunk driver. When I woke up in the hospital I was seeing talking animals and characters from old sitcoms. A few hours later, a crazy old Cherokee shaman turned up and explained my options. In the white world, talking to invisible animals made me a candidate for the loony bin. In the Nation, it made me a holy person. It was not a tough choice.

And so, though I am of the Nation, I am at home among neither the Purebloods nor the Returned. I am an outsider. But it is a role that suits me.

We reached the seventh floor, and First Robin led us down the hall and into the conference room. She was right. The situation was a mess.

Roaring Grizzly and Stan Fallen Dove were yelling at each other across the conference table. Everyone else was hugging the walls, not wanting to get caught between the two of them. Jason Storm Chaser, lead counsel for the Nation, caught my eye as we entered. I saw him mouth the word "Help!"

I sat down quietly, determined to get the lay of the land before I stuck my nose into the middle of this one. Stan was banging his fist on the table, looking like he was about to blow a blood vessel. Stan is normally a pretty controlled guy, but Roaring Grizzly can bring out the worst in him.

Come to think of it though, so can I. Stan is president of the Tribe's corporation, and we've locked horns several times in the past. He's never been quite sure what to make of me. He has to admit that my information is good, if not always precise. I can't see specific movements in the stock market or next week's price of oil.

But I do catch most of the major things: wars, droughts, floods, hurricanes. And Stan can usually figure out how the tribe can make a buck off it. I actually respect Stan. At least, more than he thinks I do. Stan's a good manager. Under his leadership, our casino businesses have been more profitable than ever, and more importantly, Stan has been extremely successful at turning our new wealth into political clout. A number of entirely legal, if somewhat underhanded, campaign contributions. It doesn't quite have the moral pique of warriors doing battle on horseback, but it is how modern wars are fought.

The problem with Stan is that his way of doing things will eventually leave us as empty and barren as the white man. What good is it to finally beat them, if we wind up becoming them? Greedy, exploiting the land like a slave, bent on acquiring endless goods in the vain belief that they will make us happy. And losing our sense of who we are and where we come from.

The two men continued arguing over the table, but I noticed that Roaring Grizzly's totem seemed to be losing interest. It had crawled out onto the table and was poking around the flower arrangement. It is indeed a bear, although it has always manifested itself to me as a teddy bear.

"If there were any justice," I said under my breath, "you would be a weasel."

It must have heard me, because it turned and pulled the draw-string in its back.

"Hey Mack, I didn't *ask* for this gig."

Roaring Grizzly was wearing a bearskin cloak, the bear's head forming a sort of ridiculous hat, its jaw poking out over his forehead, its glass eyes staring out. Beneath the bear's white teeth was the dark face of Roaring Grizzly himself. Like many of the Returned, he feigns the look of a Pureblood. Black hair dye, dark contacts, and full body tattooing to darken his skin tone. I suppose it's harmless. Still, I wonder what his viewers would think if they knew about the hour he spent each morning with an iron, straightening his hair.

I guess it's not so much that I hate Roaring Grizzly, as that I'm scared as Hell of him. As a shaman with the sight, he has a legitimate claim to be my successor. Probably a better one than Forgets-to-Smile. But Roaring Grizzly is a fanatic believer in tradition, who would have us return to the land and live as our ancestors did. But what does that mean? To go back before the gun? Or before horses? Or before the introduction of corn? The truth is that the Cherokee have always made use of new technologies as they became available to us.

So what does it mean to be a Cherokee? I don't think that either Fallen Dove or Roaring Grizzly knows. I'm not sure that I do either. Our language is lost. We can no longer speak the words of our grandfathers. And so much else is lost as well. Most of our sacred rituals are gone forever. We borrow where we can, from the Plains Indians, from the Iroquois, sometimes even from the Pueblos. Anyone who can remember their sacred ways. But it's not the same.

What does it mean to be Cherokee? I have wrestled with that since the day I returned, and I have tried to give the Nation guidance. And my successor will have an even tougher road to follow. Which is why I am so nervous about this test. I can only hope that Forgets-to-Smile has the strength within her, for my mantle must not fall on Roaring Grizzly. For he would lead the Nation to oblivion. It must be Forgets-to-Smile.

The two men were still yelling at each other. I looked around. The rest of the room broke down neatly. The defendants all belonged to Roaring Grizzly; the lawyers were Stan's. Not that Stan gave a rat's ass what happened to a bunch of crazy ghost dancers who went around getting into fights with equally crazy Baptists. But he had recognized the possibilities of the case, and what it could mean to the Nation.

Stan didn't care about who'd fired first or who'd fired in self defense or just what all these gun toting lunatics had been doing out there in the first place. Nope. All that mattered to Stan was that the firefight had taken place in North Georgia, on the land of our fathers. On the land which the U.S. Government had recognized as ours in the treaties of 1816 and 1817. The land which the U.S. Supreme Court had confirmed as ours in its ruling of 1831 and then again in 1832. The land which President Andrew Jackson and his army nonetheless drove us off of in 1838 to make room for white settlers. Marching us on the Trail of Tears to dry and dusty Oklahoma. Until they finally decided that they wanted that land, too.

Guilt and Innocence were irrelevant concepts to Stan. Jurisdiction, on the other hand, was everything. For by using Jurisdiction, Stan hopes to regain the land of our fathers. His lawyers will argue that under the Supreme Court Ruling of 1832, the case belongs in Cherokee tribal courts rather than Georgia State courts. It's a small beginning, but it is a beginning. Next year we will file suit in the Hague's court of International Law, demanding that the U.S. Government return the land promised us under the treaty, which now constitutes the northern half of the State of Georgia. A jurisdictional ruling in the present case would be a powerful admission by the Yankees that we are in the right.

Of course, I'm sure that the State of Georgia isn't going to just sit still and see itself chopped in half without a fight. The Attorney General will no doubt argue that we haven't been on the land for 200 years or so. But we have the treaty, and a Supreme Court decision upholding it. The Whites may have history on their side, but we have the law. And finally, we have the money to make the law work.

Still, Fallen Dove and Roaring Grizzly bicker on. I try to follow their argument, but the details elude me. Have they lost sight of what we're doing? It is a momentous undertaking, and should be treated with reverence. To be once again on our father's land, the places they knew, the spirits they talked to. That is too sacred a goal to let two spoiled brats ruin it at the last moment.

I lit up one of my hand-rolled cigarettes. Everyone around me, my husband included, instantly wrinkled their noses. I can't blame them. I smoke *tobacco rusticana*, the wild and more pungent variety. The smell is quite...attention-getting.

The smoke dispersed through the room, and Stan and Roaring Grizzly had to stop arguing long enough to cough and wipe the tears from their eyes. Roaring Grizzly looked at me and spoke. "Is that such a good idea, Grandmother? They tell me you have emphysema." He feigns concern because he knows that I won't last much longer. And a power struggle with a dying old woman would only weaken him in the eyes of the Nation.

"I saw the possibilities for my death long ago," I said, blowing a smoke ring at him. "And I made my choice. Trust me, one more cigarette now is not going to make any difference."

Then, before the two of them could remember what they were arguing over, I started reciting poetry.

"And as I spit out my last breath,
It's not my errors I regret,
Nor stupid things I did for love,
Nor sins against some God above.
But seconds wasted on details,
Ticking by like coffin nails,
And all the dreams and all the rhymes,
I leave undone for lack of time."

I turned to Jason Storm Chaser, the lead lawyer on the case. "If these two butt out, do you know what needs to be done?"

Jason looked from Stan to Roaring Grizzly, not wanting to alienate either of these powerful men. I shot him a look which reminded him that *I* was the one he'd better not piss off.

"Yes, Grandmother."

"Then come forward."

I nodded to Forgets-to-Smile, and she took the small pots of paint out of her bag and set them on the table. Jason stood before me, and I painted the marks on his face, saying:

"Go now, and be strong,
Go now, and be wise,
Go now, and be joyous in your battle,
For you fight for the Nation,
And the land that was our fathers',
And the land that will be our children's."

Then the other lawyers came forward. I painted them each, repeated the blessing. Then they went down to the courtroom and into battle.

Laughing Bear, Forgets to Smile, and I followed them down. Seats had been reserved for us in the gallery, of course. And I tried to pay attention. Really I did. But it was just all *so boring*. Lawyers quoting case law back and forth for hours on end. I started going into nicotine withdrawal and had to light up another cigarette. A bailiff glared at me and pointed to the no smoking sign on the wall. I glared back at him, and let him see just enough of the cold snake in my eyes to let him know whom he was dealing with. His face went pale. Then he realized that there are much scarier things in this world than the dangers of second-hand smoke, and went on about his business.

I passed the time watching totems. The lawyers totems all manifested beautifully whenever they spoke, even if it was just for some dry technical motion. There was one from the other side who caught my attention in particular. Whenever he addressed the judge, his totem appeared as a swirling cluster of shields behind him. It was a symbol that I knew from somewhere, but I couldn't place it. Until, just for a second, the swirling cluster resolved itself into a male form with outstretched arms. His sword flashing brilliant, his wings like burning gold.

Oh, boy. The Archangel Michael?! I sent a note to Jason telling him to watch out for this guy. He was going to be trouble.

After awhile, I got bored watching the lawyers, and switched to watching the spectators. Every so often one of their totems would come out to play. A cartoon dragon. Zorro. A giant robot. A gargoyle. I sat there and watched them for almost two hours before I saw the dark form pass over the crowd.

It was like the shadow cast by a hawk circling overhead, and it sent all the little totem spirits diving for cover. It circled silently, a harbinger of death. Exactly what I had been waiting for. Because only in the face of death can one be reborn and awakened to new, and different, life.

"Go get me some coffee," I said to Laughing Bear.

He looked back at me, puzzled.

"You don't drink coffee."

"I didn't say I was going to drink it, I said that you were going to get it."

For a second, Laughing Bear looked like he was going to try and argue with that logic. Then he shrugged and left. He knows better than to try and reason with me.

The shadow circled the courtroom three more times, then flew out the exit at the back.

I turned to Forgets-to-Smile. "Come."

She looked up from her notebook, then followed me without asking any questions. Roaring Grizzly saw us leaving and came chasing after us. I should have known I wouldn't be able to avoid him. He caught us at the door.

"Grandmother, where are you going? We need your spiritual guidance at this..."

"The test is come," I said. "I suppose you should be there." One of the perks of being a shaman is that you don't have to explain cryptic statements like that.

Out in the hall, I found no trace of the Shadow Hawk. I looked around for some sign, and saw a clerk with a stack of papers walking by. His black leather shoes left bloody paw prints on the floor. I followed him, the two candidates for my successor in tow.

We rounded a corner, and the prints stopped abruptly.

"Where are we going?" insisted Roaring Grizzly.

"Shhhhh!" I responded.

A woman approached us wearing a stole of mink, or sable, or some other rodent with a pedigree. As she passed us, the rodent opened its eyes and growled at me.

I growled back. The woman turned around and looked at me. The mink laughed and spoke.

"Come on then, little sorcerer, if you're so eager to die."

"I *know* the hour of my death, vermin, so none of your tricks. Take me where I need to go."

The woman, realizing that she was dealing with a crazy person, backed away from us slowly, then turned and walked briskly for one of the elevators. My entourage and I followed her, and we managed to squeeze onto the same car, even though she didn't hold the door for us. The mink kept giggling. We were close.

On the next floor, a boy got on. He was wearing an Atlanta Cubs T-shirt and jeans, and looked like he was all of 19. Probably here to pay a parking ticket. His totem spirit, a Tyrannosaurus, peeked out nervously from behind him.

Two floors later, a middle aged man got on the elevator. He instantly put me on edge. There was something very strange about him. I studied him for a few seconds, trying to figure out what it was. Then I realized it: I couldn't see his totem.

Totems only fully manifest at times of great passion, like battle or sex. But even in a relaxed state, they usually appear every few seconds. Sometimes as little more than smoke, but you always see something. But this guy was showing nothing.

I mean, he had to have a totem. Everyone does. But he'd buried his deep. Or maybe he was just very self-controlled, self-contained. Either way, he had to be the one. He had to be the assassin.

I saw him glance at me, and then do a double take. He looked over my dress, my face, my throat. A confused expression crept over his face. Then he smiled, and a glimmer of recognition twinkled in his eyes. He knew my secret!

Damn, this guy was good. Not many anglos guess my real secret. But then, not many of them ever stop to think that an old Cherokee woman in a buckskin dress might not be *quite* what she appears to be. I wondered if this guy might even have a little of the sight.

He saw me staring back at him, and we shared one of those awkward moments when you both know something you're not supposed to.

I smiled at him and said, "Hello, my name is Ice-in-Summer." If he was going to try and kill me, I thought we ought to at least be introduced.

"Oh," he said. "Hello…ma'am, my name's…"

Then the elevator stopped abruptly, between floors, and the alarm went off. Which was odd, because I hadn't seen him touch the emergency stop. Then I heard the T-Rex roar, and felt the pain in my stomach.

How could I have missed it?

I looked down to see the kid pull the knife out of my gut. It was transparent acrylic, and my blood didn't stick to it, but ran off, leaving it clean like some gleaming piece of crystal. Laughing, the boy grabbed my hair and jerked my head back as he brought the knife up in a wide arc.

But I look away from the knife, to Forgets-to-Smile. This is it. The moment that will push her over the edge and awaken her powers, if they ever can be. It must be her, and it must be now. I look into her eyes and wait for the cat to emerge. The cat that sees and understands and looks straight into your soul. The cat that will paralyze this child with fear and stay his hand. I look at her, and I wait. And nothing happens. Nothing.

The knife starts down in a long, slow arc to cut open my neck. And I force myself to look at Roaring Grizzly. Barely able to stand my defeat. Not wanting to see him transformed, the sad little teddy bear turned into a grizzly. But I see his eyes, and they are as empty as Forgets-to-Smile's. And the knife keeps coming down.

This cannot be happening. To have the wrong successor would have been a disaster. But to have none? To be the last. To die here and now, my work unfinished.

And this last thought brings me back to myself. I am no helpless old woman, to be murdered by some child with a knife. I unleash the snake, and its power fills the small space of the elevator like a storm. The woman in the coat, standing across from me, gasps. Already shocked by the sudden appearance of the knife, her face now goes white, her heart almost stopped by the terror of what she sees in my eyes. And I turn to deal with this upstart little child who thinks he can kill *me*!

But he has gripped my hair too tightly, and I cannot bring my eyes around to his. And the knife comes down. And it's just too pathetic. And all I can think as the pain rips through me is that it was not supposed to end like this. This was not the death I chose!

Then I am holding the back of my head. And I look up to see the laughing child pinned up against the elevator doors, still gripping a handful of my hair. And the one whose totem I can't see has him in some sort of hold.

"You may as well stop squirming, kid. I've been getting a lot of practice at this move lately."

Then the man turns to me. "You OK?"

I put my hand to my throat, relieved to find that the moisture is only sweat.

Forgets-to-Smile starts fussing over the blood on my dress, and Roaring Grizzly is trying to support me. But I'll be damned if I'll lean on him. I stand on my own feet and look the stranger in the eye.

"It won't kill me."

Then Forgets-to-Smile recovers her wits enough to push the start button, and the elevator begins moving again.

And everything seems strangely quiet. Like the world is getting further and further away from me. And all I can think is that I am alive. But without a successor. The last. Dying. And old. And the last.

And it's too much. And I find myself speaking.

"The last week, the last day, the last hour,
Tick on.
And all my youthful dreams

Of glory, fame, and power
Die with the passing minutes.
And I am forgotten."

The man who is holding the boy listens to me recite the verse, and I can see it moves him.

"It's by my favorite poet," I say.

"Yes," he says, "I've always liked that one." He tightens his grip as the boy tries to squirm again. Then he turns back to me and finishes it.

"And in the end, it comes to this,
That I never was the first or best.
But hey,
Who ever said that life's a test
Anyway?"

Then I am lying on the floor, and the doors are open to the lobby, and there are police everywhere. Someone is screaming for paramedics, and someone else is trying to staunch the slow bleeding from my stomach.

I am falling, falling, falling into the coils of the snake. I see the man slipping away into the crowd. I try to yell after him, but there is no more breath in my old body, and no one hears my words.

"Who the Hell are you? And how do you know the words to a poem that won't be written for another fifty years?"

## Chapter 9: The Chosen
## Monday the Ninth, 10:55 AM

I was looking at it, but I still couldn't believe it.

D-.

My face was burning, and I was having trouble reading the message on my notebook. I realized there were tears building up in my eyes. Oh great. That's just what I needed now.

I put a hand over my eyes while I tried to get control of my face. I didn't need to have the whole school know that I was about to fail English. I turned and faced the wall and read the rest of the evaluation.

"Nice idea, and good arguments to support your thesis. However, you will note the following three grammatical mistakes that I have highlighted in your report. As you know, I deduct a full letter grade for each such error. Rely less on the grammar checker and proofread your work more carefully. J. Chandler."

"Nice idea?" I'd come up with a friggin' brilliant paper proving that Heinlein was really just an extension of Thoreau and the Transcendentalist movement of the 1800s. Yeah, I know it sounds crazy, but it's all right there in *Stranger in a Strange Land*—once you realize what you're looking for. And I'd gone through *Walden Pond* cover to cover pulling quotes to nail down my argument. And all I get for my trouble is "nice idea" and a D-.

I forced myself to read through the three mistakes that Chandler had highlighted. She was right, of course. They were just the sort of stupid mistakes that the grammar checker can miss. I'd used "herse" instead of "horse," I had a pronoun with an unclear antecedent, and I had an adjective that had gotten separated from the noun it was supposed to be modifying. Well, to Hell with Chandler. Who cares what she thinks, anyway? I told the notebook to delete the message and started down the hall toward my locker.

I had long ago resigned myself to the fact that I am the chosen of God. And I don't mean that in any messianic, second-coming, kind of way. No, I just figure that every few hundred years God decides that he needs a good laugh, so he picks out some poor sucker to be the butt of all his jokes for the next century. And I guess it's only fair. After all, the Big Guy does work pretty hard keeping the universe running and all. Who's to deny him his little sitcom?

Anyway, the Chosen thing explains a lot of the facts about my life. Like, for example, the fact that I have the locker next to Kyle Gordon, a.k.a. God's gift to the basketball team. Although we are nominally the same age and species, Kyle is 2 feet taller than I am, with a build that no fifteen year old is entitled to. He's probably the best basketball player in the Baptist school league.

Of course, I would be too, if my parents had sprung for the kind of pharmaceuticals that Kyle has charging through his system. I've seen his lunch regimen—two tablets of DHEA, a chromium pill, a growth hormone capsule, a packet of creatine that he has to dissolve in juice, and a DRC tablet. And that's not even including all the weird stuff that his sports doctor injects him with twice a week.

I wouldn't minded it all so much if his parents had stopped at turning Kyle into the wonder jock. But no, they'd decided that he had to be good looking, too. It started a couple years ago, when Kyle came back from Christmas vacation with a new nose. Then last year it was a slightly stronger chin. And finally, this Easter he'd come back with higher cheekbones. Sigh. I guess they figure there's no point in turning him into the uber-athlete unless he's pretty enough to land the endorsements.

Right now, Mr. Wonderful was leaning up against my locker, chatting with a couple of his goon hanger-ons. I managed to squeeze past Tweedle-Dee and Tweedle-Dum and press my thumb onto the key plate of my locker. Of course, I couldn't open it with Kyle's 215 pounds of bulk propped against it. I waited, in the vain hope that Kyle would notice me and shift his weight. How silly of me.

"Hey, Kyle," I said, daring to interrupt what I'm sure was a fascinating conversation on whether he was better in last night's game or the one a week before. He stopped talking and looked down at me. "Yeah?"

We've been locker neighbors for nearly a year now, and he still hasn't bothered to ask my name.

I pointed at my locker. "You mind?"

"Oh," he said, then stood up and went back to talking with his remoras.

I opened my locker and swapped the battery in the recharger for the one in my notebook. I also grabbed a nut bar to munch on during civics.

Just then Scott came galloping up, with Tim riding on him piggyback. They were wearing blue jeans and matching rugby shirts.

"Hey Benji!" they said in unison. It was disgustingly cute.

Kyle stopped talking to look at them. Then he looked at me. I briefly considered pretending not to know them, but I guess it's better to have geeky friends than no friends at all.

"Hey guys. See you at lunch?"

"Of course," said Scott, giving Kyle a wink.

"You betcha," said Tim. He gave Scott a kiss on the cheek and then dug in his heels. "And now, ON MIGHTY STEED! WE RIDE TO...ALGEBRA!"

As they galloped down the hall, the warning bell sounded, so I took off for civics class.

As I walked in to the room, I saw Julie, the girl who stars in all our school plays. She looked up and smiled, and for a second, I felt all warm and happy inside, like someone had just a thrown a light switch on in my heart. Then I thought to look behind me. There was a whole stream of guys pushing in the doorway behind me, so she could have been smiling at any one of them.

But it might have been for me. Hope springs eternal.

Julie has the sort of face that can only be adequately described by certain metaphors involving angels which have all been used up and turned into cliches, so I won't bore you by repeating them here. I would like to say that when you look at Julie you feel absolutely sure that she must have a beautiful soul. Because there are some things that God would never let be counterfeited. When Julie smiles, it is like the sun coming out.

Not that she's a saint, by any means. For example, I suspect a little vanity. Someone must have told her once that green brings out her eyes, because she always wears some shade of it. Forest green, pea green, emerald green, sea green. Today her blouse was spring green, the color of the first new leaves in March.

There were three empty seats next to Julie, but I knew better than to take any of them. Just as the final bell rang, Kyle and his entourage came sauntering in and slipped into the chairs around her like they owned them.

Which I guess they did.

Mrs. Bradley, our civics teacher, called the class to order, then switched on the monitor to play the news clips we'd be discussing that period. The BNN logo flashed on the screen, and then slowly faded to make way for the all too familiar face of Sandy Roberts.

"Hi, I'm Sandy Roberts, and welcome to Baptist News Network's school news break!"

Sandy's teeth are an almost radioactive shade of white. I sometimes wonder how she gets them that way. Does she brush with bleach? Or do they just run her image through a program that recolors her teeth before they broadcast?

"Our top story this hour: Police in Atlanta uncover the grisly remains of a satanic ritual!"

Sandy has a real gift for perkiness. No matter how depressing the news gets, she never lets it faze her. Last month she reported on a tidal wave that wiped out a whole city in India without ever dropping her winning smile.

On screen, Sandy's cheerful face was replaced by an aerial shot of a graveyard.

"A chalk pentagram, black candles, a sacrificed rooster, and a mutilated corpse were discovered at Forest Green Cemetery this morning by a patrolman responding to a complaint by neighbors."

Sandy used to have an up-beat co-anchor named Carl. They would have good natured discussions about the news and what it meant to their viewers. Carl hadn't been on the show in a few weeks. I'd heard a rumor that Sandy had gotten him canned because she was jealous of his ratings.

"Police are refusing to give out further details of the crime. However, Lieutenant Megan Strand of the Special Investigations Bureau is optimistic about the APD's chances of solving the case."

The screen filled with the image of a black woman with messy hair. "This case is being pursued with the full resources of the Atlanta Police Department. Whoever did this, and whatever their motives were, we *are* going to catch them. *Period.* That's all I'm going to say right now."

I'd also heard a rumor that Sandy isn't even a real person, that she's just some computer-generated character that they programmed to read the news.

"BNN asked Dr. Terrence Whiteside, professor in the Department of Occult Studies at Freedom University, to speculate on the nature of the ritual that was performed."

The screen shifted to Dr. Whiteside, who was a surprisingly young man sitting behind a tidy desk with a fern on it.

"Well, Sandy, as you know, the Satanic Conspiracy is the biggest threat facing the U.S. right now. Unfortunately, because the Conspiracy operates on so many different levels, it's difficult to guess just what they're up to this time. Its ultimate goal is to turn the U.S. away from the Christian faith of its founders to a darker, malevolent religion. A religion that celebrates perverse sexual acts, the worship of pagan idols, and the murder of unborn children. Most experts agree that the legalization of abortion was the Conspiracy's first step toward one of their ultimate goals—state-sponsored child sacrifice. Now, the particular details of this ritual lead me to believe that..."

While Dr. Whiteside droned on, Kyle slid his foot under Julie's desk and nudged her foot. She kicked him. I wished that I could see her face from where I was sitting. Was she glaring at him when she did it? Or was she smiling?

When I looked back up at the monitor Sandy was talking again. "...leading the Reverend Senator Zachariah Stonewall to announce that the Christian Alliance would be conducting an independent investigation into the crime."

The picture changed to Reverend Stonewall, standing in the cemetery with police in the background. I know the old guy turned 53 last month (yes, my parents actually celebrated his birthday), but he doesn't look nearly that old to me. He was on the move, answering a question while walking.

"Now don't get me wrong. As one of the Senators of this fine state, I have great faith in the ability and courage of the Atlanta Police Department. Your average policeman is a good, God-fearin' individual. However, the good work of the many is being undermined by a certain element...Well, are we to believe that it is simply a coincidence that the APD allows unrepentant, practicing, self-proclaimed *witches* to handle evidence, and that it has not arrested one single solitary Satanist in the last ten years?"

There was heroic music playing softly in the background during Stonewall's speech. Something classical, with a lot of drums. Stonewall always gets good background music. But of course, he does own the network.

The picture cut away to Stonewall, with his head bowed and his eyes closed tight in concentration. The camera pulled back to show that he was holding hands with a little old white-haired lady and some college guy in an Emory T-shirt. Then it pulled back further to reveal a long line of people holding hands outside the police cordon.

"The Reverend Senator concluded his remarks by leading a prayer vigil outside the crime scene," explained Sandy.

"We gather here, to pray for the souls of the men who committed this desperate act. May God open their eyes to the wickedness of their ways. And may he protect us from what they have unleashed here."

The picture suddenly changed to a line of Indians in war paint, screaming and waving tomahawks behind a line of police.

"In related news, the court case of five Cherokee accused of murdering four Baptists in the King National Park went to trial today. The Cherokee were attempting to perform the 'Ghost Dance,' an occult ritual by which they hoped to summon up spirits to murder all the whites in America, when they were interrupted by a group from a local Baptist Militia. In addition to the four Baptists who were killed, 17 more were injured. 6 Cherokee were also killed in the ensuing fire-fight."

Of course, it really doesn't matter whether she likes Kyle or not. At least she's aware of him. She knows he exists.

"The trial was briefly interrupted by news that James Singleton, a sixteen-year-old who attends Furman Memorial Baptist
School in Augusta Georgia, had attacked one of the Cherokee
witch doctors attending the trial. After stabbing the witch doctor
once with a small acrylic blade, Singleton was tackled by a by-
stander and prevented from continuing his assault. Singleton has
been arrested and charged with attempted murder."

I don't know why I worry. After all, what could Julie possibly see in Kyle? I mean, besides the gorgeous wonder jock thing.

"That's the news this morning. I'm Sandy Roberts, and thanks
for joining us for BNN's School News Break!"

The monitor went dark, and Mrs. Bradley turned to us.

"So class, who has some thoughts on today's news?"

Jeff, a fat kid at the front of the room chimed in. "Well, why
can't the police just go and arrest the witches?"

"Well, Jeff," Mrs. Bradley responded, "if you hadn't slept
through our section on the Constitution you might remember the
first amendment, which guarantees our freedom of religion."

It was a leading statement, designed to get the ball rolling.
Seeing a chance to score a few easy class-participation points,
one of Kyle's goons jumped in.

(OK, I admit it. I don't know the goon's name. But hey,
it's not like he's a real person who has an existence independent of Kyle. No, he's more like some zit of Kyle's that suddenly sprung arms and legs and started following him around.
But I digress.)

Anyway, the goon jumped in and said, "Yeah, but witchcraft isn't a religion. It's devil worship which is sort of
a...well...an *un*-religion."

From there we were off, with Mrs. Bradley asking who gets to
define what a religion is. A couple of kids took a shot at it, and I
eventually chimed in with my opinion that it was a matter of original intent—that is, what did the founding fathers have in mind when
they wrote it? Would they have considered witchcraft a religion?
Probably not. (Hey, I needed the class participation points, too. I
might as well try to pass at least one class this semester.)

From there we went on a fairly standard tour of civics subjects. We talked about how to be tolerant of religious diversity
while remaining intolerant of sin. We talked about the kid who'd
stabbed the Indian, and whether it's ever acceptable to take the
law into our own hands. We talked about the commandment not
to kill, and how we can reconcile that with our lives in a violent
world. And we talked about the Cherokee problem, and the dangers of putting parts of the country under Indian rule.

Then we kind of went off on a tangent about the connection between the Satanic Conspiracy and the Indian witch doctors, which Mrs. Bradly didn't really seem to mind because she was getting bored with the discussion, too, so she pulled out some really cool clips of these Indians doing some ceremony called a sun dance where they were driving wooden hooks through their skin and one guy cut off a piece of his finger. Then I think she decided that we were having too much fun, because she put on this really boring clip of some legal professor from Liberty explaining that the Cherokee's case doesn't really hold any water, but they've been bribing congressmen right and left, so they might win anyway.

I was just starting to nod off when the volume suddenly doubled, and a deep alto voice came slithering out of the speakers.

"Your attention, my loyal subjects," it cooed. I looked up at the screen to see a woman with an angular face, her dark eyes accentuated by black lipstick and eyeshadow. "It is I, Madame Palaprince, your benevolent ruler. I must note with...displeasure, that there has been yet another attack by the rebel calling himself 'Zero.' Fortunately, his plans were thwarted by our mighty thewed champion, Captain Cool, who at the same time manage to thwart an attempt by the alien brain stealers to infiltrate our just and fair society."

There were a few chuckles at this. Anyone who had been following the comic knew that it was really Zero who had thwarted the brain stealers, even though Captain Cool, as usual, got all the credit.

The silky voice continued on. "Any citizen having knowledge of this 'Zero' would be well advised, for their own safety, to contact Captain Cool immediately."

Then the screen filled with an image of Captain Cool and the room broke into laughter. Tall, barrel chested, square jawed...and a dead ringer for Kyle.

"That's me! Captain Cool!" The voice even sounded a lot like Kyle's. "Sworn protector of Planet G-8! Remember, with your help we can capture this dangerous traitor and see that he gets the psychiatric treatment he so desperately needs!"

The image of Captain Cool slowly faded from the screen as heroic music played. But under it, softly, could be heard laughter. Not just of the kids in the room. But there, in the background, as if echoing up from some hidden subterranean lair, the deep bass laughter of Zero himself.

As the last of the music faded, there was a chorus of electronic beeps, as every notebook in the school registered a priority message. Since mine was already out in front of me, I tapped on the mail icon in the corner of the screen. Sure enough, there was this week's issue. "Captain Cool and the Lust Puppets of Palaprince."

Mrs. Fitzpatrick, who had been frantically yelling into her desk, finally got it to accept the "off" command for the monitor. (Of course, she could have just unplugged the darn thing, but I think that would have been too revolutionary a concept for the woman.) I saw her grimace and mutter "not again," just before the end of period bell rang. I noticed that Kyle's face was a delightful shade of crimson as we all piled out of the room. Everyone else went running off to lunch, but I hung around outside the door for a minute. On a hunch, I poked my head back into Ms. Fitzpatrick's room. Sure enough, shes was hunched over her desk, reading something on its screen. I had a pretty good idea what.

On the way to lunch I called up the new issue. Just out of curiosity, I checked out the return address. This time, it had come from a system in Finland. The time before that, Malaysia. The time before that, Buenos Aires. Interesting. I had time to open the first page before I got to the lunchroom.

It was a picture of a man in a black mask, sitting in a dark room, dimly lit by glowing electronics. The caption said, "Zero, in his underground Fortress of Secrets, monitors the actions of all who dwell in the totalitarian state above." I touched the page and the light shifted a little. A glint came into Zero's eyes, and the soundtrack played.

"Oh, darlink, touch me there." It was the voice of Madame Palaprince, the mad dictator of Planet G-8. Of course, it's not hard to recognize, since it's just a thinly filtered version of our principal's. "Oh, yes. Touch me there. Pleasure me now, Drake. And if you are good...perhaps we'll talk about that promotion."

Righteous.

I got to the lunch room. Everywhere, kids had their notebooks out, reading the latest issue of the comic. I saw Scott at our usual table and went to join him.

"Hey Scott," I said. "Where's Tim?" You don't often see one of them without the other.

Scott took a bite out of a tuna sandwich and nodded his head in the direction of the in-crowd's table...where Tim was sitting. In Kyle's seat, no less.

I looked at Scott in alarm. "Has he gone suicidal?"

Scott winked at me and smiled. "Wait."

A minute late, Kyle came back from the juice machines, his entourage nipping at his heals. He said something to Tim, who said something back. I have no idea what either of them said, but the conversation ended with two of Kyle's goons picking up Tim by his underwear and lifting him out of the seat. They dropped him on the ground, and a third goon tossed him his lunch bag.

Tim stuffed his underwear back into his jeans and came over to our table, smiling broadly.

"What was that about?" I asked.

Tim sat down with us and pulled a black cube out of his pocket. He plugged it into the side of his notebook. Suddenly I heard Kyle's voice saying "...not that I can think of. Hey Tom, get me another OJ. No, there's nobody I've ticked off so badly that they'd..."

There was the squeak of a chair and a clank like a bottle or a cup being set down, but weirdly amplified.

"It's on the underside of the table," explained Tim with a certain note of glee. Tim is the intelligence wing of our three-headed conspiracy, and I must say he does an admirable job of it. I suspect that one day he's going to make some CIA section chief a very happy spook.

"It is a pity we don't have video feed from the principal's office," Tim mused. "I would love to see her face right now. Well, maybe I'll make that my project for next week."

Yes, Madame Palaprince's sex scene was the big bomb we were dropping this week. Our comic is a delicate blend of fact and fantasy. Figuring out just which is which can be half the fun. At that particular moment, I suspect that a certain Madame Principal was desperately trying to figure out how the anonymous creators of an underground comic could possibly know about her affair with the PE teacher. The truth is that her office is one of the easiest places in the whole school for us to bug. After all, Tim gets called in there practically every week.

Anyway, like I said, Tim handles the intelligence department. He gets us the dirt on everybody, and the voice recordings we used to program the synthesizers for the characters' voices. Scott does the artwork and the animation, and helps out some with the plotting. Basically, though, the comic book is my brain child, and I do most of the writing. I came up with character of Zero and I write all his dialogue. He's this nobody who lives on this planet called G-8 that's run by the mad despot Madame Palaprince. But he's been pushed just a little too far, and he's become a rebel. He's got no superpowers at all—no super flight, no super strength, no super nothing. So he has to survive by his wits, using whatever devices he can build or steal or scavenge. Captain Cool has all the really neat powers—as the genetically engineered defender of G-8, he can fly, and bounce bullets off his chest and benchpress a star cruiser and all that kind of stuff. But he's really just a tool of the mad Madame.

There was a senior at the next table over who started laughing so hard she almost fell out of her seat. I caught sight of our comic on her notebook as she waved it around, pointing to the scene where Madame Palaprince has Drake lashed to her desk. Ah, it was good to have fans, even if they didn't know who we were. Scott pulled me out of my reverie.

"OK, writer-boy. Enough lounging around on our laurels. What do you want to do for the next issue?"

"I dunno," I admitted. "I haven't even started thinking about it. You got any ideas?"

"Well," said Scott, "I thought we could have Jade kidnapped by alien slavers who take her away to a space harem..."

Jade is one of Captain Cool's allies, another of Madame Palaprince's genetic creations. She has green eyes that can hypnotize men if they meet her gaze, and she always wears a green costume. I suppose you can guess who we based her on.

"Yeah, right," I responded, "you just want to draw Julie naked again, don't you?"

"Can you blame me?" said Scott, cocking an eye at Julie, who was sitting at the table next to Kyle's.

"Careful," I said, cocking an eye at Tim, "your boyfriend's gonna get jealous."

Tim was too busy making notes on Kyle's conversation to follow ours, so the comment was wasted.

"No really," Scott went on. "I've got it all worked out. Jade gets kidnapped, and so the Mad Dictator sends Captain Cool off to rescue her. Only Captain Cool follows the wrong clue, and winds up battling some completely innocent, but heavily armed, starship in another quadrant. So it's up to Zero to go rescue her."

I chewed on my peanut butter sandwich and thought about it.

"Not bad," I said, "but kind of linear. We need to add a few complications."

"Well you're the writer. Complicate."

"Well..." I said slowly, trying to buy myself some time to think. "Suppose Zero follows the slavers and sneaks into the space harem. Then he figures our where Jade is being kept, and he sneaks through the air filtration system to a place where he can talk to her from behind a ventilation grate, and he tells her that he's come to rescue her. Now Jade, of course, assumes that it's Captain Cool who comes to help her, so she tells him she loves him, and Zero responds, and they have this really erotic whispered love scene. Then Zero loosens her slave collar, and goes off to create a diversion so that she can break free and steal a shuttle. So Jade gets back to G-8 and thanks Captain Cool for saving her. Only Captain Cool doesn't remember any of the romantic things he's supposed to have said to her. So now she's in love, but she doesn't even know who with, and..."

Scott looked at me in disbelief. "Boy you must have an interesting fantasy life. OK. As long as I get to draw her naked and in chains. Now, what other sorts of interesting alien sex slaves do you think we should have in a space harem? I have this great idea for a cat woman with eight breasts and retractable claws..."

I probably should have said something at this point to get us back on track, but I decided to let Scott run with it. I sometimes wonder what sort of job he's going to get when he grows up. Probably something doing either children's cartoons or pornography.

"And this woman who is made up of nothing but mist, so she can reshape herself to look like anyone you want her too, but you can't *touch* her. Oh! and this snake girl with no arms or legs who is really slinky and sexual, and she's got this prehensile tongue that she can hold things with, and..."

"You know," I interrupted, "the slave girls do sound like a lot of fun. How about instead of just stealing a shuttle, we have Jade lead a slave rebellion? Then we can have some great fight scenes between the alien slave girls and the harem guards."

"Yeah!" Scott said, expanding on the idea. "And I can think of some great scenes where the harem girls turn on their former captors and do all sorts of horrible kinky things to get even with them. And..."

I finished off the rest of my peanut butter sandwich while Scott raved on about alien S&M in freefall. This chaos was about par for the course on our story sessions. Somehow it would get hammered out into a plot by Friday, and then we'd spend the weekend writing dialogue and doing the graphics.

I glanced over at the notes that Tim was making on the in-crowd's lunch banter. Four lines down he had triple-underlined the words, "KYLE SLEPT WITH A CHEERLEADER LAST WEEKEND." Noting my panicked expression, he scrawled a couple of extra words next to it. "No, not Julie."

Ah. There are some days when it's good to be alive. It looked like Captain Cool would have more than a star cruiser to tangle with in our next episode.

The bell for next period rang. Tim waited until the in-crowd had vacated their table, and then went to retrieve his bug. Then he and Scott took hands and skipped off to Spanish class. Me, I had math lab next, which is another one of the many things that isn't my best subject. Not that I suck at it, either. You have to get twenty problems in a row correct before the program will let you go on to the next unit. I was two units behind the average for my grade, but that's not too bad. If I have to, I can force myself to concentrate and make that up in about a week.

Normally I manage to muddle through the lab without calling too much attention to myself. But I kept thinking about Kyle, and trying to figure out which cheerleader he was sleeping with, and wondering if Julie knew yet, and wondering what she would do when she found out, or if she would even care. Then that got me thinking about whether Julie was sleeping with anybody. And anyway, none of that was helping me with this polynomial I was supposed to be differentiating. Normally when you make a mistake, the computer figures out what you did wrong and explains it to you, and then gives you another problem of the same kind to make sure that you get the point. But I kept getting those really stupid wrong answers that the computer couldn't recognize, so it kept calling the teacher over to take a look at what I was doing and put me back on the right track. By the time the bell for fifth period rang, I had received no less than five such personal conferences with the math teacher, and we were both finding this sudden burst of familiarity a bit wearing.

After math class is PE. Personally, I am convinced that PE is required for the sole purpose of teaching us humility. I mean, what is the point, really? OK, maybe I could understand it if they taught us something useful, like karate, or fencing, or ninjitsu. But basketball? I mean, when is my life ever going to depend on being able to throw a ball through a hoop?

Mr. Drake, our PE teacher, divided us into two teams based on who we were standing with when he walked into the gym. As a result, Scott, Tim, and I all wound up on one team facing off against an opposing squad led by Kyle. Well, at least none of his goons were in this class. Still, there didn't seem to be a lot of doubt as to the outcome of the game. I proposed that our team be named the "Sacrificial Lambs." We could have a bleat as our team cheer.

We were getting set for the tip-off when I noticed Scott and Tim exchanging suspicious looks. Scott wrinkled his forehead, and then Tim raised his left eyebrow in return. I sometimes think that they've worked out a code that consists of nothing but facial expressions.

The other team was skins, so Kyle was taking off his gym shirt.

"Ooh, Kyle," Scott said in an admiring tone, "looks like you've been working out."

This confused Kyle. "Well, yeah," he admitted. Lots of things confuse Kyle.

"Yeah," said Tim, "nice box."

"What?" asked Kyle.

"I said, 'Nice Boxers.' Are those Calvin Klein?"

The waistband of Kyle's boxers was indeed peeking up over his gym shorts.

"Well, uh, yeah," stammered Kyle, trying to figure out where this was going.

"Well, they suit you," added Scott.

By this time Mr. Drake had noticed that we weren't playing ball, and decided to round up the usual suspects.

"Tyler, Breckin, what are you two doing now?" he said, walking over.

"Just making conversation," said Scott.

"Well, knock it off," said Mr. Drake. Then he caught sight of the piece of jewelry that Tim was wearing over his gym shirt.

"Tyler, is that a crucifix?"

Tim looked down at the ornament around his neck as if seeing it for the first time.

"Oh yeah. I'd never noticed the little man on it before."

"Well put it away. You're not supposed to wear those in school."

"But why?" asked Tim, all wide-eyed innocence.

I could see Mr. Drake's frustration level starting to build. He knew that Tim wasn't really gay. I mean, we'd all had a blood test before the school would accept us. Mr. Drake made some polite attempt to explain that the crucifix was a homo thing, but Tim cut him off.

"But...my Aunt Melissa left me this. YOU MEAN SHE WAS A LESBIAN?"

"No, I didn't...I mean...Oh go run twenty laps."

"But I didn't do any..." Tim started to protest.

"JUST DO IT!" Then he looked at Scott. "You too."

"Yes Sir!" they said in unison, and made a dramatic show of starting their laps. It was clear that they had no intention of finishing them before the end of class.

Kyle looked at what was left of my team, and then actually said something to me.

"Why do you hang with those two, anyway?"

Good question. I guess, it beats hanging by myself.

With Scott and Tim out of the game, that pretty much ended any pretense of running a scrimmage, so we broke up into pairs to play one on one. I should have realized how that would work out. I mean, nobody wants to play with Kyle because he's seven feet tall and mops the court with anybody who goes up against him. And nobody wanted to play with me because I'm five feet tall and suck at this stupid game. So guess who the two leftovers were?

"So," said Kyle, looking me over. "You want to play some one on one?" His tone made it clear that he knew how absurd the suggestion was.

"I'd rather play chess," I responded.

He actually smiled at that one. "OK. So what do we do for the rest of the period?"

We eventually settled on a game of H.O.R.S.E., where he had to make every shot from twice as far away as I did. He still beat me three times before the end of class, but it wasn't a completely horrible experience, and I even managed to get him up to 'R' in one game.

Of course, he still didn't bother to ask my name.

Thankfully, gym is the last class of my day. I grabbed a quick shower, got out of the locker room before any of the jocks could get a fix on me, and headed for my locker. On the way I passed a group of seventh graders huddled around a notebook, reading about the latest exploits of Zero. Kyle came walking by, and they all burst into giggles. He pretended not to notice. Then I saw the Principal coming down the hall at a brisk walk, scanning the faces of the students, looking like a volcano about to blow. Apparently she'd seen a copy, too. The seventh graders flipped off their notebook as she passed, and pretended to be talking about something else. I tried to play casual too, although I had one really bad moment when she locked eyes with me. But she went on, and I made it to my locker.

God, I love being a writer.

## Chapter 10: The Witch
## Monday the Ninth, 11:35 AM

Almost done. I rubbed my eyes and looked at the screen. "Ghost Dance Trial Opens with Assassination Attempt." I paged down through it, re-reading my prose. It was one blessed good piece.

According to the file that the Research Department had sent up to me, some guy had foiled an assassination attempt against one of the Cherokee Shamans, turned the attacker over to a cop, and then...left. In all the confusion, he just walked off. And nobody knows who he is. A mystery man.

Is that a great story, or what?

A guy saves a person's life, and then just walks off without leaving his name. And for some reason, no one can even remember what he looks like. The police tried to pick his face out of the security camera footage of all the people coming into the courthouse that morning, but couldn't recognize him. There was also a white woman who had been on the elevator and seen the whole fight, but apparently she was too traumatized to remember much of anything. And then there were the three Cherokee, who wouldn't say anything about the guy. Not a single word. I thought that was interesting.

The guy must have used a glamour. A potent one, too. It was the only way to explain why no one could remember his face. I'd heard rumors that the Cherokee have magick like that. Something about a secret order of Shadow Hunters, who can pass unnoticed until they strike. I wondered if this Shaman had one of those for a body guard. A guy whom no one ever paid attention to, who could hang around practically invisible until he was needed. It would explain why none of the Cherokee was willing to say anything about him now.

I went to one of the magick databases and pulled up some quick information on the Order of Shadow Hunters. The data was kind of sketchy, and I didn't have any hard evidence that this guy was one of them, so I settled for putting the information in a two-paragraph sidebar to the piece. My readers could make their own speculations.

I went back to the main piece and made a few wording changes, then pulled up the image file to see what the girls down in graphics had come up with to accompany the piece. I tapped my way through about thirty pictures, and wound up choosing a photograph of the Cherokee lawyers going into the courtroom. There was something about the juxtaposition of their business suits and the warpaint that I liked. I pasted that one in next to the second paragraph, where I was doing a recap of the trial itself. Then I grabbed a picture of the assassin being carried off by police, and pasted it in near the bottom. And lastly, I decided to use a line drawing they'd assembled of a man's silhouette with a question mark inside it. It was a little bit obvious, but I decided to put it up near the headline, to help draw people into the piece.

I closed the story and sent it off to my editor for review, then checked the time. 11:40. Good. Almost time for lunch.

I blinked repeatedly, trying to moisten my eyes. So far this morning I'd already written up five stories: "Canadian Scientist Points to Disturbing New Evidence of Advancing Glaciers", "Congress Links Brazil's Trade Status to Advances on Eco-Crimes", "California Separatists Stage Tax Revolt Against Fed"—and one really sad little piece, "Actor Eddie Rockland Arrested for Drug Possession."

I've always felt kind of sorry for that kid. I mean, talk about having a pushy stage mother. OK, it's not like Virginia Rockland is the only single mother ever to buy genetic material from the estate of a dead movie star. In fact, there are several boys at Summer's high school who bear a suspicious resemblance to Tom Cruise. Most such mothers, though, are content to keep the identity of their child's father as a delicious secret. And they certainly don't try to push the child into following in its father's footsteps.

Not Virginia Rockland, though. She'd opened up her own little franchise. Had five of the little nippers incubated by one of those big commercial firms. Now, I may be old fashioned, but I still think the whole idea of subcontracting your pregnancy to a corporation is pretty darn cold. I mean, I didn't have an easy time being pregnant with either of the girls. But I wouldn't have given up that time with them for anything.

Anyway, Rockland started marketing her boys about seven years ago. Since they're identical quintuplets, they're supposed to be interchangeable, so that you can shoot five different scenes with the same actor at one time. Need an actor who can work 80 hours a day? Well this one can do it! Three of the boys—Bernie, Charlie, and Doug—actually do work that way, and have their own television series. Albert, for some reason, just acts too differently from the others, and can't sub for them. But he does commercials, and gets a movie every once in awhile.

Then there's Eddie. Poor Eddie, who just couldn't act. He did some underwear modeling for awhile, and now he does mostly porn. Just once I'd like to go to a party and *not* have someone tell me the latest joke about Eddie.

11:42. I rubbed my eyes again, which were burning from the dry recycled air. Normally the office air doesn't bother me too much, but some days the sterile environment can get to me after awhile. I needed a minute to ground myself.

I put my headset on my desk and slipped my shoes off. I ran my toes over the office carpeting. Synthetic. Lifeless. But beneath it I feel the floor, cool and slick. And beneath the floor I can sense the metal crossbeams, running in a web to the structural supports. I feel how the supports connect to the giant steel girders which form the skeleton of the building. Girders that run down. Down through the offices. Down through the street, through the basement, through the foundation. Down into the earth, the dark and powerful earth. I follow that connection down into the earth, and I draw some of its power up into me. My spine tingles with the energy. Thank you, Mother.

I slowly let out my breath, and follow it as it mixes with the sterile office air. I can feel it racing around the office, brushing against the sealed windows, looking for a way out. And somewhere, it finds it. Somewhere there is a leak, and cold office air spills joyfully out into the warm summer day. It is caught by a breeze, and the two mingle playfully in the sunlight till they have forgotten which is which, till they have forgotten that they were ever separated.

I came back to myself much refreshed. I glanced at my screen. 11:47. Jen would be here at noon to pick me up for lunch. Just enough time to crack open the research file on another story. I pulled up the list of waiting fact kits. There was an interview with the Prime Minister of Quebec, but that looked boring. Then there was something on the Christian Music Awards, but since I write for the company's Wiccan newsite, my readers wouldn't be interested in that. I scanned through the rest of the list, looking for something that would be attention-getting.

...Dietary Study on Foods that Prevent Impotence...

...Cyber-Democrats form surprise coalition government with Neo-Confucian Party in Chinese Parliament...

...House introduces bill to defund National Endowment for the Arts after Pyrotechnic Display...

...Local high school teacher accused of running protection racket using students...

...Graveyard vandalism incident upsets North Atlanta Neighborhood...

Graveyard Vandalism? I called up the file just to see what it was about: Mutilated corpse found in cemetery. Evidence of occult activity. Baptist Senator babbling about black magic and witchcraft. Wiccan Anti-Defamation League issues statement. Special Investigations Bureau called in.

I opened up the accompanying graphics file. Wow. Pretty grotesque stuff. Like something out of an Edgar Allen Poe story. I clicked through several different images, and finally stopped on a diagram. Unfortunately, the police had removed the corpse from the scene before our photographers had been able to get a picture. However, the company's field agents had interviewed people in the crowd of onlookers, and had been able to find a few witnesses who had seen the body before it was packed up. Based on their statements, the graphics department had put together a line drawing showing what had been done to the body, and how it was positioned with regard to the rest of the elements of the scene.

The image was disturbing, and not just because of the savagery. It was disturbing because whoever had done this had actually known a thing or two about *real* magick. This wasn't just an act of anger, or even a well-planned hoax. It was something much more dangerous.

I found myself studying the details of the scene, trying to figure out what sort of ritual they had performed. Trying to decipher what sort of spell they had loosed on the world. I could recognize certain elements. The candles, for example, told me that they knew enough basic conjuring to build a circle of power to contain the magick as it built up during the ritual. And some of the things they'd done to the body looked like a form of sympathetic magick. Had they sewn up the lips of the corpse in an attempt to silence someone else? Or were they just trying to show that the corpse had been silenced in life? And what to make of the incisions in the stomach?

I started making notes, assigning possible meanings to each of the elements in the scene. But there were some parts that I didn't know how to interpret. The inverted cross, for example, was clearly a reference to something from the Christian faith. And while I could guess that turning the cross upside-down was probably a bad thing in their book, I didn't really understand the nuances of their symbol set. My only real exposure to Christian mythology had been skimming *Paradise Lost* for a lit course in college. I was going to need some help with this one.

I poked my head into a few cubicles and got some quick pointers. Thomas, who works for our Catholic News Site, had already written up his version of the piece, and was able to explain all the old myths of a "Black Mass" at which witches were supposed to drink real blood and eat human flesh. Felicia, who writes for our Gay and Lesbian Site, turned out to be a Zen Buddhist, and couldn't really help me much. Terrence, who works on our Black Interest News Site, hadn't gotten around to looking at the research file yet, but when I told about it he seemed to think that the sacrificed rooster might be an element from a Voodoo ceremony. Everybody else had already gone to lunch, except for Susan, who writes for our Baptist News Site. Susan has managed to be civil to me so far, and I have returned the favor. I saw no reason to ruin such a perfect relationship now by actually talking to her.

I got back to my cubicle and started running down the new avenues of research that Thomas and Terrence had suggested. I contacted a database on Religion at Harvard and set up a search for various elements of the ritual. There was a medieval text called the *Malleus Mallefactum*, translated, "The Witch's Hammer", which was a handbook for members of the Inquisition on how to find and deal with witches. It included some diagrams detailing various spells that witches were supposed to use. Then there were some accounts from anthropologists who had seen voodoo rituals which were done over corpses in the hope of animating them or affecting their relatives. Then there was a book from the 1970's called *The Satanic Bible*, which seemed to mostly deal with philosophy but had some odd ideas about magick rituals that seemed to have been applied to the situation. And lastly there was a huge body of literature being put out by the Baptists on occult activity and how to recognize the hand of Satan at work in it.

It was all fascinating reading, and I completely lost myself in the research until my stomach finally reminded me that I hadn't eaten yet. I glanced at the time. 12:43.

12:43? Where in the Goddess's name was Jen? I called her up and got her voicemail, so she must have been on the phone with someone else already. I left her a sarcastic message concerning her promptness and reminding her of our lunch date. Then I went back to my reading while I waited for her to return the call.

Ten minutes later, I called her again, and got her voicemail, again. This was getting weird. First she misses a new moon ceremony. Then she pulls a no-show for lunch. And now she wasn't answering her phone.

Well, Jen's office is only a few blocks away. I signed out for lunch, and started the walk down Spring Street. It was a hot day, and the air was full of the smells of summer in the city—rotting garbage and sweaty people, and every now and then a whiff of something green and fresh...they were mowing the grass over in Peachtree Park. And underneath it all was the smell of rain. Still far off, but coming. A storm that would be here by evening.

Four blocks down Spring, I took a right onto Eighth, and then a left into the building where Jen and her partner rent space. It's an old converted warehouse that's a warren of little offices inside. I never can find my way around the place. No matter how many times I go there, I always have trouble finding their office. Of course, it doesn't help that there's a different name on the door every time I visit.

I eventually found the office, halfway down a zigzagging corridor on the third floor. Today the name on the door was "Fortress Security". I'd asked Jen about the door once, and she showed me how they do it; they have a whole set of brass name plates with little magnets on the back, so that they can take one off and slap another one on whenever they want to. Apparently, the name of the business at any given moment depends on which client is coming in for an appointment.

I knocked on the office door. No one came.

I shouted Jen's name. There was no answer.

I tried the knob. Locked.

Something was definitely not right.

I left the building, walked up to the Midtown MARTA station, and caught a train out to Decatur, where Jen lives. On the way, I tried her phone again. Voicemail.

I reached the station and hoofed it the three blocks to her apartment complex, a collection of low brick buildings. I climbed the black metal staircase up to her front door and knocked.

Once again, no answer.

I pressed my thumb against the doorknob, and felt it unlock. I'm supposed to feed Jen's cat whenever she's out of town, so her door is programmed to recognize my print. I swung the door open slowly, then stepped out of the warm sunlight and into the cool darkness of Jen's apartment.

The shades were drawn, and it took a few seconds for my eyes to adjust from the sunlight.

"Jen? You home?"

"Jen? You home?"

Something brushed against my leg. I almost jumped out of my skin before I realized who it was and bent over to pick her up.

"Hey, cutie. Where's your mistress?"

Medea purred appreciatively as I scratched under her chin, but provided no useful answer to my question. I put her down and took a look around the apartment. Nothing seemed to be obviously amiss. In the kitchen nook, I found Medea's food bowl. I noticed that it was empty, but then Jen had been threatening to put her cat on a diet for more than a year now. There was also a big bowl of water out. (Medea's an Abyssinian, and they like to play in it.) I dipped in a finger and tasted it. It had lost that chlorinated tang that tap water has for six or seven hours after you dispense it, which meant that Jen hadn't been home to change it this morning. Unless, of course, she had taken to feeding her cat bottled water. I could just see Jen doing that.

I poked my nose into the bathroom, which could have used a thorough cleaning but was otherwise unsuspicious. That left the main room.

A sliver of sunlight was sneaking in through a crack in the drapes, dancing through Jen's collection of crystal balls. She's got at least a dozen of them, made out of different minerals. Quartz. Obsidian. Aquamarine. Amethyst. A couple of gargoyle-shaped candlesticks sat guard over them all, and overhead a squadron of paper dragons hung from the ceiling, twisting in the draft from her air conditioner.

It was all appropriate to Jen. I could feel her energy running through the place. Powerful, erratic. As beautiful and unpredictable as lightning. Like her, the apartment was long on flashy nick-nacks and short on permanent furnishings. What furniture there was didn't match. The desk with her computer on it was a huge corporate affair, probably bought surplus from an office supply firm. The bookcases were made out of two-by-fours stacked on cinderblocks. An inflatable Tyrannosaurus Rex served as a coat-rack.

Then there was the bed. A big, wooden, ornately carved, Victorian canopy bed. I've always wondered how it came to be in Jen's possession. I bet it must have been a gift, and I'm hoping there's an interesting story that goes with it. Did she get it from an old lover? A client she saved from ruin? I wonder. The thing is enormous, hand-carved, and looks like it would cost me half a year's salary. And it was glowing.

I hadn't noticed that before. I walked over to the bed to see what was up with that. I stared at it for a few seconds, trying to figure out where the light was coming from, and then looked up into the canopy. A thousand points of light burned in a midnight blue background. I recognized Hercules and the Southern Cross, so it must have been displaying the summer constellations. I'd never notice that before. It was a nice trick—to be able to lie in bed and look up at the stars. I wondered if it was a static display, or if the stars changed with the seasons.

I stood back up and looked around the rest of the apartment, but there was no sign of Jen. I checked her closet to see if she might have packed clothes for a trip, but the only useful thing I learned was that Jen hasn't organized her storage space in at least a decade. There was no way to tell what she may or may not have taken out recently. But I did find a blouse I'd loaned her four years ago.

I was running out of things to check. I looked at the computer on her desk. It was running a complicated screen saver. Clips from old detective movies segued into each other in an endless dream sequence. Bogart pointed to Mr. Moto, who drew a gun on Basil Rathbone. If I could break into Jen's system I might be able to find out something useful—maybe what case she was working on—but I had no idea how to do that. How did info-thieves do this sort of thing? Just keep guessing passwords till they got lucky?

I realized how ridiculous this was getting. What was I really looking for? OK, so Jen had dropped out of sight without telling anyone else in the coven. Still, what had I expected to find here? Broken furniture and signs of a struggle? A half-finished breakfast, mysteriously abandoned? Or maybe a cryptic message scrawled in lipstick on the bathroom mirror? I've got to stop reading so many detective novels.

Of course, there was one more thing I could check. It was sort of an invasion of privacy, but under the circumstances...

I went over to the bed and studied the intricate carving on the front panel that faces her desk. It was a mermaid, her long hair flowing out in all directions, carried by some unseen current. Jen had once told me how to work this, in case anything ever happened to her.

Every witch has a hiding place. A secret place where she keeps her Book of Shadows, the tome in which she records the mysteries of her personal magicks. It is deeply private, and no one else will ever see its pages. And when the witch dies, one of her friends comes to collect it, so that it may be burned with her at her funeral.

Things hadn't reached that state of affairs yet. But I did want to see if the book was there. Jen would never let herself be without it for more than a few days. If she had planned on being gone for longer than that, she would have taken it with her.

I pressed the mermaid's eyes, and the panel popped off. There was a dull thud as the book and some loose papers fell out of their hiding place. I only had to glance at the tome to know that it was indeed Jen's Book of Shadows. It was bound in leather, with a silver oak leaf on the cover and an elaborate silver lock.

Well, there was my answer. Jen had not planned on leaving town, at least not for more than a few days. If she was not back soon, I would know that something had happened to her.

I picked up the book and gently put it back in its hiding place. Then I stooped to gather up the papers. They'd fallen out of a folder. I picked up the first to put it back in... and stopped. I had not intended to read any of Jen's private papers, but there was a drawing on this one that I recognized. It was a page from the *Malleus Mallefactum*.

The Witch's Hammer.

I quickly looked through the rest of the loose sheets. There were eleven of them. Ten were diagrams and instructions for black magic rituals. Several were from sources that I had been consulting just a couple hours ago. Taken together, they were a diagram for the ritual that had taken place in the graveyard last night.

Last night, when Jen had missed our new moon ceremony.

What in the name of the Goddess had Jen gotten herself into?

The eleventh page was even more interesting, because it didn't seem to fit in with the rest. It was a biographical profile.

"Sex: Male. Birth date: 5/12/10." Hm. That would make him 14. I kept reading.

"Eyes: Blue. Hair: Brown, Curly. Nose: Roman, Small. Height at Adulthood 5'11". Sexual Preference: Hetero. Manual Preference: Left."

The bio went on down the page, listing all sorts of details about this kid. The shape of his ears. His blood type. His propensity to allergies involving molds. But nowhere did it give his name. There was no phone number. No e-mail address. No way to get ahold of him.

Which was going to make things more difficult. Still, one way or another, I was going to have a conversation with this kid. I only hoped that when I found him he could tell me what was going on. Because whatever this thing was, he was right in the middle of it.

## Chapter 11: The Gumshoe
## Monday the Ninth, Morning

It was turning into one of those days. And by that I do not mean a cute "one of those days," like when you wake up to discover that your waterbed has sprung a leak, find out the hard way that your ex-boyfriend still has one of your credit cards, and learn from the vet that your small dog is actually a South American rodent that's about to enter its breeding cycle. No, I mean "one of those days" in the sense of a giant asteroid hitting the earth, frogs raining from the sky, and some crazed promoter thawing out Boy George's frozen head and sending it out on a comeback tour. It was one of *those* "one of those days."

First off, it had taken me nearly an hour to get into the courthouse. For some reason, a couple hundred Indians and Baptists had chosen this particular day to re-enact Custer's Last Stand on the courthouse steps. So first I had to fight my way through them, then I had to wait in line for the metal detector, and then finally I had to pass muster with the security guards who were grilling everybody about what business they had in the building.

Anyway, I finally got in the door and up to the courtroom where our divorce case was set to start and...no Jen. Nope. My partner was nowhere to be found. Figuring that she might have gotten stuck with the crazies outside, I tried calling her.

No answer.

Which left me with a bit of a problem. Or, more accurately, it left my client with a bit of a problem, who in turn made it a problem for me. You see, I could only testify as to my part in the investigation. I could show the court the photos I had taken of my client's wife and his business partner having sex, and I could assure the court that the pictures had not been altered in any way. Unfortunately, I could not testify about Jen's end of the investigation. Oh, I could produce the documents proving that our client's wife and his partner had been embezzling from his business. However, I couldn't verify that those papers were the same ones that Jen had taken from the company safe, and I could not really explain how she had gotten her hands on them. (I knew it had something to do with posing as a temp worker and faking an epileptic fit, but after that the details were a bit hazy.)

So around 11am the whole proceeding ground to a halt, because my firm could not deliver what it was supposed to. My client was not amused by this. The judge was not amused by this. Both of them conveyed their lack of amusement to me in concrete terms. Then they postponed the the hearing till next week, because, aside from making my life miserable, there was nothing else they could do about the situation.

And so, thinking that by now I must have finally worked through all the bad karma I could possibly have coming for a single day, I got on the elevator to leave. And found myself right in the middle of a knife fight between some teenage white kid and a geriatric Cherokee drag queen. (Like I even want to know what that was all about.) Anyway, I managed to wrestle the kid into an arm lock and keep him from killing anybody.

Having been a policeman, I knew what would happen next. First, they'd take me downtown as a material witness. Next, I would spend all afternoon waiting to be interviewed by some overworked detective who would ask me the same questions five different ways, just to make sure that I could keep my story straight. Then, finally, I would have the pleasure of a long trial to look forward to, during which I might spend weeks on end waiting around the courthouse for my chance to testify—all the while not getting any work done and thus not making any money. Yeah. Sounded like a real treat. But since I couldn't afford to take a few weeks of unpaid vacation just now, I handed the kid over to the first cop I saw and slipped away while she had her hands full with him.

I suppose the police might come looking for me, but I doubt they'll put much energy into it. After all, they've got four other eye witnesses to the stabbing. I guess they could go ahead and bust me for leaving a crime scene, but I doubt they could find a DA who'd be willing to prosecute the case. I mean, can you see him trying to explain it come the next election? "He saved some guy's life, so we busted him for not sticking around to fill out the paperwork." Besides, if it came to that, I still had some friends on the force.

Once I was finally out of the courthouse and the surrounding war zone, I tried giving Jen another call. She still wasn't answering her phone, which was really beginning to tick me off. I sicked Sherwin on her, telling him to call her every five minutes until he got through. Then I walked over to Commerce Street and popped into a RUSH-IN for a quick bowl of borscht and a chicken Kiev sandwich.

I was still kind of annoyed after lunch, so I grabbed my gym clothes from the office and headed over to The Inquisition for a workout. I don't really have any sort of organized fitness plan. I just exercise whenever I'm frustrated and need to blow off some steam. Which probably explains why I'm in such good shape.

The guy at the front desk was wearing a monk's robe with the hood pulled back and a big rip from the collar all the way down to his solar plexus. A golden crucifix gleamed against his smooth, tanned chest. His name was John. Or Jim. Or Joe. One of those really common J names that I can never keep straight. He smiled at me while I signed in.

"Hey, Drew."

I noticed that he'd had to glance at the sign-in sheet to remember my name. I smiled back.

"Hey cutie," I said. "Just out of curiosity: You wearing anything under that robe?"

He winked.

"You'll just have to find that out for yourself."

John or Jim or Joe and I had been flirting ever since he started working here, but we've never quite managed to connect for a date. We were now at that awkward stage where we'd asked all the easy questions—"So, what's your name? Where are you from? Where'd you go to school?"—and forgotten all the answers. So we were kind of running out of things to say. I keep thinking that I should take notes when I flirt, to avoid situations like this.

I changed, threw my stuff in a locker, and pressed my thumb against the lock plate to seal it. There were three other guys in the changing room getting dressed. Nice bodies, but they all had black wavy hair and green eyes; the disco clones were out in force today. Not a big surprise. The Inquisition was the "in" gay gym this year.

I went up to the aerobics room to stretch out, but there was a class in there using the space. It was being taught by some guy in manacles and chains—I think he was supposed to be one of the heretics being imprisoned. I watched him for awhile, expecting to see the chains swing up and smack him in the face, but I guess he'd been getting a lot of practice avoiding them. The other members of the class were wearing more conventional wrist and ankle weights.

The gym had gone to this theme just six months ago, and it was already tired. Before this, it had been The Colosseum, and the theme had been Roman gladiators. I had actually found that one kind of amusing, if only because the centurion outfits they'd had for the staff had been so cute. Before that it had been The Cruiser, and the staff had all been in navy uniforms. Well, at least the music was interesting this time around. I'd had no idea that there were so many rock groups doing covers of Gregorian chants.

I went down to the weight room and did some pull downs on the rack, then climbed into the iron maiden to do some pec flies. Next to me a guy was doing tricep dips on the stocks. It really was uncanny how well the machines had been adapted to the decor.

But then, I have often suspected that modern fitness equipment owes a lot of its design to medieval torture devices.

I finished my flies and took a quick look around the gym. The lunch hour crowd was thinning out. Seven or eight of the disco clones, and a couple other guys whom I sort of knew were the only ones left. I waved to a lawyer I'd done some work for. I'd been hoping that Daniel might turn up. I was still in a foul mood from the whole morning ordeal, and Daniel can usually bug me out of my moods.

I did a round or two on the punching bag, and then hit the showers. One of the disco clones followed me in. He took the shower next to mine, and then kept staring at me while I rinsed off. Which is odd, because most of the clones won't give me the time of day. And I mean that literally. I asked one a couple days ago and he just sneered at me. I took a careful look at this one, trying to figure out what he wanted.

Like most of them, the kid was a walking advertisement for better living through chemistry. He had that sort of hyper-muscular build that you can only get through steroids, and that dizzy-happy sort of look that comes with doing bliss. I'd tried bliss once, just to see what it was like. Didn't much care for it. It was sort of like ecstasy, only more so. It made me horny, and affectionate, and wanting to cuddle. And not particularly discriminating.

Still, you got to hand it to the pharmaceutical wizards. Where would gay men be without them? They came up with steroids to make guys muscular, and bliss to make them affectionate. Now if someone could only invent a drug that would also make them considerate, funny, and pleasant to be around. They could market it as "personality in a pill."

I couldn't help but notice that my attentive friend was also beginning to sport a hard-on. That's when I recognized him.

"Hello, Lance."

He smirked and lathered up a place he'd already lathered twice before.

"Hey, Drew. Wow! The workouts must be going well. You're putting on some muscle there."

Lance used the remark as an excuse to put his hand on my chest. Lance was not particularly subtle. Or well-informed. His sudden interest in me had started a couple weeks ago, when he saw how much time Daniel was spending around me, and jumped to the conclusion that I must be rolling in money. I hadn't bothered to correct him on this point yet. After all, somebody needed to teach the boy about the dangers of not doing his market research.

Lance let his hand slide down my chest, and finally withdrew it about the time it reached my belly button. Although my brain knew that I didn't want to sleep with Lance, some other parts of my anatomy were starting to respond to the come-on. I found myself doing a visual inventory of his muscles, starting with the calves and working my way up. Lance looked to be in his mid twenties, and the boy did have some very nice parts. By the time I'd gotten up to his shoulders, my brain had come to the party as well, speculating on what he liked to do in bed, what positions we would find ourselves in. Then I got to the smile. Those slightly sharpened canines. Then those weird, unnaturally green eyes. Somehow, I knew that sex with Lance wouldn't be nearly as much fun as the flirting had been. As is all too often the case.

I managed to extricate myself from the showers, dry off, and get dressed. As I clipped the throat mike back to the inside of my collar, I checked in with Sherwin.

He still had not gotten through to Jen.

This was getting a little weird. Why wasn't she answering her phone? The only possibility that I could think of was that Jen had gotten caught up in her undercover work and forgotten to come up for air and make our court date. I could see her doing that. She's good at undercover, but she does this whole method acting thing for "getting into character," and it can be a bit hard to snap her out of it sometimes.

Anyway, if Jen was undercover, that would explain why she wasn't answering her own phone. She'd be using one of the numbers we set up for her alternate personae. It has to work that way. After all, it wouldn't do for Darlene Debromowitz, temporary secretary, to be getting calls for Jennifer Gray, private detective, now would it? You never know who might be listening.

I had Sherwin pull up the numbers for all the cover identities we'd set up for her, and called them all. In order, I got the voicemail for:

Darlene Debromowitz ("Hey. Dis is Darlene. Leaves me a message.")

Susan LaCroix ("I am terribly, terribly sorry that I can't make it to the phone just now. Do be a dear and leave me a message.")

and Ivana Mantrap ("Ooh. My hands are full right now, Tiger. If you'd like to get…ahold of me, leave something hot and steamy at the sound of me screaming in ecstasy. OH!").

I left a message on each. I was going to have to talk to Jen about toning these characters down a bit. There's a difference between detective work and running a freak show. Although, given the class of clients we get, not a lot.

OK. So she wasn't answering any of those numbers, either. Where was she? I had Sherwin pull up a list of our open cases. We were down to a lousy three of them. And not a one of them involved anything that should have kept her away from her phone for more than a few minutes.

Now I was getting worried. I decided to swing by her apartment. It seemed vaguely possible that she might have gotten sick and turned off the ringer on her phone in order to get some rest. I walked back to our office and got my car, and then drove down Ponce to Decatur.

Jen lives in a two story brick building, in a complex consisting of mostly Wiccans, college students, and old married couples. I pulled into her parking lot, climbed the stairs to her front door, and banged on it. No answer.

OK. Scratch "worried" and upgrade it to "afraid".

It took me almost three minutes to bypass the security sensor on her front door and jimmy the lock. I must be getting out of practice. Fortunately, no matter how complicated they make the print locks on these things, they never seem to make the actual dead-bolts any tougher.

Inside, everything seemed to be normal. No Jen, but no dead body on the floor either. Perfectly normal, except for one odd detail—her cat was missing.

I looked around to make sure. After all, cats can hide in the darndest places. But it was nowhere to be found. There was water out for it, and a litter box, and a few crumbs of food left in its bowl. But no cat.

I checked the door and windows. Except for some scratches on the front door that I had made on my way in, there were no signs of a forced entry. And it certainly didn't look like she'd been burgled. Her computer was still on her desk. Some expensive-looking crystals were arranged in front of the window. Nothing was missing.

Except her cat.

I sat down on her bed and tried to figure that out. I could imagine a few reasons why someone might want to kidnap or harm Jen. After all, you don't become a PI to win popularity contests. But why in the world would they go after her cat, too? My brain was beginning to hurt, so I filed the subject under "things I will lie awake worrying about at 2 in the morning," and finished searching her apartment.

I found her suitcase under her bed, so she hadn't packed for a trip. There was also a carton of milk going bad in the refrigerator, so she had probably been gone for at least a couple of days. Aside from that, though, the apartment didn't seem to have anything useful to tell me.

Well, like I said before, I still have some friends on the force. I punched Megan's number into my phone...and got her voicemail.

"I'm sorry, I'm too busy to come to the phone right now..."

By this point, I was getting really sick of voicemail. I had Sherwin pull up her priority code from my phone list. It was seven years old, but she might not have changed it. I punched it in. She answered on the first ring.

"Strand here."

"Hi Megan."

It took her a couple seconds to place the voice.

"Drew? Is that you?"

"Yeah. Look Megan, I need a favor, could you..."

"Drew! Talk about a blast from the past. Look, I'd love to talk, but...hold on a sec..." She shouted something to someone on the other end of the line. "Drew, this is going to have to wait. I'm in the middle of a real mess right now and..."

"It will just take a minute, Megan. I need..."

"No, Drew, you don't understand. I'm *really*..."

"It's *important*. Jen's missing."

"Jen? You're still hanging out with that dizzy wench?"

"Yeah, the 'dizzy wench' is still my partner, if that's what you mean."

"Well, it's your life, Drew. But she's going to get you in trouble one of these days. So what do you need?"

"Just run a search on APIN for any Jane Does or hospital admissions that match her prints. It won't take you more than a minute."

"All right, all right." She turned away from the phone for a second to yell something at someone in her office. "OK. You got her prints on file?"

I told Sherwin to zap her Jen's fingerprints.

"OK, got it." she said. "Just a second...Nope. No hospital matches. No Jane Does. Let me take a quick look through the unidentifiables... How long has she been missing?"

"I talked to her a couple days ago."

"OK. We've had three bodies come in that were too burned to fingerprint, but two of those are men, and the third is a child."

"Thanks Megan, I owe you."

"No more than usual. Say Drew, why don't we get together and do dinner sometime, I know this place where... OK, I *really* have to go now. Call me next week?"

"Yeah. OK."

Click.

OK. So Jen wasn't in the hospital. She wasn't in the morgue. She wasn't at work. And she wasn't at home. So where the Hell was she?

I sat down at her desk. Her computer was running some scene from a Charlie Chan movie. I hit the return key, and the movie dissolved away, to be replaced by a cartoon drawing of an old roll-top desk. The top was closed, and there was a blinking cursor over its lock.

OK. What would Jen use for a password? I cleared my mind and tried to think of things that she might have used. Sometimes I can break into systems this way, just by dumb luck. And with Jen, I had the advantage of knowing her habits. I got it on the third try: MAGICK. The cartoon lock opened and the top rolled back to reveal the desk top. Jen's system was a little funny looking, but not too far from the standard. There was a blank sheet of paper in the middle of the desk that I guessed was for launching applications. To the side, there was a stack of letters, which was probably her e-mail. An old-fashioned phone with a crank, which would be her voice-mail. And an ornate picture frame with a painting of a mermaid in it. The mermaid's eyes were blinking red. I had no idea what that icon was for.

I read through her e-mail. Most of it was pretty routine, but there was one message that seemed out of place. I checked the profile of the sender, and it turned out to be an art dealer at one of the shi-shi galleries over in Virginia Highlands.

"Jen,
Was finally able to ID that piece off the photo you sent me. Not an easy job. Where'd you find this thing anyway? Some mysterious trove of stolen art? There was no record on the piece, so it's never been exhibited or sold by a *reputable* dealer. However, a friend of mine recognized the style and that squiggle in the corner that I can only assume is supposed to be a signature. Turns out the piece is a St. Cloud, done in her later style. You may remember the name from the newsites a few years back—Alicia Calerant-St. Cloud was stabbed to death by her husband. Anyway, everybody in the art world knows the story, so her work has a certain cachet. Tell the owner that if he's interested in selling, I can get him a good price.
Good luck with whatever it is you're working on,
Estevan."

Stolen art? None of our current cases had anything to do with a missing painting. Or I should say, none of our cases that *I* knew anything about. Apparently, Jen had taken on some extra work and neglected to leave me a note about it. Hm. When I found her, a lecture on proper record-keeping procedures would be in order.

I went into her mail program, retrieved a copy of the outgoing message she'd sent to the gallery, and had a look at this painting she was checking into. Now, I don't know much about art, but I could tell this wasn't the sort of thing you'd find hanging in a Holiday Inn. It was a picture of some guy in medieval armor, fighting off a hoard of demons with a sword shaped like a crucifix. There was even a little tiny figure of Jesus on it, splattered with demon's blood. A couple of little devils were crawling up the guy's legs, and another one had climbed up on his shoulder and was biting his ear. It kind of reminded me of a painting I'd seen once of St. George fighting a dragon. There was even a big beam of golden light shining down from above. Only, it wasn't shining on the big guy wielding the sword. It was focused on a spot off to his right, so that it just caught one of his feet and a little piece of one elbow. I'm sure it was supposed to mean something big and metaphorical, but to me it just looked like the guy needed to hire a better spotlight operator. Anyway, I forwarded a copy of the image to Sherwin, so that I'd have it for future reference.

Then I started in on Jen's voice mail. It took awhile to listen through all her messages. Me calling her Sunday night. Someone named Shard asking why Jen had missed some big Wiccan pow-wow. Sherwin calling her 32 times. A friend asking why she'd missed lunch. The only calls that seemed out of place were a series of three from someone named Justin Weir. I tapped on the name and played them again.

JUSTIN WEIR, 7/7/23, 2:42p : "Hi Jen, it's Justin. Just called to see how things are progressing."

JUSTIN WEIR, 7/8/23. 3:14p : "Hi Jen, Justin again. How's the case comin' along? If you can get back to me before the show tonight, it would make my life a lot easier."

JUSTIN WEIR, 7/8/23, 8:22p: "Hi Jen. It's Justin, again. I know you said you'd be hard to get ahold of, but when you pick up this message could you call me and let me know how the case is coming? Thanks."

Justin Weir. He wasn't one of our current clients, but the name was familiar. I had Sherwin do a search for him in our files, but he wasn't in there. Not as a former client, not as a former suspect, not even mentioned in passing.

So what case was Jen working on for him, and why the Hell hadn't she told me anything about it?

I listened to the messages again, trying to form a mental picture the guy. His voice was mature, but it hadn't yet picked up the gravelly sounds that come with age. At a guess, he was somewhere between 20 and 40. Slight southern drawl, but he was trying to suppress it. Didn't sound like the Georgia variety, but I wasn't good enough with accents to pick out where it was from. At any rate, it was a nice voice. Deep and masculine, but kind of melodic. I would certainly be able to recognize it if I heard it again. I tapped on his name, and her system gave me the return phone number.

I was about to sign off and go back to the office when my brain started playing tricks on me again. Out of the corner of my eye, I saw the mermaid icon waving at me, and when I looked at it, I saw Jen's face staring back at me from atop the mermaid's body. Then I blinked, and it was gone.

Great. I knew I should have included psychiatric care in the company health plan.

Anyway, out of curiosity I tried touching the mermaid icon. The desktop vanished, and a line of text appeared at the top of the screen saying, "Vault opened at 1:48 PM July 9." A video clip began running.

A woman was removing a heavy board from the front of a canopy bed. I glanced over my shoulder and recognized the angle. This footage must have been shot by the little video-conferencing camera on top of Jen's computer. As I watched, the woman took a secret panel off the bed. She picked up a book that fell out, put it back behind the panel, and then read some papers. The light was bad, and I couldn't see much of her besides a silhouette, but there was no way it could be Jen. This woman was shorter and stockier than Jen, and the look was all wrong.

Whoever the woman was, she gathered up some papers in a folder, replaced the panel, and then left with the documents. The clip ended a few seconds later.

I rubbed my forehead. First the missing cat, then some mysterious painting, and now this. I went and took a look at the bed. It took me a good ten minutes to figure out how to open the panel, but I finally found the trick. Once it was off, I examined the edges and found the contact points for the sensor that tripped Jen's little alarm. I looked back at her computer and waved, knowing I was being recorded.

There was nothing left in the vault now but the book, which presumably wasn't important because the thief had left it behind. Still, you never know. It was locked, so I pulled out my pocket knife and cut the leather strap that held it closed. The stuff inside was all mystical mumbo-jumbo, and I couldn't make heads or tails of it. Maybe I could find a witch or a New Ager to explain it to me, though.

Well, I had probably found everything that I was going to here. I replaced the panel on the bed and went back to Jen's computer. I forwarded copies of all her e-mail and messages to my own account, along with the footage of the burglar. Then I logged out of her system, relocked her front door, and walked back to my car.

OK. So far I had a vanished partner, some clues for a case that she was working on but never told me about, a mysterious painting, photos of someone breaking into her apartment to steal some papers, a missing cat, and a book full of magic that I couldn't understand. It didn't add up to much, yet. Good thing I also had a name.

It was time I had a chat with Justin Weir.

## Chapter 12: The Chosen
## Monday the Ninth, 3:07 PM

By the time I had gotten everything out of my locker and packed my book bag, Scott and Tim were waiting for me.

"Did you see Kyle's face?" asked Scott with a grin.

"Did you see the Principal's?" I responded.

"Ah yes," said Tim with a malicious gleam in his eye. "Gentleman, I pronounce this issue an unparalleled success. So what are we doing to celebrate?"

"Well, here's an idea," I suggested. "How about we buckle down and get to work on the next issue."

Tim frowned. "Taskmaster."

Sigh. Good help is so hard to find. "What did you two have in mind?"

Tim and Scott looked at each other and then said a single word in unison.

"Mall."

Well, we did have a few hours to get into mischief. My parents don't get home from work till seven. Of course, they are the sort of raging control freaks who check the house door logs to make sure that I came straight home after school. Fortunately, Tim found a way around that. He planted a bug in my parent's room, and got their passwords. So now I can reprogram the locks to say I got home anytime I want them to. But I still have to get back before my parents do to make it all work.

Anyway, knowing that I was outnumbered, I agreed to the mall idea, and we had a short argument over which one to go to. I like Lenox because it's close. Tim likes South Point because they have the best electronics store. And Scott likes Lost World, because it was built back in the teens and has all that funky themed architecture that they were doing back then. We odd-evened for pick, and Scott won, so we caught the south train down to Lost World.

Personally, I think the guy who designed the place must have read way too many Edgar Rice Burroughs novels. Lost World's subway stop is designed to look like the inside of some ruined Aztec pyramid. Now, I don't really mind all the faux stone blocks and the big concrete snakes and the little bats with the light-up eyes that hang upside-down from the ceiling and flap their wings and screech. And I actually kind of like the little robotic monkey that swings around on the vines, always staying just out of reach. (I know, because we tried to catch it once when there was no one else in the station. Scott got up on my shoulders and...well, at any rate it didn't work.) But I really think that designing the benches to look like sacrificial altars was going a bit too far, and I definitely could have done without the fake bloodstains and manacles.

We took the escalator up to the third floor, where Scott and Tim vanished into the men's room to change into their bad kid drag. I braced myself for what was coming. Tim emerged a couple of minutes later, wearing a huge gold crucifix and a t-shirt with a picture of two shirtless men kissing. Oh, well. What are friends for if not to embarrass the Hell out of you in public places? Scott came out a minute later wearing...

"Oh, no." I said. "You can't be serious."

"What, too subtle?"

Scott's t-shirt depicted the crucifixion, with an extremely muscular Christ sporting a goatee and an earring. But what really caught my attention was Christ's huge, erect...

"Oh, don't worry," Scott said. "I brought something along for you."

He pulled out a big, dangly crucifix and clipped it onto my right ear. I sighed loudly but left it there. It's not like I was going to meet any girls anyway.

And so, properly attired, we set off to leave our mark on the mall.

Tim, of course, headed straight for the spy store. His mom and dad got divorced a few years ago, and he's worked the guilt angle beautifully. He's collecting an allowance that's five times the size of mine— from *each* parent. I'll bet that even the CIA envies his budget.

Anyway, knowing that Tim would not emerge from his electronic wonderland for at least half an hour, Scott and I wandered over to the Poster Pagoda. I headed for the racks with the pictures of naked women, while Scott delved into the art section. I was drooling over a photograph of a particularly wholesome young woman in a haystack and trying to figure out where I could hide it in my room when Scott let out a yelp.

"What's wrong?" I asked, jogging over.

"I've found it!" he said exultantly. "This is the one I've been hunting for!"

He was looking at a knock-off of the Last Supper. It was actually a pretty good copy, except that the apostles were all having sex with each other and Jesus was shoving a loaf of french bread down Judas' throat. The title was "Eat Me."

"I saw this in an art book once," said Scott. "It's a CALERANT, one of the ones he did while he was in prison for killing his wife. Wicked, huh?"

Actually, I thought that "wicked" was a rather tame description. Scott noted the number and went up to the counter to place his order. He had the sales girl print it on a t-shirt for him. I had a feeling that I knew what he'd be wearing on our next mall outing.

After that, we started over to the music store, because I wanted to hear the new Justin Weir album. Scott gives me a hard time about listening to Christian Rock, but even he admits that Justin is different. The other Christian singers are all a bunch of whining ass-kissers who do song after song about what a great guy God is: Gee he's perfect. Gee he's wonderful. As if God doesn't hear it enough all ready. But Justin writes about people trying to deal with God, and that's a lot more interesting. His songs are about doubt, and searching, and wondering why things are the way they are. Sometimes, when I've had a really big fight with my parents, I'll just sit up in my room with the lights off, listening to his songs over and over again all night.

Anyway, before we even got to the music shop my phone went off. It was Tim letting us know that he was done at the Spy Store. So we all agreed to meet at Jeremy's Jungle Jambalya for a quick snack. After that, we all headed for the Temple of Zoom at the far end of the mall.

The Temple's entrance is kind of neat. They've got a couple of big stone snakes with eyes that light up and rotate to watch you as you go in, and their mouths blow dry ice fog across the entryway, so it's like you're walking into another world. It's all so tacky that it's cool.

Just past the smoke there's a bank of SkyLord machines. Scott wanted to play, but there was a gang of Mormon kids taking up all the machines. As we watched, one of the cockpits flipped upside-down. Not bad. Some hot-shot must have pulled an Immelmann. A second later we saw another cockpit shake and go into a flat spin. I guess we know who he'd been lining up a shot on.

Tim wanted to rent laser guns and play zap-tag, but there were already 23 kids in the maze, and that's just too crowded for my taste. Besides, I knew where I wanted to go.

Casually, I steered my friends toward the row of Slip Stream machines at the center of the temple. There were still four empty drop zones. Scott put up a bit of a fuss, because I always want to play this game, but Tim took my side for once and we outvoted him. I don't care if the game is three years old. It's still the coolest thing anybody's ever come up with.

We went over to the keeper's desk to get our gear, and Tim put our games on his card. (He always does. I kind of feel guilty about letting him pay for all our arcade time, but I can't very well have charges from Lost World on my card when my parents pay my bill, now can I?) I zipped myself into one of the baggy jumpsuits, and then put on the clunky metal arm and leg bands. By the time I finished, Scott and Tim were already dressed. We saluted each other, grabbed our helmets, and headed into our separate machines to face each other in combat.

The inside of a Slip Stream machine isn't much to look at. Just a small circular room with padded walls, a grate on the floor, and some little holes in the wall where the game cameras look in to monitor your body's position. I put on my helmet and activated it.

The padded room faded away, and I found myself in the dark, surrounded by a circle of menacing characters. I turned around until I found the one I wanted—a reptile man, with big wings and a tail. I pointed to him.

"That one."

The characters all disappeared, but when I looked down, my arms were covered with scales. I had claws on my hand. A barbed tail twitched about my feet, and when I looked over my shoulder I could see my mighty wings flexing. Righteous.

I felt a draft from the floor as the game started up. I waited for it to build to a strong wind, then leaned into it and felt my feet leave the floor. I got myself leveled off, floating on the breeze, and waited for the world to come alive.

It appeared suddenly. Rocks. Rocks all around me. Little rocks, drifting past me. Big boulders, turning slowly and catching the sunlight in interesting ways. I guess it was supposed to be an asteroid field. I hadn't seen this part of the game grid before, but they're always upgrading it, adding new areas.

I put my arms out in front of me to indicate that I wanted to move forward, and heard the beat of my monstrous wings. I zoomed in and out among the rocks, looking for Tim and Scott.

I heard the squeaking before I saw anything. I looked around. Nothing in front. Nothing below. I flipped over onto my back and saw them coming. Bats. One of the computer generated opponents, not too dangerous. They don't have a ranged attack, but if they catch you they start draining off your life points. I sighted down my arms at the lead bat and clenched my fists to fire a shot. My plasma bolt seared off his flesh, and a little flaming bat skeleton plummeted down out of sight.

I threw myself into a dive to buy some time, since the game only lets you fire one shot every two seconds, and then fried the second bat. The third gave me a good chase, hanging tight on my tail, but I managed to play hide and seek with him in the asteroid field until I could double back and get a clear shot on him. I seared off his right wing, and he made little squeaking noises as he fell out of sight. Then I went in search of bigger game. Bats are tasty little morsels, but you score the big points by taking out other players.

I flew past a few more boulders and then emerged into a big open space. In front of me was a huge flat planetoid that looked to be a few miles across, with some sort of city on top of it. Towers of colored glass shooting up for hundreds of feet, with bridges and floating platforms and all sorts of crazy stuff between them. I started in carefully, keeping an eye out for an ambush.

I flew between a couple of towers, and was just slipping in under a hanging garden when a plasma shot barely missed my left wing. I glanced behind me just in time to see a blue cape disappearing behind a balcony. Ah ha! So that's where Tim was lurking. He always plays that Superhero character.

Tim would be expecting me to take off after him, but I knew better. Instead, I flew up into the roots that were dangling down from the garden and waited for him. Tim's a good flyer, but patience has never been his strong suit. Sooner or later, he'd come looking for me.

Sure enough, I spotted him a few seconds later, coming out from behind the balcony. He flew over to the garden cautiously, but didn't spot me. I waited until he was just a few feet away before I let him have it.

I dropped out of the roots and hit him square in the chest with a plasma bolt. He went spinning out of control, loosing altitude. I followed him close, but he regained control before I could get off a second shot, and barrel rolled out of the way of my bolt.

Which left me with no attack for a few seconds and Tim with an armed plasma bolt. I saw him flip over to line up a shot on me. I was about to dive back into the dangling roots, hoping they would buy me some cover, but just then a blast came out of nowhere and knocked Tim back into a bridge. The bridge shattered, glass flew everywhere, and Tim's persona broke up into little fragments.

"My, but they don't make superheros like they used to." The voice was deep and kind of metallic-sounding.

I turned to see who the newcomer was, but the kid wasn't gonna wait around for me to line up a shot on him. I saw a figure disappear behind a tower. At first I thought it might be Scott, but this guy was zooming around in powered armor with boot jets, and Scott usually plays an archangel.

I started around the tower in the opposite direction, figuring I'd run into him on the other side. I passed over a couple of those funny bridges, a couple of balconies. But I didn't see him anywhere. I started doing a slow corkscrew spin, so that I could keep an eye out above and below me. The problem was that I should have been keeping an eye out behind me.

Out of the corner of my eye, I saw the armored guy zip out from under a bridge I'd just passed over. He must have been hovering there, waiting for me to come by. He was already lining up a shot, and there was no way that I could turn in time to fire on him. I tried to bank off into a roll, but I never had a chance. The bolt hit me in the shoulder, and I felt the game's magnets grab hold of my wristbands and send me into a flat spin. I heard a tinny, mechanical laugh, and then that metallic voice saying.

"Ha. Ha. Gotcha, snake boy."

Wow. What an insightful observation. I wanted to put this kid in his place, but it's hard to think of a snappy comeback when you're spinning like a top.

I managed to stabilize myself, but the kid was right on top of me and blasted me again before I could even get my bearings. This time he sent me crashing through one of the towers. Glass exploded around me, and my life points dropped even lower due to the collision. As the world spun around me I could see the guy in the armor, his little bootjets aflame, still coming after me.

OK. I'm no novice at this game. There was no way I could take another hit like that, and he's not gonna finish me off that easily. This time I came straight out of the spin into a power dive. I was yielding the high ground, but it was worth it to avoid getting nailed by old metal head again.

I dropped a couple hundred feet and then leveled off, zipping between a series of towers. I glanced behind me. Metal head was still on my tail. He was playing cautiously, not wasting shots on anything but a sure hit. He was waiting for me to stop zig-zagging for a second so that he could nail me. I made sure that he didn't get the chance.

I have one trick up my sleeve that I'd never seen anybody else pull. Apparently, neither had metal head. With him on my tail, I suddenly balled up into a half-somersault, then flattened out again. For a split second, I was flying backward. And a split second was all I needed.

I blasted him in the face at point blank range, sending him into a tumble. Of course, I went out of control as well, which is the problem with this maneuver. I'd hoped to come out of my spin first, so that I could shoot the little twerp again, but he pulled out of his as fast I did. I was running out of options. Even after that shot, he still had at least half his life points, and I couldn't even take a glancing hit. There was no way I was gonna win a straight shoot-out with this guy.

So when he came back at me, I threw myself into another dive, trying to lose him. He followed me. We flew down for what seemed like miles, out of the sunlit tower tops. The light grew dimmer. The bridges and skyways grew more numerous. But no matter how I zigged or zagged between them, I couldn't lose the armored geek. Down and down we dove. The shadows grew darker. The bridges gave way to pipes and girders. And still I couldn't loose him.

Down in the twilight depths of the city I was forced to slow as I picked my way through the maze of pipes. But at least they kept metal head from lining up a clear shot on me. We wove in and out among the pipes, but I could never quite lose him. Finally, I saw a building up ahead with a big opening. A slow fan blade turned in it. I guess it was supposed to be a ventilation port. Well, any port in a storm.

I timed the blade and managed to fly in without getting whacked. Maybe metal head wouldn't be so lucky, but I wasn't counting on it. Once inside, I had been hoping to flip over and ambush him as he came through, but there wasn't enough room to turn around. The air duct was pretty narrow, and any attempt to turn would have sent me crashing into the walls. And with my life aura this low, that would have finished me. So I zoomed further into the system.

The ventilation ducts kept turning abruptly at all sorts of weird angles, and it took all the flying skills I had to keep from slamming into the sides. I forked right, then up, and then right again, hoping to lose metal head and find some way out of this crazy maze. The sound of metallic laughter echoed weirdly in the system. But it never seemed to get any further away.

I forked right again, then slalomed through a crazy series of S-turns, and then...I found exactly what I needed. The tube suddenly widened out by a couple of feet. Not a lot, but just enough to turn around. I let myself glide to a stop, and then carefully did a half somersault. I lay there, hovering, waiting for my nemesis to come barreling down the corridor.

I didn't have to wait long. In the dim light of the ventilation ducts, I could see the glare of his bootjets reflecting off the walls as he came through the S-turns. I put out an arm, sighted along the corridor, and waited for him to come around the last corner.

Then I let him have it.

The shot went home. It hit him squarely in the shoulder. He started to spin and bounce off the walls. Now it was my turn to laugh. He was going to take a lot of extra damage from crashing into the walls, and with any luck he'd be too turned around in these narrow quarters to do anything before I could get another shot off at him. I began to gloat.

"He who laughs last," I said, the game modulating voice and stretching out the S's to make it sound more reptilian, "laughs..."

Then I realized what was going to happen, and I stopped laughing. He was ricocheting off the walls and completely out of control, but his momentum was still carrying him toward me.

"Oh sh..."

There was nothing I could do. No time to turn around, no room to dodge. He bounced twice more and then crashed into me. The damage from the impact was enough to put my life total over the edge. The world went black, and glowing letters appeared in front of me.

"Benji the Reptilian slain by Vengeance the Space Knight after 7 minutes, 32 seconds of play. Score: 687." Six hundred and eighty seven. It was the first time in two months that I hadn't cracked two thousand.

The air stream began to slow down. Sometimes I'll flatten out, just so that I can ride the stream for as long as possible before I reach the floor. Today I just turned myself up vertical and waited for my feet to touch bottom.

Scott and Tim were waiting for me when I got out of the cabin. I took off my helmet and looked at Scott. "I take it you met our little mechanical friend as well?"

Scott looked disgusted. "I didn't even last two minutes. He finished me off before you two even turned up."

"Well," I said, "I think it's about high time we met laughing boy."

We walked around until we found the booth with a display that read "Vengeance". He was still playing, so he must have survived his crash into me. Still, according to the display he was almost out of life. We waited a couple minutes till his life ran out and his final score flashed. I noted with some annoyance that it was 70 points higher than my best score ever.

Well hey, I'm not too bitter to admit it when someone out-flies me. When he stepped out of the cabin I stuck out my hand.

"Hey, nice flying," I said, trying to sound sincere. "I'm Benji— I was the reptilian you blew away in the tunnels."

He shook hands and climbed out of his jumpsuit while Scott and Tim introduced themselves. He had a really cool shirt on that was black with all the constellations on it, and it must have had a battery somewhere because the stars were all lit up. I was going to ask him where he got it when he turned toward me and I noticed...he had breasts.

Uh?

He took off his helmet and smiled at me. I mean, she took off her helmet. She had long brown hair and green eyes.

"Oh, hey!" she said with a smile, "So you were the hot shot that almost punched my ticket. Nasty little trick you pulled in that ventilation system. By the way, how do you do that maneuver where you flipped over and shot me backwards? I tried something like that once, but I couldn't stay stable long enough too... Uh, sport? My face is up here."

I hadn't realized what I was looking at. I mean, I had realized what they were, I just hadn't realized I was staring. I could feel my face turning red and I was wishing I could just spontaneously combust and get it over with.

"Uh...sorry," I stammered. "I didn't mean..."

"Oh, don't sweat it," she said. "They only started coming in a few months ago, and I'm still getting off on this strange power they seem to have over men. It's like hypnotic or something." Then she paused. "Of course, it usually doesn't work on gay men."

"HEY! What makes you think I'm..." Then I remembered the earring, and yanked it off. I was going to have to come up with a particularly inventive way to kill Scott. Maybe something involving Liquid Plumber and an enema.

"Oh, don't sweat it," she said. "Whatever side of the fence you want to play is fine by me. By the way, what's your name again?"

"Um... Benji." Oh, that was just great. Um Benji? Did my name suddenly have an extra syllable? Why couldn't I have just said "Ben" in a confident voice?

"Well, hi um-Ben-ji." she pronounced it like an African name, but for some reason the teasing didn't bother me. "I'm Summer. So how long have you been playing Slip Stream?"

"Well..." Did she say that they'd only come in a couple of months ago? How fast do those things grow?

"Uh...Benji? Ben? Earth to Ben? Oh dear." She handed me her helmet and jumpsuit and I took them absent-mindedly. Then she crossed her arms over her chest.

"OK, Ben. Am I going to have to walk around like this just to carry on a conversation with you?"

Actually, holding her arms like that just pushed her breasts together and made them look even bigger. But I tried not to notice that. Really I did.

I can't quite remember how the rest of the conversation went. For some reason Scott and Tim went off to do something else and Summer and I wound up splitting a mango shake at Jane's Jungle Juicery. I kind of remember that we talked about video games, and how stupid my Baptist school is, and how stupid her Wiccan school is, and all the stupid little things our parents do just to drive us crazy.

Suddenly she looked at her watch.

"Oh, darn," she said. "I've got to go. I have to be home to meet my little sister when she gets back from her nature appreciation class."

She paused for a moment.

"So, uh...You want to come over?"

## Chapter 13: The Police
## Monday the Ninth, 3:20 PM

K'yon from Data Services was waving at me from across the conference table, trying to get my attention. I held up my hand in the "give me five minutes" signal, then answered the call that had been beeping in my ear for the last fifteen seconds.

"Strand here, what is it?"

There was a pause at the other end.

"Uh...It's Shard Lewis. And you don't need to bark at me."

I forced myself to count to 5 and slow down. Ordinarily it would have been 10, but today I didn't have the time.

"Sorry," I said. "Things are a bit hectic up here."

"Yeah, I can imagine. But I think you'll be happy with the news from forensics. It looks like we've caught a few lucky breaks."

"Just what I want to hear. Hit me with it."

"Well, first off, we got a positive ID on the corpse. The dental records were a match to the name on the tombstone. Carl Phillips. Which saves us all kinds of trouble trying to lift prints off what's left of his fingers."

"Great." At least something about this case was straightforward. "Do you have a cause of death?"

"Yeah. I called up the original death certificate and uploaded it to the casefile. You should have it by now."

I glanced down at the conference table, and noticed the large number of blinking red numbers, indicating files I hadn't read yet.

"Probably," I said. "But there's a whole stack of stuff here I haven't gotten to yet. Want to give me the highlights?"

"Sure." There was the sound of clicking keys on the other end of the connection. "Cause of death was pulmonary failure due to blood loss, due to internal bleeding, due to massive blunt trauma to the chest and abdomen. The guy was in a car accident. Manslaughter charges and civil suit pending."

"OK. One second." Across the table, K'yon was dictating a document. I flipped the mike of my headset down and waved to get her attention. She looked up.

"We've confirmed the ID on the corpse as Carl Phillips. Have someone pull together a bio on him. In particular I want to know about any enemies this guy might have had."

K'yon rolled her eyes in frustration, then nodded agreement. I flipped my mike back up.

"OK Shard, I'm back. What else have you got for me?"

While I talked, K'yon walked around to me, mumbled something into her headset, and pressed her thumb onto the table surface in front of me. A document came up. I glanced at the title. "Bio profile on Carl Phillips: 1/12/1978 - 4/14/2023." She scrawled something on the table next to it and gave me a superior smile. I read the note. "As if I wasn't on this already?" I forced myself to smile back and flash her the OK sign.

"Well," said Shard, calling me back to the conversation on my headset, "I managed to work up an approximate time of death on that rooster using liver temperature. I'll spare you the gory details on how I got the comparison data. Let's just say that death occurred between 2 and 3 in the morning. Can't pin it down much past that."

"Two or three in the morning? Good. That narrows down the time a lot. Thanks a lot Lewis, I appreciate it."

"No problem. Just don't give me any grief when you see my expense report on those thirty live chickens."

"I...I wouldn't think of it," I said.

"Great. Also checked our bird's DNA against the patents of commercially available livestock. Turns out he was a Monsanto 'Prize Fryer.' I checked with a vet, and he said that's a pretty common breed. Most of the agribusinesses in the state use them. Of course, most farms only keep a few roosters around, so you might have somebody call around to see if any of them sold a live one or had one stolen in the past few days."

"Good idea," I said. "I'll put data services on it." I got K'yon's attention again and scrawled a short note for her on the table while still talking to Lewis. K'yon read it, nodded, and set to work at it. "Anything else I should know about?"

"Let's see. A few interesting fibers we found on the body. One white linen thread, probably from a handkerchief or dress shirt. One dark blue cotton thread. Looks like it came off a dress jacket of some sort. Hm...other than that, nothing too exciting. At least nothing you can't wait to read about in the case file...oh, except for the candles."

"What about the candles?"

"That's our other lucky break. We managed to get a partial print off one of them."

"A print! Lewis, I could kiss you!"

"No thanks, my girlfriend's the jealous type. Anyway, the thing's right there, embedded in the wax. Well, actually it's not wax. Turns out to be animal fat of some sort. Roger is trying to pin down what kind right now, but the stuff was boiled. All the proteins are pretty thoroughly denatured which means DNA tests aren't going to...

"Excuse me," I said, getting a bit impatient. "Can we get back to the print?"

"Yeah," said Lewis. "Looks like the edge of an index finger. Not a lot there to work with. I don't know if we'll be able to get a ID off AFIS, but we can certainly match it to the perp if we find him."

"Well that's useful. Do what you can with AFIS. Even if you can just narrow down the possible matches to a few thousand, that would be a big help. We'll be able to narrow things down further based on other criteria."

"I'm on it. Anything else?"

"Not now. Do you have any idea how much longer the ME will be with the body?"

"No, but give me a second and I'll poke my nose in and see how they're doing." I heard Lewis calling up the video feed from the ME's lab. "Oh. Shouldn't be more than another ten minutes or so. Looks like he and Browning are wrapping up things now."

"Great," I said. "Tell Browning to give me a call when they're through." I'd sent Tony in to witness the ME's work on the corpse. It's procedure to have an officer on hand at the autopsy to take possession of any evidence that might come off the body. And it was good politics to have Tony in there. When this was all over, I was going to have to sell our findings to the Baptists. And I wanted to have Tony in there to assure them that there'd been no hanky-panky with the evidence. Some of them would probably still scream cover up, but it was the best I could do.

I hung up on Lewis and took my headset off. I'd been wearing it almost continuously since visiting the crime scene this morning, and the darn thing was pinching my temples and giving me one Hell of headache. I stretched and glanced up at the clock. 3:27pm.

I put the headset down on the conference table and took a look at what we had so far. Most of the table was taken up with a schematic of the crime scene, with control numbers next to important features. Eleven or twelve of these were blinking red, indicating that there was new information that I had not reviewed yet. At the other end of the table was a smaller but more detailed  schematic of the corpse. New numbers were lighting up on this one every fifteen seconds or so as the ME finished his report and the information got entered.

Across the table from me, K'yon was reviewing a document she'd called up. Her fingers tapped on the table at a steady pace as she flipped through the pages.

"Anything interesting?" I asked.

"Just going over the reports from the phone pool."

"Any useful tips?"

"Well," K'yon said, "I've got one report of a giant demon rising from the graveyard, another from someone claiming to have a 'psychic impression' that the Brazilians are involved, one sighting of suspicious looking poodle leaving the scene, three reports of witches riding in on broom sticks, and a whopping seven reports involving flying saucers hovering over the graveyard. I actually called the last group back, thinking they might have seen a helicopter."

"And had they?"

"No. But they'd all seen *Plan Nine from Outer Space* recently."

"Well, you never know when we'll get lucky," I said.

"I think we're overdue," K'yon responded, then flipped her mike back up to answer a call.

I stretched again. I was really starting to notice those two hours of sleep I'd missed this morning. I was about to put my headset back on when the door to the conference room opened. A uniform came in with a stack of boxes. I caught a whiff of something spicy, and suddenly realized that I hadn't had breakfast or lunch yet.

Darn. I hadn't even noticed that anybody was putting together an order. I enviously watched K'yon accept her box from the uniform. She must have noticed the way I was looking at her food because she leaned across the table.

"I hope you don't mind. You were busy when the rest of us were deciding on lunch, so I went ahead and placed an order for you. Hope jade curry is OK with you. By the way, credit me a twenty when you get the chance, to cover it."

I smiled at her. K'yon is an acquired taste. But she was beginning to grow on me.

The officer worked his way around the table, passing out boxes to the various techs and detectives I had working on this thing. He finally got around to me.

"Here you go Lieu..." he started to say, then suddenly grimaced and turned a pale shade of green.

Well, it's not my fault. I'd squeezed in time for a shower as soon as we got back to HQ, and shampooed twice. And I still smelled like old, rotten corpse. I don't know where that darn smell hides. It must get into your pores or your hair follicles or something. I don't think anything short of shaving my head and going though a sand blaster was going to get rid of the stink.

"Thanks," I said, taking the box. The private backed off, tried to smile politely, and then left as quickly as he could. I glanced around to see if I was turning anybody else's stomach. I was the only one in the room who'd actually been at the crime scene. They were all chowing down, though, so I guess their noses must have adapted by that point.

I opened up my box. Green curry chicken. Good call on K'yon's part. I unwrapped the plastic fork and dug in. As I chewed my first mouthful, I saw another three blinking numbers light up on the table. No rest for the weary.

I touched a blinking number next to the white pentagram and read the report on it while I ate. The lab had run the lime through a gas chromatograph and identified the brand as Pru-Chem Lawn Care. Probably not much help. It was a common brand, and lots of people buy it in small quantities. Still, if we found the bag this came from, we could probably match it as belonging to the same lot as the stuff from the crime scene.

I finished off the chicken and moved on to another number. The report linked to the footprints proved to be a bit more helpful. Two sets had been usable. The first was from a boot, a size 10 1/2 Nike Outlander, while the other was a dress shoe, a size 8 Pripyat Accordance, with a cut in the sole. Both were men's shoes. Based on the depth of the prints and the compression of the soil, the techs were putting the Nike Perp at 190 lbs, and the Pripyat at 210. There was also a partial print of a size 9 boot, another Outlander, but not enough to get a reliable weight estimate.

I was about to call up another report when I remembered the bio on the corpse. I glanced down at the table. The bio was still there, right where K'yon had pulled it up for me. I slid my chair over to it, and was starting to read the report when I heard my headset beeping again. I picked it up and put it on.

"Strand here."

"Hey Megan, it's Tony."

"Tony, great. What have you got for me?"

"Well, your ME is dictatin' the final report now. Looks like it's going to run forty or fifty pages by the time he's done with it. Thought you might like a heads up on the exciting bits before he throws the whole thing in your lap."

"Fine. Hit me with it."

"OK. Let me pull up my notes. Let's see. Per your idea, we checked the abdominal wound for semen. Negative.—I might add that I am relieved on that score. The instrument used to make the wound was sharp, and had a slight curve. Your techs also picked up some microscopic traces of metal in the lining of the wound. It's a funny alloy, mostly copper. It's not used in modern weapons, so they think we're looking at some sort of antique knife or ceremonial dagger. Oh, and he's pretty sure the same knife was used on the abdomen, the tongue, and the rooster.

"No good latent prints on the body. Word from your other techs is that they haven't found any good prints on any of the crime scene surfaces, just one partial embedded in the candle wax. So it's a good bet that most of the perps were wearing gloves. We did find one faint impression of a knuckle on the body, about 1.5 cm to the left of the ring impression. Our guess is that there was at least one person at the scene with bare hands, probably someone who wasn't supposed to handle anything. He must have bumped into the body as it was being moved."

"Good. Is there any way to make an ID off a knuckle print?"

"I already asked about that. Your techs don't seem to think so. The impression is pretty faint to begin with, and apparently there's not much detail to work with on a knuckle, at least compared to a finger print."

"Darn. That would have been a nice break. Well, we've still got the ring."

We'd learned from the officer at the scene that he'd gotten his ring as a gift from his father. A call to the old man had revealed that he'd gotten the ring after making a donation to the Christian Alliance. A couple calls to the Alliance had verified the fact that the rings were indeed sent out as "thank you" gifts to some campaign volunteers and individuals contributing $10,000 or more.

"Yeah," said Tony. "How are things coming with that?"

"Slow. We need someone to get the Christian Alliance to cough up a list of everyone they sent those rings to."

"Ouch. They are not going to be happy about that. Those donor lists are political gold."

"Which is why I want you to be the one to ask them. I figure you've got a better chance than any of us. Try blinking those blue eyes at them and see how far you get."

"I'll try. But you may have to issue a subpoena."

I groaned. "I'd rather it didn't come to that. Stonewall's got a lot of pull, and if he thinks we're trying to go over his head he'll take us to court to block the release of the information. It could take years before we ever get our hands on that donor list. Let's just ask nicely and see what we get."

"All right. Let me just grab a quick shower and I'll be on it."

I took the headset back off and settled down to read the bio on our corpse.

"Carl Phillips: Born 1978. Died April 14, 2023, of injuries sustained in an automobile accident. Manslaughter charges have been filed against the driver of the other vehicle, Fritz Roth, and a grand jury has indicted. Criminal trial and civil suit pending.

"Phillips was born in upstate New York. Father employed as an inventory manager for a chain of shoe stores. Mother employed as an elementary school teacher. Family moved to New Jersey when Phillips was age 7. Graduated public high school in 1995. Enlisted in army same year. Saw active duty in Yugoslavia. Left army after one tour of duty in 1999, worked a succession of personal security jobs from 2000-2004. In 2004 was hired by Liberty Media to provide security services for then Representative Stonewall. Remained in employ of Liberty Media until 2020, when in recognition of his service he was given an extremely generous compensation package. He retired to open a gun and ammunition store in Marietta."

So our corpse had worked for Stonewall. The same guy who had been making speeches over the crime scene this morning. Interesting coincidence.

"Married once, to Pamela Reese-Phillips. One child, Jessica Reese, born 2007. Divorced in 2021. Wife and daughter now living in Orlando, Florida.

"Known Associations: National Rifle Association, Christian Militia, North Atlanta Bowling League, and volunteer counselor at Fellowship Summer Bible Camp.

"Arrested once in 2006 for carrying a concealed weapon. Pleaded guilty in exchange for suspended sentence. Investigated in 2021 on a tip that he was dealing in stolen guns. No corroborating evidence was found, and investigation was dropped.

"No known ties to organized crime. No known occult ties."

And that was it. Nothing that suggested why our perps might have targeted one Carl Phillips over all the other bodies in that cemetery.

I looked across the table at K'yon. She looked up from the document she was reading and met my stare.

"Yes?" she said. "What is it Lieutenant?"

"I want to dig a little deeper into Phillips', background," I said. "Pull a couple interviewers from the phone pool and have them call the guy's wife down in Florida. See if she can think of any enemies the guy might have had. I also want a list of who this guy's friends were. Everything from old army buddies to guys from his bowling league. There's got to be something about Carl Phillips that we don't know, something that singled him out for this treatment."

"I've already got some people on it," said Kyon. "I'll let you know if we find anything." Then she went back to issuing orders into her headset.

I looked back down at the table and called up a chart of the humanpower we had assigned to this case. We had ten officers out canvassing the neighborhood around the graveyard, but that effort was winding down now. It hadn't turned up much. A couple more people remembered hearing weird noises last night, but no one had any reliable descriptions of suspicious characters or strange cars lurking around the area.

I read over the list of officers who would be on their way back in soon. I noticed that Konig was still hanging in there. I put my headset back on and told Mindy to put me through to Torcelli, the officer I'd put in charge of the canvassing effort.

"Sure thing, sugar," Mindy chirped.

A moment later I got through.

"Torcelli here. What's up?

"Hey Torcelli, it's Strand. How soon till you guys finish up the neighborhood?"

"Just wrapping things up now. Konig and I have another block to go. Most of the others are about done. A couple of the guys are already on their way back to HQ."

"Tell 'em not to bother. I want to keep your unit up North. We've identified the corpse, and Data Services is pulling together a list of the guy's known associates. We'll work the out-of-state names through the phone pool, but I want your uniforms to track down all his local friends and do face to face interviews. Find out if this guy had any enemies, anybody he might have ticked off, any possible ties to occult groups. There's got to be some reason that they picked his body for this special treatment."

"All right, sir. We'll get moving on it as soon as we're done here."

"Oh, and another thing. Tell Konig to go home and get some sleep. She's been on duty for 14 hours straight now."

"OK. But she's not going to be happy about it. She's kind of excited to be working a case like this."

"Well tell her I'll promise not to solve it in the next six hours. You can put her back to work after she's rested. I don't want someone to get tired and miss something."

"OK. You got it."

"Good."

I hung up and looked back at the main display. Another ten blinking numbers had lit up. Down at the other end of the table, the schematic of the body was even worse. The thing had so many blinking numbers it looked like a Christmas tree.

I leaned back in my chair for a second and closed my eyes. I was drowning in details, but I didn't seem to be any closer to understanding what had happened. I needed to start putting the pieces together.

I grabbed one of the paper napkins that had come with my lunch, took out a pen, and started drawing a flowchart. I could have done this on the conference table and saved my work, but I don't necessarily want all my doodling preserved in the case file.

I drew a box with the name Carl Phillips in it, and then I drew
arrows to all his connections I knew of so far. To start with, I drew
an arrow to a box labeled "Occult Ritual Site". Then I drew arrows to boxes labeled "Army", "Gun Dealership", "Bible Camp",
"Bowling", "NRA", and "Christian Militia". None of these boxes
seemed to lead anywhere else. Then I added the box "Senator
Stonewall."

Well, I could draw an arrow from Stonewall to the Christian
Militia, but that was no big surprise. Phillips had probably joined
the militia because he worked for Stonewall. I could also draw
another arrow back from Stonewall to the "Occult Ritual Site"
box, since he'd turned up with protesters to make political hay out
of it. Again, no big surprise, though it was an interesting coincidence. We hadn't released the name of the body when Stonewall
made his speech, so he couldn't have known that the body belonged to someone he knew.

I drew in a new box labeled "Ring", and connected it by arrows
to both Stonewall and the Occult site. Now that was an interesting
one. It suggested that someone who was connected to Stonewall's
party was involved in mutilating the corpse. But why? I couldn't
see Stonewall ordering it as some sort of publicity stunt. It doesn't
improve his political standing that much, and if it was ever proven
that he faked it, his career would be over. So what was the alterna-
tive? That some secret Satanic Conspiracy had infiltrated the Christian Alliance? I wasn't wild about that theory either.

I was still puzzling over these connections when the priority
beep on my headset went off.

"Strand here."

"It's Davison. I'm briefing the mayor in ten minutes. What do
you have so far?"

The Watch Commander had been handling high profile stuff
all afternoon. Briefing panicky VIPs, performing at press conferences, holding the hands of various community leaders, and generally stepping into the spotlight wherever it turned. And not that
I blame him. The Commander has a good shot at making Chief of
Police in the next few years, and right now he needs to be seen by
all the right people doing all the right things. And besides, it's not
like the Commander hogs the glory. He's smart enough to take
care of the people under him. He's looked out for my career in
the past, throwing me enough good cases for me to prove myself,
and then making sure I got the credit I deserved. But this case
was something else. The fact that he had assigned it to me said a
lot about his faith in me. And the fact that he was willing to stay
out of my hair and let me do the job said even more.

I gave the Commander a brief rundown on the new technical data that had emerged in the hour since he called, and then explained how I'd deployed our resources to run down new leads. I described my conversation with the folks at the FBI Behavioral Sciences Lab. I'd given them the data on the crime scene, and they'd said they could get me back a psychological profile of the perps by the end of the week. I had the feeling they weren't taking the case too seriously because it was just vandalism. I'd tried to make them understand how volatile things were down here, but I wasn't sure I'd gotten through to them. Anyway, Commander Davison agreed to give them a call and light a fire under them after his briefing with the mayor.

Lastly, I described our work running down the ring impression, and our efforts to get the Christian Alliance to give us a donor list.

"Tony said he would try," I explained, "but he's pretty dubious about his chances of..."

"Don't worry. I've got some connections. You'll get it in an hour or so."

That surprised me. I had always been impressed with how well the Commander played the political game, but I would never have guessed that he had any pull with the Christian Alliance. Of course, I didn't know much about Davison's life outside the office. He was a career civil servant, and smart enough not to talk about things like religion or his personal life. Come to think of it, I didn't even know if he was married or not.

I thanked my Watch Commander, and he hung up. I made a note to myself to do some checking on his connections to the Christian Alliance when this case was over. I have career plans of my own, and it pays to know who's in bed with whom.

## Chapter 14: The Chosen
## Monday the Ninth, 4:45 PM

Summer and I caught a south train down to Civic Center Station, then switched over to an east train for the ride out to Little Five Points where she lives. On the way we talked about music. I was surprised to find out that she actually knew who Justin Weir was. I didn't think that witch kids listened to his stuff. Mostly, she was into this group called Iambic Predator, which she figured I'd never heard of, but I had. They're not on the approved list that my parents programmed into my media agent, but Scott plays them sometimes when I'm over at his house. They've got one song I really like called the "Hellbound Haiku", which is all about always trying to do the right thing and always having it blow up in your face. Summer and I wound up singing the whole thing on the subway with people watching, but for some reason I didn't feel stupid doing because she was doing it with me. Afterwards she told me that I'd earned a bonus point for knowing all the words.

We got to Little Five and walked seven blocks to this house with a tall, holly hedge around it. There was an iron gate at the front, with pictures of a lion and a unicorn worked into it. Summer said something to the gate, and it unlocked. Inside, the yard went back further than I'd expected. It was full of big trees, climbing vines, and roses, and had a kind of wild look to it. The house itself was a big, old-fashioned thing, with a tall pointed roof, long windows, and one of those weird sort of second-story patios around the second floor. A widow's walk, that's what they're called. It was a pretty house, in a creepy sort of way. It reminded me of the haunted house at Disneyland. Which I guess makes sense. After all, she is a witch, right?

It looked even more like a haunted house from the inside. Not in a scary sort of way, just in an odd sort of way. The first room off the front hallway was a library. The windows were stained glass, and the setting sun threw pictures of dragons on the wood floors. There were shelves full of weird books, crystals, and a big metal thingamajig that looked like something Portuguese sailors would have steered by in the Middle Ages. I was trying to decide if her parents were weird or just rich.

We walked down the hall, past the front staircase which had a wooden banister carved to look like some sort of snake, and into the kitchen, which seemed pretty normal except for all the strange-smelling plants they had growing in window boxes.

Summer got us some soda, and I noticed that there was a really cool drawing on the refrigerator of a woman's face as she was turning into a wolf.

"You do this?" I asked.

"Yeah," she said, grabbing a handful of ice from the freezer. "You like it?"

"It's good. Particularly the eyes. You managed to get the same expression in the human eyes and the wolf's eyes. Like she's thinking about something...something she's lost. Like love, or innocence, or..."

"Like love or innocence? That's not bad. You should be writing greeting cards."

"Thanks," I said, accepting the dubious compliment.

"Didn't know you had a poetic bent, Benji. You get another bonus point for that. Anyway, she's a character in a game I play. Her name's Petunia BoneCruncher."

"Petunia?"

"Yeah, it's sort of a family curse. All her siblings are named after flowers. You see, her dad ticked off this..."

Doorbell.

"Oh, joy," said Summer. "The brat is back."

She went to answer the door and I followed along. An orange cat that I hadn't seen before came sprinting out from underneath the kitchen table and joined us. We walked down the hall to the front door, and Summer opened it to an old lady in a sun hat who was holding a little blond girl by the hand.

"Thanks for bringing her home, Ms. Peterson," Summer said. "She didn't give you any trouble, did she?"

The old woman beamed. "No trouble at all. Such a nice little girl."

Summer looked down at her little sister. "Yeah, right."

The little blond girl smiled at the old woman. "Thank you for bringing me home, Ms. Peterson."

The old lady patted her on the head and left. The little girl stepped into the house. Summer closed the door and looked at her suspiciously.

"So runt, have fun at nature appreciation?"

"Yeah, it was COOL! We went out and looked at wildflowers, and Ms. Carpenter taught us all their names. We saw black-eyed susans, and coral honeysuckle, and wild roses, and..."

"And chocolate ice cream, I see." said Summer.

The little girl looked genuinely puzzled. "That's not a flower, silly."

"No, but there's a big smudge of it on your left cheek. I take it you zapped poor Ms. Peterson into making a small detour on the way home?"

The little girl folded her arms across her chest and gave Summer a "you can't make me talk, copper" glare.

Summer laughed and turned back to me. "Sorry, Benji. I should introduce you. Winter, this is Benji. Benji, this is my rival sibling, Winter. How about you two go into the family room and get acquainted while I get something to wipe her face off."

Summer vanished into the kitchen. The orange cat jumped into Winter's arms. She stroked its head while she looked me over. I felt like a used car.

"Well," I tried, "Winter is a nice name."

"Uh-huh. But Benji's a goofy one."

"Yes," I said. "Yes it is. And one day I will get even with my parents for sticking me with it."

Winter smiled at that, then looked at me slyly.

"So Benji, you like to play with dolls?"

By the time Summer joined us in the family room, I was trying to squeeze Rebecca the Receptionist in behind her desk—which I swear was made for a much skinnier doll—while Winter, playing Maxine the Mogul, was barking orders to me:

"Get me Fox-Warner on line one! And that jerk of a director on line two! And what's a person got to do to get a cup of cocoa around here?! Hello, Spencer? Baby! Love ya! Let's do lunch."

Summer just stood there, looking at the two of us. I tried to salvage the situation.

"Excuse me," I asked, "but do you have an appointment?" I swung Rebecca around in her little swivel chair to face Summer. "I'm afraid no one sees Maxine without an appointment."

She glared at Winter. "Now I know why baby birds eat their younger siblings."

I turned the doll back to her desk and got up.

"No, go ahead," Summer went on. "You might as well get used to taking orders from her. She's probably going to be running the whole planet by the time she's twelve."

Winter frowned at me. "Benji, you're not playing the game."

I sat back down and picked Rebecca back up…and then stopped myself. Something was not right here. I mean, of the two girls in the room I definitely knew which one I wanted to play with. Err…well, you know what I mean. So why was I holding this doll?

Summer grabbed me by the collar and yanked me to my feet. I dropped the doll. Summer held me up in front of her sister and growled.

"MINE. Got it?"

Winter shrugged, then picked up Rebecca and put her back in her swivel chair. The orange cat came over and started sniffing around the tiny office suite. Summer led me over to the far side of the family room.

"Sorry about that, Benji. Should have warned you about Little Miss Mind-control. Now, where were we before the tiny terror descended upon us?"

"You were showing me the drawing of the wolf-girl. You got any more pictures?"

"Sure."

She seemed pleased that I'd asked. She got out a notebook and called up some of her other drawings.

I had to admit that they were really good. She had a couple more drawings of the wolf-girl, one of this really creepy-looking vampire mime, and an intensely cool one of this girl with a katana who was hacking apart some Nazi zombies. That made me think that she might be into comics, which it turned out she was, so then I started telling her about our comic, which I hadn't really meant to do, but she was standing close to me and I wasn't thinking very clearly. Then she wanted to see it, so I opened up my notebook and showed her the first couple issues.

And she liked it! I mean, she *really* liked it! She thought Zero was cool, and the dialogue and the fight scenes were great. But then we got to the scene where one of the alien brain stealers is trying to sneak up behind Jade in the shower, and Summer sort of got quiet and stopped talking. And I could tell she didn't like it.

"What's wrong?"

Summer wrinkled up her nose. "Well, it's just that…good grief, you guys really haven't seen many naked girls, have you?"

"Hey! I'll have you know I've seen hundreds."

"I mean real ones, not centerfolds, testosterone boy."

"Oh," I said. "Well. That would cut the number down a bit, then."

"I mean, COME ON! Look at the size of this girl's breasts. Do all the super-heroines in your world have implants? Or is that like one of her powers? She's got cyborg breasts that shoot lasers or something?"

"Hey! Those are real!" I said.

"And how do you know?"

"Because I write this thing! I didn't give her any cyber-breasts, so she doesn't have any. She's just well-proportioned."

"Well-proportioned? Get real! The woman's got more saline in her than Sea World!"

"Does not!"

"Does too!"

"Does not!"

"Does too!"

"Does..."

She cut me off. "OK, I'll prove it to you."

She closed the comic and sent her agent out on the web for some photos. It came back a second later with the last three Hustler centerfolds.

"Wow," I said. "Your parents let you download this stuff?"

"Sure, why wouldn't they? Anyway, this is probably what you think a woman's body looks like," she said, tapping the screen. The woman under her finger was lying by a pool. One of her hands still held the bottom of her swimsuit. The other was cupping one of her breasts, so that the fingers were just brushing against...

"Uh, Benji? Could you try to stay with me here?"

"Oh. Yeah. Sorry."

"Boys. Sheesh. OK, now watch this." She called up pictures of a couple more centerfolds, cut out everything except for their breasts, then arranged those side by side. "OK. Now what do you see?"

"Uh...six breasts?"

"Yes. Anything else?"

"No. I have trouble getting past the six breasts part."

"Figures. Haven't you noticed that they're all exactly the same shape?"

"Oh, yeah. They are."

"That's because those are assembly line tits, Benji. Now this is what breasts really look like."

Summer sent her agent out after some more photos, and it came back with a whole boatload of them: some old oil paintings, some arty black and white photos, and a bunch of what looked to be amateur pictures of women taken by their boyfriends.

"See, the real ones are all different shapes," she said, clicking through the pictures in the file. "You can tell the fake ones because they're always perfectly centered. They point straight forward like car headlights. Real breasts usually point a little in or out."

"Really, I'd never noticed." I snuck another look at her chest, trying to figure out which way hers pointed. She caught me looking. She put a hand under my chin and turned my head back to the monitor. But she was smiling while she did it.

We talked about breasts some more, and then we kind of expanded the subject and started arguing over which of the models were pretty and which ones were gross. Then I said that one of the women she'd pulled up was *really* pretty, and it turned out to be some singer that Summer liked so she told me I'd earned another bonus point for having good taste. Then at some point I heard the front door open and some footsteps in the hallway.

"Who's that?" I asked.

"Oh, probably just my mom."

"Oh. OK." Then I remembered what we were looking at. "YOUR MOM!"

I reached out to flip off the notebook, but Summer slapped my hand away.

"Hey," she said. "Cut it out. I believe you were about to explain to me why little Miss Twelve Gauge here is such a turn on."

"Uh, Summer, shouldn't we turn this thing off..."

"Hello Family!" shouted an adult voice as her mother strode into the living room. The woman had an arm full of papers and a pet carrier.

"Mommy!" shouted Winter, and ran to her. The woman put the pet carrier down and picked up her daughter.

"Hello, my darling children. And what mischief have we been up to today?"

"I got to see wild flowers, and I learned all their names! I saw black-eyed susans, and..."

"Hi, mom," Summer said, talking over her sister's babbling. "This is my new friend Benji."

Her mother nodded in my direction, trying not to drop either Winter or the papers. "Pleased to meet you, Benji. Oh, by the way, dinner's going to be a little late, kids. I have some things I need to look over tonight, so your dad's going to pick up Thai food on his way home."

She kept talking as she walked down the hall away from us. I heard a door close at the end of the hallway.

"Well, that was weird," said Summer. "She usually gives us the third degree when she comes home. 'So what did you do today? What did you see? What did you learn? What did you feel? Why don't we all sit down and have a good *share*.' I can't believe she didn't want to know more about *you*."

The orange cat was sniffing around the pet carrier, and there was a low yowling coming from inside. Summer and I went over to investigate. There was a big black cat inside. It didn't look too happy about being there.

"Wow, mom *is* distracted," Summer said. "She didn't even introduce us to the new house guest. Well, I suppose we should let her out."

"How can you tell it's a girl?"

"I just can. It's a witch thing."

Summer opened the carrier's front grate. The black cat paused for a second, then poked its nose out. The orange cat tried to slice it off with a claw, but wasn't quite fast enough. The black cat sprung out of the box, and the two felines started circling each other, hissing and arching their backs.

"I'm not sure that was such a good idea," I said.

"You may be right," Summer admitted. Then her face suddenly lit up with an idea. "Hey, Benji. You want to see some real magic?"

"Sure."

"OK. But you have to know the magic word."

"And what's that?"

"WINTER!" Her shout almost split my eardrums. The six-year-old came stomping down the hall back to the family room. "What do you...OOH! Kitty cat!"

The little girl scooped up the black cat in her arms and squeezed it. It just sort of looked confused. The orange cat followed them as she carried her new friend over to the other side of the family room. She put it down to get out some toys, and the two cats sat watching her in rapt attention as she got out a T-set and some large dolls.

A few minutes later, the cats were both wearing little sun dresses and sniffing politely at tea cups full of milk that had been set out before them on a little table.

"Wow. She really is a witch."

"Yep. That's my little sister. Just call her Xarena. Say, you want to stay for dinner? I could call my dad and tell him to pick up another order of Pad Thai."

"Nah. I got to get home before my parents do."

"All right. I'll walk you to the gate."

She led me out the front door and down the path to that weird iron gate in the hedge. We sort of stood there while I tried to think of some really suave way to say good bye.

"Well, it's been fun," I said. "Guess I'm kind of glad that you kicked my butt at Slip Stream."

She laughed at that, which was a little strange since I hadn't said anything particularly funny.

"Gracious in defeat. OK. I'll give you another bonus point for that. Good night Benji."

"Good night. Uh...by the way, just what do I get to do with all these bonus points I'm earning, anyway?"

She smiled at me coyly.

"I'll let you know when you have enough to trade in," she said. Then she kissed me.

No, I mean *really*! She kissed me!

Then she closed the gate and walked back to the house. I watched her go in, and then started the walk to the MARTA station. It was a glorious evening.

## Chapter 15: The Gumshoe
## Monday the Ninth, 5 PM

Justin Weir. I mused on the name as I drove back to the office. There was something familiar about it. He wasn't in our casefiles, so I wouldn't have run across him in connection with work. So where did I know the name from? I flipped on my throat mike and told Sherwin to comb the Web for any information on a Justin Weir living in Atlanta. I normally don't use broad searches like that, but I figured a name like "Weir" had to be pretty uncommon. Sherwin grumbled something about being overworked and under-appreciated, and informed me that he had located 14,872 websites referencing an individual meeting those criteria.

I almost ran into a telephone pole. Fourteen *thousand*!? What the Hell? It wasn't like I'd asked Sherwin to pull in all the information on a John Smith or Kim Li or Elijah Mohammed. How many people named Justin Weir could there be living in one city?

As it turned out, none. At least, not according to the directories. There was no publicly listed phone number for a Justin Weir in the greater Atlanta area. Or in the entire state of Georgia, for that matter. Nor was there a publicly available street address for such a person. Nor a publicly listed e-mail address. I put in a call to an information service and learned that no one named Justin Weir had ever filled out a warranty card on a major appliance, or responded to a Publisher's Weekly Sweepstakes offer. The guy was a ghost. An extremely high-profile ghost, judging by the amount of press he was getting.

I told Sherwin to scan all the websites and pull together a short bio for me, then I switched off my earphone for awhile and tried to concentrate on my driving. Maybe if I could just clear my head, this darn case would start to make sense while I wasn't looking at it.

Fifteen minutes later I pulled into the parking lot, stopped the car, and went up to our office. Inspiration had not struck yet. I opened the door and looked the place over. Nothing had been moved, and all the clutter around Jen's desk was at least a couple of days old. I guess she hadn't stopped by while I was out. Not that I ever get *that* lucky. I made myself a cup of Kona and sat down to read the information that Sherwin had put together for me.

"Justin Weir: Born March 27, 1995 in Boone, North Carolina. Only child of Virginia Weir (1957-2019), a software sales rep, and Thomas Weir (1951-2020), a software helpline rep."

Interesting. That would make his mother 37 when he was conceived. A bit late in life.

"Marital Status: Single. Racial Mix: Caucasian. Hair: Brown. Eyes: Blue. Height: 5'11". Residence: Atlanta. Profession: Musician."

"Attended Fairview Memorial Baptist High School in Boone. Three years at Freedom University before failing out in 2015. Limited information available for years 2015-2018, although he appears to have been playing at small clubs and revival meetings. In 2019 he released a self-published album for sale on the net, which became a modest success due to strong word of mouth. Picked up by Trinity Music, a subsidiary of Liberty Media, in 2020. Next album went platinum, as did the following one in 2023. Two-time winner of "Best Vocalist" at Christian Music Awards."

OK. So the kid was a rock star. That was why the name was familiar. And why his phone number would be unlisted.

Yep. This was all starting to make perfect sense now. Some famous Christian rock star had called up Jen, a third-rate psychic detective, and asked her to help out with some private problem. Never mind that the guy is a Baptist, one of those nice folks who think that psychics are all channeling demonic spirits. (Of course, they've accused the Pope and Mickey Mouse of the same thing, so it's not like they're singling the psychics out for special treatment.) And never mind that this guy was probably rich enough to hire the entire Metro Atlanta Police Force if he wanted to.

Yeah. Peachy. Everything was really starting to fall into place now. I stood up, walked over to the wall, and banged my head into it a few times.

After satisfying myself that this maneuver was not going to produce any new insights, I went back to my desk and tried to think things through again. OK. Vanished partner. Christian rock star who had hired said partner. Thief who breaks into partner's apartment to steal some papers, leaving behind a book of magic spells. And of course, there's the missing cat. I was beginning to feel like Alice, chasing a white rabbit and finding that everything makes less and less sense the further I go.

Well, no help for it but to keep collecting pieces in the hope that they'll eventually all fit together. Right now the only live lead I had was Weir. He had to have at least some idea of what was going on. Of course, he wouldn't be easy to see. I couldn't just turn up on his doorstep and expect to get an appointment. That is, if I could even find his doorstep, which was unlisted.

I had Sherwin call up some pictures of Weir from the newsites while I figured out how to play the situation. The guy was kind of cute. Curly hair and a friendly smile. And he didn't have that plasticy Ken-doll look that a lot of celebrities get from having way too much cosmetic surgery.

OK. Weir had a couple of advantages. He was rich enough to afford protection, and he had more information about the situation than I did. I, on the other hand, had two things going for me. First off, I had his private number from Jen's voicemail. And secondly, the guy had no idea just how little I really knew. I ran through a few different ways of playing this set of cards, and finally decided on the "Cryptic Spy" gambit.

I had Sherwin dial up Weir's number, after first routing the call through a service in Nashville that strips off the return number. Weir answered on the first ring.

"Hello?"

I recognized the Carolina drawl from the messages on Jen's voicemail.

"I'm a friend of Jen's," I said. "We need to talk."

"Who are you? Wait... Why did she give you this..." He sounded confused. Good.

"Eight o'clock," I said, cutting him off. "At the latest. After that I'm gone. Where?"

"I don't understand..."

"Where? Where do you want to meet?"

"Meet? Um... I guess here would be best..."

"Here? I'm afraid 'here' isn't a big help, guy. How about giving me some map coordinates?"

"Oh. Sorry. Come to...Should I tell him to come to..."

He was talking to someone on the other end, but I couldn't make out their conversation. A moment later, a woman's voice came on.

"Come to 4322 Crestview Circle in North Marietta. What time shall we expect you, Mr..."

"Seven-thirty." I said, and hung up.

OK. I know. The whole thing sounds like a scene from a bad spy movie. But that's the way the gambit works. You make the appointment, count on the other guy's curiosity to get you in the front door, and then hang up as fast as possible. Because the longer you talk, the more chances he has to figure out that you don't know what you're doing. After that conversation, Weir probably had as many unanswered questions about me as I had about him. And maybe that would level the playing field a little.

At least, until he found out I was bluffing. There was no telling what he would do after that. The only thing I knew for sure about Weir was that he had hired my partner to do a job, and now she was missing. And we were going to be meeting on his turf. I decided it might be smart to take out a little insurance.

I only had one piece of physical evidence, the spellbook, so I grabbed that and walked the two blocks down to the Inquisition. John-or-Joe-or-Jim was still on duty at the front desk. He'd let his monk's robe slip down off one shoulder to show off a tanned bicep and a rather nice bit of chest. After we'd worked our way through the usual flirtation, I got him to rent me an overnight locker in the changing room. I put the spell book in and sealed it up with my thumbprint. Before I left, I took a look around the gym for Daniel, but he must have been at work. I made a note to give him a call tomorrow if I wasn't doing anything else. Like lying dead in a landfill or something.

On the way back to the office I dictated a letter to Megan, explaining who I was going to meet and why, and detailing everything I knew about the situation so far. I had Sherwin bundle the letter together with the locker number, the photograph of the painting, and the video footage of the woman stealing the papers, and told him to send the whole thing off to Megan at 10 o'clock. Then, just to play it safe, I changed Sherwin's password. I do that about once a month anyway, but it was just possible that Jen had overheard my current one or could figure it out the same way I'd figured out hers. And at the moment, there was no telling who might have access to the contents of Jen's head. Better safe than sorry. I chose "Vengeance of the Tap-Dancing Walrus" as a random but easy to remember phrase.

My meeting with Weir was at 7:30. If everything went well, I could tell Sherwin to cancel the message sometime before ten. And if not...Well, at least Megan would have a head start on investigating *my* disappearance. Then she could figure out what the Hell that damn missing cat means.

I got back to the office and had Sherwin check the traffic advisories. He estimated that it would take 45 minutes to get out to the address that Weir had given me. That left me a little over an hour to kill around the office.

I decided to spend the time doing a bit more reading on Mr. Weir. I had Sherwin call up some stuff from the Web: interviews, personality profiles, tabloid gossip stuff. I even had him play a couple of Weir's songs, which weren't nearly as bad as I'd been expecting. My only prior exposure to Christian Rock had been a song about modern day martyrs called "Going Down for Jesus," which, due to an unfortunate double-entendre, had been picked up by all the gay clubs last summer and played over and over and over again for three agonizing months. Then just when I thought I'd finally heard the last of it, someone came out with a new dance mix of it, and the whole thing started all over again. If there is a God, She's got a really twisted sense of humor.

The news sites gave me a better handle on Weir, or at least on his public face. But they weren't helping me with the big question: Why had some billionaire Baptist boy hired a two-buck psychic detective? It seemed vaguely possible that we might have been recommended to him by a former client. I had Sherwin run a comparison between a list of our old clients and names appearing in articles about Weir. He found one match, a reporter who had done a story on Weir and who had also hired Jen to find his missing cocker-spaniel. (Don't ask, it was a lean year.) Seemed like a pretty tenuous connection, though. I couldn't see the reporter suddenly jumping up in the middle of an interview and telling Weir about what a great job Jen had done finding his pet. Particularly since the dog had been dead for three days when we found him.

No, there had to be some stronger connection between the two of them, some reason he had come to her. I ran a search for common relatives. No. I checked old phone books to see if they had ever lived in the same town. No. Common newsgroups or mailing lists? No. Finally, I set up a massive search for any news article mentioning both their names. And that netted me seventeen hits. Sixteen of those were old articles from a small paper in Nickelclintelok, Wales. Apparently back in the teens there had been two city council members whose names were Justin Weir and Jennifer Gray. No relation to my partner or the rock star.

However, that left one article from the Freedom Gazette, the school paper for that fundamentalist university up in Virginia that Weir had attended. It was a review of a production of the musical *1776* done by the school's theater department. At first I thought it was another coincidental match, some other Jennifer Gray. But there was a picture attached. The woman was younger, and dressed up as Mrs. Jefferson, but there was no doubt that it was my partner.

My partner? The poster girl for radical in-your-face feminist psychic wiccans had gone to a fundamentalist university? The things you don't know about your co-workers. And come to think of it, I didn't really know much of anything about Jen's past. Over the years, we'd talked about a lot of things, but never our families, never where we grew up. It was a sort of understanding we had, not to bring up the subject.

At any rate, I had found a link between her and Weir. I did some more digging into Liberty's records. Jen and Weir had been there at the same time. Jen was five years older, but she'd started college later and was in the class behind Weir. They did three musicals together, so they had to have known each other. And there was something else interesting. In 2015, her Junior year, Jen had transferred out of Liberty and gone to Emory—which is where she'd told me she'd graduated from. That was the same year that Weir had failed out at Liberty. Maybe the timing was just coincidence. Or maybe something had happened?

There was still a lot I didn't know, but things were beginning to make a little more sense. At least I could fit two pieces of this crazy puzzle together. Weir had hired Jen, because of some past relationship; he knew he could trust her.

I glanced at the clock on my desk. 6:40. Time to get moving.

## Chapter 16: The Gumshoe
## Monday the Ninth, 6:40 PM

I walked down, got in the car, and had Sherwin pull up a map on the dash screen highlighting the fastest route to Weir's house. Then I pulled out of the parking lot, headed down West Peachtree, and picked up I-75 heading North.

Once I was on 75, I flipped on the cruise control and let the car do the driving, while I let all the weird pieces of this case bump around randomly in my head. Maybe I'd get lucky and a couple of them would match up. In the meantime I watched the scenery go by. It's interesting how things change as you drive north from the center of town. Somewhere around I-285 you cross an invisible line between two worlds. The billboards showing almost naked men hawking vitamins and underwear and cologne suddenly disappear and get replaced by advertisements for local churches. The cars with pink triangles and rainbow flags on their bumpers become fewer and fewer, and you start to see stickers like "Jesus Saves", "Abortion is Murder", "*One* Nation Under God".

When we reached Marietta I took the wheel again, left the interstate, and navigated my way through the maze of surface roads to Weir's street. Crestview Circle, it turned out, was in one of those "secure" communities. I pulled up to the front gate, a big iron sliding number with retractable tire spikes on the far side just to let you know they meant business. Stretching out from the gate, a thick hedge formed a perimeter barrier, protecting the homes beyond from the riffraff, like me. I recognized the bushes: P&T plants, short for "Pain and Terror," a little something that the Army had genetically engineered a few years back to provide subtle defense for facilities in unstable countries. You'd need a machete *and* a flame thrower to get through that hedge. P&T bushes are tough, dense, and loaded with inch-long thorns. They also have really pretty white flowers in the springtime.

There was a pillar next to the gate with a thumb print reader and a numeric key pad, but Weir hadn't mentioned any code to me. I turned on the throat mike and had Sherwin dial his number.

"Hello?" someone answered. It wasn't Weir. It was the female voice that I'd heard the last time I called.

"I'm here."

"I thought that might be you. Just a second."

I heard a car door open, and turned to see a woman getting out of a black Transcendental parked down the street. She was tall, with short black hair. Which was a good match for the black shoes, black slacks, and black silk shirt she was wearing. She reminded me of that year in college when I'd figured I could eliminate laundry by only wearing dark colors.

Anyway, the woman in black walked over to my car, leaned down, and took a look at me through the passenger-side window. Well, actually, she she took a look at me through the hole where the passenger side window is going to be one of these days when I finally have the money to get it fixed. She must have been satisfied with what she saw because she opened the door and climbed in. And she just sat there, as if waiting for something to happen.

"Well?' she finally said, nodding forward.

"Well?" I responded, pointing toward the gate.

"Oh, yeah."

She unbuckled her seat belt and leaned across me to press her thumb on to the gate's print reader. In doing so, she managed to rub up against me in all sorts of interesting ways—and also feel me up for a concealed weapon. It was a pretty slick maneuver. If I'd been as distracted by her curves as she'd been expecting, I would probably never have noticed it.

The gate cranked open, and I drove into the complex. It was a nice neighborhood, if a bit odd. Big houses sitting on small lawns. Every porch flying an American flag. Dogs and kids running around loose, without a fence or a leash in site. I guess their parents felt they were safe enough with the wall around the place. Well, that and the security cameras hanging from every streetlight.

The woman in black extended her hand to me.

"I'm Linda."

I gave her my hand.

"Hi, Linda. I'm Drew."

We shook, but she didn't let go right away. She turned my hand over and seemed to be studying it.

"You a palm reader or something?" I asked.

"No," she said, pulling a small print reader out of her pocket and pressing it up against my thumb. "Just wanted to make sure you're not wearing a false print. They've been real popular with ID thieves the last few years."

She let go of my hand and plugged her print reader into a palm display.

"Let's see," she said, reading something off the display. "So it is Drew. Drew Parker. And you're...you're a *cop*?"

She sounded unhappy about that, and I was going to explain, but the palm display beat me to it.

"Oh," she continued. "Ex-cop. Now you've got a Class-H license to be professionally nosy. Work for three different firms...all of which you co-own with Ms. Gray. Ah, so that's how you know Jen."

"Yep," I said, wondering what database she was running my prints through. Maybe she had a friend on the force. I had expected the veil of mystery to start unraveling as soon as I arrived on the scene. I just hadn't expected it to happen so quickly. "I take it you do security for Mr. Weir?"

"Nah. More like trouble*shooting*." She had a strange way of emphasizing the word *shooting*, and I decided that I did not want to find myself under her definition of trouble. If I could help it, that is.

"Now let's see," she continued. "Born in Charlotte, North Carolina in 1990." She turned to look at me. "Huh. You don't look 34. You had some work done?"

I didn't say anything. I look my age and I know it.

"Hm?" she pressed. "Nah. You don't seem like the type. Besides, if you had they certainly would have fixed that thing with your nose."

I made a mental note that I owed her one for that comment, and turned left past a small school with a playground. Some kids were playing on the merry-go-round. Across the street was a pool with a bunch more kids splashing around. I couldn't get over how many kids seemed to be running around this place. Based on what I was seeing there had to be five or six kids for every house in the complex.

"Graduated Metro Atlanta Police Academy in 2011," Linda continued. "Made detective in 2016. Left the force just two years later after blowing the whistle on..."

"I know my rap sheet, thank you."

A soccer ball bounced across the street in front of me, and I had to brake for the kid who was chasing it. An older couple out for a stroll on the sidewalk recognized Linda and waved to her. She waved back.

"Hello, Mr. Johnson. Mrs. Johnson."

The kid waved at us, too, and jogged back across the street with the ball. I drove on through the neighborhood. In front of every house, there was somebody sitting on the front porch, watching us drive by. I wondered what they were all doing, just sitting out there. Maybe they were all mannequins, or robots or something, put out there to scare off burglars.

We finally reached Crestview Circle, which turned out to be a cul-de-sac. The lot next to Weir's place was vacant, but it seemed to be a deliberate sort of vacant. There was a treehouse with a tire swing, and a big grassy area that some kids were playing Capture the Flag on. As we parked, a woman came out of the house next door with some paper cups and a pitcher of something pink, and all the kids went rushing over to her like jackals descending on a wounded gazelle.

Weir's place itself was a two-story colonial number, a bit bigger than average for the neighborhood, with white columns supporting an overhang for the front porch. Linda and I got out of the car, and were starting up the lawn to the house when I heard footsteps behind us. I turned just in time to see a little Asian girl, four or five years old, launch herself at Linda, who caught her adeptly. She looked like she'd had some practice at this.

"Come play with us, Linda!" squealed the little girl.

Linda turned the girl upside down and swung her around by her feet. The girl giggled.

"Maybe later, Susie." Linda said, flipping the girl back around and putting her down. "Right now I need to go in and see Justin."

"OK," said the little girl. She stomped off a few feet, then turned back and shook her finger at Linda. "You've got five minutes." Then she ran off to rejoin her diminutive street gang.

"Yours?" I asked Linda.

"Foster kid," she answered. "She's been with us for about a year. All the families around here try to take in one or two, or adopt a couple kids. Part of the whole pro-life thing. You know, adopt rather than abort."

We turned back to the house, and she put a hand on my back, as if to guide me. It was also a convenient way to check for a holdout pistol or a knife back there. We walked up the steps of the porch, and Linda opened the big front door for me. I stepped inside and found myself facing a white haired woman in her mid-fifties, wearing an apron that said "One Rockin' Granny". There was a picture of a blue-haired lady in a rocking chair with an electric guitar.

"Well, hello there," the woman said, smiling at me. The accent sounded like something from the northern plains states. Maybe Wisconsin or Minnesota. Some place where they make a lot of cheese.

"Uh, hi," I mumbled. "I'm Drew."

"Well nice to meet you, Drew," the white-haired woman said as she pulled a metal detector out of the apron's pocket. "Now, if you'll just hold your arms out to the sides for a moment."

"You're another...trouble-shooter?" I said, not meaning to make it sound so much like a challenge to her competence.

"Oh, heavens no. I'm Mrs. Templeton, the housekeeper. Now, I did ask you once nicely to put your arms up."

I did as she asked. For some reason I had the distinct feeling that Mrs. Templeton would have no trouble dislocating both my kneecaps if I decided to be difficult. My sixth sense trying to keep me out of trouble, I guess.

Mrs. Templeton finished with the wand, then proceeded to pat me down for any non-metal weapons. Well, "pat me down" is a rather tame description. Let's just say that she stopped short of a cavity search—but not by much. Anyway, the combined search turned up my throat mike, my palm display, a fiber optic snake, a pocket camera, a little recording device I have that's designed to look like an old button, my Swiss army knife, a few inches of copper wire and a set of wire cutters, my cash card, and an old one dollar coin that I keep around for making those really hard decisions. Mrs. Templeton arranged them all neatly on an end table while Linda looked it all over.

"What's this for?" Linda asked, holding up the coin.

"Image," I said. "I walk it back and forth on my knuckles when I'm trying to look cool. It's a private eye thing."

She looked it over carefully, as if expecting to find a secret camera or explosive charge, or something.

"No weapons?" she asked, trying the knuckle trick with the coin and almost dropping it. It's harder than it looks.

"Just my razor wit."

"Oh. That. Any *dangerous* weapons?"

She finished looking over the coin and flipped it back to me. "You can get the rest of the stuff back on your way out. Come on, I'll introduce you to Justin now."

"Do you kids want anything to drink?" Mrs. Templeton asked as she pushed past us into the hall. "Some lemonade? Maybe a glass of ice tea? Water?"

"I'm fine," said Linda. "Anything for you, Drew?"

"Uh. No. Thank you."

I was still a little off my game. I had been all ready to deal with big gorillas in designer suits, but something about Templeton made me really nervous. I was glad when she disappeared into the kitchen.

Linda led me down the hall toward the back of the house. It was a nice place, though it was showing a bit of wear and tear from the kids. I noticed some roller-blade scrapes in the wood floor, and a crayon drawing on one of the walls that Mrs. Templeton hadn't gotten around to removing yet.

At the end of the hall was a set of French doors. Linda opened one and showed me into a library. It was a plush room—I had the feeling the kids weren't allowed back here—with a soft Persian rug on the floor and a nice English landscape painting hanging over a real fireplace. There were bookshelves full of old hardcover books and knickknacks, and in the middle of the room was a table with a computer and a guitar hooked up to it, I guess for transcribing music.

And there was Weir. I didn't spot him right off, but I could feel him there even before I turned around. He was sitting in a chair in a corner back behind the door, wearing jeans, a white t-shirt, and boots. A gold cross hung against his chest. I recognized the face from his pictures on the Web, but now I couldn't imagine why I had thought he was only cute. In person, the boy was a knockout. He had a beautiful smile, and big, trusting blue eyes.

He was also radiating sexual energy like a fusion reactor. Literally. I could feel it filling the room like some sort of electric charge, making the hair on my arms stand up. Among other things. No wonder the kid sold so many records. I found myself staring into his eyes, not saying anything, and all too aware that my darn blush reflex was going off.

Then my brain finally kicked in to gear and coughed up a clip from an old film noir that I'd seen a couple months ago. It was the scene where the gumshoe first meets the femme fatale and goes so gaga over her gams that he completely fails to notice a couple of important plot points that almost get him killed later on in the movie. I thanked my subconscious for coming through in the clinch, and tried to put a leash on my hormones. Weir was pretty. But he was also the reason my partner was missing.

Weir was staring right back into my eyes.

"Hey. I'm Justin," he said, standing up and sticking out his hand. It was the same Carolina drawl I'd heard on the phone.

I walked over and shook his hand, and was relieved when no actual sparks flew between us. I was trying to play it cool, but Weir had to notice that my face was burning. I could only hope that with this much charisma the kid was used to people being a little starstruck around him.

"I'm Drew…" I started to say, and then my eyes locked on to his again and I forgot what I was going to say next. Sometimes I hate being a man. Linda came to my rescue.

"Parker," she said. "Gray's partner. Seems to be on the level. Ex-cop. Mostly clean, except for a disturbing the peace charge a few months ago for a bar fight at some strip club called The Monastery."

Ouch. I had forgotten about that little incident being in the public record. Weir looked like he wanted to laugh, but he didn't. But then, he probably didn't even know what gender of strippers they have at The Monastery, anyway. From the amused look on

Linda's face, though, I could tell that she did. Weir gestured to the chair facing his, and we both sat down while Linda leaned up against a bookcase.

"I'm real glad you're here Mr. Parker," Weir said. "I was startin' to get worried."

"Don't stop on my account," I responded. "When's the last time you spoke to Jen directly?"

"Three days ago," Weir said, without taking time to consider his answer. Which meant that he was either telling the truth or had worked out his lies in advance. All I knew for sure was that Jen had gone to work for Weir, and now she was missing. Maybe she'd run across one of Weir's enemies. Or maybe she'd found out something that Weir didn't want her to know about.

"And she hasn't gotten any messages through to you since then?"

"No," said Weir. "She'd told us she might be out of touch while she was undercover. I was hopin' she'd get back to us before the broadcast. She'd seemed pretty sure that she was on to somethin'."

The broadcast? I wondered what that was all about.

"You know, gumshoe," said Linda, "you seem to ask a lot more questions than you answer. So how about telling us what's up with Gray?"

"Yes, is she all right?" asked Weir.

I'd been watching Linda, but I couldn't get a good read on her body language. She played everything too close to the vest. Weir, on the other hand, seemed like an open book. He was sitting with his legs apart, leaning forward with his elbows on his knees. The message was pretty obvious—he was anxious, I had his undivided attention, but he wasn't defensive.

"I don't know," I admitted.

I watched Weir's eyes closely. If he'd had something to do with her disappearance, there should have been at least a momentary glimmer of relief that I didn't know about it. But all I saw was frustration.

"But, I thought you said you had a message from her?"

"No," I corrected him. "I said that I was a friend of hers, and that we need to talk."

"OK," said Linda, "So why don't you do some talking, Dick Tracy." She gave me a look that made it clear I had just crossed over into the "trouble" part of her job description.

"All right," I said, not sure what I was going to say next. I'd arrived at the big decision point—whether or not to trust these two. My gut said that I could trust Weir, but my gut was connected to other parts of my anatomy that wanted to do business with Weir for reasons having nothing to do with the case. I was having a real tough time keeping up my usual healthy paranoia around him. Still, his concern did seem genuine, and I'm pretty good at telling when someone is faking an emotion. Lord knows I should be, with my dating history.

Linda was another story. She seemed capable of all sorts of unpleasantness, if the circumstances called for it. On the other hand, I couldn't see her doing anything to Jen without orders from Weir, and somehow I just couldn't see Weir ordering it. Besides, in the end, these two were the only good lead I had on Jen. I either had to give them something and hope they'd fill me in, or else take my toys and go home.

"Here's what I know," I continued after a long pause. "I know that my partner is missing. She pulled a no-show for an important court date this morning, and she hasn't been back to our office in a couple of days. I know that somebody broke into her apartment this morning, looking for some papers. And I know that she was working on a case for you."

Weir looked me over, his guard going up for the first time. I saw him glance up at Linda, who shrugged. I could tell they were both wavering, unsure whether to trust me or not. I decided to try playing my wild card. I just hoped it would turn out to be an ace and not a deuce.

"Look," I said. "I realize you guys don't know me from Adam. But I know that you trust Jen. I know all about that business back at Freedom and why you *know* you can trust her. Well, Jen trusts me. Otherwise, she wouldn't be my partner. So how about you two cut me some slack and tell me what she was working on?"

Weir looked up at Linda, and they exchanged facial expressions for what seemed like thirty seconds. Finally, Weir broke the silence.

"I didn't think she was in any danger."

"Well, she is," I said, taking the opening. "Someone broke into her apartment to steal some papers from a secret compartment. And they didn't have to trash the place to find it, either. They knew exactly where it was, and how to open it. Which makes me think that somebody has made Jen do some talking."

That sure got their attention. Weir's eyes widened. Even Linda looked a little panicked. Weir looked into my eyes, trying to decide if I was serious, then turned back to Linda.

"What do you think?"

"I think..." she started to say, then paused. She gave me a look like someone sizing up a cut of beef. "I think that if someone's got Gray, then the cat's already out of the bag. Parker seems square. I'd chance him."

"I don't see that we got a choice," Weir said back to her. "If Stonewall knows what we're up to, then things just got a whole lot more complicated."

"Look," I said, "I don't know what sort of secrets you two are trying to keep, and I don't really care. The only thing I want right now is to find out what happened to my partner. And for the moment, I think that means we're all playing on the same team. So how about sharing the play book with me?"

Weir looked back at me, and finally nodded. "Agreed. But only on condition that everything you learn about me during this case remains strictly confidential."

"I'm not in the blackmail business," I said to Weir. "If I were, I would have retired from the PI game and gotten that beach house in the Bahamas a long time ago."

"Good point," said Weir. "What is your usual fee, Mr Parker?"

"Five hundred a day, plus expenses." I shouldn't have answered so quickly. Based on what I knew about Weir's net worth, I could probably have quadrupled that figure and he wouldn't have blinked. But I don't work that way. Besides, I had a feeling the guy was about to pay me to go looking for my own partner.

"Plus a five thousand dollar bonus when I solve the case."

"That's reasonable," Linda said to Weir. "A little on the cheap side, even."

"...and," I interjected, "an additional five thousand if anybody starts shooting at me. I got to pay my medical bills."

"Very well," said Weir, "I'll see that..."

"Wait a minute," interrupted Linda. "Is that if they hit? Or just if they aim at you?"

"That's just for aiming. I try not to be an easy target."

"Well, that doesn't seem fair," she said.

"Seems damn fair to me," I responded.

"Well, how about knifings?" asked Linda. "Do you charge extra if someone pulls a knife on you?"

"No, I throw those in for free."

"OK. But what about grenades?"

"Hasn't happened," I said with a smile. "Yet."

"As I was sayin'," Weir said, raising his voice, "I believe we can accept your terms. Linda will see that your first week's salary is paid in advance. And I assume that anything you learn in my employ remains..."

"Our little secret, of course."

"Good," Weir said, relaxing visibly.

"So, Drew," chimed in Linda, "now that you're on the payroll, how about you tell us everything you've found out so far?"

I wasn't wild about spilling my guts, but I had decided to trust these two. They were paying my bills now. And besides, if I was wrong, and they were behind Jen's disappearance, at least I wouldn't be telling them anything they didn't already know.

So I gave them the whole story. I explained how Jen had missed her court date this morning, and how I'd determined that she wasn't working on any of the cases in our file. I gave them a rundown on the condition of her apartment, including the video of the thief stealing her papers, the spell book I'd recovered, and the voice-mail messages that had lead me to Weir. I showed them the photograph of the demon-fighter painting, which they looked at with some interest but no indication that they recognized it. And of course, I told them about the missing cat. Eventually, I'm going to find somebody who can tell me what that's all about.

"Strange." Weir said when I was done. "I can't imagine what a spell book, or a painting, or a cat have to do with my case. And I have no idea what the papers were." Then a thought seemed to pop into his head. "By the way, you say Jen never mentioned me?"

"No. She doesn't talk about her past a lot."

"Hm, Then how did you know about the incident back at Freedom."

"Oh, that," I said. "It wasn't that hard. I just pulled some facts together from the online databases and made some lucky guesses."

"Not bad." said Linda, visibly impressed. "You want to share with me? Justin still hasn't told me the whole story on that fiasco during his senior year."

"Sorry," I said. "Client confidentiality and all that. Now, do you two want to tell me what you hired Jen to do, or would you rather watch me stumble around in the dark for awhile longer?"

"All right," Weir said, and then spent the next twenty minutes giving me the whole story. It was a doozie. Apparently, the kid had political aspirations, and had hired Jen to dig up some dirt on Senator Stonewall, the big blowhard behind the Christian Alliance. Hence Weir's reasons for not going to a Baptist detective agency. Wasn't sure that he could trust his own people on this one. So he'd gone to the one person he figured he could.

Personally, I wasn't sure that Weir was cut out for politics. He struck me as a bit naive, and his whole plan to turn a bunch of heavily armed Christians into some collection of smiling do-gooders struck me as a bit loony. I just couldn't see the kid getting into office. But then, stranger things have happened. Like Reagan in 1980. Or Stallone in 2012. I noticed that Weir did all the talking about the plan, and Linda just let him gab. I had the feeling she wasn't any more sanguine on this scheme than I was. But if Weir was gonna try it, she was going to do her darndest to make it work. I wondered what exactly the deal was between the two of them. Anyway, the job Weir described was tricky, but certainly something Jen should have been able to handle. It would involve finding old acquaintances and subtly pumping them for information. Finding old girlfriends, business partners, that sort of thing. Weir and Linda already had a pretty good dossier on Stonewall, so Jen had a lot of leads to start running down. She'd been working for Weir for the last three weeks, squeezing in time between our cases—not much of a trick, given how slow business had been lately. The last thing Jen had told Weir was that she was on to something big, and would have the smoking gun he needed in the next few days. Unfortunately, she hadn't told him what her lead was or how she was going to pursue it. Chalk it up to Jen and her sense of the dramatic. Always wanting to spring the big surprise.

Weir wound up the whole story and looked at me expectantly. "So, what do you think, Mr. Parker?"

"I think," I began, "that Jen should have told you to bring me in when you started this whole caper three weeks ago."

"She wanted to," said Linda, "but Justin and I wanted to keep the risks of a leak to a minimum."

"Yeah, well, you've risked a Hell of a lot more than a leak if Jen got caught snooping," I shot back.

"OK, OK," said Weir. "So we've got a mess on our hands. What are we goin' to do about it?"

"*We* are not going to do anything," I said. "*I* will go out and deal with this. *You* are going to sit tight, right here, where Linda and Mrs. Templeton can keep an eye on you. If Stonewall is holding Jen, then she must have stumbled onto something really big. And it won't take him long to find out who sent her. The only question in his mind will be how much you know, and what you plan to do with the information. Hopefully, that will buy us a little time before he moves against you."

Weir looked like he wanted to argue, but Linda nodded agreement.

"Good," I said. "Now, I'm going to need all the data you've put together on Stonewall, and recordings of all the phone calls you got from Jen. And if you've got any ideas on where Stonewall might hide a prisoner, I'd love to hear them."

"You think Gray is still alive?" asked Linda.

"Yes," I answered, a little too quickly, and then had to think fast to justify my answer. "First off, we don't know that Stonewall is desperate enough to actually kill anybody. Even if he is, he's certainly not going to do anything to her until he's figured out what to do with Justin. He might need to use her to get at you." That sounded plausible enough. But it wasn't the real reason I was so sure Jen was still alive. The truth was that I just couldn't believe that Jen could be dead and I wouldn't know about it. She'd been my partner for four years. We'd spent a lot of time together, talking on stakeouts and stuff. She knew me about as well as anyone ever does. If she were dead...I'd know. Somehow I'd just know.

Anyway, Weir promised to think about locations where Stonewall might hold someone, and Linda transferred the files I'd asked for to Sherwin. She also made arrangements to have my first week's pay wired to my account from some bank in the Cayman Islands, so that no one would be able to trace it back to Weir.

"I'll check in with you every 12 hours," I told them. "Sooner if I've got something good or have some questions. If I miss a check-in...well, you two should seriously think about going to the cops or taking a long vacation in Buenos Aires."

They both walked me to the door, and Linda returned the possessions the housekeeper had frisked off me on the way in.

"Take care of yourself, Drew," Weir said as I was leaving.

"I always do," I said, thinking that if Stonewall really did have Jen, then he would probably be looking for her partner by now. Great. I wondered just how much trouble a U.S. Senator could make for me. I must be working off some serious bad karma from a previous life.

Then I walked back to my car and drove out of their weird little Stepford world. Once outside the gates, I drove around Marietta in circles for half an hour, just to make sure that no one was following. Once I was positive that I didn't have a tail, I pulled into a service station. While my car recharged, I got the snooper out of the trunk and checked it for bugs or trackers. Apparently my luck was still holding; the car was clean. I got on line with Sherwin, and told him to cancel the message to Megan.

Then I started the long drive back to Midtown. Things were finally starting to make a little sense now. But they were also getting a Hell of a lot more dangerous.

## Chapter 17: The Gumshoe
## Monday the Ninth, 8:10 PM

I got the car heading south on I-75, then flipped on the cruise control and let it do the driving for awhile. I didn't have a particular destination in mind yet. I just wanted to go south. Out of the Baptist end of the city and back to mine. If somebody was going to come hunting for me, then I wanted to be on my own turf.

I ran through everything I knew about the case so far. The whole idea that a United States Senator was holding my partner hostage because of some dread secret she'd dug up seemed pretty far-fetched. Like something from a bad conspiracy movie. But it was the only theory that made any sense right now. And if Stonewall did have Jen, then it was a good bet that he was looking for me, too. Avoiding a run-in with Stonewall's goons so far had probably used up my quota of dumb luck for the entire week. I was going to have to be more careful.

While the car drove south, I read over the files that Linda had put together on Stonewall. They were surprisingly thorough, and I got the impression that she'd done this sort of thing before. She'd broken down the sleaze by category: suspicious campaign contributions, influence peddling, overly lucrative business deals, and tax evasion. Scattered among these four categories was a lot of dirt on the good Senator. But I could see why they'd called in Jen to find a smoking gun. None of this stuff would stick. For one thing, there probably wasn't a politician over the rank of dog catcher who hadn't done all this and more. And for another, it was all way too complicated to explain in fifteen second sound bites, so the public would ignore it.

I did, however, notice the complete absence of sex scandals. Either Stonewall really was living clean, or he covered his tracks well. Still, Linda had gone ahead and put together a complete list of Stonewall's bodyguards over the years, figuring that if the Senator was sleeping with anybody, they'd have to know about it.

By the time I finished reading through all this, the car was back inside the perimeter and coming up on Midtown. I took the wheel and caught the Peachtree Industrial exit, still not exactly sure where I was going. The office was out. That would be the first place that Stonewall's Christian Stormtroopers would come looking for me. My apartment would be the second, so it was out too.

Then I hit upon the idea of breaking back into Jen's apartment and crashing there for the night. I toyed with that one for about a mile. The image of the Salvation Army Rangers tearing up the city looking for Jen's partner while I was sleeping safe and sound in her bed had a certain amusement value. But I decided it was too risky. If any of the neighbors spotted me breaking in, I'd have one Hell of a time explaining all this to the police.

Eventually, my caffeine addiction settled the matter. I couldn't risk going to my usual coffee shop, so I caught Ponce de Leon heading east, then took Moreland south into Little Five Points—one of the more unusual neighborhoods in this town. I hit a red light at the main intersection, and watched as a gang of kids dressed like vampires crossed the street in front of me. It was a retro look, popular with kids who wished they'd been teenagers back in the single digits. As the light changed, another gang crossed going the other direction, dressed in clothing so hideous that I decided they must be committing some intentional act of fashion terrorism.

A block further down I pulled into an alley and found a parking place in the lot behind the Bridgetown Grill. I cut the engine and dug out the fifty dollars in cash that I keep taped under the passenger seat for emergencies. I wasn't sure if Stonewall actually had the resources to trace my bank card, but I wasn't going to bet my life that he couldn't.

I got out of my car and walked back to the street, then over to the psychedelic skull face that forms the entrance to Cafe Diabolique. I'd been there a couple of times before, but not often enough that anyone would come looking for me there. Inside, I took the only empty table. A woman in an elaborate Renaissance gown came and leaned over my table.

"Good evening. I'm Lucrezia Beorgia, and I'll be your server. What would you like?" She leaned over the table a bit further, displaying her cleavage to full advantage. (Hey, even though I'm not in the market, I still notice these things.)

"How about a mocha?" I asked.

"Mm. Would you like that with arsenic, or without?" she purred.

"Uh...unleaded, if you don't mind."

"Of course. That will be eight-fifty. We'll talk about the price of the antidote later."

I handed her a ten-dollar bill, which she looked at a little funny, like she wasn't sure what to do with it. I could tell she was about to give me a hard time about paying in cash, so I handed her a five as a tip, which she looked on much more favorably. She waltzed away, humming the funeral dirge.

While I waited for her to come back with my order, I looked over the crowd. Mostly high school kids, and mostly in costume. Based on the prevalence of pasty white makeup and latex gore, I guessed it was some sort of undead theme night at the Cafe Diabolique. The girl at the table next to mine was dressed as a zombie flapper, with a red beaded dress, feathered hat, and an axe sticking out of her back. Her date was a mobster, complete with spats, a pinstripe suit, and a violin case leaning against his chair. There was a bullet hole in his forehead, and a little trail of dried blood and brains wound its way down his face. Well, if any of Stonewall's goons did turn up in this place, they certainly wouldn't be hard to spot.

Lucrezia brought my mocha, and I went back to work on the files. I was hoping that I could reconstruct some of Jen's case-work. If I could figure out what sort of dirt she'd found on Stonewall, I might be able to use it as a bargaining chip. I went through all the possible leads from Linda's file, prioritizing them by how easy they would be to investigate and how likely they were to yield the smoking gun.

Linda's files were extensive, and three mochas later I was only halfway through them. I was looking around for Lucrezia, trying to score another refill, when I noticed a guy come in the front door in an Indian costume. Jeans, ponytail, a feather in his hair, some sort of quill breastplate. Bare arms. Very nice, muscular, bare arms. And a steel tomahawk tucked into his belt.

The tomahawk got my attention. OK. It was actually the guy's arms that got my attention, but the tomahawk did seem a bit odd for somebody to be carrying around in public. He noticed me staring at him, and he stared back. He looked to be in his late twenties. I smiled, trying not to look too goofy, and then I felt the blush reflex kicking in again. One of these days I am going to have to find a doctor who can fix that. The guy in the Indian costume looked me over...then turned and walked back out the door.

Hm. Me and my darned animal magnetism. Now if I could just get it to attract instead of repel.

I was still pondering this and the deeper mysteries of my social life when I saw him come back in, pushing a wheelchair. I recognized the occupant immediately. After all, I don't meet that many octogenarian drag queens who dress up like Princess Tiger Lily.

I looked away quickly, hoping that this was all just some incredibly improbable coincidence. Maybe we'd both just picked the same eccentric coffee shop to hang out in. But like I've said before, I never get that lucky. The guy in the breastplate pushed my friend with the Pocahontas fixation over to my table, and then stood behind her wheelchair like some sort of honor guard.

I waited for her to say something. She didn't. She lit up a hand-rolled cigarette and started blowing smoke rings while she stared at me. Stared at me in a really weird way, like she was trying to read something written on the back of my head. I even turned around once, thinking that she might be looking at something behind me. Eventually, the stench of her cigarette started getting to me, and I had to say something.

"Uh. Shouldn't you be in the hospital?" I asked. The last time I'd seen her, someone had been doing an unscheduled appendectomy on her in an elevator. Now, aside from the wheelchair, she was looking pretty healthy. I mean, for someone who's a hundred years old with one foot in the grave.

"I was," she answered. Her voice was a bit hoarser and weaker than it had been this morning.

Well, that was a conversation killer. We sat there staring at each other for another thirty seconds. Finally she extended her hand across the table to me. I wasn't sure if I was supposed to shake it or kiss it. I opted for the former.

"I guess our introduction got interrupted," I said. "My name's Drew."

We shook and she said, "Ice-in-Summer." I wasn't sure whether to interpret that as a name or an attempt at conversation on the weather.

Lucrezia finally came around to the table, but instead of refilling my mocha, she started to say something to Ice about no smoking in the restaurant. Ice gave her a nasty glare, and Lucrezia went a little pale and seemed to forget what she was saying.

"Uh..."

"Yes," Ice said, her face suddenly breaking into a smile, "a peppermint tea would be lovely. And my husband here," she nodded to the guy with the tomahawk, "will have a black coffee."

Lucrezia nodded that she understood, then left the table in a hurry, without asking if I wanted anything.

Ice and I sat there, staring at each other again.

"Well," I said. "Did you want to see me?"

It was a stupid question. She was here, after all. But I was kind of hoping that the question might lead to a conversation. It didn't.

"Um...Would you mind telling me how you found me?" I asked.

More silence. Finally she blew a smoke ring and said, "A bit of a surprise, actually."

"Excuse me?"

"Not at all what I expected."

She sat there and stared at me some more, blowing smoke rings. Lucrezia appeared briefly to drop off their drink orders, then vanished again before I could ask for a refill. Ice picked up her tea and sipped it.

I was getting tired of staring at Ice staring at me, so I switched to staring at her husband. He was, after all, decidedly more pleasant to look at. He had dark skin, and dark eyes that looked back at me with mild curiosity. I couldn't quite decide if he was really an Indian or if he just spent a lot of time out in the sun. But he was certainly getting his exercise. I looked back and forth from the muscular guy to the little old drag queen in the chair. I began wondering if there was any chance that Ice would let me in on some of her man-catching secrets.

I was distracted by a smoke ring that caught me in the face. My eyes started watering and I had to clear my throat. Whatever she was smoking had one Hell of a kick to it.

"So, how often do you see things that aren't there, Drew?" asked Ice.

"Uh, what do you mean?"

"Oh, you know exactly what I mean. Those 'hallucinations' that you carefully ignore, because you know that nobody else can see them. The flashes of intuition that you can't explain. The voices that whisper to you in the dark, of secrets that you couldn't possibly know. Spirits. Portents. Talking animals. That sort of thing."

I raised an eyebrow like I had no idea what she was talking about. It occurred to me that I had gotten into a boxing match with St. Peter just last night, but I was not about to be psychoanalyzed by a drag queen.

"Is there a reason you're here?" I asked.

She blew another smoke ring at me.

"Of course."

I waited. She continued smoking.

"Any chance you'll tell me what it is?" I went on.

"Certainly. I'm here to give you some advice," she said, taking another puff on the cigarette.

"And what would that be?" I asked.

She looked around, then leaned over the table and motioned for me to move closer. The smell of her cigarette was overpowering. Then, finally, she whispered something to me.

"1776."

I waited for her to say something else, but she didn't.

"1776?" I repeated.

"Yes," she said, as if this was somehow profoundly important.

"What, like the musical?"

"If that helps you remember it," she said, leaning back in her wheelchair.

"Lady, do you ever make any sense?"

"I try not to," she said, putting out her cigarette in my empty coffee cup. "It kills the aura of mystery around me."

Then she looked up at her husband and nodded, and he turned her around and wheeled her away. They were already out the front door before I realized that they'd stuck me with the tab for their drinks.

Well, this whole day had seemed like one long episode of the Twilight Zone, anyway. I dropped a twenty on the table, grabbed my palm display, and left through the side door. Right now the only thing I knew for sure was that some crazy Indian drag queen had been able to find me, and I didn't want to bet my life that Stonewall couldn't do the same. I grabbed my car and drove around the neighborhood a few times, doubling back to check for tails. When I didn't spot any, I started driving west, weighing my options.

I didn't want to check into a hotel, because that would mean using plastic or a thumb print. And I didn't want to sleep in my car; I'm not a kid anymore, and my back notices when I pull stunts like that. But I did have one friend with a perfectly good couch. Someone who would likely be up late, and who only a few people knew I hung out with.

I called up Daniel and asked if I could crash at his place for the night. He answered with one of his standard flirtatious come-ons, which I took for a yes. I told him I'd be there in twenty minutes.

Daniel lives in a block of brick apartments on a street that dead-ends into Piedmont Park. Low rent, but within walking distance of a lot of stuff. I parked behind his building with my license plate up against a wall, climbed the stairs to the second floor, and knocked on his door.

Daniel took a couple of minutes to answer. When he finally came to the door he was dripping wet and wearing a towel. His hair was sandy blond again today. It was all mussed up and wet, and he looked like a puppy that had gone swimming. Well, a puppy that goes to the gym a lot.

"Oh, hey Drew!" he said, his facing bursting into a type of smile that is usually reserved for small children getting surprise gifts.

"Hi, Daniel," I said, then glanced down at the towel. "Nice outfit."

"You caught me in the shower," he said, shaking his head and sending water spraying over me.

I'd bought that story about the shower the first time I came over to his apartment. The second time he answered the door in towel, though, I was beginning to suspect that there might be some agency at work here beyond mere chance. This was the third time, and I was beginning to see a pattern.

Daniel closed the door behind me, and went back to his dresser. I poked around his apartment while Daniel made a dramatic presentation out of drying off and getting dressed. Sort of a reverse strip tease. I glanced at him just often enough to let him know that I wasn't deliberately ignoring him.

Daniel's apartment is one of those single-room efficiencies, with a little kitchen nook and a bathroom. Half the main room was taken up with his bed, and the other half with a couch and TV. He'd put up some prefab shelves, from which a collection of stuffed dinosaurs kept watch over the room. Hanging on the bathroom door was one of those muscleman calendars. I flipped through it. Artsy black and white photos of beefy guys in improbable poses with driftwood. I wandered over to the couch and noticed a Raymond Chandler novel propped open on the arm.

"Hey, when did you start reading these?"

"What?" Daniel asked, looking up from buckling his belt. "Oh, that. About a week ago. I thought it might help me understand that whole silent machismo thing you've got going."

Hm. Well, at least he was reading something. I got out my palm display and settled into the couch to do some work. I'd started prioritizing leads in the coffee shop, but there were just so many to work with. While I clicked through the list making notes, Daniel plopped down on the floor in front of me and started watching television. It was some science fiction show about political intrigue on a Martian colony. At least, I think it was supposed to be Mars. Daniel had the sexual content filter jacked through the roof, so half the dialogue in the show had been replaced by shots of men grabbing each other and having sex in improbable places. The airlock. The hydroponics garden. The Prime-Minister's desk. Still, there was a good storyline buried in there somewhere. All sorts of plotting, double-crossing, and twisted relationships. Sometime during the second act I realized that I was no longer working on my case and had joined Daniel down on the floor.

After the second act, we ordered pizza—no garlic, since Daniel was working that night—which we ate while we watched the third act. Well, most of the third act. With about ten minutes left in the show, Daniel got a call and had to go out to work, so we paused it.

With Daniel out of my hair for a couple hours, I settled back to work on the files. I spent another hour and a half prioritizing leads before I realized that I was going about it all wrong. I was flagging the ones that *I* would have started investigating first. What I needed to know was which one's *Jen* would have started working on first. Back to square one.

I thought about how Jen would tackle the problem. She's not bad at running down an electronic trail, but that wouldn't be her first choice. Her real strength had always been reading people and manipulating them. Figuring out what makes them tick. How to make them do what she wants them to. She would have looked through the files with an eye toward the characters involved in all these near-scandals, searching for the one that she thought she could turn, or trick into telling her what she needed to know.

With this in mind, I went back into the files and looked for someone who might have caught her attention. But the files were so damn large. Stonewall had been in office for more than twenty years, and there were thousands of people he had been involved with. Jen could have started with any one of them.

This was giving me a headache.

I set down the display for awhile, went over to Daniel's kitchen nook, and rummaged through his cabinets looking for some coffee. No luck. Not even instant. Daniel's entire stockpile of food consisted of three packages of instant noodles, four protein bars, two frozen dinners, and a six-pack of Coke. Oh, and one bottle of olive oil. I don't think that was for cooking.

I popped open one of Daniel's Cokes, wandered back to the couch, and stared at the ceiling for half an hour, waiting for something I'd overlooked to walk up and slap me in the face. But it wasn't there. I was going to have to face facts. The only way to reconstruct Jen's work would be to have her case notes or a couple of months to chase down all the blind leads. I didn't have either.

I was stumped. So far, I had based all my thinking on finding out what dirt Jen had stumbled onto and then using it to bargain for her release. If that was out, what other leads did I have?

I was wrapping my brain around all this when Daniel came back from his call, all bouncy and talking a mile a minute. At first I thought he might have been doing bliss, but his pupils were normal and he wasn't showing any other side effects, so I guess it was just normal Daniel bounciness. He showered, then threw on a clean pair of boxers (I noted the Tasmanian Devil printed on the crotch), and snuggled up on the couch with me to watch the last ten minutes of the show, which I finally found out was called "Mars Rising". Then he got another call, and started getting dressed to go back out.

"He's got three of us coming over," Daniel said, pulling on his jeans. "I'll be gone for at least a few hours. If you get tired, go ahead and take the bed."

"I'll be fine on the couch," I said. "It sounds like you'll need your rest when you get in."

"Oh, don't be silly," Daniel responded, slipping on a white tank-top. "I may be gone all night. And if I do get back before you wake up, I'll just crawl in next to you. Which side do you sleep on, anyway?"

I gave Daniel a suspicious look.

"What?" he said, all innocent. I continued giving him the look. "Oh, come on, Drew. Will you get over yourself? This is my third call today. How much sexual energy do you think I have, anyway?"

"*Your* sexual energy is not the problem," I responded, looking over his rather nice physique.

"Oh," Daniel said, his face lighting up. I could tell he liked that answer. He smiled and winked at me. Then he pulled on his sneakers and left.

With Daniel gone again, I settled back to work on the problem at hand. Sometime during our conversation, it had hit me that even if I couldn't find Jen's dirt, I might still be able to find Jen herself. After all, there are only so many places that you can stash a live body. Linda's files included a list of all the properties in Stonewall's name, all the ones held by businesses he controlled, and all the ones that were effectively in his control through close allies. It was a long list.

I put myself in Stonewall's situation: I've got a nosy gumshoe who knows too much. I don't want to kill her until I can deal with the people who hired her. So where would I keep her?

Well, first off, I'd worry about security. I couldn't very well have people wandering through my office asking about the woman handcuffed to my cappuccino maker. That meant the site had to either be physically remote, like a cabin up in the woods, or some-place with restricted access, like a business with trade secrets.

Secondly, I'd have to worry about my own employees. Who-ever the staff were at this place would have to be absolutely loyal and able to keep a secret. And they'd have to be the sort of people who could hold onto a prisoner and not get squeamish about it.

That made me think of Stonewall's mansion. He probably had an extra room somewhere he could keep her in, and he could assign some of his personal bodyguards to watch her. But that didn't feel right. Too risky. If a servant talked and the police turned up with a warrant, there'd be no way to explain the situa-tion. He'd be caught dead to rights. I didn't think Stonewall was that stupid.

So I added a third criteria: plausible deniability. Someplace that Stonewall controlled, but that couldn't be traced back to him too closely. That way, if anything went wrong, he could deny knowing about the woman in the basement. That cut the list down considerably.

I was left with a short list of five properties. They all seemed like decent possibilities, but one leapt out at me immediately. The National Headquarters for the Christian Militia. I ran through a description of the site. It was part of an old industrial park on the edge of the city. Several of the buildings in the park were vacant, and the Militia had bought theirs at a bargain basement price eight years ago. The land around it had been turned into a weekend training site for militia units from around the country: a firing range, an obstacle course, a wooded area for paint-gun battles. The building itself housed the militia's fund-raising, recruiting, and political action committees. A fence surrounded the whole area, with a guard shack on the road leading up to it.

It was perfect. Tight security. Loyal staff. And not actually in Stonewall's name. If anything went seriously wrong, he would have no trouble claiming that some rogue faction in the militia was behind it all. It felt right.

I had Sherwin pull up the architectural plans for the place from the building inspector's office, but those were ten years old. I needed something more current before I could plan a reconnaissance mission into the place. I glanced at my watch; it was 4:30 in the morning. I called up Linda on the number she'd given me, expecting to get her voicemail. Instead, I got a groggy, "Huh? Who is it?"

"Parker."

"Parker?" she mumbled.

"Your friend from earlier this evening," I reminded her.

"Oh, yeah. Parker. You got something?"

"Maybe. I ran over a list of places where Stonewall might be holding Jen, and one of them jumped out at me as the best bet."

"Where?"

"The National Headquarters of the Christian Militia," I said, and explained why the place seemed like such a logical place to keep a prisoner on ice. Linda listened, asking a couple questions to clarify my logic.

"Hm," she finally said. "You may have something there. So what's the game plan? You gonna ride up on your big white stallion and break her out?"

"Uh...something like that. First I want to make sure she's in there. I've got some architectural plans, but they're a bit out of date. The Militia have probably made some modifications to the building. Do you have any sources who have been inside recently, who could tell me how the layout has changed?"

"Let me think. Justin or I might have a friend of a friend who's been inside."

"Good. Find out everything you can about the place. Particularly, how tight their security is."

"OK. I'm on it. I'll start calling around. But I probably won't get anywhere until people start waking up and checking their messages. I'll call you as soon as I have something."

"Thanks," I said, and hung up.

Well, I finally had a plan of action. But I also had a colossal headache. Well I couldn't move on anything until Linda got back to me with a layout on the place anyway. I pulled the phone out of my ear and unclipped my throatmike, then peeled my way down to my boxers and crawled into bed. I think I was out before my face hit the pillow.

I had weird dreams all night. In one of them, I was in a pit of lime jello, wrestling with a giant snake that turned into a lawyer. I wouldn't have noticed the difference, except the lawyer was wearing a deerskin shirt with a long fringe that kept tickling me. He pulled out an eagle feather and started drawing some map on my chest while he tried to explain some complicated land treaty.

In another, I was back in Justin's library, and he was telling me about the details of the case. Only he was singing all of it. I took notes through the first couple of verses, but then I noticed that he was taking off his shirt and I got kind of distracted. He handed me the shirt and kept singing as he pulled off his boots, took off his belt, and finally slid out of his jeans. I noticed that that the boy didn't believe in underwear. I followed him into the next room, where a team of makeup artists smeared him with baby oil, while the technicians made some final adjustments to the lights. Justin apologized for the interruption. Price of fame and all. Then he laid down on a stone block they'd set up for the shoot. A technician laid out a tape measure next to him, the director on the shoot posed him, and the photographers started snapping pictures. I remember thinking that I would have to find out what magazine these were going to appear in.

Then there was the dream where I was directing the Ukranian Water Polo team in a water-ballet version of *Psycho*.

You know, it's a good thing I can't afford psychotherapy.

Anyway, I woke up the next morning to light coming in through the blinds and a face full of blond hair tickling my nose. I could hear my palm display buzzing on the table next to the bed, but I couldn't seem to get my left arm to move and turn it off.

It took me a few seconds to wake up completely and realize that I couldn't move my arm because it was wrapped around Daniel. He stirred a little and mumbled something as I disentangled my arm, but he didn't wake up. Poor kid. He must have had a late night. I got out of bed as quietly as I could. I grabbed my throat mike and my earpiece off the table and went into the kitchen to take the call.

"Hello?"

"Good morning, Drew. It's Linda."

"Great. What have you found out?"

"Quite a bit, actually. I did a little networking, and found someone who used to work in the building. Secretarial stuff, but she knew a fair amount about how the building is laid out. I've e-mailed a rough drawing of what she described. I also managed to wring a few details of the security system out of her, without tipping our hand too much. Told her Justin was going to be visiting the sight, and I needed to make sure it was safe. Looks like we're talking about a perimeter fence with a guard house at the front. She didn't seem to think they had anyone patrolling it, but it's probably got a basic motion detector and breach alert system. The building itself has a standard system: thumb print entry on the front doors, cameras on the main entryways. Sensors on the windows. Apparently, security isn't too awfully tight once you're inside the building."

"Good work," I said. "Now, do you think..."

"Oh, yeah," she interrupted, "and I also got us invitations."

"You did what?!"

"I got us invitations. I got on the phone with their vice-president in charge of fund raising and fed him this whole story about how Justin was all upset that he'd never done anything for the Militia, and now he wants to do a fund-raising concert on their behalf."

"And this guy bought it?"

"More or less. At any rate, I figured it would give us a chance to poke around the place and see what's there."

"Perfect," I said, trying not to sound *too* impressed. "When do we go in?"

"I figured we'd better move fast. I've set up our appointment with them for 2pm. Can you be in Marietta by one?"

"Uh..." I stalled while I walked back to the table and grabbed my palm display to check the time. It was 11:12 am. "Sure, no problem."

"OK. Go to the service station on the corner of Main and Cavalry. My car will stop there on the way to our meeting."

"I understand. See you there," I said, and hung up.

I shaved and jumped in the shower. It took me a few minutes to locate the shampoo from among the dizzying array of hair care products in Daniel's bathroom. It turned out to be something with herbs harvested from what's left of the Amazon Rain Forest. Oh well, it smelled nice and it didn't turn my hair any funny colors. I toweled off, threw on my clothes, and made a quick breakfast of a Coke and a protein bar. Then I went back to the bed to put on my shoes.

Daniel was still asleep. I needed to get moving, but I couldn't resist taking a minute to look at him as I tied my laces. Sleeping there in his underwear, his legs all tangled in the sheets, the muscles of his back slowly moving as he breathed, the sunlight catching the gold in his curls. I gave him a pat on the head, and then went out to face a day full of heavily armed militant Baptists.

I have got to get a better job.

## Chapter 18: The Police
## Tuesday the 10th, 3:50 AM

Dad is carving the turkey, while mom and sis stare at each other from across the dining room table. So far, things have been quiet. But we all know it's not going to last.

"Well," my mother says, as dad makes an incision in the breast between the third and fourth ribs, "isn't it nice to have everyone home for..."—a warning glare from my sister—"...for the weekend."

Dad puts down his scalpel and picks up a set of forceps. A moment later he digs a 9mm round out of the turkey and puts it on a tray next to the cranberry sauce.

"Yes," my sister says, her voice dripping with sarcasm. "Isn't it it just so nice that we all got together to have turkey dinner at the end of November for no reason in particular."

Sis only came home this break because mom promised not to try to make a holiday out of it. Dad makes a valiant effort to change the subject.

"Hm," he says. "Look at these powder burns around the entry wound. I'd say the fatal shot was fired from no more than six inches away. I'll bet this bird knew his killer."

I push my plate forward, hoping to get a drumstick before the fireworks start.

"Well, it really is so good to have both you girls home from school," says Mom. "I'm just so *thankful* that we could be together..."

"That's it!" shouts my sister, jumping up from her chair and throwing her napkin on the table. "I knew you were going to try this! Well, I am not going to sit here and celebrate the fact that some white racist pilgrims landed on some stupid rock and started 200 years of genocide and slavery.—No offense dad.—In case you've forgotten mother, our people did not land on Plymouth Rock, Plymouth Rock landed on..."

"Oh, do not go getting self-righteous with *me,* young lady!" Mom shouts back. "I'm the one who talked you into reading Malcolm X in the first place. And is it really too much to ask for us to have one nice family Thanksgiving where you don't..."

Sis doesn't wait for her to finish, but jumps in with a nasty comment about Uncle Toms. Now they're both yelling, neither of them hearing a word the other one says. Down at the end of the table, dad has opened up the turkey's stomach and is spooning the contents into an evidence vial. He looks up from what he's doing, and we smile at each other.

"Megan?"

"Yes, Daddy?"

"Megan?"

Something isn't right. My dad always calls me "Meg". And besides, his accent is Boston, not Southern.

"What is it, Daddy?"

Now my own voice was starting to sound funny. Like I was slurring my words. I felt dizzy, and realized the lights were off. Someone was standing over me and saying my name.

"Megan, you OK?"

I knew the voice. It was Tony.

I managed to sit up and get my bearings. I was on a cot in a dark room. There was some light coming in from under the door. Tony was standing next to the bed.

Oh, yeah. I was at the station. I'd gone in to the back room to grab twenty winks while we were waiting for the psych profile to come back from the FBI. That had been a little after one in the morning.

I started pulling myself together, but it takes me a few minutes to get coherent when I first wake up. I groped around next to the bed, trying to find my watch, and finally realized that it was still on my wrist. 3:52 am.

"What's up?" I struggled to say through a yawn.

"There's been another incident," Tony said. "Downtown this time. In the Second precinct. We need to get movin'. Your commander wants us at the crime scene."

I rubbed my eyes. "Huh? What happened?"

"I'll explain it to you on the way. Now close your eyes, I'm going to turn on the lights."

I did as he suggested, and a second later the world lit up in red and orange. I blinked a few times, but by the time my eyes adjusted to the light, the door was open and Tony was gone. I felt around under the cot and found my shoes, and even managed to get them on the right feet. By the time I was standing up, Tony had reappeared with a travel mug full of coffee. I took a swig as he pointed me toward the elevator.

By the time we'd reached the auto pool, I was coherent enough to realize that I was leaving the building without my headset. I told Tony to get a car while I went back up to grab it. But as I was turning around, Tony tapped me on the shoulder and handed it to me. He's going to make somebody a wonderful husband one of these days.

We climbed into the back of a cruiser that was being driven by some uniform I didn't recognize. As we pulled out of the parking lot, I searched through my pockets and finally found a roll of perk-ups. I swallowed two with a gulp of coffee. Contrary to the advertising on the package, the things don't actually replace sleep. But they do keep your serotonin levels all bubbly. So even though you're still dead tired, you're less likely to bite people's heads off because of it.

"OK, I'm here," I said, trying to sound more alert than I was. "More or less. Where are we going?"

"The Family Planning Clinic on the corner of Eighth and West Peachtree," Tony said as he read over some documents on a notebook. "We're still tryin' to pull together a clear picture of just what happened. There's a team from the Second on site, but they're just keepin' the site clear while our techs set up shop."

I was not too tired to notice his use of the words "we" and "our". It was good to know that Tony was finally thinking of himself as one of the team.

"So what happened?"

"Vandalism. Couple of assaults. Maybe a robbery, but they haven't run an inventory yet."

"So why are we on this?" I asked. "Do they think it's related to the graveyard business?"

Tony called up something on his notebook and passed it to me. It was a picture of a room with a chalk pentagram drawn on the floor. There was a dark smudge at its center, with what looked like a circle of wet rope around it. I glanced at the control code in the lower left hand corner. It was feed from a headset.

"Who shot this?"

"First officer on the scene. Fellow named Spivey. Run the image forward a few seconds and you'll see what really spooked him."

I touched the forward arrow in the upper right-hand corner and started playing the clip forward. The picture swung around to the corners of the room as the uniform checked his perimeter, making sure nobody was going to come jumping out at him from a blind spot. The room looked like some sort of lobby. Marble floors. Reception desk. Some sort of wall hangings. Then the picture swung back down to...

I touched the pause icon. I was looking at a nude woman, lying on her back, her legs spread around one of the points of the pentagram. A dark trail led from her  legs to the smudge in the middle of the pentagram.

"Good God."

For once, Tony didn't give me any grief about taking the Lord's name in vain. I enlarged the section of the image with the woman's face. Her eyes were closed, and there was a mark on her forehead, as if a child had drawn an upside-down cross in red fingerpaint. There was something wrapped around her forehead, something that had pricked her skin in several places, causing her to bleed. I had to look at it for a few seconds before I realized that it was barbed wire.

"Is she alive?"

Tony had taken out another notebook and was still reading.

"She was when the patrolman found her. We haven't gotten any word back from the paramedics yet."

I stared at the image on the notebook for a few more seconds, trying to get my mind wrapped around this. Then I closed it out and called up a menu of available documents on the case, but there was barely any time to start making sense of it all before we arrived at the scene. The clinic is only ten blocks from HQ, and at this time of night there wasn't much traffic on West Peachtree. We pulled up behind seven cruisers, four or five unmarked cars, an ambulance...and three news vans.

"Damn it. How did they get here so fast?" I asked as we got out of the car. I'm not used to having the media beat me to a crime scene.

"Well, the perps are practically flashin' the bat signal for 'em," said Tony, gesturing up to the clinic. The big ground floor window of their lobby had been splattered with what looked like blood, splashed into the crude shape of a dripping, inverted cross. The light from inside made it all glow a dull red.

"Oh, great," I muttered. "That's going to look real good on the newsites. Just the sort of thing to inspire people to stay calm."

Tony nodded as we walked toward the scene. "Yep. I'd say we're about to have a lot of scared people on our hands."

We pushed our way past a camera crew from the Microsoft News Service and then circled around behind that androgynous blond reporter from "Atlanta Today" who was already offering up unsubstantiated theories on the crime. At the bottom of the clinic's steps I flashed my badge to one of the uniforms keeping the crowd back, and he waved us through the line.

On the way up the steps we passed a team of paramedics carrying down a gurney. I got a good look at their baggage as they went by. It wasn't the woman from the video. This one was a beefy-looking guy in a security guard's uniform. He was unconscious, but they didn't have him on a respirator, so he might not have been too bad off.

At the top of the steps, Tony and I edged around a tech who had propped the front door open and was already lifting prints off the handle. Inside, a couple of three-person teams were photographing the scene. Two officers to hold the tape measure, a third to work the camera.

I looked around for the person in charge and settled on a short Asian woman who seemed to be giving the orders. I walked over to her and waited for her to finish pointing out something to one of the photographic teams.

"I'm Lieutenant Strand, SIB."

"Oh, hi," she said. "You guys move fast. Your techs are just breaking out their equipment now. I'm Tang, Second Precinct."

We shook hands.

"Pleased to meet you," I said. "This is Lieutenant Browning, from the Fourth."

"Hi," said Tang, taking his hand. "I saw the news reports on the incident out in the Fourth this morning, that whole mess out at the cemetery. That's why I sent the SIB a heads-up as soon as I saw this thing."

"Good thinking," I said.

"So, you figure they're related?" Tang asked. "Right?"

"Why don't you just tell us what you've got so far." said Tony.

"Yeah, sure. Mostly I've just been holding down the fort since I got here, keeping the crowd back so that your techs can do their job. I have picked up a few interesting tidbits, though..."

"Such as...?" I prodded. I hate it when people drag out information to make it seem more dramatic.

"Well, for starters, we've confirmed that the stuff on the windows is real blood. So is that stain in the pentagram. One of the techs ran a quick fluorisol test just to see. Nobody's had a chance to do a DNA typing yet, though, so we don't know if it's human or not."

"Any idea where it came from?" Tony asked.

"Yes," said Tang. "I'd say it's a pretty safe bet the stuff came from the clinic's medical supply. We've found eight or nine empty blood bags scattered around the room. Techs are checking them for prints."

"What about the woman?" I asked. "How is she?"

"Alive. Looked like she was drugged. Dilated pupils. Slow breathing. We couldn't bring her around. The hospital will run a toxicology screen. I sent an officer with a rape evidence kit to ride to the hospital, too, just in case. We should hear back on that in half an hour or so."

"Do you have an ID on her yet?" I asked.

"Yes," said Tang. "That turned out to be pretty easy. There's a pile of clothes over there near the hall. We found a security badge pinned to the shirt, had her picture and name on it. Her name is Delilah Collins. She was one of the security guards on duty."

"*One* of the guards?" pressed Tony.

"Yeah. Apparently, this place is a bit jumpy about security. Worried they might be bombed or burned down, something like that. There were three guards on duty tonight. Also a doctor up on the fourth floor who was babysitting the artificial wombs. The perps never went up that far. The doc was reading a novel. He didn't even know that anything had happened until we turned up and told him."

"So what happened to the other two guards?" I asked.

"One of them is on his way to the hospital," said Tang. "We found him in the lounge, passed out in a chair, displaying the same symptoms as the woman. There was a dirty coffee cup and a dark stain on the floor next to him. There were also a couple other half-drunk cups on the table in there. I mentioned to your techs that they might want to get samples."

"And the third guard?" I asked.

"No sign of him. I've got some officers doing a floor by floor search of the building, but I don't think we'll find him."

"Why? You think he's involved?" asked Tony.

"Well, there are no signs of a break-in," said Tang. "None of the external doors or internal doors were forced. It looks to me like whoever did this had an access badge and the relevant codes."

"All right," I said. "We should know for sure as soon as we check the security camera footage and the door logs."

"Maybe," said Tang. "We haven't gotten access to their system yet. I got through to the clinic's chief of security, though, and she should be here any minute now."

"Good. Was she able to tell you anything about the third guard?"

"Yeah. Knew the duty roster right off the top of her head. Says the third guard's name is Clinton Tanner. She hired him three weeks ago when another guard got mugged and had to take some medical leave. She says the guy came with good references."

"Do we have an address?"

"Yes. I sent a car out to his house to pick him up if he's there, but..."

"But you never know when you'll get lucky," I said.

I caught sight of Tony kneeling at the edge of the pentagram. He was looking at the dark circle around the inner edge of it. I went over to see what he was examining.

"Is that what I think it is?" he asked.

I examined the circle. It appeared to be made from short lengths of bloody flesh, knotted together.

"Yes," said Tang. "Those are umbilical chords. I asked the Doc, and found out that the clinic keeps them after the delivery and puts them in cold storage. Every so often they ship a bunch of them out to some university doing fetal tissue research."

Tony and I looked at each other. We were both thinking it. Whoever these perps were, they were really working the womb imagery. So what was next?

"You mentioned the artificial wombs," I said. "Do you know if any of them might have been tampered with?"

Tang shrugged. "I don't think so. The doc says he was up there with them the whole time. You can go ask him yourself. He's being interviewed in the hall over there right now."

"I'll do that. But in the meantime have him double check to make sure none of them have been tampered with." The artificial wombs were used by women who couldn't—or chose not to— carry children to term. I hated to think what the perps might have done if they'd broken into one of those.

"Oh, there was something else that the Doc did notice. When we brought him down here, he noticed the lights."

"The lights?" asked Tony.

"Yeah," said Tang. "Apparently, the lights in this room aren't usually set up this way. He seemed pretty certain about that."

I looked up. The lobby had an extensive track lighting system, which had been focused to throw all its beams on the center of the pentagram. The effect was a bit unnerving.

"You mean whoever did this stopped to adjust the *lighting*?" asked Tony.

"Yep," said Tang. "Theatrical bent, I guess."

"Actually, that makes some sense," I said. "Both these sites were obviously designed to shock and scare people."

"Well, it's workin' on me," said Tony.

Just then, a disheveled-looking woman in slacks and a white shirt came in through the front door, escorted by a uniform. Tang waved the woman over and dismissed the uniform with a nod.

"Dahlia Cole, I'm the chief of security for the clinic," the woman said as she approached us. We did the introduction thing, then I sent Tony off with her to call up the clinic's security camera footage and the personnel records on the missing guard. While I was doing that, I noticed Tang take a call on her headset. I waited for her to finish, hoping she had some good news for me.

"We've found the third guard," she said after a moment. "He was home asleep. Claims he's never heard of this place. Says he's been working security at a hospital over in Connyers for the last six months."

"Can we confirm that?"

Tang held another mumbled conversation on her headset. A minute later she got back to me.

"Yeah, the personnel manager at the hospital confirms his story. Apparently he didn't get off *there* until midnight tonight, a couple of hours after he supposedly came on duty *here.*"

"Identity theft?" I suggested.

"Sounds like it to me. Somebody must have applied for the job here using this guy's name and references, maybe a fake copy of his thumbprint as well."

"Pretty slick," I said. "You want to lay odds that the same guy created the job opening here by arranging for his predecessor to take medical leave?"

"Maybe," said Tang. "I could look into that if you want."

"Do that. Find the previous guard and get the details on the mugging that..." A beep went off in my ear. Now it was my turn to take a call.

"Strand here."

"It's Tony."

"What have you got?"

"You'd better pull out a notebook. You're gonna wanna take a look at this."

I still had the the notebook with me from the car. I flipped it back on and called up the feed from Tony's headset. I found myself looking at some stubs of melted fiber optic cable and some charred crystal fragments.

"What is that?" I asked.

"That was the secure memory core for this little operation," Tony answered. "Looks like somebody took a blowtorch to it."

"Great," I said. "What about the backup?"

"It's thirty feet down the hall, in exactly the same shape."

"They keep their backup in the same building as the primary?" I asked, incredulous. "Haven't these people ever heard of an off-site backup? You know, in case they have a fire or something?"

"I had a word with them on the matter," Tony said. "Apparently, they're a bit uptight about data security around here. Worried someone might get a list of employees, or abortionists, or adoption records, or women who've had abortions, or..."

"I get the picture."

"Anyway, they figured the risk of moving the data outweighed the risk of having it all in one buildin'. And they did have one dandy security system in place around these things. Fireproof vault. Motion detectors. Laser..."

"Any idea how the perps breached it?"

"No signs of any force. I'd say they must have had the access codes."

"Yeah, that fits. So where does this leave us?"

"Well, unless the techs can work some sort of miracle on these crystal fragments, I'm afraid the personnel records are a total loss. But the door locks and the security cameras all have 24 hours, worth of backup memory built into them—just in case they get cut off from the rest of the network for some reason. We can start downloadin' those one by one. 'Course' the perps might have messed with a few of the cameras, but I can't imagine they had time to take out every single one. There must be picture of this guy on some piece of hardware in this building."

"Good," I said. "We'll use Tang and some of her uniforms to start checking out the cameras and the door logs. In the meantime, I want you back up here so that I can bounce some theories around with you."

"Yes Ma'am," answered Tony. "I'll be up in a flash."

I told Tang what I wanted done with the cameras, and she started rounding up uniforms to make it happen. In the meantime, I went outside to get a breath of air and collect my thoughts. I walked out the front door, then around to a dark corner of the building where I wouldn't be standing in silhouette. Across the street a dozen more newscrews had set up camp, and a large crowd was gathering. Amazing how many people were up at five in the morning. They must have heard the story on the news and come down to see it for themselves.

In the next few hours, a lot more people would be waking up to see this on the news. A lot of people who were going to be scared by this thing. I just hoped they wouldn't be scared enough to do anything stupid.

## Chapter 19:  The Reverend Senator
## Tuesday the Tenth, 7:30 AM

I rounded the corner and started toward the elevator at a fast walk, surrounded by people who work for me and can't get out of my way fast enough.  Some days, I just want to bring a machete to work and cut a path through them.

"Will you hold still for a second!" Kate said, smearing some more base under my left cheekbone and trying to smooth it out.

"I don't have time," I barked back at her, a little more harshly than I should have.  Kate's one of the best makeup artists in the business, and she knows it.  I should treat her with more consideration.

"Would you rather go on television with rouge smeared all over your face like a fifty-dollar whore?" she said, spitting into her hand and erasing a mistake.

She was right, of course.  No sense getting out there only to make a fool of myself.  I stopped walking, and Kate proceeded to smooth out the rouge on my cheeks.  Then she got out a pencil and started darkening my eyebrows.  The end results of all this tends to seem a bit odd when I look at myself in the mirror, but on camera it always looks just right.  Which is what counts.

While Kate penciled in my other eyebrow, I looked around impatiently for a wall monitor, but there wasn't one in this hallway.  Just a crowd of lackeys.  I counted eight of them. You'd think they'd realize that there isn't room for all of them to lick my boots at once, and they'd arrange to do it in shifts.

"Haven't any of you eggheads got a display handy?" I growled at them.  "How am I supposed to know what's going on in the world?"

Three of them flipped open palm displays and held them up for my approval.  All of them tuned to my station.

"Fascinatin'," I said.  "Just what I want to see at a seven thirty in the mornin'.  Every other network in the country is broadcastin' a story live from the clinic, and we're still showin' a documentary on missionaries in South America."  Is it any wonder I haven't made it any further than the Senate yet?  "Can somebody tell me when our team is going to get there?"

Several of the whiz kids started scrambling for the information. A young woman I didn't recognize beat them to it.

"We have two vans en route, Reverend. The driver of the closer one expects to reach the clinic within eight minutes, but I think he has severely underestimated the amount of traffic around the sight. It will probably be closer to fifteen or twenty minutes before they are in position and broadcasting live."

I looked at her more carefully. She was blond and wearing a dark blue business suit. She also had a nice chest, but I'm not supposed to notice things like that.

"You're new," I observed.

"Well, actually, Reverend, I've been interning in the demographics department for the last six months. But since Ms. Phillips isn't in the building yet, I though I would jump in and fill in for her."

Self-starter. I'd have to keep an eye on this one. I glanced at her nametag.

"All right, Natalie. Do you think you could find me a network that has a crew out there, so that I can see what's going on?"

"Of course, Reverend." She handed me her display, which was already set to another network. "Microsoft has had a team broadcasting on site for the last ten minutes. I thought I'd better stay on top of what they were showing."

I took a look at the picture. They were panning the crowd. Mostly spectators. I caught sight of some of our people waving crosses. A few had signs. I tried to read them, but there were two many words on the posters and the lettering was illegibly small.

"Good grief. Hasn't anybody given these people some slogans?" I asked, looking pointedly at Natalie. "I can't read a thing on those signs they're wavin'."

"Well..." Natalie started to say, but it was obvious she didn't know the answer. She looked longingly at her palm display, but I held onto it. "I believe..." Then she reached out and yanked a display out of the hand of the guy standing next to her, cleared whatever he was working on, and called up the data she needed.

"Yes," she said, reading something off the screen. "We have ten organizers en route to the site with supplies of new signs. Message Department has put together the following slogans."

She tapped the borrowed palm display, and then passed it to me. I read over the stuff my genius speechwriters had come up with. It was mostly old standbies. "One Nation Under God." "Abortion is Murder." A couple new ones. "Abortion *is* child sacrifice." I kind of liked the one one that just said "Business as Usual," but I was worried that most people wouldn't get it.

"Not bad. But not great, either. Nothing that really gets to the terror of the situation. And these three are too long," I said, flagging them with my finger. "Axe them."

Natalie recorded a note to that effect, mumbling it into her watch. In the meantime, Kate finished with my eyebrows and started on my hair.

"And I want some professionals out there, too. These losers are all amateurs. They have no idea how to get a cameraman's attention. Call up thirty of our best protesters and get them out there."

"Yes, sir," Natalie said, making another note.

"Oh, and get another twenty of them out there to lead an abortionist counter-protest."

"Sir?" Natalie said, seeming genuinely surprised. Well, she might have ambition, but she was still a bit naive.

"A counter-protest," I said again. "You don't think we're going to leave it to the pro-death faction to organize their own protesters? Granted, the abortionists are all a bit loopy, but you can't always count on them to be suitably absurd in front of the cameras. I want at least ten guys out there with signs that say "Abortion is a Right!" and the same number of women with signs saying "My Body! My Right!" Have the Message department dream up some good publicity stunt. Oh, and make sure all the women are unattractive."

Natalie paused a second, then started dictating the relevant memos to get it all done. In the meantime Kate was just finishing up my hair. I glanced at my watch. 7:38. We needed to be on the air by eight if we were going to make the morning news cycle.

"What's my ETA once we hit the chopper?"

Natalie scrambled to pull up the data, but Jerry beat her to it this time. "About ten minutes. We've negotiated landing rights on a nearby building. You may even beat the news crew there."

"OK. Now show me what the speech writers have for me."

Jerry said something into his watch and called up the speech on the display I was already holding. I read through it. It went on for almost thirty seconds. Way too long.

"No. No. No. I want something short, snappy, and scary. This dang thing meanders on for almost half a minute. There's no telling which parts the other networks would pull out of it for their coverage." I turned back to Natalie. "Get in touch with the lamebrains who wrote this. Tell them I want a couple five-second sound bites that I can spit out. If it's the only thing I say, they'll have to run it."

Kate finally finished with my hair, and I started forward again. At the end of the hall I boarded the elevator with two of my security guards. I motioned Natalie to join us for the ride up.

"I want you to go ride herd on the speech writers. Light a fire under them, and don't let up until they give you ten seconds of material with some bite to it. This is a big chance for us. All those liberal churches that have been laughing at the idea of Satan are gonna be feelin' pretty silly when they see this on the news. We're not just preachin' to the choir with this one, so it's got to count."

The doors to the elevator opened onto the roof. The helicopter was already juicing up for takeoff.

"You got maybe fifteen minutes before I go on the air," I yelled over the noise. "Get me something I can use!"

She nodded to indicate that she understood. I started to go, but remembered something else I needed.

"Oh, and have them write me a two minute speech as well, to run on our network. We'll shoot it in front of a bluescreen when I get back, and then paste in the protesters before we broadcast. Make it something special."

Then I took off running for the helicopter with my bodyguards in tow. This was it, our big chance to open the country's eyes. Maybe our last chance. I said a silent prayer for the souls of whatever lunatics had done all this. They may be real sickos, but they have inadvertently done the nation a great service. They have focused the public's attention.

The hand of Satan is subtle. He corrupts slowly and by degrees, until what was once obviously repugnant and sinful, over time becomes familiar and acceptable. Until a nation founded by Christian pilgrims finds itself condoning the murder of babies, sanctifying perversion in the holy cloak of marriage, and awarding voodoo and witchcraft the status of protected religions, equal to the light of Christ.

Oh, there is a Satanic conspiracy, all right. It may not be the guys in black robes and sacrificial daggers, but it's just as real. You only have to look around to see it at work. At the advertisements, telling us that we can fill the emptiness in our lives with a new car or expensive clothes. At the movies, telling us that we can find the meaning of life in a sexual encounter. At the psychotherapists, telling us that there is no right and wrong, only different mental disorders. At all the forces trying to drain the sacred from our lives, trying to tell us that there is nothing more to the human soul than a series of appetites to be sated.

It's all there, for anyone who looks. Only people don't pay attention. So we have to make it a little more obvious, a little more colorful. So that they will pay attention. And they will be afraid.

I looked at some of the pictures coming back from one of the other networks. Yeah, when people woke up and saw this, they would be afraid all right. And I would be able to ride that fear all the way to the White House.

Then I would set about makin' things right again.

## Chapter 20:  The Witch
## Tuesday the Tenth, Morning

I'd been awake for awhile, watching the morning sunlight inch its way down the far wall. Watching Alex sleeping, his breathing slow and regular, punctuated every so often by a little snore. It's not often that I'm both happy and have a free moment to notice the fact. But sometimes, in the morning, I'll suddenly realize just how good my life is.

I rolled over to look at the clock, and the green smell of crushed ash leaves filled my nostrils. I'd picked them last night from the tree in the back yard, and put them under my pillow. They're supposed to give you dreams that make everything clear. And with all the questions I had right now, a little clarity would have been useful. But if I'd had any dreams, I couldn't remember them.

Last night I had started looking for the kid described in the paper I'd taken from Jen's apartment. I had a birth date and a gender, so I'd set up a search on the birth records for the Atlanta Metro area. A task made no easier by the fact that the city of Atlanta sprawls across four different counties, each with its own database, and none of them compatible with each other. It turned out that there were 104 boys born in Atlanta on the sixth of June, 2010. Unfortunately, though, birth certificates don't list blood type or eye color or anything else like that. So I was stuck with 104 possible candidates, and no idea which one was my man.

The clock said 6:57. I let it roll around to 6:59, then switched the alarm off. I got up, showered, brushed, and dressed, and then crawled back into bed next to Alex, who was still out like a light. The plan had been to wake him up with a kiss, to get his day off to a good start. But the lout managed to kiss me back without ever really waking up, then rolled over and went back to sleep. I had to resort to pulling the covers off the bed and dumping them on the floor, which produced a series of little whimpering noises as he hunted around for them and a slow return to consciousness.

While Alex was pulling himself out of bed, I went to start the wake up sequence on the girls. First I went to Winter and gently shook her awake, telling her it was time for school. This was was met with an incoherent groan that I took for an acknowledgement. Then it was off to Summer's room, where I repeated the process. This time I got a mumbled response to the effect that she was not

in the army—yet. Then it was back off to Winter, who had made
the titanic effort required to crawl out from under her covers, only
to collapse back on top of them. (Honestly, the girls must get this
behavior from their father. I have always been a morning person.) So I tickled Winter's feet for a couple of minutes, until she
was all giggly and squirmy and awake, and then I packed her off
to the bathroom to brush her teeth. Then it's back to my moody
teen, who assures me that she is getting up, and that I don't need
to watch over her like a child. Yeah, right.

I went downstairs to get started on breakfast. I had loaded the
breadmaker with dough the night before, and the loaf was just beginning to cool. I broke a warm piece off and munched on it while
I listened to the footsteps upstairs. I could make out the sounds of
my husband getting dressed, and the pitter-patter of Winter's little
feet as she finished in the bathroom and ran back to her room. But
I didn't hear the stomp-stomping of my favorite, moody teen. Hm.

I munched on another piece of bread as I picked a flower off
the jasmine plant by the window. I carefully crushed the blossom
in my hand as I repeated the Charm of Sending, and then I blew
across the petals and sent a little something fluttering into Summer's
dreams. A nice image of her turning up for class in her nightgown, with unwashed hair and dingy teeth.

I took a couple more bites of bread, and then I heard a pair of
feet hit the floor in Summer's bedroom and go stomping off to the
bathroom, followed by the sound of water running in the shower.

Children. I wonder how anybody ever manages to handle
them without resorting to magick?

Well, with the household finally in motion, I set about getting
breakfast on the table. I got out the fruit for the salad, and as I cut
it up, I began to recite the Charm of Making. After all, cooking is
a kind of magick. You take ordinary things, and make something
wonderful out of them. And if you do it all just right, you get
something truly magickal—almost fifteen minutes of peace with
the whole family together. That's the great thing about eating:
You can't chew and fight at the same time.

The Charm of Making is a long one. I'd tell you the words, but
then someone who didn't know what they were doing might be
tempted to use it, and that could cause all kinds of mischief. Anyway, by the end of the first speaking, I'd finished chopping the fruit.
By the end of the second, I'd mixed the honey and yogurt for the
dressing and heated up the pan for the eggs. And by the end of the
third speaking, I had a pan full of fried egg whites and turkey bacon
nearing completion. Magick, and the magickal smell of food, filled
the house, calling my family down to breakfast.

They all came tromping down the stairs at once, and descended on the kitchen table like they hadn't eaten in weeks. Breakfast itself passed in a flurry of giggles and two dreadfully serious conversations: one about the theatrical merits of the play that Winter's kindergarten class is doing (she's playing a fern), and one on the correct behavior for Alex and me at Summer's upcoming parent-teacher night. ("Just don't embarrass me, Mom, OK?") When the meal was over, I sent the girls out to collect the herbs for the day's charms, while Alex and I cleared the table and loaded the dishwasher.

The girls came back a few minutes later with all the things that I'd asked them to gather from the back yard, and I set about making the charms. For Summer and Winter, I make bags filled with Dogwood leaves for protection and Sage for wisdom. I add a sprig of dill to Winter's bag, because it is a special protection for little children. Of course, it's also induces lust, which is why I leave it out of Summer's charm bag. Even if she thinks she's ready to start dating, *I'm* not ready for her to start dating.

In Alex's bag I put a Basil leaf, which helps lovers understand each other, and a sprig off the Juniper tree in the backyard, to protect him against accidents. And in my own charm bag I put Basil, a leaf of Holly for luck, and one Sesame seed, which is supposed to help unravel secrets. Let's hope it works.

When I was done, we all recited the Charm of Making three times while I tied up the bags, and then everybody took theirs. The girls and I wear ours on silver chains around our necks, while Alex prefers to carry his in his pocket. Then I left Alex to finish cleaning up the kitchen while I walked the girls to school.

It's a good five block walk. When we got there, Summer spotted some friends and took her leave with an abrupt "Yeah, bye Mom." Winter made a better show of it, giving me a kiss on the cheek as I handed her off to her Kindergarten teacher, Ms. Greenbriar.

From there it was a three block walk for me back to the MARTA Station. On the ride back into the city, I turned my mind back to the problem of Jen's disappearance, the black magic rituals, and the boy whose profile I'd found in her apartment. I played around with different ways of putting the whole thing together. Maybe Jen had been hired to find the boy, and had found out that he was involved in a cult. Or maybe she was investigating the cult, and had found out that they were planning on doing something to the boy. Was he slated for a human sacrifice?

There was a nastier possibility which I kept trying to avoid thinking about, but which I kept coming back to: that Jen was actually involved in the black magick. It was a nasty thought to have about a friend and a member of my own coven. But I had found the papers detailing the ritual in her apartment. She did have the magickal knowledge to set up something like this. And...and while I hated to admit it, it was not impossible to imagine her getting caught up in something like this. Jen was intensely proud of her magickal abilities, and could be a bit of a show off. As a warrior type, she could get caught up in accomplishing an end without adequately thinking through the means. It was all too easy to imagine her being seduced by the powers afforded by black magick. Particularly if she had a score to settle with someone.

My train arrived at Arts Center Station. I walked the two blocks to my building, and was at my desk by 9:07, ready to face the work day. But first...

I made a call down to Sally in Research.

"Research, what'cha need?"

"Hey Sally, it's Holly."

"Oh, hey Holly. What can I do for you?"

"Well, I have kind of a strange favor I..."

"Oh, no. This isn't going to be another one of those weird ones, like that time you asked me to find out the average humidity at each of the last 12 Summer Olympics, is it?"

"Uh...no, not exactly. See, I..."

"Good, cause Julia over on the young women's site has had me running around all morning finding out what the most popular shade of lipstick was for every year going back to 1957. Would you believe that in 2008 it was a shade called 'Vampire blood'?"

"Huh. Well, that is strange."

"And Sam, over on the Libertarian page, wants to know the seasonal variation in the surface area of Mars' polar ice caps."

"I see," I said. I had learned a long time ago not to interrupt Sally when she's pretending to complain about weird data requests. After all, it's the only chance she ever gets to show off, and she's entitled to it. Her research makes all us reporters look good, but because she never gets a byline, we're the only ones who know just how talented she is. And everybody needs a little recognition. So I let her rave on about three other choice assignments she's already had today, muttering sympathetically, until she finally seemed to be running out of steam. When she paused, I jumped at the opening.

"Well," I said, "that's what you get for cultivating a reputation as a wonder kid."

"Yeah," she responded, "me and my big mouth. I should have played stupid when I first started working here. Once they find out that you can do the impossible, you never get a moment's peace. So, what do you need, Holly?"

"Well, you're gonna hate me for this," I began, knowing full well that this was the sort of challenge that Sally lives for. "I need to find a certain kid who lives in Atlanta. I have his birth date, his original hair and eye color, and the original shape of his ears and nose. I also know that he's left handed and blood type O positive. The only thing I don't know is his name."

There was a long silence at the other end of the phone

"Do I even want to know what sort of story you're working on this time?"

"No, you don't. But I'll tell you all about it when it's done, anyway."

"OK. Do you know what facility the kid was born at? Hospitals tend to have lousy data security. I might be able to bribe an orderly and get access to their records."

"Uh. No, I don't."

"Rats. That's going to make it a lot tougher. I can't go breaking into every hospital computer in town. Give me a minute to think what other databases this guy might be in." There was a short pause. "How old is he?"

"Fourteen."

"Hm. Too young for a driver's license or a military record. Do you know if he's in high school?"

"No, but it seems like a good bet."

"OK. Let's take that bet. Most high schools have year-book Web pages, which means there might be a photo of this guy somewhere online. Send me everything you've got on the kid, and I'll set up a program to search for someone his age with the right hair and eyes and features. But it's going to take me awhile to set up."

"Great," I said. "But what if the kid dyes his hair or wears tinted contacts? Won't that throw off your search?"

"Not the way I do things, Holly," Sally said with a sniff. "I'll have my program check every photo on these kids going back to kindergarten. They must have had their real hair and eye color at some point. And if they were ever a match to your mystery man, my program will flag them."

"Thanks. You're a genius, Sally."

"Well, wait until I've done something to earn the praise. Get me the data and I'll call you as soon as I've got something."

I hung up, scanned in the page describing the kid, and zapped it down to her. Then I tried to put the whole thing out of my head for awhile and get some work done. I called up our newsite and read the headlines that had been posted by the night shift, just to get caught up on what was going on in the world.

"WTO launches suit against Brazil for breach of Greenhouse Emissions Treaty."

"Asteroid Surveyor VII finds major platinum deposit."

"Technical problems threaten Europa Lander mission."

"Princeton Botanist announces creation of 'vaccine' for Dutch Elm Disease."

"California Separatists gain 30% of seats in State Legislature."

"Black Magicians attack guards, vandalize Family Planning Clinic."

The last one caught my attention.

I called up the full story. Not one of our better-written pieces. It was long on words and short on hard information. A few quotes from the police, saying that they wouldn't say anything. The usual round of comments by pundits, who didn't know anything about the case but were still willing to give opinions. A few reactions from bystanders at the scene.

But the pictures spoke volumes. A night time shot of the clinic, its windows splashed with blood, glowing a dull red. Pictures of drugged guards being wheeled out to an ambulance. And a particularly disturbing drawing, based on an interview that our field agents had done with a doctor from the clinic who'd seen the crime scene. It depicted a naked woman, her legs spread around the edge of a pentagram, in the center of which lay an aborted fetus. I started to get sick, and had to get up and away from my desk for a few seconds.

I took a walk around the floor and tried to clear my head. I had already been thinking about calling the police, reporting Jen as a missing person and turning over her papers to them. The incident at the clinic only made it more important that I do so. But I still didn't know how Jen was tied in with all this. And how could I go turn over evidence to the police that seemed to prove that a Wiccan was behind all this? The Baptists have always accused us of being closet Satanists. If hard proof ever came out that one of us really was mixed up with black magick, well...the situation could get very ugly. I had to find out what was going on before anyone else did.

As soon as my stomach settled, I went back to my desk and called up the same story on our Baptist Newsite, just to see what their take on it was. The article consisted of the same sketchy information that had been on the Wiccan newsite, with a slightly more apocalyptic spin put on it, and some additional video clips. I touched on the still frames to play them. Footage of some Christian and Pagan protesters throwing beer bottles and rocks at each other. A clip of Reverend Senator Stonewall giving a speech. He had a cut on his head that was bleeding down the side of his face. His voice reminded me of Charleton Heston, the way he had delivered his State of the Union address.

"We will retake our country from the forces of Darkness! From the pornographers and perverts, from the child murderers and demon worshippers!" At the end of the speech, Stonewall announced that the Christian Alliance was creating a strike force of professional "Witch Hunters" to track down the culprits and bring them to justice. And of course, there was a 1-800 number to phone in pledges for the group's funding. According to the article, they had already received 7.8 million in pledges by 9:30 this morning.

That made me think of the time. I glanced up at the clock. It was 9:55. Good grief, I hadn't realized how long I'd been poring over this stuff. I'd been here for almost an hour, and I hadn't even started my first story of the day. Well, getting myself fired wasn't going to help matters, so I forced myself to stop worrying about Jen and Stonewall and whatever those black magicians were up to. I took a moment to ground myself, then I opened up the queue of stories that Research had waiting for me and got down to work.

First up, I tackled an interview with Gene Dark, TNTC. (The Next Tom Cruise, there's one every year.) I checked his bio and wrote up a fast intro for the piece, stressing the fact that he was a practicing Wiccan. Then I dove into the interview itself. Most of it was usable. I kept the parts where he talked about his latest film, his career, and how he used his magick to enhance his acting. But the naive political ramblings had to go, along with all that really boring stuff about his new house. Finally, I picked a nice shot of him in a towel from the publicity stills for the film, laid the whole thing out, and shipped it off to my editor for review.

I doubletimed it through a couple more quick stories, getting myself caught up. A piece on poachers in the Amazon park, and a profile on an ornithologist who was trying to save the Emperor Penguin from going extinct as global warming wiped out its habitat. Finally, at 11:20, I got a call back from Sally.

"OK. *Now* you can tell me I'm a genius."

"All right, you're a genius, Sally. What did you find out?"

"Well, I would have had this for you a lot faster, but Flanders called up all panicked and had me drop everything to go find all the nitty gritty on elephant mating. It turns out to be a lot more complicated than you'd think."

"I can believe it. Now, you were telling me about the results of the search?"

"Oh, yeah. Here's the deal. Of the 104 boys born in Atlanta on the day in question, I can write off 83 of them as definite negative matches. Wrong ethnicity, wrong facial structure—No way they could be your guy. Then I've got 14 guys who are positive matches; that is, they have the right nose and ear structure, and their hair and eye color matches your guy's at some point in the last few years. I've found death certificates on three of those, which leaves you with eleven live matches. I hope that's helps."

"Excellent. 14 will be a whole lot easier to sift through than a 104. But what about the rest? 83 and 14 only make 97."

"Glad to see you remember your arithmetic. Yeah, the other seven are the maybes."

"What does a 'maybe' mean?"

"Well, two of them died before they reached the age of five, so there are no yearbook pictures of them. The other five just vanished off the face of the earth. No school records, no death certificates, no nothing. My guess is that those were probably adopted."

"OK. Got it. Thanks again Sally. You're a wonder worker."

"Ah, don't mention it," she said. Then, "Well, actually, do mention it. Preferably to one of the senior editors come performance evaluation time."

"Consider it done."

"OK. I'll zap you the list of matches and maybes. Good luck with it. Bye."

She hung up, and I looked over the list of names she'd just sent. At least I was down to 14 now. But none of the names jumped out at me. There were none that I recognized.

So I dove back into my work. My editor hadn't called down yet to ask about my mysterious drop in productivity for the first hour of my shift, and maybe if I made up the deficit by lunch she wouldn't notice at all.

By one o'clock I was finally caught up. I was ravenous by then, but I still wanted to get another look at Sally's list. So rather than going out for lunch, I grabbed a brie and watercress sandwich from the vending machine and munched it at my desk while I looked over the names.

I still had no idea what I was looking for. I just had to hope that I would recognize it when I saw it. I started with the eleven live matches. I pulled up their yearbook photos and read the descriptions of their activities. Soccer, track, science club, chorus, drama club and so on. If one of them was into black magick, he hadn't been thoughtful enough to list it among his hobbies.

I did a search for news articles mentioning the names and got a few hits. There was a photo on one of them with his prize winning science project. Another was mentioned in an article on the state track meet. And a third was briefly mentioned in an article about his father, who was the chief fund raiser for a charity which finds homes for retired racing dogs. Again, nothing that suggested a connection to black magick.

I moved on to the three dead matches. One had died in an auto accident, along with his father. Another got caught by a stray bullet from a fight at school. The last died of bone cancer. All of them had been dead for at least a year. None of them were buried in the cemetery where the mutilated corpse was found. Nothing suggested that any of them knew a thing about magick.

I racked my brain, trying to think of a reason why one of these kids would have come to the attention of a group of black magicians, but it was no good. At one-thirty, I put the whole thing aside and went back to work, burying myself in articles about illegal child labor in the software industry, a recent border dispute between Quebec and Ontario, and the growing influence of the Russian Virtual Mafia.

Normally I'm pretty good about concentrating on one task at a time, but all afternoon my mind kept wandering back to the list. What should I be looking for? What was the thing that made this kid so special? And how was I going to recognize him when I found him?

The afternoon passed slowly, and I was relieved when I glanced up and the clock finally said 5:30. I signed out and walked the two blocks to the MARTA station through the remnants of a glorious summer day. What was left of my frustration melted in the warm evening breeze. I gave up, and stopped trying to force the problem. Maybe if I just let it lie in the back of my mind for awhile, something would hit me. I walked down out of the sunlight and into the cool of the station, waiting for some sort of insight to come.

Hm. Maybe it wasn't the boy himself. Maybe it had something to do with his parents, or his siblings. I could start checking the families of the boys on the list. Maybe there was something interesting about one of their relatives. I thought about ways to check up on that, as I made my way toward my train.

I must not have been paying too much attention to where I was going, because the next thing I knew I was standing at the edge of the platform, surrounded by a crowd of teenage boys.

Something was wrong. They were all standing a little too close to me. They were staring at me. I followed their eyes, and realized that they were examining my accessories: the charm bag, the crescent moon dangling from my ear, the silk headband with the third eye painted on it. What, they've never seen a witch before?

Then I took a good look at what they were wearing, and suddenly felt a lot less comfortable. One had on a T-shirt that said "Campus Crusade for Christ." Two of the others had shirts printed with the slogan "One Nation Under God." And there was a preponderance of gold cross earrings.

Nobody said anything. We all just stood there, looking at each other. I had a feeling that they'd seen the news about the clinic and the riots. Then one of them, a blond boy, pulled out a cigarette and lit up. But he didn't put his lighter away afterward. He just held it there, staring at me through the flame for a few seconds. Somebody else whispered the word "witch".

The message could not have been clearer.

Then a train came, and the boys all pushed their way past me to get on it, the blond boy with the lighter getting on last. He was still staring at me when the doors closed and the train pulled away.

I had decided to wait for the next one.

## Chapter 21: The Chosen
## Tuesday the 10th, 10 AM

Mrs. Chandler was off on some roll about Melville and the forma-
tion of a uniquely American voice in literature. I flipped open my
notebook, trying to look like I was interested in what she was
saying and wanted to take some notes. When she turned and
paced away from me, I tapped on my mail box. The latest message from Summer was there.

"Yech. I'm in Geometry now. Something about proving that
two cords have to intersect at a right angle or something like that.
Could they make this stuff any more boring? What have you got?"

I picked up my stylus and wrote her back.

"English. Melville. Dull."

A few seconds later a message came back.

"Melville? Has she mentioned that he was gay?"

I had to bite my lip to avoid laughing out loud.

"No," I wrote back, "she hasn't mentioned that yet. Though I
did kind of wonder about those whipping scenes in Billy Budd.
So, you think he and Hawthorne were getting it on?"

I glanced up and noticed that Mrs. Carpenter was pacing back
toward my end of the room, so I switched over to a blank screen
and quickly scribbled Melville's name, the title "Development of
America's voice," and several short, nonsense phrases with big
words in them. It was a good thing, too; she looked down at my
screen on her way past. After that, I had the feeling that she was
keeping an eye on me, so I wasn't able to get back to Summer
until the bell rang for the end of class.

Out in the hall I opened my new mail. There were three messages from Summer.

"Nah. You ever seen a picture of Hawthorne? Major dog-boy.
Whitman seems more his type. Anyway, you free this afternoon?"

"Benji? You there? Earth to Benji…"

"Oops. Guess you've been busted. Drop me a line when they
let you out of solitary."

I dictated a fast note to her while I walked to the testing room
for my history midterm.

"Got time off for good behavior. Well, for faking good behavior. So, what did you have in mind for this afternoon? (I'll
have to check with my parole officer to see if I'm free.)

"P.S.: Won't be able to talk for an hour. History test. Catch up with you at lunch."

I got into the testing room and grabbed a desk just as the bell was ringing. For once, I was not particularly stressed. History this term was on the first half of the twentieth century, with World War I and II, spies, battles, and all sorts of cool stuff, so it had been fun to do the reading. This was one test I was ready for.

I sat down at the desk, gave it my thumb print, and began the test, starting with the short answers. I breezed my way through the multiple choice section in about 6 minutes. The timeline took a little longer, but once I'd gotten the Battle of the Somme into the right slot, everything else fell into place.

The AI-moderated essay was, as usual, the real bitch of the test. The topic was the underlying cause of World War I. I decided to go with an argument that the real cause of World War I was technological. Europe was always having small wars between the great powers every few years. World War I was just another in the series—except that modern transportation, industry, and weapons allowed it to escalate beyond the usual border skirmish into a massive confrontation where whole nations could devour each other.

I thought it was a pretty clever argument. It wasn't particularly original, but it wasn't one of the theories that Mrs. Sheffield had beaten to death in her lectures. The AI really jumped on my case, though. It brought up the American Civil War, and pointed out that it had been a complete blood bath. So why hadn't the Europeans learned their lesson from that?

I wrote a short counter-argument to that, saying that the Americans were dismissed as barbarians who didn't know how to fight a proper war, so the Europeans were not going to alter their tactics based on the experience of ignorant Yanks.

Then the history AI brought up the Russo-Japanese war. It predated World War I by only a few years, and used almost all the same technologies. Yet it had not erupted into a global bloodbath.

Unfortunately, I wasn't particularly up on the Russo-Japanese war. So I punted, trying to argue that it was only the Japanese that were employing fully industrial tactics, while the Russians were fighting on the fringes of their empire, far from their transportation net and industrial base. Thus the quick and relatively decisive victory for the Japanese. I hoped.

The AI caught me on a few factual mistakes, but seemed to buy that general line of reasoning. Then the two of us settled down into a debate about the interaction of technological and diplomatic forces. The AI is ruthless, but I felt like I held my own pretty well until the bell for lunch rang.

At lunch, I caught up with Scott and Tim at our usual table. They were already working on the next issue, arguing over the design of alien geisha girls. Scott had his notebook open with a sketch of some sort of frog woman with webbed hands and feet and big eyes. And big breasts, of course. Scott thought her skin should look wet and slick like an amphibian's, but Tim thought that was gross. While they debated the point, I put my own notebook on the table where they could both see it and opened my mail. There was a message from Summer waiting.

"Ug. Sorry to hear it. History of what? Anyway, my Dad is picking up my sister from school today, so I'm free. You want to meet at Lost World so I can obliterate you at Slip Stream again?"

I started dictating a response into my notebook.

"Hm. I'll have to check. Scott and Tim and I are supposed to be having a story meeting on the comic after school. We have to get everything decided soon so that we can get the artwork and the dialog done in time for next Monday's issue."

Scott paused in the middle of his diatribe about personal lubricants and looked over at my notebook.

"Who are you messaging?" he asked.

"Oh, just a girl," I said, trying to sound nonchalant.

Both of them looked at me in astonishment. My social stock with my peer group had just shot up twenty points.

"You're messaging a *girl*?" said Scott.

"Who is she?" asked Tim.

"Oh, you know her," I said, playing it cool. "Summer. The girl who beat us at Slip Stream yesterday."

"Wow!" exclaimed Tim. "She's like a giga-babe! Let me see what she's saying."

I pushed my notebook forward a bit so that my buds could cluster around it. Summer's response had just come back.

"Cool? Can I sit in? I want to meet the brains behind this sick little rag."

"Hey!" Scott complained. "You told her about the comic!"

I gave him a sour look. "Like, who's she gonna tell? I mean, she doesn't even go to this school."

He looked uncertain, so I gave him the bait. "And she did say that she liked your artwork."

"She did?"

I knew I had them both hooked now. But I couldn't resist giving them one more tease.

"Yeah, but there's even more."

"What?" said Tim, leaning in close.

"She's a *witch*."

I swear that Tim and Scott's eyes both went about three inches wide. Faking homosexuality was quite a coup on the bad kid ladder of success. But it was nothing compared to dating a witch.

Tim took my notebook and started dictating.

"Hey Summer, it's Tim. Can we use you as a model for one of the alien harem girls?"

I grabbed my notebook back from Tim and repressed my urge to smack him over the head with it. I was about to send a message apologizing for him when the answer came back from Summer.

"Sure. But only if you get my breasts right. I'm not going to have my character walking around with those basketballs that you've been drawing on everybody else stuck to her chest."

Tim and Scott read the message, then looked at each other in disbelief. Not only was I dating a girl, I was dating a *bad* girl. My cool stock had suddenly eclipsed theirs.

I was trying to think up a suave reply when the next message came in.

"So? Can I come to the story meeting, or what?"

I looked at Scott and Tim, but there was no real need for a hand vote. I wrote her that she was more than welcome. We messaged back and forth a few more times, and it was agreed that we would meet her at the North Finch MARTA Station, near Scott's house, after school.

I passed the rest of the day in a fit of restless excitement. I broke two test tubes in chemistry. I wound up at loggerheads with the computer in my math lab a record-breaking eight times. And PE was the usual exercise in humiliation.

Finally, the school day came to an end. I caught up with Scott and Tim at my locker, and the three of us walked the five blocks to the Fairfield MARTA stop, where we hopped an eastbound train to the mainline, and then a southbound train to the North Finch station. Once there, we set up surveillance from a position on the upper platform, from which we had a view of both the escalators and the exits.

It was about three-thirty in the afternoon, when all the other kids were trying to get home from school, so there were lots of people pushing past us. I was looking around for Summer, in case she'd gotten there before us, when I noticed this old lady in a funny hat working her way through the crowd. She was carrying a couple big wire mobiles, and everybody was trying to get out of her way as she shuffled along. I took a couple of steps backward as she passed by, not wanting to get poked in the eye with one of those things.

At least, that was the plan. Unfortunately, as I stepped back, she made a right hand turn and smacked me in the back of the head with one of the sculptures. I mean, OK, it wasn't very heavy, it didn't hurt, no harm done. At least, not until she turned around to try and apologize. Which is when we discovered that the wires had gotten tangled in my hair.

Anyway, she practically pulls me off my feet. Then I'm grabbing the back of my head, and she's apologizing even louder, and we're both trying to get the darn thing loose from my hair. (Tim and Scott are laughing too hard to be of any help whatsoever.) About now I'm expecting to see Summer come trotting up the escalator to see me being eaten by some carnivorous piece of wire sculpture. That's just the way my luck runs.

But she doesn't come trotting up. The old lady and I finally manage to get me loose from the thing without ripping too much of my hair out by the roots. And she's saying she's sorry, and offering to buy me a candy bar by way of an apology. But I explain that I'm not supposed to take candy from strangers, and besides, it's not her fault anyway. Nope. Just another part of my job to keep God amused. If only he weren't so bent on physical comedy.

Anyway, the old lady eventually went off to catch the train, and I pulled out a comb and did my best to fix the damage. Which, of course, produced another bout of giggles from Scott and Tim. I was about to warn them to be on their best behavior when Summer suddenly turned up.

"Hey boys, been waiting long?"

Scott and Tim reintroduced themselves, and she shook hands with them. Then she turned to me. I was kind of hoping that she might kiss me in front of them, but she didn't. Not that I could have handled the sudden rise to fame that such an event would have entailed in my social circle, anyway.

We all left the station and walked the three blocks to Scott's house. His mom works late, so we have the run of the place till 8 or so. Well, they would have the run of the place. I would still have to be home by 7 to beat my parents.

In the kitchen, we all grabbed cokes and a bag of those eggplant chips that Scott and Tim really like and that I think are gross. Then we all sat down on the living room floor to start work.

Well, that was supposed to be the idea. We all got out our notebooks, but then Tim and Scott suddenly clammed up and wouldn't say anything. They just sat there, looking at Summer. Not that I can blame them.

"Uh. You guys want to tell me what you're working on?" she asked.

Since Tim and Scott had clearly disengaged their brains, that left it to me to get the meeting started. So I told Summer all about how Jade was going to be kidnapped by space slavers in this issue, and the romantic subplot with Zero, and the whole plan for the slave girl rebellion. She started asking questions about it, and even had a couple good ideas on how to improve it, like how the slavers were going to lure Jade away from planet G-7 with a phony distress call. As it became clear that she really was interested in the comic, Scott and Tim started chiming in with their ideas. Before long, the meeting was really rolling, with everybody throwing things out faster than we could write them down.

Then we hit the alien slave girls. Scott had called up his proposed sketches, and then Summer started drawing some changes on them, and then they were both riffing off each other's ideas. Tim and I watched, and lobbed in a suggestion every so often, but it was pretty clear that the two of them were off on some creative roll, and all we could do was watch.

Anyway, Summer and Scott went off on their mad sketch-a-thon for about twenty minutes until they hit the breast problem. Scott had called up the eight-breasted cat woman, and Summer was giving him the same lecture she'd given me the day before, on the proper size, shape, and consistency of female breasts. But Scott wasn't buying it. Apparently, big breasts are like a religion with him. He's arguing that women in outer space would develop bigger breasts because of the free-fall, and there is no way he's going to downgrade the cat woman from a double-D to a C cup. And Summer is trying to point out that even if they were that big, there was no way that they would point that way when she does a flying side-kick like she was in the drawing. Then Rick jumps in with some comment about how cat breasts might be naturally perkier than human breasts. Then finally Summer just says "Men," and pulls her t-shirt off over her head and tosses it to me.

"Hold that, will you Benji?" she says, as she undoes a hook on the front of her bra and takes it off.

Then she stands up and puts her arms up in some sort of kung-fu block, and starts moving around the floor like a boxer.

"See, even when I punch," she said, striking the air, "my breasts don't move like that."

Then she hit some of the poses that Scott had drawn the cat woman in. "See. I know I've only got two, but even with eight there's no way they could be doing *that!*"

Finally, Scott managed to recover his wits enough to start sketching some of what she was doing. Tim and I just sat back and enjoyed the show. Heck, if I'd known art lessons were this much fun I would have taken up drawing years ago.

Then Summer leapt up and did this really impressive spinning crescent kick.

"Wow," I said. "Where did you learn all this karate stuff?"

"Oh. My mom made me take it. She's kind of big on self-defense. She says she's not going to let me date until I earn my blue belt."

Summer did a couple more kicks. Then she showed us some arm blocks. Then some strikes. Then Scott's mother walked into the room.

I know that as a writer, I'm supposed to be good at finding the right word. But I'm still not sure how to describe the sound that Scott's mom made when she walked into the room and saw Summer doing topless karate strikes. Something between a gurgle and a screech, I think. Summer turned around to see what could be making such a noise.

"Oh, hi!" said Summer, offering her hand to shake, "You must be Scott's Mother."

Mrs. Breckin made a few more gurgling sounds and then managed to articulate a few words. "You...You're naked."

Summer glanced down at her breasts. "Oh, yeah. But don't worry. It's for art's sake."

Mrs. Breckin glared at Scott, who looked like he wanted to crawl under the rug. I just hoped he would leave some room for me. His mom's face turned a deep maroon. She stepped over to me and grabbed Summer's shirt out of my hands.

"Cover yourself!" she barked, shoving the shirt at Summer.

"Sure," Summer said, still perfectly calm. She stuck an arm through to pull the thing back right-side-out. "But you can relax, Mrs. Breckin. It's not like anything was going on. We were just drawing. See your son has some very odd ideas about breasts, and..." The rest of her sentence was mumbled from inside the shirt as she pulled it over her head.

"And you just stripped down and showed him?!"

"Well, yeah," said Summer, her head emerging from the other end of the shirt. "Why not? Boys take their shirts off in public all the time. What's the difference?"

"The difference is..." Mrs. Breckin stammered, turning even redder. "The difference is that you are a *girl*!"

"Yeah, that was sort of the point," Summer responded.

By now Scott's mother was reaching the "because I said so" point. You know, that moment in every argument when the adults stop pretending that what they're saying makes any sense at all and fall back on being older. Scott's mom screamed a couple more things, and Summer answered her calmly and politely while Tim and I looked for some way to get out of the room without actually having to walk between the two of them. I was seriously entertaining the idea of breaking a window and escaping that way.

Anyway, the debate went on while we waffled: Scott's mom shrieking and Summer trying to calm her down. I had to hand it to Summer. No matter how crazy Mrs. Breckin got, Summer kept her cool. Of course, it's a lot easier to keep your cool when the crazy parent you're arguing with doesn't know your mom's phone number.

I'm not sure how long this all went on, but at some point Mrs. Breckin called Summer a Godless heathen, which did seem to get under Summer's skin a bit. Summer shot back that the term was Goddess, not God*less,* and she preferred the word Pagan, thank you very much. Then things started getting really interesting. They started circling each other like boxers, and I was beginning to wonder if Summer really did have some heap bad ju-ju that she could call in to solve the problem. Some spell to turn Mrs. Breckin into a frog would have been really handy about now. Not that I actually believed in all that stuff. But it sure would have been convenient.

The whole scene eventually ended with Scott's mom screaming "GET OUT OF MY HOUSE!" and Summer saying something catty about "Gee, I guess that means I'm not invited for dinner," and storming off down the hall and out of the house. As the front door slammed, I realized that I was still holding her bra. I hurriedly stuffed it behind the sofa, then tried to slip past Mrs. Breckin. But she caught me by the ear.

"Oh, no," she said. "You're not going anywhere. That goes for you too, Tim. The two of you can just sit here and think about what you've done while I call your mothers."

The next 45 minutes were the worst of my life. Well, my life so far. No telling what tomorrow has in store. Mrs. Breckin called my mom at work and told her what had happened in pretty graphic terms. Hell holds no horror for me after what I went through waiting for my mom to come and get me.

The doorbell rang, and there were footsteps in the hall. My heart leapt at the sight of Tim's mom. At least it wasn't mine. I could tell by the expression on Mrs. Tyler's face what Tim was in for. They left, and my relief quickly faded as it sank in that my own doom had only been postponed for a few minutes.

My mom finally got there ten minutes later. Her expression was like ice. She apologized to Mrs. Breckin for my behavior, then grabbed me by the arm and dragged me out to the car. She started the engine and drove for five minutes without saying anything, without even looking at me.

If I'd been smart, I would have done the same. Just shut up and kept my head down till the worst of it blew over. Unfortunately, this was one of life's little lessons that I had not mastered yet.

"Uh...Mom? You know, it's really not as bad as Scott's mom made it sound."

That opened up the floodgates. There was a squeal of tires as she made an abrupt right hand turn into an Arby's parking lot. She pulled into a space at a crooked angle and killed the engine.

"Not as bad as it *sounds*? It *sounds* like you were dancing around naked with a witch! Just which part isn't as bad as it sounds?"

By now, I knew that I'd made a mistake. But it was too late to reverse course.

"No. Well, not exactly. I mean, I wasn't naked. And nobody was dancing. See, she was just posing for Scott, so that he could draw..."

"JUST HOW FRIGGING STUPID ARE YOU?!" Mom screamed at the top of her lungs. It scared me, and in the confined space of the car it hurt my ears. I shrunk back against the door.

"You know what THEY do!" she shouted, at a slightly lower volume. "You've been warned enough times. Jesus, don't you pay attention? This is how they work. They lure boys like you away with sex and then they sacrifice you. Or even worse, they drag you into their worship of Satan. Is that what you want? To wind up dead, or a pawn of Satan? Are you really stupid enough to sell your immortal soul just for some cheap sex with some teenage whore?!"

"Jesus Mom, you're really blowing this thing out of..."

"DON'T YOU TAKE THE LORD'S NAME IN VAIN!"

"But Mom, you just..."

"Has she got you hooked on drugs?"

"What? No Mom. If we could just..."

"'Cause they do that, you know. Get you hooked on drugs and bound to Satan..."

"...try to calm down a little."

"...How could you! Your father and I..."

"...It's really not what you..."

"...raised you better than..."

"...think it is. She's just this..."

"...this. After all we've done for you..."

"...girl who came over to help Scott with..."

"...and this is how you repay us! What is it..."

"...his drawings. And yeah, things got a little..."

"...with you? We send you to a good school..."

"...out of hand, but nobody was having sex!"

"...But you get lousy grades. You won't..."

"...I mean, she wasn't even really naked..."

"...play any sports no matter how many times I..."

"...she had her pants on.  And we were..."

"...ask you to try out for the teams at school..."

"...practically on the other side of the room..."

"...And now you get mixed up with some whore..."

"...from us.  So nothing was going on! Are you..."

"...of Satan. I swear, Benji, your father and I..."

"...listening mom?  Nothing was going on, it's..."

"...adopted you, we've fed you, we've clothed..."

"...not..."

"...you.  And what do we get in..."

"..."

"...return?  We deserve better..."

"..."

"...than..."

"..."

"..."

"...adopted?" I asked.

I felt like someone had hit me in the solar plexus.  My gut hurt, and my eyes started watering up.

I turned away from her, opened the door,  and started running. Behind me, I heard the crazy woman yelling after me, telling me to come back.  But I didn't have to listen to her.

Not anymore.

## Chapter 22: The Singer
## Tuesday the 10th, 12:00 PM

I was sitting on Linda's bed, picking random notes on my guitar. She was at her make-up table, putting on her face, getting ready for battle. I started fingering chords.

"Will you knock it off!" she said as she put on her lipstick. It was the dark red color, the one that she uses for contract negotiations. "If you're going to play something, play it. But don't just pick at the strings."

I stopped with the strings. But a few seconds later my hand started thumping on the side, working out a rhythm. Hey, I have to do something when I'm nervous. Linda glared at me in the mirror.

I stopped with the thumping.

"I just hate waiting around and worrying while other people take all the chances," I explained.

Linda finished with her lipstick and blotted on a piece of tissue.

"Hmph. If you're going to worry about someone, worry about those poor little lambs in the Christian Militia." She took a leather sheath out of her desk and strapped it to her inner thigh, where it would be covered by the skirt of her business outfit. Then she got out a plastic knife and slipped it into the sheath. "If things turn ugly, *they* are going to be the ones on the receiving end of the makeover. I am not somebody they want to mess with, and I get the impression that Parker can take care of himself."

She straightened up and looked at herself in the mirror. There was no sign of the hidden weapon. A security guard would have to buy her dinner and a movie before he would find that knife.

I strummed a few more notes before she glared at me again.

"So what do you think of Drew?" I asked.

"Parker? He seems to be reasonably good at what he does. It was probably smart to bring him on board. Why?"

"Nothin'," I responded casually. "He just seems kinda interestin'."

Linda turned to look at me. She'd noticed that I'd slipped into the drawl again.

"Why?" she asked.

"Why what?" I said, plucking a couple more notes and giving her the innocent smile. Usually, it puts people at ease and throws them off the scent, but Linda has been around me long enough to build up a resistance to it.

She raised an eyebrow. "Why do you keep bringing Parker up? And why do you get nervous every time you do it?"

I switched to the clueless smile and shrugged, then went back to strumming my guitar. She let it drop. For now. But I know her; she never let anything drop forever.

"So you're pretty sure Jen is there, right?"

Linda was slipping on a pair of black shoes. "I think it's worth a look," she said. "Parker's right. It would be the best place for Stonewall to try stashing her."

I plucked a few more notes. She looked over at me, exasperated.

"Sorry," I said, and stopped again. She was putting on a pair of subdued black earrings to go with her black business suit. "But you know what's bothering me?"

"No. But I can guess that it's not the same person who is bothering me."

"It's Stonewall. Do you remember how he was behaving on Sunday night?"

Linda added a gold cross on a chain to her outfit. It hung strategically between her breasts, causing even a casual observer to start speculating on what might lie beneath her suit.

"You mean screaming and turning purple?"

"Yeah, exactly. Like we'd really surprised him."

"Well, that was the plan, Justin. Take him down on his own show when he didn't expect it."

"Yeah, but if he had Jen, shouldn't he have seen it coming? I mean, he would have known that I was up to something. And he would have acted different, too. Sort of smug, 'cause he had an ace in the hole. You think he could have been faking all that rage?"

"I don't know," she said, making the final adjustments to her outfit. "I'm not sure what goes on in that man's head."

"No," I agreed. "But I sure wish I did."

She was ready to go, so I got up and walked her to the garage. She promised to call as soon as she and Drew had taken a look through the Militia's headquarters. She kissed me goodbye as she climbed into the car, and I waved as she drove off. Then I went inside to wash the lipstick off my cheek.

I gave her a fifteen minute headstart—during which time I made myself a quick peanut butter sandwich—then grabbed my own car and started the drive into Atlanta, to the Liberty Media Tower.

It's about a forty-five minute drive, but I've got a blue Aries convertible that's just a hoot to drive, so I don't mind. I took down the top and put some music on. But I found myself thinking about Parker again. He reminded me of this character in a western I'd seen when I was a kid, this grizzled old gunfighter who'd lost everything, but who still lived by the code. Not because he believed in it, not because he had any faith left, but just because it was the only thing left that was his. His code. I couldn't help but be curious about Parker, how he'd gotten that way.

I got to Freedom Plaza and pulled into a parking garage across from the tower. I checked my hair in the rear-view mirror, made a few adjustments. I brushed a curl down, so that it fell in front of my forehead. That looked a little too calculated, so I shook my head and brushed a few stray strands down to join it, then checked the mirror again. Yeah, that was more like it. Kind of accidentally cute, like a lost puppy. God gave David a sling, and Samson strength. I figure I'd better use what he gave me.

I got out of the car and walked across the plaza to the big front doors of the Liberty Media Tower. As I stepped into its shadow, I almost lost my nerve. What was I doing here, walking right into the hands of someone who probably wanted me dead?

Then I reminded myself that I was here because Zachary was leading this country into war. I was here because sooner or later he would have Christians out killing people in the name of God. And I was here because somebody had to find out just how much he knew about our plans, and what he was up to now.

There's a story in the Bible, about Daniel walking into a lion's den, armed only with his faith. In the story, Daniel walks out unharmed. I don't know that I have Daniel's faith, but I was willing to bet that Zachary wouldn't have me shot in his own lobby.

A guard was at the front door, checking people's ID badges. He stopped me, but I smiled at him and all of a sudden he realized who I was.

"Hey, you're Justin Weir!"

"Uh...yeah," I said, blushing a little and going into the "aww shucks" routine.

"You know, my daughter is crazy about you."

The guy had a big smile and was making a lot of eye contact. I got the feeling that nobody ever paid any attention to him.

"Really? What's your daughter's name?"

"Elizabeth. She'll be thrilled when she finds out I met you."

"Well, tell Elizabeth I said hi."

He was still smiling at me, a little starstruck.

"Uh, I've got an appointment with Reverend Stonewall."

The guard looked down at his monitor.

"That's funny, you're not on the guest list."

"Oh. Well, could you call him up or something? I'm supposed to be having a meeting with him in ten minutes. I'm running kind of late."

"Ah, don't sweat it," the guard said. "I guess I can trust you. I'll just sign you in."

He tapped a few keys, then handed me a guest badge.

"This one has an access code on it, so the elevator will take you all the way to the top. Just make sure you wear it where the camera can see it."

"I'll do that. Thanks a lot..." I read the name off his badge, "...Mr. Carter."

"Ah, you can call me Stephen."

"OK. Well, thanks, Stephe."

We shook hands, then I walked across the lobby to the elevator bank. I caught a ride up to the 51st floor and got off outside Zachary's office. I snuck up to the door and stole a peek inside to see what was up. Luck was with me. I knew the secretary who was on duty.

She was on the phone, but she looked up and waved when I came in. I just sauntered up and sat on a corner of her desk.

"No, Governor, but there is an opening on his schedule for the sixteenth."

She looked up and brushed the hair out of my face.

"All right, then. I'll pencil it into his schedule. Yes...Of course... Good day, Governor Vasquez."

She ended the call and swung down the microphone on her headset.

"Justin! What are you doing here?"

I sort of shrugged and threw in that expression of remorse that always got me out of trouble with my parents.

"Hey Berta. Good to see you. I just got tired of feudin' with Zachary, and I figure one of us needs to be big enough to make the first move. So here I am."

She looked at me like I was out of my mind.

"Justin, I don't think he's gonna want to see you."

"Well," I said, looking down at my feet and doing the guilty kid act, "I gotta do somethin'. What's his mood like?"

She rolled her eyes back. "Justin, the boss doesn't have moods. Cattle have moods. Actors have moods. The boss has weather patterns. And where you're concerned, we're looking at something between a tornado and a class five hurricane."

"Oh." I said, and gave her the wounded puppy expression. She looked at it for almost five seconds before she cracked.

"All right. I'll see what I can do. But I'm not making any promises."

She swung the mic back up and put in a call to her boss.

"Reverend Stonewall, you have an unexpected visitor...Of course sir, but in this case I thought you might want to know who it is...Justin Weir."

There was a burst of sound from the other end that even I could hear. Berta reached up with both hands and pulled the earphones away from her head to spare her ears. She looked at me and mouthed the words "told you."

After about thirty seconds, the volume died down and she put her headset back on.

"No sir, he doesn't have a lawyer with him."

On a pad in front of her, she wrote the words "DO YOU?" I shook my head no.

"Actually sir, I think he wants to apologize."

There was a long pause, and she looked at me and shrugged. Finally he said something, and she responded.

"Yes sir. Of course sir."

She swung the microphone back down.

"Well?" I asked.

"Well, you must be living right. The boss says you can take a seat. He'll try to work you into his schedule."

"Thanks, Berta. You're a lifesaver." I said, and kissed her on the forehead. It's a little corny, but with my persona I can get away with it.

She actually blushed. "You're lucky I'm a married woman, Mr. Weir."

"Now, why would that make me *lucky*, Berta?"

She slapped me on the back as I hopped off her desk. "Take a seat, you rascal, and I'll let you know when the Reverend can see you."

I grabbed a chair in the waiting area in front of her desk and waited. Five minutes went by. Then ten. I picked up one of the reading screens off the table and tapped through the latest copy of *Revelations* Magazine. An article detailing Biblical principles for investing in the stock market. A story tracing the satanic roots of the Psychic Phone Counselors Network. And a feature analyzing verses in Revelations to prove that the Anti-Christ will arise from Brazil. Apparently Zachary was still against the trade deal with the South American trading block.

I finished reading the magazine and glanced at my watch. I'd been here for an hour. I should have expected this. Zach was going to make me do penance in his waiting room before he'd see me.

I picked the reading screen back up and looked over the list of available publications. They had a Christian Music trade publication, so I called that up and read through it. They managed to do a whole spread on the Christian Music Awards without once mentioning me or the fact that I'd won best male vocalist. Zachary hadn't been kidding about the media black out.

I finished the trade magazine, which took me another hour, and then I took a stab at *Christian Science*. It was a little over my head, but I struggled through the simpler parts. Finally, a little after four, Berta said Zach would see me. She gave me a thumbs up signal on my way in. I smiled back as I took a deep breath and got ready for this. Then I screwed on my "little kid who knows he's in trouble" face, and walked into the presence of the Reverend Senator Zachariah T. Stonewall.

He was sitting behind that big wooden desk he has. Some sort of antique, I think it used to belong to Ronald Reagan or something. Behind it, there are glass walls on two sides, looking out over the skyline of Atlanta's convention district. I noticed that there was no chair out for me. He was going to play this the hard way.

I waited for him to say something, but he didn't. Figures. He was going to make me do all the work.

I dropped my head a couple more degrees. "Reverend."

He gave the slightest nod to indicate that he was aware of my presence.

"Look, I know I screwed up…" I said, then put in a long pause, to indicate how painful the statement was. I looked down at my feet and shifted from one foot to the other. Zach still didn't say anything. He was enjoying watching me twist. "…and I guess I just wasn't thinking."

I lifted my eyes so I could watch his face. I'd been hoping that I could figure out something, just by gauging his mood when I first came in. Was he gloating 'cause he thought he had me? Or was he scared 'cause he thought I had something on him? I looked over his face, but he wasn't giving me anything to work with.

So, I went in to plan B, and laid it on thick. I talked about how much the movement meant to me, and how important his approval was to me, how I never wanted to do anything to disappoint him, yadda-yadda-yadda. I even let myself start crying after awhile. By the end of the production, I had Zachary convinced that he was practically a father figure to me. And let's face it, nobody can stay mad at me for long.

He softened up a little, and had Berta bring in a chair for me so I could sit down. Then we started discussing the nature of my sins against him. I played dumb (which, like I've said before, is not a big stretch for me) so that I could get him to define my crimes. And he did. He went on at great length, talking about the song I'd done on last Sunday's show, how it could lead people to think that there might be ways other than accepting Jesus Christ that could lead them to heaven, and how I was damning such people to Hell as a consequence. I took it all sorrowfully, looking hang dog. Waiting for him to move on and talk about the sin of sending a PI to dig into his dirty laundry.

He never did. After about twenty minutes of chewing me out for the song, he said that he realized that it was an honest mistake, but that I had to realize what a dangerous mistake it was. That if I would apologize, he would welcome me back into the flock.

I was momentarily confused, trying to decide if he really didn't know about Jen, or if he was just playing his cards really close to his vest. Zachary is a slippery one. But if he was holding back on me, he was doing one heck of an acting job.

He ended the meeting by saying that we should do lunch next week, and then dismissed me. I turned to go, still trying to figure out what was going on…and that's when I saw it. The painting he had mounted on the wall across from his desk. All the times I'd been in his office, and I'd never really paid it any attention.

A man, standing near the top of a mountain, with one shoulder in a beam of light, fighting off a hoard of demons trying to pull him down. And suddenly I realized who the guy in the picture was. I turned back to look at Zachary. The face in the painting was a good fifteen, maybe twenty years younger, but it was him.

He had already taken his attention off me, turning to read something on his desk.

"What an interesting painting," I said. "Is it a portrait of you?"

This time, there was no mistaking the reaction. Zachary tensed up and looked up at me. And for an instant, a shadow of fear passed over his face. He regained control almost instantly, but I was sure of what I'd seen. I apologized for disturbing him, and then turned to go again. I stopped to say goodbye to Berta on my way out, and then headed for the elevator.

Hm. A painting that was in Jen's files, that she was making inquiries about before she disappeared. A painting that Zachary keeps on his wall, and yet scares him to death. There was something dangerous about that picture. And I was going to have to find out what it was.

## Chapter 23: The Gumshoe
## Tuesday the 10th, 12:10 PM

I hit the interstate, put the car on cruise, and let the miles between me and my appointment in Marietta roll by. I should have been thinking about the case, about my partner, my client, and how I was going to get us all out of this mess. But instead I was thinking about Daniel. How cute he'd looked when I left him this morning, all curled up and sleeping in the sunshine. My subconscious was working overtime, trying to manufacture some daydream about the two of us together. But every time it came up with a scenario, my practical side shot it down. I know Daniel too well. I know how short his attention span is, and I've never kidded myself about what I am to him. Oh, we probably had a couple more weeks of hanging out together, but eventually he would get bored and move on to chasing someone else. It wasn't that he was bad or shallow. It was just that he was 22.

There's a poem that I read once about a situation like this. I can't remember the words exactly. But it was something about hard-won knowledge of the true nature of love, and half-regrets at leaving behind the illusion. And how sometimes the wise envy the foolish. Something like that.

My subconscious continued to spit up new images of Daniel and I together. Daniel and I with a white picket fence and puppies. Daniel and I in Casablanca. Daniel and I in an airlock on Mars. Probably my libido's way of telling me that I'd been single for too long. My last date had been…good grief, a whole year ago. A lawyer I did some work for. We went out once after the case was over. I thought we hit it off; he suddenly became busy for the next few weeks. Well maybe it was time I went out on a date again, if only to remind myself why I don't do it more often. Maybe Joe-or-Jim-or-John would like to grab a pizza.

I hit Marietta and took the wheel back. I got off the interstate at the Main street exit, then cruised west toward Cavalry. Coming up on the intersection, I saw the service station that Linda had told me about. Her black Transcendental was parked around the side.

I drove past the station without slowing down. At the next intersection, I made a turn and circled the block a couple of times to see if anyone was following me. Once I was sure I didn't have a tail, I drove down the street to a strip mall and left my car in front of a Christian Diet Center. "EXPERIENCE THE MIRACLE OF

WEIGHT LOSS TODAY!" I popped open the trunk and got out a couple of smoke bombs and then walked the half-block back to the service station.

Linda was waiting outside her car. I went into the station and bought a coke, then walked outside and stood by a charger where she could see me. She looked around carefully, then gave me a little nod. I climbed in the passenger side and we were off.

"So how you feeling, Drew?" she asked as we pulled back onto Main. "Good day to storm a castle?"

"I don't know. Guess it depends on whether or not these guys are heating a cauldron of oil for us."

"You worry too much, Drew. By the way, reach around behind you. There's a briefcase and a change of clothes on the back seat."

I unbuckled myself and got the things she was referring to. It was a dark business suit with a white shirt, blue tie, and dress Nikes. The briefcase was an expensive leather number with brass bindings.

"Nice," I said, taking off my shirt. "So what's my story?"

"You're my personal secretary. Mostly you're there to take notes and make me look important. I'll turn to you a couple of times and ask questions about my schedule or Justin's. The answers are already programmed into the notebook in the briefcase, so just read them off in order. The notebook is also loaded with the floorplans and architectural records on the compound, plus a few extra goodies I was able to squeeze out of someone who used to work there."

I had gotten the white dress shirt on, and was struggling my way out of my jeans. Linda glanced down.

"Bugs Bunny boxers? I would have pegged you as a Calvin Klein man."

I had borrowed a clean set of underwear from Daniel's closet before I left this morning, but I didn't feel like explaining that. Linda was still staring down at the picture of Bugs Bunny doing a muscle man pose.

"Get your eyes back on the road," I said, pulling on the dress pants. She complied, but she had an evil smile on her face.

"Besides," I said, "I thought you and Justin were an item." I watched her reaction carefully, but she was too careful to let anything slip.

"Tsk tsk, Drew. I know what you're really asking. And you know I'm not gonna tell you. So quit fishing."

I shrugged as I tied my tie. I dug out my fiber optic snake, my Swiss army knife, my taser, my lock picks, and my lucky dollar out of my jacket and transferred them to the suit pockets. Then I opened up the briefcase, put the smoke bombs in it, and took out the notebook. I called up the building plans and looked them over. Then I thought about what sort of room I would put a prisoner in, if I owned this building.

"So, what do you think?" Linda asked.

"I think we may actually have a chance," I said. "It looks to me like there are only a few places they might try to keep Jen."

"How do you work that out?"

"Well, they're going to want to put her someplace out of the way. No matter how loyal his people are, Stonewall's not going to want every janitor and secretary who walks into the building to know that he's holding a prisoner. And if he stores her too close to the employees, Jen might be able to make some noise and let someone know that she's there."

"OK. So where does that leave?"

"Probably either the upper or lower stories. On the top floor there are a couple of conference rooms. According to the schematics, they're soundproofed and protected from eavesdropping, so they might try putting her there."

"But you don't sound like you believe it."

"Not really. It's too close to the offices of their Chiefs of Staff. They might want to hold her close, but I think they'd be more likely to put her at the far end of the building, so if someone turned up with a warrant she could be quietly disposed of without implicating them."

"So you're thinking the basement?"

"Yeah. There are a lot of small rooms down there with concrete walls that they could lock someone up in. According to your friend who worked there, most of the basement is used for storage: emergency rations, ammo, water barrels. Stuff to have on hand when the country falls apart, I guess. Anyway, there probably aren't a lot of people who go down there. If I were them, I'd use one of these." I highlighted five rooms on the map of the basement. "They're not too close to an elevator or stairwell, and according to the schematics, there are no exposed pipes."

Linda took her eyes off the road to glance at the map.

"Why are pipes important?"

"Because they conduct sound. If there's a pipe in the room, Jen might be able to crawl to it and start tapping on it. The pipe would carry the sound to other places in the building, and someone might hear it. I'm betting these guys are smart enough to think of that."

"OK," Linda said. "So how do you want to play this?"

I outlined what I had in mind. Linda listened, then put forward a few contingencies I hadn't thought of yet. I refined my idea, and she refined my refinements, and before long we'd arrived at a plan of action. Which was good, because we were also arriving at our destination.

I stuffed my old clothes under the seat as we pulled up to the gate. The perimeter fence boasted warning signs about being electrified, but I had a feeling that they were bluffing about that. I couldn't sense that low hum you usually hear around an electric fence. Plus, they would be forever having trouble with dogs pissing on it and getting electrocuted. More likely, they had the ability to charge the fence if they were expecting trouble, but didn't keep it on all the time. At least, I hoped that was the case.

At the gate, a couple of guards asked our business, checked Linda's name against a guest list, and finally waved us through to the main compound. I pegged them as weekend warriors, probably doing volunteer work for a merit badge or something. They were taking the job way too seriously, and seemed to be getting a real kick out of walking around with guns.

We drove through the militia's campus toward the main building. It was an interesting setup. Obstacle courses. A shooting range. A big artificial cliff for rock climbing. We passed one field full of old junked cars, where a couple squads were having a paint gun duel. Down the road, another squad was learning marching drills, and still another was learning how to put on camouflage makeup. It reminded me of boyscout camp. Well, boyscout camp with a lot of automatic weapons.

The militia's headquarters was a big glass parallelogram. Sort of like someone had built a rectangular building, then nudged it so that it leaned a little in one direction. We parked and walked up the front steps to the main door, where another guard checked Linda's name against the guest list. I noticed that he only checked for her name. As an assistant, I didn't rate my own invitation. Which was good.

The guard made a call, and a couple minutes later a secretary came down and welcomed us, saying how nice it was that Mr. Weir had finally taken an interest in the militia. She led us back to the main elevator bank, then up to the fourth floor and the vice-president's office.

It was a big office, with lots of open space to emphasize its bigness. One wall was all glass, with a view looking out over the campus. In the distance, I could see a squad running laps, carrying their rifles above their heads. Another wall was adorned by a picture of the Vice-President shaking hands with Senator Stonewall. And for the wall behind his desk, our host had selected a framed poster of the Ten Commandments.

The secretary who showed us in introduced her boss as "Lieutenant Colonel Stevens, Vice-President in charge of Fund Raising." He was wearing a dark blue dress uniform with a prominent white cross on the left breast with the motto "One Nation Under

God" stitched above it. He seemed kind of young to be the vice president of anything, maybe mid-thirties. Clean-cut, brown hair. A bit stuffy, but he seemed happy to meet Linda.

"Ah, Miss Jordan. A pleasure to finally meet you face to face."

They shook hands, he offered her a chair, then they started talking business. What sort of benefit concert Justin could do for them, when there were openings in his schedule, what would and would not be acceptable locations and terms. I stood behind Linda's chair, answering questions from the notebook when prompted, and trying to look like I was making notes. Not that anybody was really watching my performance. The Colonel was leaning across his desk, hanging on Linda's every word. But who could blame him? Linda was wearing a subtly seductive business dress, one that hinted at all her curves without actually showing any of them. And she was sending all the right subliminal signals. Leaning forward when he talked, staring right into his eyes, smiling in the middle of a sentence for no reason at all. And of course, it didn't hurt that she was talking about a deal that would net this guy's organization a few hundred million, and probably win him a nice bonus. Poor guy. She was teasing with both sex and money. He never stood a chance.

Thus, the Colonel did not particularly remark on it when I began to feel a bit queasy. Linda, however, did notice that I was not my usual efficient self, and asked if anything was the matter. I confessed that the sushi we had eaten for lunch was disagreeing with me. Being an understanding employer, she suggested that I step outside for some fresh air, maybe get an antacid and lie down in the car.

"After all," she said with a warm smile, "I do think the Colonel and I can get along without you for awhile."

I nodded, and backed out of the room slowly while they talked flirtatiously about broadcast rights and percentages of net.

Once out of his office, I caught his secretary and asked her for an Alka-Seltzer and directions to the men's room. She reached into a drawer and gave me the former, and then—as anyone who had seen a map of this place could predict—she pointed me down a hall that led past the two soundproofed conference rooms.

I walked down the hall slowly, coming up on the doors to the first conference room. I looked around. There was a guy coming toward me, wearing another one of those dress uniforms and dictating something into a headset. I nodded to him, but he walked past me without even looking up.

Once his back was to me I put a hand on the door to the first conference room and gave it an experimental twist. It was unlocked. I opened it and looked inside. Table, chairs. Some big monitors on the walls. No Jen, and no sign that they'd been hold-ing a prisoner there recently.

I closed the door and continued down the hall to the next one. Looked around again; there was no one coming. Turned the handle slowly. Once again it was unlocked. I opened it slowly.

And found myself staring at a conference table full of men and women in dress uniforms who were all looking back at me.

"Can I help you, son?" asked someone wearing a General's star.

"Uh…" Fortunately, I didn't have to fake the embarrassment "…I was looking for the men's room?"

The general let out a friendly laugh. "That's OK, son, it hap-pens all the time. Keep going on down to the end of the hall, and it's on your right."

"Thank you, sir," I said, looking around. There were six people in the room, but none of them was Jen. "Sorry to interrupt." I backed out sheepishly and closed the door.

Back in the hall I smiled to myself. She wasn't in the confer-ence rooms. I'd been right. They were keeping her as far away from the top brass as they could, in case something happened. She had to be in the basement.

I went into the men's room, splashed some water on my face, pulled out the notebook, and checked out the floor plans for this place again. My best bet for getting down to the basement unno-ticed was a stairwell at the back of the building. All right, I was getting close.

I went over to the air vent, unscrewed the cover with my Swiss army knife, and put the first smoke bomb inside. After I found Jen, I was going to need a distraction while I got her out. I put the cover back on, went back out to the hallway, and then down to the eleva-tor, making sure to wave to the nice secretary on my way out.

I got off the elevator on the second floor and walked toward the back of the building. There were several other people in the hall, but I looked like I knew where I was going, and no one stopped me. Along the way, I went into another restroom and put my second smoke bomb behind its ventilation grate. Then I continued on my way, and two turns and a couple doors later I was in the back stair-well. From there I made my way down to the basement.

Which is where things would start to get tricky. I had no good reason for being down there, and I couldn't very well claim to be looking for a restroom this time. I would have to be care-ful. I listened at the door to the basement, and didn't hear any voices, so I uncoiled a few feet of the snake and slipped the end under the door. The area on the other side looked to be storage, with no one in sight.

I opened the door. In front of me was a stack of crates labeled "MREs". Old army surplus food. I called up the map, and got my bearings. I had highlighted five rooms where they might be holding Jen. The nearest was in the northwest corner.

I made my way there quietly. A couple of times I heard someone else walking around, but with all the stuff stored down here there was plenty of cover for me to duck behind. I never saw whoever it was, but they never saw me, either. Probably good for both of us.

I got to the first room, and looked around. They hadn't posted a guard outside it, at any rate. I walked up and listened at the door. Nothing. I ran the snake underneath it. It was dark in there, but fortunately the snake can carry light in both directions. I turned on its little headlight, and then boosted the gain on the picture all the way up.

I found myself looking at a stack of ammunition crates. I ran the snake around behind them just to make sure Jen wasn't stashed in the back, but no luck. Well, one down, four to go.

The next two rooms proved to be dead-ends as well. The first wasn't even locked. It held a collection of those collapsible water barrels that they used to keep in fallout shelters. The second was stacked up with spare components for assault rifle computers.

On my way to the fourth room, I almost collided into a janitor. Fortunately, I heard the music playing on her headphones right before she came around a stack of crates, and I was able to step back into the shadows. Lucky for me she liked tunes with a lot of bass.

The fourth room was another disappointment. Stacks of helmets and body armor.

One chance left. I pulled out the notebook and looked over the location of the last room I'd highlighted. It was off in a corner, furthest away from the main entrance and the buildings through-traffic. Yeah, that made sense. Had I'd been thinking clearer, I would have started with that one. If I were in their shoes, that's where I would keep her. Of course, if I were in their shoes, I also wouldn't leave her unguarded. I got my taser out and started moving quietly to my target. I was about halfway there when a voice barked, "Can I help you, sir?"

My heart politely reminded me that I had been getting way too much fat in my diet of late, but declined to actually go into cardiac arrest just then. I turned around to see a kid in his early twenties, dressed up in those camo fatigues that all the guards around here wear, and carrying a flashlight. He had a pistol in a holster at his side, but he hadn't gotten it out yet.

I smiled, tried to look relaxed, and left it to my lightning-fast brain to come up with a plausible excuse for being down here.

"Uh......................................."

The guard walked up and shined the flashlight in my face.

"Do you have a reason for being down here?"

"Actually," I said, finally coming up with something, "I just came down here to collect my thoughts." The guard was looking me over skeptically. I went on, "You know, get a few minutes of quiet away from…"

I saw his eyes move down to the taser in my right hand.

## Chapter 24:  The Gumshoe
## Tuesday the 10th, 2:41PM

He glanced from the taser back up to my eyes.  Then he went for his gun.

Big mistake.  Apparently he hadn't gotten his merit badge in close combat yet.

I caught him with a left uppercut to the chin while he was still fumbling with the snap on his holster.  His head jerked up and he wobbled back a couple of steps.  I thought about finishing him with a shot from the taser,  but I figured his uniform might include some body armor that the dart wouldn't penetrate.  So I stepped in and tried to take him down with a blow to the solar plexus.  That didn't accomplish much besides bruising my knuckles and confirming my guess about the body armor.

The kid recovered his balance, but apparently hadn't learned his lesson.  He went for the gun again, and I went at his head again.  Same results as before, except this time while he was wobbling I put a foot behind him and pushed him over.  He landed on his back with a thud, but he was still moving.  So I put a knee on his chest to hold him still and fired the taser into the side of his neck.  That finally put him out.  It probably hurt like the dickens, but I didn't have time to play nice.

OK.  I recoiled the taser and set it to recharge while I thought about what to do next.  I was going to have to move fast.  My young friend here wasn't going to stay unconscious forever, and even if he did take a nice long nap, someone would eventually notice that he was missing.  I searched the kid's pockets and came up lucky—he was carrying a pair of handcuffs.

I picked him up in a fireman,s carry and hauled him over to an out-of-the-way corner behind some crates, and cuffed him to a pipe.  He was stirring a little now, but his nerves were still pretty thoroughly scrambled.  I took off his headset so he couldn't call in when he woke up.  I thought about breaking it, but that would probably turn up as a red light on someone's board, so I just tossed it up on top of a stack of crates where he couldn't get at it.  That would buy me a couple more minutes after he woke up, while he yelled for help and tried to get someone's attention.  If I played it just right, I might even be able to use his shouting to distract the guards they had on Jen.

I checked the taser; the ready light had come back on. Then I checked my map again, gave Sleeping Beauty a pat on the cheek, and took off for the last room at a jog. A careful, quiet jog.

I came up on the room cautiously from behind a stack of cardboard boxes. There was no one posted outside the door. Maybe I was finally getting a lucky break. I walked up to it and listened at the door for a full minute. Nothing. Which was good. Either no guards, or only one. Two or more and they would be talking or something. I got out the snake, and was just getting ready to slide it under the door when sleeping beauty woke up and started yelling for help.

I shoved the snake back in my pocked, stepped to the side of the door, and drew the taser. If my luck held, the guard in there would hear the shouting and come out to see what was going on. I gave him thirty seconds. Either the walls were too thick for him to hear, or he had orders not to leave his post. Dang. I gave him another ten seconds, then pounded on the door.

"Hey, we need some help out here!"

I stepped back to the side and waited for him to come out. Still nothing.

OK. That meant either one damn stubborn guard, or none at all, which would be even worse. They would only leave Jen alone if she was in no danger of going anywhere on her own. Drugged. Or worse.

The shouting stopped, which probably meant that somebody had found my sparring partner, and they were now phoning in a report. I had to do this quick. I checked the door. Hinges on my side. A standard thumbprint reader lock. If I had time, I might be able to bypass it without setting off the alarm. But time was running out. I would have to settle for distracting them.

I flipped on my throat mike and had Sherwin call the numbers that would detonate the two smoke bombs I'd planted upstairs. A few seconds later, the fire alarm went off. Hopefully that would keep them too busy to worry about one door being jimmied open down in their basement. I went to work on the lock. The plan was to grab Jen, carry her upstairs, blend in with the crowd pouring out the fire exits, and then hop in Linda's car and blow this clam bake before anybody realized what was going on. Simple. If the door would just cooperate.

It looked like such a simple little lock. The sort of thing I could get through in under thirty seconds. Yeah, right. This one took me almost two minutes. By the time I finally got through, I could hear the sounds of other people moving around in the basement. People in army boots. The reinforcements had arrived.

I readied my taser, stepped to the side, and pulled the door open. I could see the lights in the room come on, probably automatically. I risked a quick glance inside. When no one took a shot at me, I risked a longer look. Then I stepped inside.

Ice cream. Box upon box of freeze-dried ice cream. That was it. No guards. No secret cell for holding prisoners. No Jen.

I moved a couple of the boxes to make sure there wasn't a secret room behind them or anything. Nope. I opened up a box. Chocolate. It really was just freeze-dried ice cream.

Out in the basement I heard someone else opening up doors. They were looking for me. I had to get out of here now.

I pulled out the notebook and consulted the map for the fastest way out of the basement. There was one elevator, but it would have shut down as soon as the fire alarms went off. That left a staircase, about fifty yards to the east of me. I headed for it as quietly as I could.

I had to stop once, to let a couple guards go past me. Good thing they make so much noise, stomping around in those boots. Once they were out of sight, I pressed on.

OK, Jen wasn't here. I'd have to figure that out later. But if I could get up to the ground floor I could still blend in with the crowd and get out of this mishap scott free. If I could just get to the stairwell...

No dice. I stuck my head around the corner and saw a guard posted by the door to the stairs. Great. These people were more organized that I'd given them credit for. And unlike my last dance partner, this guard already had his gun out.

Great. I wasn't getting past him, even with the taser. I had one shot that wouldn't do me any good unless I hit him in the head or the hands, the only places not covered by body armor. He had a 15-round magazine that would blow holes in me no matter where he hit. Not much of a contest. I worked my way back down the hall and checked the map again. Maybe I'd get lucky with another staircase.

I never had a chance to find out. Working my my way south down the hall, I saw a guard checking doors, walking in my direction. No problem. I doubled back, crossed over to the east hallway, and tried it. Another guard, also coming my direction. I was getting a bad feeling about this.

I went back out to the open area, and scouted around carefully. A line of three guards working their way toward me, doing a sweep; looking up on top of crates, shining flashlights in among the boxes, poking their noses into any place a guy could hide. Great. Apparently boyscout camp included lessons on how to do a manhunt.

I turned north to keep ahead of them and checked the map again. They had me in a pickle. I was already cut off from two of the stairwells, and they had a guard posted on the third. I was running out of options. I could try to find a hiding place and hope the sweep passed by without finding me. I could make a suicide run at the guard watching the stairwell. Or I could just surrender and hope they had a sense of humor about the whole thing.

I decided to go with option one. I worked my way north, staying ahead of the sweep, looking for a hiding place good enough to fool them. I could hear the guards behind me, opening doors and moving boxes. It sounded like they were being pretty thorough. I considered prying open a crate and crawling inside, but then I'd have to do something with whatever was already in there. No good. I kept moving, looking for a place to hide. But I was still looking by the time I hit the north wall.

They were only thirty or forty yards behind me, and steadily getting closer. I couldn't keep moving away from them, so I worked my way laterally along the north wall, hoping I could find something to hide in. An air vent. A drainage grate. Anything.

I was almost to the west corner when I found a metal hatch that seemed out of place. Unlike all the other doors down here it was round, and had both a thumbprint reader and a numeric keypad on the lock. I checked the building plans. It wasn't listed on any of them. A little something the Baptists had added since they took it over.

I heard the sound of boots on the pavement, real close. I had run out of time to consider my options. Wherever this thing led, it had to be better than here. I tried typing in the usual idiot codes. 1234. 1359. 2468. 69. 666.

Damn. Sometimes I can do this. Just by dumb luck. Or by knowing something about the person who set up the code. But I was flying blind this time.

I tried the year. 2024. No good.

Behind me, I could hear the guards poking around some boxes. No more time .

I tried a few more codes. 9876. 1111. 2222. Nothing.

I heard footsteps, even closer. I tried to ignore them and think. A numeric code. They had to make it something easy to remember. One lousy number and I could get out of this jam.

3333. 4444. Zip.

Then it occured to me that someone had given me a number recently. Had even repeated it, to make I sure I remembered it. I tried tapping it in.

1776.

The hatch opened.

## Chapter 25: The Gumshoe
## Tuesday the 10th, 2:49 PM

I was almost too surprised to move. Almost, but not quite. I hopped through the hatch and started down the tunnel on the other side. For the moment, I would shelve the whole question of how Ice-in-Summer happened to know the access code for a hatch in the Baptist's basement. But if I got out of this alive, there was going to be one Indian drag queen with some serious explaining to do.

The tunnel was just big enough for me to stand up in hunched over. I ran along it, following a set of tiny green lights in the floor. Behind me I heard shouting, and I guessed that my pursuers had found the open hatch.

I kept running. And running. And running. The tunnel went on and on and on. I must have covered a couple thousand yards before I came to an intersection. It was a choice between a vertical shaft that ran up, and continuing on straight down the tunnel.

About then, somebody behind me started shooting. I could hear the bullets ricocheting off the walls down here. Well, that made up my mind. I noted that the bonus clause in my agreement with Weir had just kicked in to effect. Now if I could just live long enough to spend it.

I jumped for the first handhold and started climbing. About twenty feet up I hit another one of those metal hatches. I punched in the 1776 code again, and it opened. I blinked as the sunlight came pouring in, but forced myself to crawl out.

It took my eyes a few seconds to adjust to the light. I was staring at a brick wall. Some trash cans. Graffiti. The hatch I had crawled through looked like a manhole cover from this side. I seemed to be in an alley, somewhere in the inner city. But there was no way I could have crawled that far.

I jogged to the open end of the alley and had a look around the street. Something was wrong. There were parked cars, but no moving ones. And no people around. I looked up, and saw that all the buildings were cut off at the third story. And the street was only a block long, and dead-ended into open fields at both ends.

It took my brain a couple of seconds to realize that I was in another one of the training areas, probably a set for running urban combat exercises. I was still on their campus.

OK. Think, Drew. The Baptists had probably put the tunnels in as part of the compound's defenses. That way they could pop up behind anyone who attacked the place, or sneak in and out unseen if they needed to. So there was probably at least one tunnel that would take me all the way out of the compound. If I had just kept going, I might have...

Behind me, I heard the sound of the hatch grinding open again. No time to worry about tunnels now. I took off down the street at a dead run—no pun intended. Since no one had shot me by the time I reached the field, I turned right to get out of their line of fire and kept running. That took me through an obstacle course and then a shooting range. Luckily, no one was using either of them.

I glanced over my shoulder and saw the top of the headquarters rising over the fake cityscape. Great. I was running the wrong direction, away from Linda and the car. But that might be just as well. By now they'd have the whole hue and cry out for me, and there was no sense in taking Linda down with me.

I made it across the firing range and into a little wooded area with a jogging path running through it. Since the trail and I were heading in about the same direction, I took it, and stuck with it through a couple of S turns until it finally ran into the fence and turned left to follow it

The fence. That lovely little fence with the cheery yellow "Danger: High Voltage" sign and an open road beyond it. I just hoped that I had been right about them not keeping this thing on all the time.

There's supposed to be some trick for telling whether an electric fence is on or not, but I didn't have time to think of it. I held my arm next to the wire, and it didn't make the hairs stand on end or anything, so risked a quick brush against it. Nothing. It was dead.

At least something was going right today.

The climb up was easy, but on my way over the top I got my right leg caught in the barb wire. Damn barb went right through those thin dress pants and lodged in my thigh. It was painful, but certainly nothing that was going to kill me. I was working to untangle myself when I got a really bad feeling.

Have you ever had one of those moments when you know that you are totally and completely screwed? I did. Because sitting on top of that fence, with a hunk of wire embedded in my leg, I suddenly knew that somewhere, one of the guards had thought to turn on the fence to keep me from getting away. He was making the call now, to tell them to do it.

I panicked. I grabbed at the fence and tried to pull my leg off, but only succeeded in jamming another barb in just above the knee. Then I looked up and saw a limo pulling up on the road outside the fence. Great. They'd already sent someone around to cut me off. I must have tripped a sensor when I started climbing.

OK. Stay calm. One crisis at a time. Deal with electrocution first. Plenty of time to get shot later. And who knows? Maybe they'll just take me prisoner. Maybe we can talk about this. Sit down, have a cup of coffee, work through our differences. For now, just work the barbs out methodically, and GET OFF THIS FENCE BEFORE IT FRIES ME.

That really bad feeling that had been lying in the pit of my stomach suddenly leapt into my throat, and I knew that I was out of time. I jumped.

The barbs ripped a good chunk out of both my pants and me. I felt blood gushing down my leg, and it occurred to me that I might have managed to sever my femoral artery. Not that I had the time to worry about minor details like that, though. You see, I'd still had both my feet on the fence, pushing off when the charge came through. Oh, nothing too big. Just a short, ten thousand volt love tap, a little something to let me know what I would have been in for if I hadn't broken contact when I did.

I tumbled off the fence in a heap, bleeding and half-electrocuted, and landed on my back with a thud that would have knocked the wind out of me if other forces hadn't already seen to that. I heard the limo's door open, and footsteps coming toward me. Something in the back of my brain still had the sense to think about getting up and running away, but it was no longer connected to any part of my body that was capable of following the advice. I tried to sit up, but even that was too much. It took everything I had left just to lift my head and see who was coming for me.

That's when I began to suspect my body wasn't the only thing that had gotten fried. Because either my brain was seriously cooked, or there was a Cherokee warrior in war paint and leather breeches walking up to me.

He knelt over and looked at me. Half his face was painted blue, the other half white, except in a band around the eyes, where the colors were reversed. He leaned closer, and then he kissed me. A long slow kiss.

Then the world went away.

## Chapter 26: The Reverend Senator
## Tuesday the 10th, 5:42 PM

It had been the perfect end to what had already been a glorious day. First the incident at the clinic, then the riot, and finally Weir crawling his way into my office to beg his way back into the fold. I really should have made him grovel a bit more before I forgave him, but I was in too good a mood. And it was good to have him back.

I needed the boost he would give me in the 15-25 age range. Particularly now. Maybe I could have him write a campaign song. Yes. That was a good idea. He's got a pretty face, and a natural ability to tug at people's heart strings. And he's also got some critical cross-over appeal outside of the Conservative Christian base. A really good song from him, getting radio play, might be good for a whole percentage point in a national election.

And we would need every percent. The Christian Alliance's share of the vote has never managed to top 17% in national elections. We can win House and Senate seats from a few states, mostly in the South and the Midwest. But we've never been able to make a serious run for the Presidency. Not till now. This thing...This could finally give us a chance to win the big race.

I sat down at my desk and played the coverage of my speech again. First the clips from CNN, then the Microsoft News Network, then Newsweek. I watched as I shouted out the words, blood streaming down the left side of my face.

"It is time for the just and the righteous to stand and be counted! It is time for us to say that there is such a thing as right and wrong!"

The imagery was pure gold. It was Churchill. It was Reagan. We'd gotten lucky with the riot breaking out just before we got there. Of course, you can't count on luck for everything. Certainly you can't count on getting hit by a bottle or a rock when you need it. I'd had one of my bodyguards give me the cut on my head, then we waited for the blood to well up and start running down my face before I made the speech. Hey, the Lord helps those who help themselves.

I touched the stitches. They were still sore. I hadn't meant for the oaf to cut me that deep, but it had done the trick. And the stitches would be a good image to have for the next couple of weeks. A reminder that a good Christian had been bludgeoned, just for trying to say that there is such a thing as right and wrong. A reminder that the forces of Satan had tried to strike me down, and failed. I touched the stitches again. I'd have to see if Kate could do something with my makeup to make them stand out more.

I played the speech a couple more times. Even the Jewish and Mormon newsites were playing it. This was our chance. Our one last chance to build a solid majority behind the idea that there is such a thing as morality, before the country slipped into darkness and debauchery. We had to make it count.

I switched off the coverage of my speech and set to work scripting the late night news shows. We were going to have to completely redo the script for "Bible Prophecies Today." The current draft was all about the rise of a dark nation and how that tied to the current Brazilian trade deal, but we were going to drop that in favor of the clinic break-in. I outlined what I wanted: something about a battle between the forces of the righteous and the minions of Satan, preferably with some tie-in to abortion, and sent it off to the boys in scriptural research to find the relevant passages. Nice thing about the Bible, you can find almost anything in there if you look hard enough.

I also yanked one of the planned phone-ins on my evening show, and set a writer to work on drafting something new. I wanted a caller that would specifically link a coven of witches to the incident at the clinic. Preferably someone unrepentant, who would make some threats about worse things to come. We'd have to be careful about which actor we cast to make the call. He had to be scary, but kind of annoying at the same time.

Then I got on the phone with Richard, our best director, and put him to work on a new video that people could download from our website.

"A nice piece on the history of the Satanic Conspiracy." I told him. "Maybe 20 minutes or so. That's as long as anyone is going to pay attention, anyway. And I want you to do it fast. Pull an interview with a satanic abuse survivor from our archives, and mix in some of the stock footage of witches dancing naked and acid rock musicians killing animals. Oh yeah, and use that clip from the homosexual march with the scary guys in leather. That always gets a reaction. Where you need to, you can stage some stuff with actors, but I want this thing up and running by tomorrow morning. Oh, and I'm sending you a list of enemy politicians. Work some clips of them into the video somehow, then at the end remind the viewer that we're raising money to unseat these known agents of the Satanic Conspiracy and replace them with responsible Christians."

I got off the phone and glanced at my watch. Only 6:30. Still plenty of time before I had to start getting ready for my nine o'clock show. I leaned back in my chair and thought about the struggle ahead. We only had a year and a half to plan the presidential race.

These two incidents had been a God send, giving us traction with constituencies we'd never been able to reach before. But the Presidency was not going to be a cake walk. To win, we'd need to soften our message a little, stick with things that most people can agree with, like the fact that there is a difference between right and wrong. The key to victory wasn't with the 10% of the country that would always vote with me, or the 10% of the country that hated my guts. The key was the vast mushy middle, the people who say that they believe in God but have forgotten His laws. And with evil finally showing its face in this world, I could be the one to remind them of why He had made those laws.

Then? President Stonewall. Had a nice sound to it. But I was not so naive as to believe that I could turn this country around overnight, even as President. Our enemies had been working for years, and it would take time to purge their subtle poison from the system. I'd have to start with the judiciary. Appoint some judges who understand where the law really comes from, that the statutes of man are nothing before the laws of God, and cannot supersede them. I had a few candidates in mind already. Then?

Then it was a matter of opening people's eyes. Our enemies have managed to make a virtue out of tolerance. As if looking the other way while evil festers is something to be commended. We would have to make people see the dangers they had been ignoring. Devil Worshippers. Baby killers. Sexual perverts. Muslims and Voodoo practitioners and all manner of heathen infidels. It was my job to make the American people see the danger that surrounded them. If I could do that, if I could frighten them into understanding, then they would go along with everything else that had to be done. And once again, America would be a Christian country, free and strong with God protecting her.

It was a pleasant dream. An America where it was safe to walk the streets at night. An America of strong, healthy families, and smiling children. I was forced out of my reverie by the ringing of my phone.

"Hello," I answered. "Reverend Stonewall here."

"Sorry to disturb you, Reverend." It was Berta, my secretary. "We've had a piece of fan mail come in for you, and it was strange enough that we thought you might want to take a look at it."

"Strange how?"

"Well, for one thing, they enclosed a thousand dollar bill. You know, *cash*."

"Hm. I see what you mean, that is a bit unusual."

"Yes, sir. And the writer also seemed to indicate that he knew you personally, so I thought perhaps he might be a friend of yours."

"Well, I do know lots of people.  What was the name?"

"Uh...he signed it with the initials J.C."

"J.C.  Really?"

"Yes sir."

I could think of one person with those initials.  But somehow I couldn't see Him returning to earth for the sole purpose of making a donation to my campaign fund.

"Interestin'."

"Yes sir.  And there were also a couple of other things in the envelope that seemed odd.  A coil of hair, tied in a knot, and a rather bizarre child's drawing."

"Did you say hair?"

"Yes sir.  Brown, if that's important."

This was a strange letter.

"What's the drawing of?"

"I...I really couldn't say sir."

"Hm.  Well, send it on in, Berta.  I'll take a look at it."

## Chapter 27: The Singer
## Tuesday the 10th, 9 PM

I heard Linda's car pull in to the garage. Good. I'd been sitting at the kitchen table banging out bad melodies on my guitar for the last two hours. She was late getting back and I'd been starting to worry about her.

I heard the door to the garage slam, and a few seconds later she strode into the kitchen. Her hair was out of place, and their were little burs and stickers clinging to her pantyhose and business suit. She reached into the refrigerator, took out a two liter bottle of coke, and started drinking without a glass.

"What happened?" I asked.

She wiped her mouth.

"You know, Justin, you really need to start keeping booze in the house. This is the sort of day God had in mind when She invented bourbon."

Linda put the top back on the coke and returned it to the refrigerator. She went over to the sink and splashed water on her face.

"What happened?" I repeated.

"I don't know," she said, drying her face. "We got in OK. Drew went downstairs to start looking around. Then the smoke charges went off, so I assumed he'd found Jen and needed some cover to get her out..."

She paused.

"Yeah, and then?"

"Then he never made the rendezvous. I waited around in the parking lot for ten minutes, and then I had to clear out. 'Cause if the militia had him, it wasn't going to take them long to come looking for me.

"Anyway, I got off the campus, and drove about a half mile away, and then waited. I figured if Drew were still on the loose, he might call needing help, so I'd better be close."

She got a glass out and started filling it with ice water.

"An hour goes by, no call from Drew. So I try calling him. Nothing. So then I head back to the compound on foot, and work my way around their perimeter. I figure maybe I'll get a glimpse of what they're up to, or spot Parker trying to get over the fence. I spend three hours crawling around in bushes and tall grass, and the only thing I found out for sure is that something had really spooked the militia. They'd turned on their electric fence, and they had at least twenty guys walking patrols on the inside."

She gulped down some ice water.

"Of course," she went on, "that could be good. It could mean that they were still looking for him."

She leaned back on the counter. "Sorry I don't have better news for you, Justin."

"It's OK," I said. "I may have a way out of this. I think I've found something that we can use to bargain with Zachary and get them both back."

She put down her glass, suddenly interested.

"What have you got?"

"I think I've found Zach's Achille's heal. I went into his office today, and..."

"YOU DID WHAT?!"

"I went to his office. Somebody had to find out what he was up to. And I think I found..."

"Do you have a death wish, Justin? We are playing a dangerous political game here, and Stonewall..."

"...Is not going to shoot me in his own office, no matter how annoyed he is. If Zach was going to have me killed, he'd have it done somewhere that wasn't connected to him. Come to think of it, I'm probably safer in his office than anywhere else on the planet. Besides, I found something we can use."

I motioned for her to join me at the kitchen table. I picked up a notebook and called up the painting that Drew had shown us last night.

"Remember this?"

"Yeah, the painting that Jen was checking up on."

"Right. Wanna guess where it's hanging?"

Linda shot me a look indicating that she was not in the mood to play twenty questions.

"All right," I said. "It's in Stonewall's office, right across from his desk."

Linda looked unimpressed.

"So? We knew Jen was looking into his affairs for us. So she took a picture of the painting on his wall. So what?"

"So, it means that she was there, that she'd somehow gotten invited into Stonewall's office. So, it means that she thought the painting was important. And I know why. You should have seen the way that Zachary reacted when I brought it up. Like I'd poured ice water in his shorts or something."

Linda put one of her feet up on the table and started picking burrs out of her nylons.

"Again, so?"

"So, remember what Parker said about the painting never having been exhibited or sold anywhere? Well, in that case, how did Stonewall get it?"

Linda held up a bramble that she'd just pulled out and examined it.

"So, you're thinking it's hot, and that you can prove Zachary's dealing in stolen art. Wake up, Justin. Zach is way too cagey to be keeping illicit goods on his office walls where anyone can see them."

"No, that's not it," I said. "I don't think he stole it. I think the painter gave it to him."

Linda extracted another bramble from her pantyhose, then gave up in disgust, stood up, and peeled them off. She sat back down and looked at me.

"Look, Justin. For the last three hours I have been out in ninety degree heat, crawling through bushes, being stuck with thorns and bitten by bugs, and ducking from guys whose ideas on religious proselytizing involve high-powered rifles. I am sweaty, I am itchy, and I need a shower. So if you've got something, drop the Socratic method and spill it."

She gulped down some more water and slammed the glass down on the table.

"OK," I said. "I'll try and make this simple. First off, take a look at the picture. That's him in there. Younger, and kind of idealized, but it's him all right."

She picked up the notebook, took a look at the picture, and gave a noncommittal nod.

"Secondly, the painter's name was Alicia Calerant St. Cloud. Sound familiar?"

Linda gave me a blank stare.

"Don't you remember that big case about fifteen years ago? It was all over the news. Her husband killed her in a jealous rage 'cause she was having an affair. But they never did find out who her lover was."

I paused, to see if she was following me. She shrugged.

"And according to that critic who e-mailed Jen, this painting was in St. Cloud's late style, so it had to be done in the last couple years of her life."

Linda rolled her eyes and shrugged again.

"Not that I don't appreciate the art lesson, Justin, but so what?"

"So what?! So, this woman had an affair. So one of the last paintings she does is this big, admiring portrait of Zachary, a portrait that she then gives to him. Can't ya connect the dots?"

Linda turned her head to the side and looked at me out of the corner of her eyes.

"Let me get this straight," she said. "You think that Zach is the mysterious guy who had an affair with this dead painter fifteen years ago?"

"Exactly!"

"Based on the fact that he has one of her paintings in his office?"

"Ah, you had to be there," I said. "You had to see the way he reacted when I brought it up. I tell you there's something about that painting that scares him."

"Then why does he keep it in front of his desk?"

"I don't know. Maybe to remind him of old mistakes or something."

Linda picked the glass of ice water back up and held it against her forehead.

"I don't know Justin, it's pretty thin."

"But it all makes sense," I insisted. "That's why Jen was checkin' out the painting. That's what she found that scared Zach silly. That's why Zach kidnapped her. And that's why Zach went all creepy on me when I brought it up. Can you blame him? Adultery would be bad enough. But adultery that resulted in a woman being murdered?" I chuckled, but the sound came out as a nasty little laugh. "You know how fast the Christian Alliance would dump him?"

"Maybe, Justin. *If* it really happened that way, and *if* we could prove it."

I was annoyed by her skepticism, but she had a point.

"Well, what if we could get proof?"

"What do you have in mind?"

"Suppose I go back in there with a tape recorder in my pocket. I tell you, me just mentioning that painting sent him into palpitations. If I hit him hard, with the whole story, and act like I've got proof, he'll crack. I could get him to make some sort of admission on tape. Then we could use that to make him give us Jen and Drew back, and force him to retire from the Christian Alliance. I tell you, it'll work."

Jen put the glass back down on the table.

"First off, Justin, I need a shower and some sleep, so I am not even going to discuss this any further right now."

She stood up.

"And secondly, you are not going anywhere near that office again. Are we clear on that, or do I have to start handcuffing you to the bathtub every time I go out of the house?"

I gritted my teeth, then smiled and gave her the "I'll be a good boy" nod, the one that got me out of so much trouble when I was a kid. She bought it.

Which was lucky for me. 'Cause tomorrow, Zachary and I are going to have a little chat, and put an end to this whole messy business.

## Chapter 28: The Artist
## Tuesday the 10th, Afternoon and Evening

I sit in your favorite tea shop, drinking your favorite tea, and waiting for you, Raven. My little mice have been following you about
for some weeks now, bringing me word of your habits. I know
that you drink jasmine tea, with no sugar. I know that you have a
cup of warm milk before bed each night. And I know that you
come here every school day, after you have finished teaching.

You arrive at 3:45, just as my little mice said you would, wearing a loose green dress, your long silver hair braided in a ponytail
behind your head. I watch you, as you order your tea. As you sit
and drink, staring out the window at the passing traffic. My mice
tell me that you're a witch now, Raven. That you're a seer, and
you can see the future. I wonder. Is some portent trying to warn
you that I am near, is there some sign predicting my arrival? It
would be more dramatic that way.

You linger over your tea for some minutes, and when the cup
is finally drained, you stare into the bottom for some time. You
look puzzled, and wrinkle your brow at something you see there.
Does the arrangement of leaves mean something to you? Does it
speak to you of danger, or justice?

You leave the shop. I follow you, casually, watching you from
across the street as you walk the two blocks back to your house. I
see you stop to watch the sunlight filtering through the leaves of a
maple tree. Do you see something in the shifting patterns? Omens
that tell you of what this night holds for you? Or are you merely
watching the pretty images that the shadows form on the sidewalk? Ah, to see the world as you do, for only a few minutes.

You get home, and I go back to the van to wait till dark. After
twilight, my little mice come, Jack and Lucien. I strap on my
forty five pounds in ballast, and then we sneak into your back
yard. We watch you, through the windows. You make your dinner, but don't eat much. You build a fire, and sit for a long time
staring into it. Does the crackle of the logs whisper to you of old
crimes? Do the dancing flames show you the faces of old friends,
ones you'd hoped to forget?

Eventually you leave the fire, and go to the kitchen to make
your warm milk. If you can taste the drug in it, there is no sign of
it on your face. Then you go up to bed.

I wait for half an hour, and then motion to Jack and Lucien that it is time to go inside. They break into the house quickly and quietly. Consummate professionals. The key to any job is getting the right help. And one does have so many interesting chances to network in prison.

We move up the stairs quietly toward Raven's bedroom. The sedative in her milk will probably render her insensitive to our noise, but why take chances.

We reach the room, and Jack and Lucien approach her to carry out my plan, but I motion them away. I want to watch her sleep for awhile. Does she have troubled dreams? Does she even remember what she did?

She mumbles something in her sleep, and then sits up with a start, looking into my face.

"You?" she says, her face more curious than afraid.

"Of course," I say. "You had to know I'd come one day."

She tries to move her legs, realizes that she can't. The agent in the milk is probably making her limbs numb by now.

"Yes. I knew," she says finally. "In a way it's a relief...to finally have the waiting over."

I stand up, and Lucien and Jack get out the equipment, to begin our night's work.

"I just want you to know," she says, "That I didn't help with it. I didn't even know. Not 'til it was all over."

"I believe you." I say. "But you also never said anything. You knew. And you stayed silent."

Her head slips back down to the pillow.

"I couldn't...I couldn't believe it. At first."

"And later?"

"I...I didn't have any proof. It would have just been a crazy accusation, something a mad woman would make up. And..."

"And?"

"And...I felt guilty. For believing in him. For not seeing it all sooner."

A tear runs down her cheek. I understand, and I am not unmoved.

"This has to be." I say, as Lucien wraps the tubing around her arm. "But I will make one gift to you."

I lean down and whisper in her ear. "Of everyone involved in this, you alone I forgive."

She smiles, but I'm not sure if it's because of what I said, or because the drug is kicking in. And for a moment, looking at her face, I waver. I think how much she has changed in fifteen years. And it occurs to me that I could just stop, and walk away from this.

Then I think of Alicia, and all hesitation passes.

And the boys and I begin our work.

## Chapter 29:  The Witch
### Wednesday the 11th, 8:30 AM

The phone rang once.  Twice.  Three times.  Then my editor picked up.

"Hello?"

Rats.  I'd been hoping to get her voicemail.  It's a lot easier to lie to a machine.

"Uh.  Yeah.  Hi, Angela." I said, trying to make my voice sound a little hoarse.  I could only hope that it sounded convincing.  I hadn't had to fake an illness since high school, and I was really out of practice.  "It's Holly."

"Holly.  You sound terrible.  What's the matter?"

Oops.  Maybe I was laying it on too thick.  I wanted the woman to think I had a cold, not throat cancer.

"I've got some strain of the flu that's just eating me alive.  One of the girls probably brought it home from school with her.  Anyway, I'm  not going to make it into work today."

"Ouch.  Sorry to hear it." Angela sounded genuinely sympathetic, which made me feel even guiltier.  "You want to try working from home?"

"Uh...I don't think that would be a good idea.  I'm running a few degrees of fever and I'm a little incoherent.  I don't think you'd want me reporting on any global crises."

"OK.  Well, you've got a  few sick days coming.  Why don't you just crawl into bed and pass out for awhile?"

"Thanks, I'll do that."

"Just take care of yourself and get healthy as quick as you can.  Call me tomorrow morning and let me know how you're feeling."

"OK.  Thanks Angela."

"No problem." she said, and then hung up.

Whew.  Well at least that was over.  I hate lying.  For one thing, I suck at it.  And for another, every lie comes back to haunt you, sooner or later.  Even the little white ones.  I just hoped that this one would wait until the current crisis had blown over.

The girls were upstairs.  I'd decided to keep them at home today.  Maybe I was overreacting, but people were getting panicky out there, and things were a little scary.  Winter had actually grumbled about staying home.  She hates to get up in the morning, but she loves to see her friends. I had expected a bigger fight from Summer—she's in those peak teen socializing years—but she's been in a weird mood since yesterday afternoon, not talking much and spending a lot of time alone in her room. Anyway, I've got them both logged on their schools' remote learning networks, so they can keep up on the lectures and what's going on in their classes. I told Summer to check up on Winter every ten minutes or so to make sure she's paying attention to her teachers.

I should be keeping an eye on her myself, but I was busy looking for the mystery boy from Jen's notes. Last night I had gone over the information on all fourteen boys who matched the description, and I'd gotten to know them all a little better. I'd read up on their after school activities. I'd read up on their parents. I'd read up on their siblings. And there was not a darn thing about a one of them that would explain why a bunch of black magicians would take an interest in him. I was at a dead end.

I brewed myself a cup of wintergreen tea, and then sat down to read through all fourteen of them again. Hoping that I had missed something. Hoping that there was some detail in there that would jump out at me and scream, "Here! This guy! He's the one who can explain everything that's going on!"

I read. But if the clue was there, I couldn't spot it.

Frustrated, I moved on to the seven "maybes"—the boys who had been born on the right day but for whom we didn't have yearbook photos to run a comparison on. Not nearly as much reading to do on these guys. I looked over some news articles on the one who had died when he was two. An auto accident. Parents sued the manufacturer of the child safety seat. Terms of settlement sealed by a gag agreement. Father was a PE instructor at a ritzy private school in Buckhead. Mother was a speech therapist. None of which suggested a connection to black magic or medieval witch hunters.

There was even less to go on with the other maybes, the ones who had vanished from the public records after they were born. Adoptions, probably. There was no information on them beyond the birth certificates, but I looked at those anyway, hoping that the name of a parent might ring a bell. Hoping that something might finally click into place.

And it did.

I was looking at the birth certificate for Maybe #5. "Name: John Doe. Father's name: records sealed. Mother's name: records sealed. Modality of Birth: artificial womb."

But what got my attention was a small detail down near the bottom. "Place of Birth: Peachtree Family Planning Clinic."

Peachtree Family Planning Clinic. The scene of the second black magic ritual.

Maybe it was a coincidence. But the more I looked at that birth certificate, the more sure I became that there was something weird going on with this kid. Like, why weren't the parents named? I checked again for any later records on this kid, and there were none. No news stories, no death certificate. Which meant that Sally was right, and the kid must have been adopted, and changed his name.

But that didn't make any sense. Artificial womb time is expensive. So some couple shelled out a few hundred thousand to grow this kid, and then they just put him up for adoption? Yeah, right. Something strange had happened with this kid. He had to be the one that I was looking for.

Which didn't help me much. So I had a birth certificate on him. Great. I still didn't know what name he was going by now, I still didn't know where I could find him, and I still didn't even know who his parents were.

But I did know someone who could find out.

I picked up my phone and punched in Sally's number. She answered halfway through the first ring.

"Hello?"

"Hey Sally, it's Holly. I need a favor."

"Holly? What are you doing calling me on an outside line?"

"It's a little complicated. I took a sick day to go run down a big story. Top secret. Even my editor doesn't know about it. So keep this under your hat."

"Wow. OK. What is it?"

I knew that Sally wouldn't be able to resist a secret.

"Can't tell you yet. But I need some help. Can you run a search for me on the QT?"

"Sure. What do you need?"

"Well, here's the deal. I found the birth certificate for the kid I'm looking for. He was born at the Peachtree Family Planning Clinic. Names of the father and mother were kept confidential. No later records, so he must have been adopted. Is there..."

"The Peachtree Family Planning...Hey, you're working on the Satanism story, aren't you! Funky. You getting close to finding the guys behind it?"

"Maybe." I said, trying to sound cool about the prospect.

"OK. I'll help. But if you win a Pulitzer for this, you have to mention my name in the acceptance speech."

"It's a deal. Now, is there any way to find out where this kid is now? I'd also like to know who his birth parents were, if there's any way to do that."

"Hm. You're placing a tall order there, sister."

"Which is why I came to the best. Can you do it?"

"Well, can't help you with the birth parents. Family Planning Clinics are notoriously uptight about data security. Worried some fundamentalist will shoot a doctor or a patient or something. And even if I had some special hacker wizardry I could work on their system, it wouldn't do you any good anyway. Word is their whole database got blitzed in the break in."

"How do you know that?"

"Because it's my job to know things like that," she snorted. "Plus I have a friend in the data recovery department of the SIB's crime lab. She's spent the last 24 hours trying to read something off charred little bits of crystal memory, with no luck."

"Oh."

"However, I might be able to help you a bit more with your boy's current location. Do you know the name of the agency that handled the adoption?"

"I hate to admit it, but no."

"Hm. That does make things harder..."

There was a long pause.

"Come on Sally," I prompted. "Your reputation as a wunderkind is on the line here."

"I said harder," she snapped back at me. "I didn't say impossible. Just give me a minute to think."

I waited. I could hear her drumming something against her desk. Finally she came back to me.

"OK," she said. "Tell you what I can do. I'll go back to the yearbooks, and I'll run a search for all the Atlanta high school kids of about the right age who fit the description you've given me. Then I'll eliminate all the ones I can find a valid birth certificate for. That will give you a short list of all the adopted kids in Atlanta that are his age and description. But you'll have to take it from there. Fair enough?"

"More than fair. How fast can you run the search?"

"Faster than I can explain to you how it works. Hold on."

She started rapidly mumbling search instructions to her agent. I could barely understand what she was saying, but I guess the program was used to her verbal short hand by now. After about a minute she came back to me.

"OK. I've got the list. Looks like there are only four of them. I'm zapping you their names now, along with whatever information my agent could put together from the yearbook entries. Happy hunting."

"Thanks Sally. You are a wonder worker."

"Yeah. I know. Just don't forget to mention me in the speech."

"You got it, bye."

I hung up and opened the file she'd sent me. The pictures of the four boys were all right there. They could have been brothers. Four boys with blue eyes, brown curly hair, and the same basic facial features.

"So which one of you is my mystery man?"

I read through the information from the yearbooks. One of them went to a public school out near Stone Mountain, one to a Baptist School up in Marietta, one to a Catholic School in South Atlanta, and one to an expensive private academy that specializes in Math and Science. A few interesting hobbies. One played tennis. Another played the violin. Neither of which explained why one of them was mixed up in this whole mess. I read through their parents' biographies, but again, nothing that pointed to which of the boys was my man.

At noon I took a break from chasing evil sorcerers, and made some grilled cheese sandwiches for the girls. We sat down for lunch together, and I asked my daughters what they were learning in school today. Winter chattered on about about how "metaphorical" everything was (I take it that was the word for the day), while Summer grunted something about American Literature and then clammed up. I tried to draw her out a couple more times, attempts which were met with monosyllabic grunts, so then I put her on warning that if she didn't snap out of whatever teenage funk this was within another twelve hours, then I would start prying. She glared at me, but other than that the threat had no immediate effect.

After lunch, I sent the girls back upstairs to finish their schooling, and then settled back into my hunt. I looked over the yearbook information on the four boys a second time, but I still couldn't spot anything to make me think that one of them was involved with black magick. So what next?

Well, I still had a few cards that I hadn't played yet, like the fact that the kid I was looking for was left handed with type O blood. Maybe it was time to start working on that angle. I glanced through the list of the four boys' activities, and settled on the tennis player as the easiest one to check on first. I looked up his mother's number and gave her a call.

"Hello?" The voice on the other end sounded perky, and I could hear chattering in the background. I must have caught her on her lunch break.

"Yes, I'm trying to reach Michelle Schultz?"

"Well, you've got me. Who is this?"

"Sorry to intrude on your lunch, Ms. Schultz. My name is Holly Jacobs, and I'm a reporter with *Left Hander Magazine*."

"Yes? What do you want with me?"

"Well it's not so much you as your son, Jared. We're doing a piece on left-handed high school athletes and the special pressures they face. I happened to run across a picture from your son's school paper of him holding a racket in his left hand. Is he..."

"Oh, no. Jared is right handed. He must have been horsing around for that picture."

"Oh. Well, I'm sorry to have taken up your time."

"No trouble. Sorry we couldn't help you." she said, and hung up. Well, one down.

I tried the violin player next. His mother seemed thrilled at the prospect of her son being used in a magazine article, but she was sorry to say that he was right handed. She couldn't imagine how I might have run across a photo of him trying to play left-handed.

Two down.

The third call was a tossup between the Catholic kid and the one who went to Baptist school. Neither had any activities that could possibly be of interest to a reporter, so I was going to have to brazenly BS my way through these two.

I tried the Catholic boy's mother first, telling her I was doing a story on carpal tunnel syndrome among left handed teenagers. The whole idea sounded wildly improbable, even to me, but she seemed to buy it. She would have loved to help out, but all three of her sons were right handed. So sorry.

Three down. One last chance. If I didn't hit pay dirt with this one, it was back to square one. I crossed my fingers and called the Baptist kid's mother. She answered on the first ring.

"Hello?" The voice on the other end of the phone was hoarse, and sounded a little nervous.

"Yes," I said, trying to sound friendly, "Hello Mrs. Danvers. My name is Holly Jacobs. I'm with..."

"Jacobs? I don't think I know any Jacobs."

"No, we've never met before. Actually, I'm calling to talk to you about your son..."

"Benji?" she interrupted, her voice suddenly full of panic. "Have you found him yet? Is he all right? Please God, don't let him be hurt!"

"Uh..." her questions and the rush of fear behind them caught me off guard, and I lost track of where I was in my cover story. "...actually, I'm just calling to see if Benjamin is left handed?"

"Left handed?! Are you crazy! Why are you all so interested in whether or not he's left handed? How will that help you find him?"

The boy was missing. I found myself giving into her panic, imagining what those black magicians might be using the boy for right now. But I fought back the image, and forced myself to listen to what she was saying. What did she mean by "all"? Had someone else been asking about the kid?

"I'm sorry, Ms. Danvers... I didn't realize that my colleagues had already checked on this..." I took a second to catch my breath and figure out where I was going with this, "...but didn't they explain to you what we need the information for?"

"Just something about having a hair sample from some boy who witnessed a crime, and you think it might be Benji. You know, you people have a lot of nerve! I ask you for help, and you won't do a thing, because he hasn't been missing for 24 hours. Then, all of a sudden, you turn up on my doorstep wanting to know where he is because he might be a witness to something. Doesn't it matter to anyone that my son could be lying in an alley somewhere, bleeding to death, while you people makes notes on which hand he writes with?! What's wrong with you people! I should never have let myself get upset with him. I should have waited till I'd calmed down until we talked. I should have..."

I let her vent for a couple more minutes. For one thing, I needed to hear what she would say. And for another, it sounded like she needed it. She was scared, and the only thing keeping her fear at bay was her anger, both at the police and at herself.

So the cops were after this kid, too. How had they found out about him? And did they know why he was so important?

When Ms. Danvers ran out of breath, I cut in as gently as I could.

"I understand what you're going through, ma'am. I have daughters of my own, and I know how worried I would be if one of them were missing."

There was no response, except for some sobbing on the other end.

"...and I am sorry if my colleagues were a little vague. Didn't they explain the nature of the case to you...?"

"No. Not a word. Said they couldn't say anything until they made an arrest."

"Oh... well I'm afraid that's true. But I assure you that the information your son has may save lives. And I'll personally do everything I can to see that your son is safely returned to you."

It took her a few seconds to answer. When she did, her voice had dropped three notches in volume.

"Thank you."

"No need. I only wish I could do more. But I'm afraid that there were some discrepancies in the reports my colleagues filed. I know you've answered all these questions before, but would you mind going through them just one more time?  It could help us find Benjamin."

I felt guilty for preying on the woman's fear, but it was only a half-lie.  While I wasn't with the police, I was looking for her son.

"Allright."

"Good.  Now, what is Benji's blood type, again?"

"O positive, like I told the other officers.  I had to go look it up from his medical records."

"And the names of his birth parents?"

There was a long silence from the other end of the phone.

"How did you know?"

"I'm sorry ma'am, I don't mean to intrude on your private life.  But we did a thorough search of his files.  There was no birth certificate for him under this name, so we assumed he was adopted. I take it the other officers forgot to ask about this?"

"Yes.  But, why do you need to know?"

"I am sorry, I really can't explain that right now.  But it would help.  Do you know who they were?"

There was a long pause.  I was worried that she might have caught on to my act.  Like I said, I'm not a very good liar.

"No." she finally said.  "I'm sorry.  The adoption agency never told us."

Rats.  I'd hoped the identity of his real parents might explain why someone was so interested in him.

"Allright.  One last thing.  I know that the other officers must have already asked you for any ideas on where Benji might have gone.  But if we could just go over the list one more time?  Just in case you think of any new details?"

"You find that whore," she hissed into the phone, "and you'll find Benji."

"Excuse me?" I said, a little surprised by her sudden burst of venom.

"That whore.  That satanist whore.  The one who seduced him."

My mind latched on to the term "satanist".  Baptists throw the word around a lot, and use it pretty freely on anyone they don't like.  Wiccans.  Atheists.  Unitarians.  Democrats.  But I was dealing with a story involving black magic.  She might be talking about the real thing.

"What makes you think she was a satanist?" I asked.

"She admitted it!  Mrs. Breckin caught her dancing naked in front of the boys, and when she told her to cover up, the little whore said she was a godless pagan."

Pagan?  My mind grabbed onto the word.  It was a strange choice for a Baptist.  They usually describe outsiders as "Heathens", or "Devil Worshipers", or "Infidels".  "Pagan" is a word that Wiccans use to describe ourselves. I was getting the uncomfortable feeling that there might really be a witch at the bottom of all this. But who? Jen? Could she really be involved in something this evil?

"And do you have a name on her?" I asked.

"Well, I talked to Mrs. Breckin on the phone when the first officers came over. Her son Tim says that the girl's name was something like Sue or Susan. He didn't know her last name."

"And could I get you to give me her description again? You might remember something new."

"Well, I never saw her. But Mrs. Breckin says she was about fourteen or fifteen."

Fifteen? Well that ruled out Jen. Not even under dim lighting with good make up. Ms. Danvers continued.

"Long brown hair. Green eyes. Big chest for that age."

There was something about that description that seemed familiar, but I couldn't quite place it. Oh well. There must be millions of girls who would fit that description.

"Anything else you can remember?"

"No. That's it. Please find him soon. Please?"

"I'll do everything I can ma'am. That's a promise."

"Thank you."

I hung up the phone. That poor woman. I tried to imagine how I'd feel if Summer or Winter was missing. One way or another, I was going to find this boy and keep that promise.

OK. So I had a 14 year old witch and a 14 year old Baptist boy that were on the run. Where would they go to hide out? I made a list of places that teenagers might try to go: cheap hotels, friend's houses, homeless shelters. But there was still something bothering me about the girl's description. I tried to figure out what it was, but the harder I tried to remember, the more elusive the thought became.

Had I seen her picture in a news article associated with the case? I took a few minutes to run through all the pictures from all the articles I'd seen about the two incidents, but there were no fourteen year old girls with long brown hair.

I brewed myself another cup of wintergreen tea, and meditated on the facts for awhile. I thought about the young witch some more, but I still couldn't remember where I'd seen her. Maybe it was just that her description was so generic. There were so many teenage girls who could fit that description, I was bound to have run into one of them. I mean, even Summer would fit *that* description...

I then had a truly ugly moment, when my suspicious nature got the better of me. But I forced the panic down. After all, the chance that Summer was the girl the police were looking for was microscopic. And there was no way that she could possibly be mixed up in something this big without me knowing about it. And besides, there has to be some limit on how much trouble one fourteen year old girl can get into.

Reassured, I took another sip of my tea. This story was starting to wear on my nerves. I was getting jumpy. I took another sip of tea.

And suddenly I had a flash back to the night before last, when Summer was trying to introduce me to some new friend of hers. I'd been distracted at the time, and hadn't paid much attention to him. What was his name? I remember it was something that ended in an "ey" sound, and I tried unsuccessfully to convince myself that it was Ricky, or Kenny, or Mickey. Then I called up Benjamin Danvers picture and stared at it, hard, for about thirty seconds.

Then I panicked.

## Chapter 30: Summer
## Wednesday the 11th, 10 AM

Benji was squirming again.

"Quit moving," I said. "You're going to drip this stuff all over the carpet."

"I'm trying," Benji said, fighting back a giggle. "But it's hard."

"Boys." I muttered, mopping up a bit of the excess with a piece of tissue. "No self control."

I'd put down a trash bag to catch the runoff, but he was wiggling around so much that it wasn't doing much good.

"And quit giggling, too." I added. "You want my mom to hear us and come up and find you here?"

"OK, OK," he said, still laughing, "but this stuff tickles."

"How can it tickle?" I asked, tipping the cartridge to wet the one part of his foot I hadn't gotten yet. "It's just ink."

"Well it's cold," Benji said, thrashing his foot out of my grasp.

"Look, do you want me to take your footprint, or not? This was your idea, after all."

"Yeah," he admitted, "but I didn't expect you to break open a toner cartridge to do it."

"Hey, I don't seem to remember that you had any better ideas. Now do you want me to do this or not?"

"All right, all right. Just do it, already."

"OK." I said, grabbing a sheet of paper off my desk. "Just try not to squirm so much." I put the paper up against his foot and then pressed it flat using a book. Then I peeled it back off to look at my handiwork. All I had was a big black smudge in the shape of a foot.

"Well?" Benji asked, sounding impatient.

"Hold still. It came out all smudgy. I probably used too much ink. Let me try making another one."

I pressed a second sheet against his foot. It was a bit drier now, so this one picked up some of the ridges in his foot print. I made a third print, which came out even clearer, and a fourth print, which was darn close to perfect. After that, the ink on his foot was too dry to work with, so I sent him into my bathroom to clean up.

While he scrubbed, I scanned in the image.

"Hey Summer," he called from the  bathroom, "I don't think this stuff is coming off."

"Well, what are you using?" I asked, as I adjusted the contrast on the image.

"Soap."

"Soap?" Boys don't know anything. "Soap's probably not going to cut it. Try my apricot facial scrub."

"Facial scrub?" He said dubiously, and I could tell that he was about to get all butch on me about using cosmetics.

"Yeah, Black Foot warrior. You need to peel off the outer layer of skin that has soaked up the ink."

He looked at me like I was crazy, but he opened up the container and started smearing some on his toes.

"And," I went on, "it will leave your feet smelling all fresh and fruity."

He looked up from scrubbing between his toes to growl at me.

I went back to my computer and checked the image of his footprint. It was still a little light, so I bumped up the contrast another notch. Then I glanced at the other half of my screen, where my biology teacher Ms. Whitefire was still rambling on about the evolution of conifers from ferns. Mom had had some weird encounter on her way home from work last night. Something to do with a gang of kids from one of the pushier Christian sects. Anyway, now she was acting all wiggy and keeping Winter and me home from school. Well, home. I still had to go to school. So half my monitor is stuck watching Mrs. Whitefire go "Yadda-yadda-yadda windborn sperm vs. swimming sperm, yadda-yadda-yadda the ability to reproduce in cooler and drier climates, yadda-yadda-yadda."

It was stuff I'd already picked up from the reading, but I had to keep at least one eye on her. I could tell from her body language that she was about to start popping questions at us. She has this nervous thing she does with her hands when she realizes that she's starting to lose control of the class.

Benji came out of the bathroom, his right foot still stained black. He pointed to it and made a pouty face.

"Oh, what's your problem?" I asked. "It'll wear off in a week or two."

He sat down on my bed. I pulled the file with his footprint up on my notebook and passed it to him.

"Here's the print. Now you set up the search. My botany teacher's about to start shooting questions at us, and I need to pay attention."

Benji went to work on the search, while I watched Ms. Whitefire. Sure enough, a few minutes later she went into the question and answer thing. I got hit with the third one, an easy one about alternation of generations that was a straight lift from the reading. I knocked it back at her for a home run, and then turned down the sound.

"OK. I'm back. She never asks the same person two questions, so I've got a few minutes free. How's the search going?"

"Nowhere." he said.

"What's wrong?"

"It's the hospital records. They're all locked down."

I went over and sat next to him so that I could look at the notebook.

"Well, it's not like we're asking if somebody's got cancer or something. We just need the birth records and footprints."

"Yeah, I know," said Benji, " but those are locked down too."

"They keep baby's footprints a secret?"

"Yeah. It looks that way."

Well that was just too weird to be true. I took the notebook from him and set up a search of my own. Sure enough, it came back with a whole string of "database non-accessible" errors.

"Wow, you're right." I admitted. "They do keep babies' footprints a secret." I handed him back the notebook. "But why? Why would *anyone* want to keep babies' footprints a secret? I mean, what do they think we're going to do with the information?"

"Who knows?" Benji said. "Who knows why adults do anything?"

He had a point there.

"OK," I said, "so where do we go from here? You got any other ideas on how to track down your parents?"

He scrunched up his forehead. "Let me think about it."

"OK," I said, then glanced at my monitor. Botany was over and World Lit was about to start. "Oops. My next class is starting. You're on your own." I gave him a hug, and then plopped myself back down at my desk.

Class started, and I had to hang close to my monitor for the next hour. My lit teacher, StarBride, is really sharp, and I've got to be on my toes for her class. Plus she's interesting. Every so often I glanced over at Benji, who was sitting on my bed, tapping out stuff on my notebook and munching on the apple I'd snagged from the kitchen on my way back from breakfast.

After class, I looked over the searches he'd set up, but none of them seemed to be making any progress. Then Mom yelled upstairs to tell me that lunch was ready. I gave Benji a kiss and told him I'd try to sneak him up a sandwich

At lunch Mom was even more nosey than usual. Fortunately, Winter owes me one for not blabbing about what really happened with the babysitter last week. I gave her the "get Mom off my back" hand signal, and she ran interference for me, babbling nonstop about new words she'd learned at school this morning. Gotta hand it to the kid. She can really monopolize Mom's attention when she wants to.

After lunch, I went back up to my room and gave Benji the half a cheese sandwich I'd pocketed. He woofed it down in three bites, then went and got a glass of water from the bathroom.

"I'll go downstairs in half hour and try to snag a bottle of fruit juice." I told him. "So, did you get anywhere on the search?"

"Not an inch."

"Well, I've got a few minutes before my next class. Let's think about it. Is there any other way to go about it?"

"Not that I can come up with. If the hospitals won't..."

My phone beeped, and I had to interrupt him. I put a finger to my lips, and then answered.

"Hey. Summer here."

"Hi Summer, it's Tim. Do you know where Benji is?"

I put my hand over the receiver and whispered to Benji, "It's Tim. Do I know where you are?"

He thought about it for a second.

"Yeah."

I took my hand away from the receiver.

"Sure Tim. He's about two feet in front of me. You want to talk to him?"

"Yeah. It's kind of important."

"OK. Just a sec."

I switched the call over from my phone and put it on the desk speakers, so that we could both listen.

"Hey Tim," Benji said. "What's up?"

"What's up! Dude, I have been trying to call you all morning! "

"Yeah, well I turned off my phone. My mom's still crazy and I don't want to talk to her."

"I can imagine," said Tim, "my mom went pretty ballistic when she found out, and she's a pussy cat compared to yours. So where are you guys?"

"Over at my house," I said.

"Yeah, she let me spend the night." Benji added.

"Oh..." I could hear the surprise in Tim's voice, and I knew exactly what he was thinking. Actually, Benji had spent the night in my bathroom, sleeping in the tub. I'd given him a couple of pillows and a quilt to make it comfortable. After all, I couldn't have my mom come in to wake me up in the morning and find some strange boy in my room.

"...Kay." Tim finished. Then started on another drawn out syllable. "Uh..."

"Look Tim," I said, "get your mind out of the gutter and tell us why you called."

"Oh, yeah." Tim said. "Benji, dude, you are in so much trouble."

"Tell me something I don't know." Benji answered.

"No, I mean *really* in trouble. You won't believe what happened today."

"I don't know." I said. "The Pope's in this month's Playboy centerfold?"

"Uh…no."

"NASA found signs of intelligent life in Washington?"

"No. It's…"

"You beat my high score on Slip Stream?"

"No. Not that.."

"Yeah," Benji cut in, "like that could ever happen."

"Hey!" Tim shouted, "You want to hear what happened, or not?"

"Sure," I said, "So get on with it already."

"Well," Tim started. "I'm busted, and Mom's keeping me home from school till she figures out whether to send me to a shrink or an exorcist or military school or what, and she gets a call from the police. And they say they're looking for you."

"Oh great," Benji said. "The police? I should have known my mother would over react."

"Oh, but it gets better," Tim assured us. "So these guys come over to talk to my mom about you. Then they want to talk to me about you."

"You didn't mention my name, I hope."

"I'm getting to that, Summer. So anyway, these two guys start asking me all these questions, but they don't flash their badges like police are supposed to do. And I'm starting to think that something is not right here. So I ask to see some ID. And they show me, but now I'm suspicious, so I memorize the names and their badge numbers."

"So?" Benji asked.

"So, after they left, I went online and checked 'em out. It turns out the Atlanta Police have never heard of these guys."

"So who were they?" I asked.

"I don't know," Tim said. "But those fake ID's were pretty good. I'm betting they were professional spooks. Maybe CIA or something."

"CIA!" I almost shouted. "Benji's mom sicced the CIA on him!" Good grief. I knew the woman was having a major cow, but I had no idea that she had the resources to pull off something like this."

"Maybe," Tim said cooly. "Could be FBI or some mercenary group. Definitely pros, whoever they were."

Oh this was just great. Mom didn't want me dating in the first place. How was I going to tell her that my new boyfriend was being hunted by the FBI?

"Well you didn't tell them about Summer, did you?" asked Benji.

"No dude, I'm way too smart for that. I told them that the girl's name was Susan. Told 'em I didn't know her last name. I think they bought it. I e-mailed Scott with instructions to say the same thing, but he hasn't gotten back in touch with me yet. His mom's probably riding herd on him this morning. Don't worry. I'm sure he'll find a way to check his messages."

I looked at Benji.

"So you want to tell me how your mom managed to get the CIA on your tail?"

"I have no idea." he said. "So what do we do about it?"

"I don't know," I said. "I hear Rio de Janeiro is nice this time of year."

"Well, before you two go booking a flight," said Tim, "why don't you at least go check up on these guys and find out who they are and what they're up to."

"And how," I asked, "are we supposed to do that?"

"Well," said Tim, "you could just follow that bug I put on them before they left."

"WHAT!" said Benji.

"Well, not really a bug. Just a tracer. It was the only thing I had in my pocket at the time. Cute little number. It's velcroed, so you can attach it to fabric. Picked it up from the spy store when we were out at Lost World..."

"You put a bug on the CIA?" I asked, still not sure that I'd heard him right.

"Yeah. You say that like it's a bad thing. Come on. Turnabout is fair play. Haven't you heard about how they eavesdropped on that poor guy down in Tampa by putting a..."

"Aren't they going to find it?" I interrupted.

"Yeah, but it may take them awhile. I managed to stick it under one of their collars. I doubt they'll spot it optically. Of course, being spooks, they'll probably run an E-M scan sooner or later. So you guys might want to get around to setting up a tail on them before we lose the locational fix."

Benji looked at me with a sort of a "Gee, I'm sorry my friend is such a freak" look.

I looked back at him with a "Don't worry about it, all boys your age are freaks" look.

Tim must have noticed the silence.

"Uh...Guys? You still with me over there?"

"Yeah!" I said. "Sure! Let's do it. I've always wanted to be a spy."

Benji smiled at me. "OK. Do I have to start calling you Mata Hari?"

"Actually," I said, "The name is Bond. Jane Bond."

"OK. I guess that makes Tim 'Q'. So what sort of funky gizmo do we need to follow this tracer?"

"Ah that's the beauty of this model," Tim said, his voice swelling with pride. "You don't need anything but a notebook or a palm display. See, the tracer uses the cell phone network. Every five minutes it checks its position by triangulating from the two nearest relay antennas. Then it makes a call, and sends the information to an e-mail box I've set it up . All you have to do is go to Spytech.com, punch in the password "TimIsCool," and check the messages as they come in. Pretty slick, huh?"

"Yeah, pretty slick." I admitted. "Now how do we recognize these guys when we get close to them?"

"Oh, that's easy," Tim explained. "They're standard issue MIBS, can't miss 'em."

"What's a MIBS?" I asked.

"MIBS. You know. Men In Black Suits. You ever see one of those spy films where the bad guys are running around in dark suits with black sunglasses and earphones?"

"Yeah."

"Well that's them. Couldn't look more like spooks if they tried. Now if I were you I'd...Oops, gotta go. Mom's coming up the stairs."

"Can we call you back later?" Benji asked.

"No, don't. They may have tapped my phone. I scrambled this call and rerouted it through Finland, just in case. I'll call back when it's clear." Tim said, then hung up.

I turned to Benji. "You know, it's kind of weird how your friends can be so geeky and so cool at the same time."

"Yeah, I know."

"But tell Tim that if he ever puts a bug on me, I'll deck him."

"I'll do that." Benji said, picking up my notebook. "I'll give you a call when I catch up with them."

"Excuse me?" I said. "You'll *call*?"

"Well yeah," he said, "I mean, you're supposed to be in school, and your mom will notice if you're not here..."

"Oh no." I interjected. "Not a chance, my favorite little fugitive from justice. There is no way I'm missing out on this caper. And besides," I said with a wink, "I have ways of dealing with my mother."

I reached under the bed and dug out the box with my spell components in it. "Now watch the door while I put up the Worry-knot spell."

"Worry-knot?"

"Yeah, I use it on Friday Nights when I want to go hang at Little Five. I tell her I'm doing homework and then I cast this so she doesn't think about me for the rest of the night."

"Will it work?" Benji asked.

I walked over and stared him in the eye. "I will attribute that question to ignorance on your part rather than to any lack of faith in my competence as a spell caster. And to answer it...well, my mom *is* pretty crafty..." I waited for him to get the joke, but he didn't, so I just pretended like it wasn't there. "But, I've got a trick or two up my sleeve."

I rummaged through my box of components and found an ash twig and a lock of my mom's hair.

"Now put your fingers in your ears and hum." I said to Benji.

"Why? Is that part of the magic?"

"No, but I'm going to have to use the Charm of Seeming and I don't want you to hear it."

He gave me a quizzical look.

"I mean it." I said. He shrugged, put his fingers in his ears, and started humming the Battle Hymn of the Republic. Off key. Remind me to test my next boyfriend for musical ability before we go out.

While Benji was distracting himself, I whispered the Charm of Seeming and tied mom's hair around the ash twig in a triple knot. When I was finished, I tapped him on the shoulder.

"OK, Benji. That part's done. Now help me find a spider's web." I opened up my bedroom window, and made a jump for the oak tree right outside it. I caught the close limb and hauled myself up. I looked back to find Benji sitting in the windowsill with an uncertain look on his face.

"You coming?" I asked. "It's perfectly safe. I've been doing this since I was eight."

Benji didn't look thrilled with the idea, but there was no way that he was going to admit that he couldn't do something a girl could do. He joined me near the trunk a few seconds later.

"See," I told him, "you didn't break your neck. Now help me find that web."

We split up to search the tree. I took the upper branches while he worked his way down. He found a web first, and whispered for me to come over.

"Oh yeah," I said, "this is a big one. It will do just fine." I got out the ash twig and told Benji to stick his fingers in his ears again. While he hummed, I said the Charm of Seeming again, and wrapped the web up around the twig and my mom's hair. Toward the end of the charm, I noticed the spider, who didn't look too happy about my efforts.

"Well, I'm sorry, Ms. Spider. But I really do need this web right now. And you can build another. I hope you understand. Thanks."

Benji pulled his fingers out of his ears.

"So are we done with this thing yet?"

"Almost. Just one more step."

We climbed back into my room, and dug the camomile leaves out of my herb pack.

"So how is this supposed to work, anyway?"

"Oh, it's actually pretty simple." I explained. "Ash is symbolic of insight, so by tying it up with my mother's hair I'm creating a link to her clarity of vision. Then, by binding that up in a spider web, I'm creating a sort of fog around her so she won't notice things. Then the camomile keeps her calm and stops her from worrying."

"And this works?"

"Haven't been caught yet. Now stick your fingers in your ears and hum so that I can finish this thing."

He complied, and I stuck the camomile leaves to the webbing while I whispered the third speaking of the Charm of Seeming. When it was done, I hung my handiwork on the bedroom door, and then loaded my back pack with my notebook and a few spell components that I though we might need.

"You're sure we won't get caught?" Benji asked.

"Trust me, I do this all the time. My mom will never notice I'm gone."

Then I climbed back out the window, and jumped into the oak tree.

The hunt was on.

## Chapter 31: The Police
## Wednesday the 11th, 11:10 AM

The car hit a bump and I woke up. I rubbed my eyes, trying to get them to focus so that I could see where we were.

"Time to wake up sleepy girl," Tony said, "We're almost there."

"That's *Lieutenant* sleepy girl to you," I grumbled. We were driving through a residential neighborhood. Up ahead I could see our destination. A house with three squad cars and a crime-tech van parked out front.

Tony pulled up behind one of the black and whites and parked. I put on a headset, then popped my seatbelt and climbed out of the car, trying not to yawn. I hadn't meant to fall asleep on the ride over, but we were under a lot of pressure to wrap this up quickly, and I hadn't gotten a full night's rest since Saturday.

I flipped on the headset and we walked over to the house. Like all the other homes on this block, it had been done in that retro art-deco style that everyone was going nuts for back in the early teens. All stucco and pastel colors and stained glass and colored tiles. Two stories. A lime green porch with a blue tiled overhang and wisteria vines climbing up the support columns. Well kept front yard with a few dogwoods in it, the big, wild variety. It must be pretty in the spring time. Tony flashed his badge to one of the uniforms keeping the neighbors at bay, and we headed up the walk and into the house.

The front door was propped open with a plastic bag over the knob to preserve any prints. Inside, the place was crawling with photographers recording the scene before the latent print and fiber teams went to work. I stepped into the living room. A fireplace, crystal ball on the mantle. Stained glass window of a tarot card labeled "The Fool". Lots of candles. A small bookcase, full of occult sounding titles. I scanned over them. Stuff on herbalism, nature worship, dream interpretation, the tarot. Pretty mild. Nothing on demonology or the Satanic Bible or anything like that. I asked one of the techs where we could find the beat cop who'd called in the report. She pointed to the back of the house.

Tony and I made our way through to the rear, watching the carpet to make sure we weren't stepping on any evidence. In the kitchen, we had to work our way around a tech who was photographing a partial shoe print left on the linoleum. A couple more techs were at work on the back door, measuring a circular hole that had been cut in the glass near the door handle. I asked them for the beat cop, and they gestured to the back yard.

Tony and I stepped out onto the back stoop. The uniform was in the garden, pointing out some more footprints to another tech. Short black hair, interesting features. At a guess he was an Hispanic Asian mix of some sort. I waited for him to finish pointing out the prints, then waved him over to join us.

"Officer Tores," I said, reading his name off the badge. "I'm Lieutenant Strand with SIB, this is Lieutenant Browning with the Fourth, assigned to SIB. You were first officer on the scene?"

"Yes sir." He said, eagerly. He was young, maybe twenty-two or twenty-three. Couldn't have been on the force for more than a year or two.

"Well, why don't you fill us in on what happened?"

The kid pulled out his palm display and started reading off it. He must have started dictating his report while he was waiting for the techs to arrive.

"The Precinct received a call at 10:47 from Edwina SeaChild, a neighbor of the deceased. She had received a call from the victim's employer, an elementary school, who became concerned when the victim did not appear for work this morning and could not be reached on the phone. Ms. SeaChild had previously been given a key by the deceased for use in emergencies, which she used to enter the premises. Upon discovering the body, she returned to her own home and called 911. As the closest officer, I was alerted. I entered the building to check the victim for any signs of life, but there were none. I then searched the premises to make sure the perps were not in the building, noting signs of forced entry on the back door and footprints in the kitchen and back yard. I then returned to the front of the house, where I apprised my dispatcher of the situation."

He paused.

"I also advised her to contact the SIB, since this looked like it was related to those occult vandalism cases that you guys are working."

He cleared his throat.

"When I exited the house, I encountered Ms. SeaChild, who had been waiting for me. Per procedure, I asked her to wait in my car, so that she would not compare her story with other possible witnesses. I then isolated the crime scene, keeping bystanders away from the premises, and awaited the arrival of the crime scene investigation unit.

"When the unit arrived..."

"Officer Tores," Tony interrupted, "You went to the academy, didn't you?"

"Yes Sir," Tores answered. This was obviously his first murder investigation, and he could barely contain his excitement, "Graduated eight months ago. Sir."

The kid looked a little lost, then decided to go back to reading his report. He lifted the palm display.

"When the unit arrived, I identified myself to..."

"Officer Tores," This time it was me who interrupted, "I assure you that I will soon read every word of your report with the utmost interest. But for right now could you just skip to the highlights?"

"Uh...Sure." He started paging through stuff on the display. Poor kid. I'd derailed his train of thought.

"You noticed the footprints," I prompted.

"Yes." he said, relieved to know where to start. "A partial dirt print on the kitchen floor, and a few out in the dirt in the back yard. The glass of the back door had been cut, and the door was unlocked when I reached it, so that's probably the means of entry."

"And the means of exit?"

"Uh... the same, I guess."

"That's probably a good guess, but we should double-check. Did you see anything that might suggest they took a different route out?"

He thought a moment.

"No. And now that I think about it, the neighbor did mention that the front door was locked. It's a deadbolt, so unless they had a key and locked it behind them they didn't go out that way."

"Good." I said. Now what else?"

"Um. Well, there's the condition of the body upstairs, but you'll see that. I only made a quick glance in the other rooms. You know, just to make sure there weren't any more bodies, or a perp hiding in a bathroom or something like that. No signs of robbery. All sorts of expensive electronics left lying around. No signs that they tore up the place looking for anything, either. That's about it."

"All right," I said. "Why don't you go back to your car and dictate the rest of your report. We'll call you in a few minutes when we get the canvassing effort organized."

Tores nodded and left. Tony turned to me with an evil smile. I knew he was about to make some wise-assed comment, so I elbowed him in the ribs.

"Ow. What was that for?"

"That's for the uncharitable comment you were about to make about a fellow police officer. Cut the kid some slack."

Tony straightened his spine, and with mock formality intoned, "I then isolated the crime scene from bystanders and awaited the arrival of the crime scene investigation unit." He snorted. "I think that's a direct quote from the procedures manual."

"Well at least the kid has read the manual," I said.

Tony and I made our way back into the house, and then up the staircase to the second floor. I found Shard Lewis and another tech waiting outside the Vic's bedroom, while a photographer shot the scene inside. I stuck my nose in to get a look at it.

I felt the blood drain from my face. It was…It was… It was almost beautiful. If you could forget what you were looking at.

The victim was an old woman, lying in her bed. They'd smashed all the light fixtures in the room, except for one reading lamp that they'd hung from the ceiling so that it shown a ray down on her face. Her long silver hair had been carefully laid out on the pillow, so that it spread out in all directions, like silver fire leaping from her mind, or one of those halos that they used to put around saints in old religious paintings. And she had this look on her face. It reminds me of a Buddha, that look of understanding, or enlightenment, or something like that. Except for the pale color of her cheeks, you might think that she was just sleeping. Well, that and the tube running out of her left arm and into a two gallon jug on the floor.

The jug was almost empty now, though we wouldn't have to look far to find the contents. A circle of blood had been drawn around the bed, marked at intervals by the stubs of black candles that had long since burned themselves out. Inverted crosses had been painted on the windows, the blood drying to a thin brown streak. And the walls. The walls they had really taken some time with.

One wall had a drawing of a monkey wearing head phones. The other next to it also had a drawing of a monkey, but for this one they had pounded holes in the wall where its eyes should have been and replaced them with a couple of palm displays. Right now they were playing a popular soap opera. The wall next to it had a picture of a monkey, with an old $20 bill glued over its mouth. And the wall behind the bed was decorated with a painting of a door. It was opened just a crack and there were rays of blood streaming out of it. Some words I didn't recognize were scrawled over it.

I took a minute just to look at it all. There was no doubt that these were the same guys that hit the graveyard and the clinic. It had the same sick dramatic flair. I stepped back out of the room.

"It means 'I come.'" Lewis said.

"What?"

"Je Viens. The words over the door. They mean 'I come' in French."

The photographer stepped out of the room to tell us that he was done with the preliminary shots, and that the other crime-techs could start the fiber and latent print search. Lewis and her associate, a short Asian girl, picked up their kits and went in.

"Wow," Tony said, as he stepped into the room with me. "They must have been here for hours to do all this."

"It fits the profile," I said. "They're planners, not impulse vandals or killers. They weren't panicked or in a rush to get out."

I walked over to the body. Shard was leaning over it, wearing a pair of magnifier glasses to do a fiber search. Her assistant was pressing the fingers of the exposed right hand up against a print reader.

"Let me know as soon as you run the prints," I said. "She fits the general description of the occupant, but I want a positive ID as soon as..."

"Her name is Raven." Shard said, without looking up from her work. "Raven Straylight. I can give you a definite ID."

Tony raised an eyebrow.

"You knew her?" he asked.

"Yes. She was the high priestess of my coven," Shard said, not showing any emotion.

Tony opened his mouth to say something, then thought better of it. He watched Shard work for a few seconds, and then went with, "I'm sorry for your loss." He sounded like he meant it.

Shard slid the magnifier glasses down her nose and looked up to gauge his sincerity.

"Thanks," she said, and went back to her work.

"You know anything that might help us?" I asked.

"I've been thinking about it," Lewis said, her voice betraying no emotion, her face showing only concentration on the task of looking for stray fibers. "I haven't really been able to get my thoughts straight on this yet. Sit me down for an interview when we're done here and I'll give you a list of known associates, that sort of thing."

"Of course," Tony said.

"I don't want to be insensitive," I said, "But you know the drill. And it is important that we wrap this up fast. Can you think of any reason someone would want her dead?"

Shard picked up a strand of hair with a pair of forceps, and slipped into a little evidence envelope.

"If you're thinking this had something to do with us," she said, "then you've been reading way too many fairy tales. Witches don't practice blood magic." Then she took her glasses off and took a long hard look at Tony. "As for somebody else who might want her dead? You tell me."

There was a long, uncomfortable silence.

"OK," I said. "If you're up to it, let's run this by the numbers. I take it we're looking at blood loss as the cause of death?"

"Maybe," Shard said, "maybe not. There are no signs of a struggle, but I can't imagine she just lay there and let them do this to her. My guess is she was drugged, maybe even dead before they started. I'll run a tox screen when we get back. I'll also take in samples from the mug on the nightstand there and the dishes in the sink, see if they might have slipped something into her food."

"What about the equipment used to drain her blood?" Asked Tony, "Any chance of tracin' it?"

"The tubing, no." said Shard. "Too common. But we may get a break with the needle. Needles all have little serial numbers burned into them when they're made. It takes a microscope to read them, and I don't think anybody without medical training would know that they're there."

"OK," I agreed. "So maybe we get lucky. What about these paintings?"

"We'll go over them for fibers. Maybe get a stray paint brush filament or two. I'll be able to tell you what company made it, but that's about it."

"What about the angle of the brush strokes?" Tony asked. "Any chance we can figure out how tall the guy was, whether he's right or left handed, anything like that?"

Shard looked up at the paintings, and let out a long slow breath. "Never heard of anybody doing anything like that. Let me see." She walked over to the wall and examined the brush work on the hear-no-evil monkey. Then she went back to her kit, got out a magnifying glass and took a closer look.

"I don't know. Maybe I could scan the ridges in and figure out the angle he was holding the brush at, figure out something from there."

"Well, see what you can do," I said. "Call me if you find something interesting."

Tony nodded at her awkwardly, and then we walked back out into the hall, and downstairs.

"So what do you think?" I asked.

"Honestly?" Tony asked. "I'd say she's either one tough woman or a borderline psycho."

"Nah, Lewis is OK. She's just one of those folks that doesn't share their pain. She'll deal with it when she's alone. I know the type."

"So where's that leave us?"

"Well," I said, "how about you go check out how the techs are coming with the shoe prints. See if any of them are possible matches to the ones we have from the graveyard. And see if there are any leads off the forced entry. I'll check in with data services and see if they've put together a profile on the victim yet. I'll meet you out on the porch in ten minutes and we'll swap theories."

"Yes Ma'am."

Tony started for the back of the house, and I walked out onto the porch. A tech was a using a laser to check the railing for prints. I had Mindy put in a call to K'yon at Data Services. I never even heard it ring.

"Greetings Lieutenant Strand. K'yon here. How is the crime scene investigation proceeding?"

"Uh, fine. Look, their should be some fingerprints on the victim coming in, how fast can you..."

"Already done, Lieutenant. While you were on your way to the scene, I put a team to work pulling together a bio of the building's occupant. I figured that even if she wasn't the vic, you'd want the information. I've added it to the casefile, so you can read it whenever you want."

"Uh...thanks." I can't figure out K'yon. She's the only person I've ever met who can give me exactly what I want, the way I want it, before I even ask for it, and still rub me the wrong way in doing it.

"I also took the liberty of highlighting a few points about the bio that I thought you might find particularly interesting."

"Yeah, good thinking, K'yon. Now there are also some photographs coming in from the crime scene..."

"Yes, I've been looking them over. I assume you'll want the shots of the paintings forwarded on to the FBI's Behavioral Sciences Lab?"

"Yes," I said, gritting my teeth. "See if there's anything new they can tell us about the perps."

"Done. Anything else?"

"Yeah. I've got Lewis working on the paintings. I'm hoping we can get a height, maybe the handedness on the painter. Can you do a search of the literature, maybe see if anything like that's been done before?"

"Of course."

"Good. Zap whatever you find to Lewis. I'll check back in when..."

"Forgive the interruption, Lieutenant, but before you go I was wondering if you'd had a chance to read that message I sent you thirty minutes ago."

"Uh, which one?"

"The one I flagged 'Priority'."

"No." I admitted. I started to apologize and explain how busy I was, but managed to stop myself in time. Something about K'yon's attitude makes me forget that I'm the one in charge. "Give me the cliff notes."

"Well, that close questioning you ordered of the two security guards from the clinic paid off. Stephens walked them through the crime scene simulation. They identified several objects that they think our perp was the last one to touch. Most of the surfaces had been wiped down: his coffee cup, his locker. But there were a couple he missed. We got lucky with the control panel on the microwave in the employee lounge. We lifted an almost pristine index print off the start button."

An index print? That was good. Usually, identity thieves only wear a fake thumb print, because that's what everybody checks. Could we finally have a break in this case?

"Great." I said. "Now tell me that the owner had a criminal record and you were able to run the print."

"OK, the owner had a criminal record, and we were able to run his print. Belongs to one Jack Banders. His full bio is attached to the memo. Arrested for assault, carrying a concealed weapon, convictions for racketeering. General history as a thug for hire. Released from Clayton State prison eight months ago. Stopped meeting with his parole officer two months ago."

"Any connection to the body from the graveyard or the vic in today's murder?"

"Nothing I can find online. But the man's profile suggests his involvement may be mercenary."

"Allright. Any ideas on where to start looking for him?"

"His records suggest several known associates and locales he frequents."

"Great. Zap those to Lieutenant Browning first chance you get. Also, get online with a judge, and get a warrant to set up a data trap on Banders. Maybe we'll get lucky and he'll use his own thumb print to cash a check or something. If so, you're to call me immediately."

"Of course, Lieutenant. I'll see to it. Best of luck."

I hung up on K'yon, and switched over to the video feed from Tony's headset. He was talking with a couple of the techs, who were pouring plaster of paris into the footprints. It looked like he was going to be a few more minutes. I walked over to the tech who was sweeping the porch for prints.

"This clear?" I asked, pointing to the porch swing.

"Sure Lieutenant. We've already checked it for latents and fibers."

"Thanks."

I sat down in the swing and called up the vic's bio on my palm book.

"Name: Raven Straylight. Legally changed from Roberta Stevens in 2013. Age 54. No criminal record. Born in Tidewater Virginia to..." The words blurred in front of me. I rubbed my eyes. I'd been up so long that my retinas were beginning to feel fuzzy. I would read the whole thing later, but for the moment I skipped down through the document, looking for the bits that K'yon had thought important enough to highlight for me. I found the first section.

"Worked as data management technician for Liberty Media beginning in 1980. Worked as Personal Assistant to Reverend Zachariah Stonewall from 1985 to 2008. (K'yon Notes: time window overlaps employment by Carl Phillips, our mutilated corpse, as a bodyguard to Stonewall.)"

Now that was interesting. I read the rest of Straylight's bio straight through. She had left Stonewall's employ in 2008, and had no recorded job for the next nine months. She then went to work as a day care attendant at Coca-Cola's corporate headquarters, at substantially lower pay. Two years later, she switched employers again, this time to take a job as a kindergarten teacher at a private school for Wiccan kids called Holy Oak.

It was an interesting story that raised a lot of interesting questions. Like why she had left Stonewall's employment when she didn't have another job waiting. And why she had moved from the world of Baptist Fundamentalists to the world of New Age Wiccans. I was pondering these questions when Tony came out and joined me on the porch.

"So Data Services give you anythin' useful?"

"Yeah, we've had a couple breaks." I filled him in on how we'd ID'd Jack Banders as the perp who'd posed as a guard at the clinic.

"Hallelujah. About time we had a break." Tony mumbled some commands into his headset and called up some data on his notebook.

"Hm. Looks like our boy Banders may have been in on last night's caper as well. One of those prints in the backyard is his shoe size. The estimated weight is 12 pounds higher than Banders was at his last prison physical, but it's not surprising that he'd put on a little weight once he's back on the street and off prison food."

"Anything else that ties this to the other crime scenes?" I asked.

"Yeah. I was about to tell you that. There's another set of shoe prints that look good to be a match for that dress shoe with the cut in the sole. Then there's a third set that might match a partial of a sneaker print that we took from the graveyard."

"OK. So now we can prove that we're dealing with same guys."

"No real doubt in my mind."

"No. Which brings up another interesting connection between these cases that I wanted to talk to you about."

Since I still had the victim's bio on my palmbook, I passed it to Tony to read.

"Start with the highlighted parts."

When he'd finished he looked up. "Interesting." He paused. "But it could just be a coincidence."

"Maybe," I agreed. "But it's the only thing we've found that ties the victim from the graveyard to this one."

"OK," Tony said, slowly. " But if that's the connection, then how does the Clinic fit into it? I can't imagine that Reverend Stonewall has a stake in it."

"No. That doesn't fit yet," I admitted. "But I think this is worth looking into. Do you agree?"

"It's a lead, we have to follow it."

"Good. 'Cause I want you to be the one to call the victim's family. According to the bio, there's a mother and a younger sister in Virginia." I didn't say that they were probably Baptist, which is why I wanted Tony to ask the questions.

"Anything in particular you want to know?"

"Yeah. I want to know why she quit her job with Stonewall back in 2008. And I also want to know about her religious beliefs. Baptists don't convert to Witchcraft every day. She must have had some sort of monster crisis of faith."

"The dark powers can be seductive."

"Maybe. Or maybe there's something more to it."

"Allright. I'll see what I can find out."

"Good. And when you're done with that, I want to put you in charge of the manhunt for Banders. Find him, but don't bring him in. Just keep an eye on him and see who he meets up with. He's not the brains in this operation, and I don't want to put the cuffs on him until I know who is doing all this and why."

"Got it."

"I'll organize the canvassing effort here. Maybe one of the neighbors saw or heard something last night. Then I'll get back to HQ. I'll let you know what forensics comes up with on the body."

"Yes ma'am."

Tony took my old seat on the porch swing and started reading up on the vic's relatives—it's always good to know who you're dealing with before starting an interview. I went out to the street and grabbed a half dozen of the uniforms that had been arriving over the last few minutes. A couple of camera crews had also turned up, but there really wasn't much for them to see from the outside of the house. I left five officers in place to keep reporters off the lawn, and sent the rest out with instructions on what to ask the neighbors. I made a point of pairing Tores up with someone a little more experienced, who could show him the ropes. Then I went back into the house, found a spot where I was out of sight of the camera crews and out of the way of the techs, and made a call to my Watch Commander.

"Hello." Commander Davison always answers his phone on the first ring. "What have you got for me Strand?"

I filled him in on the current crime scene, and the evidence that linked it to the other two incidents. Then I told him about the break we'd had in identifying Banders, and asked if we could pull in a few more plain clothes from the precincts to help with the manhunt. I was expecting him to grumble a bit about how much manpower I was using on this case, but he agreed without an argument and told me he'd see to it. Lastly, I brought up the odd connection that we'd found between the two corpses: They had both worked for Stonewall.

"Stonewall..." There was something odd in the Commander's voice. "That's an odd connection...What do you think it means?"

The Commander usually talks a mile a minute, and now suddenly he was spacing out his words, as if he was thinking about what to say next.

"I don't know..." I admitted, "...yet. It could be coincidence. But it might be important. If we can pin down a motive for these crimes, it will go a long way toward identifying the perps."

"Yes...Good idea...Let me know what you find," He said, and hung up.

Well that was weird. I spent the next few minutes trying to figure out what had just happened. I wondered if I might have imagined it, if I was reading too much into a change in speech patterns. I retrieved the phone call from the case file and replayed the end of it two more times. The more I heard it, the more I was convinced that something about the name Stonewall had really thrown the Commander for a loop.

Well, I hadn't gotten this far in the department by walking into situations with my eyes closed. If there was a political connection between Stonewall and the Commander, I was going to find out about it before it snuck up and bit me in the butt.

## Chapter 32:  The Chosen
## Wednesday the 11th, 1:30 PM

Summer was loading up her back pack.  Half a dozen weird looking herbs and wands had already gone into it.  Now she was sorting through a collection of crystals, trying to decide which ones to take along.

In the meantime, I had borrowed her notebook and zapped on over to the net address that Tim had given me for the bug.  Not that I was really that keen to find these CIA agents who had suddenly taken such an interest in my life.  Summer was all hot to play Jane Bond, but there were a number of details to her plan that were still unclear to me.  Things like:

What were we going to do when we actually caught up to these guys?

What would we do if they saw us before we saw them?

And what *exactly* would we do if they pulled out guns and shot at us?  I mean, other than bleed.

So far, Summer had glossed over these points with the assurance that we would "think of something when the moment came," a fact that I had no doubt of.  Even now, my mind was racing with all sorts of ideas.  Unfortunately, most of them involved different places where our mangled bodies might be found by the police.  Still, I wasn't about to tell Summer that I was too scared to embark on this mad adventure with her.

While I was musing on all this, the Spytech webpage came up on the notebook.  A little animated figure in a black trench coat and fedora peered around the corner of the screen, then tip-toed out into the open.  When he reached the center of my screen, he opened his coat to reveal icons for nine or ten different product lines.  He started to give me the pitch for a sale the company was having on rifle-mics, but I clicked on past him to the product support section, then on to the subsection dealing with tracers.  When I got there, I punched in the serial number that Tim had given me, along with the "TimIsCool" password.  The screen opened up onto a map of Atlanta, with a little arrow pointing out the location of the tracer.  There was a magnifying glass icon in the corner, which controlled the zoom, and an hourglass, which let me plot the past locations of the tracer.  The whole package was surprisingly easy to use.  Who would have guessed that somebody makes user-friendly espionage equipment?

"How's it coming?" Summer asked, stuffing a little crystal skull into her backpack.

"Got 'em," I answered. "They're down south, near the airport."

"Great. Let's move."

I passed her the notebook and she put it in her backpack, then we climbed out her window and down the tree into her backyard. From there, we made our way around to the side of the house, keeping our heads down in case her mom looked out a window. We slipped through a hole in the hedge, trekked across her neighbor's yard, and finally got out onto the sidewalk for the four block walk to Little Five Points

At Little Five, we caught a MARTA train heading south on the Newline over to King Memorial Station, then a west train toward Five Points station, where we would eventually switch over to the North-South line. On the way, I had Summer pass me her notebook again so that I could take a closer look at what our mysterious friends were up to. They were still at that same spot down in the south end of town. I clicked on the zoom button a couple of times to take a closer look at their location.

"Well that's weird," I mumbled.

"What?" asked Summer, leaning over to look at the screen. She was wearing a t-shirt with a wolf on it, and the collar was kind of loose, so when she leaned over that way...Well, you can probably understand why my mind went blank.

"Uh.............."

Summer grabbed my chin and pointed my face back toward the screen.

"You were saying, Benji?"

"Oh yeah. Just that it's weird. This location they've been at for the last half hour. According to the map, it's St. John's High School."

"What's so weird about that?"

"Well, if they're looking for me, what are they doing at some Catholic school? I mean, it would make sense if they were at my school, or my house, or maybe even the arcade at Lost World. But why go there?"

"I don't know." Summer admitted, staring at the little arrow on the screen. "Maybe they're questioning some friend of yours. Do you know anybody who goes to that school?"

"Oh right. Like my parents are going to let me hang out with Catholics."

"And what's that supposed to mean?"

"Nothing, it's just that you don't know my parents. Anyway, I don't know any Catholic kids."

"OK," Summer said, staring at the map. "So what are the MIBS doing there?"

"Well," I started, "we still don't know who they're working for. Maybe they're secret agents for the Pope."

"Benji?"

"Yeah. Think about it. I'll bet the Pope has a few spooks working for her. In fact, it would be kind of amazing if the Vatican didn't have an intelligence service. It is an independent country after all."

"Benji?"

"Yeah, sort of a holy CIA."

"...Benji?!"

"What? Alright, I'm kidding. I have no idea why they're there."

Summer poked me in the ribs, then went back to staring at the map.

"Neither do I, Benji. But I intend to find out."

"Uh-huh." I said, trying to sound more enthusiastic than I was. "Um, not to inject an unwelcome note of practicality into this whole spy fantasy, but what exactly are we planning to do when we catch up to these guys? This is the part of the plan I'm not clear on."

"Oh don't worry. We'll just play it by ear. I figure we'll follow them around for awhile, blending in with the other kids for cover. Then when we know what they're up to, we can..."

"Excuse me?" I interrupted. "But we're going to blend in with *who* for cover?" Summer was wearing jeans and a wolf t-shirt, with a charm bag slung around her neck. "Somehow I have trouble imagining you passing for a Catholic school girl. Don't they wear uniforms? Plaid skirts, or something like that?"

"Skirts? Ick. Well, forget that idea. But I'm sure we'll think of something by the time we get there."

I wished that I had Summer's faith in our ability to come up with a plan at the last minute. I was racking my brain, but the only thing I could think of was that trick that they use in spy movies, where the good guys lure a couple of guards into a closet, then knock them out, tie them up, and steal their uniforms. I tried to imagine the two of us tackling a couple of Catholic School kids and then dragging them into a bathroom to steal their clothes. I hoped that Summer was coming up with something better.

Fortunately, we were spared the need to implement any such drastic schemes. By the time we got to the transfer point to the North-South line, the tracer had started moving again, heading northeast. There wasn't much point in trying to catch up with our quarry while they were moving, so Summer and I popped into a Sushi Sam's to grab a bite to eat and wait for the MIBS to get wherever it was they were going. She bought me a California Roll on her cash card, and got one of those green tea sodas for herself.

"You want a sip?" she asked.

"Sure." I took a gulp and almost gagged on it. I'd never had one before, and the stuff tasted like carbonated fish guts. "Aaaaach. Oh God, that's awful."

"Huh. Well I guess it is kind of an acquired taste." She watched me make faces for a few more seconds, till I finally managed to get the taste out of my mouth with some wasabi. "So Benji, what do you want to be when you grow up?"

Wow. That one came from out of the blue. I took another bite of my California roll, and chewed slowly. It looked like I was about to have my first serious conversation with my first serious girlfriend, and I wanted to think of something cool to say. I finished chewing and swallowed.

"Taller."

She laughed at that.

"OK, but what else?"

"Hm... Better looking, too."

"Benji, come on."

I tried to think of a good serious answer, but I was stuck. We were at that age when you're too old to say that you want to be something silly, like a movie star or a bank robber or president, and too young to admit that you're going to wind up being something boring like a lawyer or an ad exec or manager of a shoe store or something.

"I don't know," I finally admitted. "What do you want to be?"

"You mean besides Empress of the World?"

"Yeah," I said, "it's always good to have a second line of work to fall back on."

"Well," she said, "I've actually been thinking that I might like to be a comic book artist. Maybe on *Mars Force* or *Underworld*, or the *Callisto* series."

"That's cool," I said, and then couldn't think of anything else to say. If I'd been smart, I would have suggested that we collaborate on a comic, with her doing the art and me doing the writing. But I didn't. I never think of the right things to say until five minutes after the conversation is over.

We sat there eating in awkward silence for a few more minutes, until I notice that the tracer had stopped moving again. I tapped on the magnifier icon a couple of times and zoomed in on the new location. It was a large building out in Sandy Springs. I read the name off the map.

"Ron Reagan High School?"

Summer leaned over the table to look at the map.

"Another high school? What can they be looking for there?"

"I don't know," I admitted, "but it can't be me. I've never even heard of this place."

"Well, let's go check it out."

I stuffed the rest of the California roll into my mouth, and Summer tossed the remainder of her soda into a waste bin. We hopped the escalators back down to the tracks, then caught a north train out to the end of the Sandy Springs spur. When we got there, we discovered that Ron Reagan High School was almost a two mile walk from the station. (You'd think that somebody in the city planner's office would have planned that out better, but adults never seem to do anything right.) Anyway, we jogged over to the school, hoping that our spy guys would still be there by the time we arrived.

Fortunately, the place wasn't hard to find. It was enormous. Ron Reagan High School turned out to be one of those big malls that the city bought up during the big real estate crash back in the single digits. I'd heard about schools like this, but I'd never actually been in one. Summer and I walked across the big parking lot, and then went in through the western entrance. A guard standing by the metal detector waved us on through. If he thought there was something strange about a couple of students turning up for school at two in the afternoon, he didn't say anything.

Inside, the place was kind of creepy. I mean, it still looked like a mall, with the big wide halls and escalators and everything. Only there were lockers along all the walls, and security cameras looking at you every time you turned around. A few other kids were walking around loose. Probably seniors with a free period and hall privileges, I guessed. I spotted a directory and walked over to it. It had maps of all three levels, and all the rooms were color coded by subject. Blue for English. Red for math. And Green for something called "Theirstory."

Summer got her notebook out and checked on the location of the tracer.

"It looks like the MIBS are somewhere around...here." She pointed to a spot on the map near the northeast corner of the building. "I can't pin it down any closer than that."

"OK." I said. "Any way to tell what level they're on?"

She looked at the notebook for a minute, and tried tapping on a couple of icons.

"Nah, not with this thing."

"Well, then that leaves us three levels and a fair amount of area to cover. Any ideas on where to start?"

"Uh, let's see what we've got here." She started checking room numbers on the map against their listings in the directory. "English 202, English 203, English 204. Girls locker room. Boys locker room. Security station. Infirmary. Maintenance. Administrative offices. Detention Center. Storage..."

"Wait a minute. Go back. Administrative offices. That would be, like, the principal and stuff?"

"Yeah, I guess so."

"Well let's try there first," I suggested. "I mean, I'll bet even spies have to check in with the Principal when they come to a school and start doing...well...spy stuff. Don't you think? Like they'd have to show him a warrant or ask permission or something?"

"OK," Summer agreed. "Sounds like a good place to start."

We took the escalators down a couple levels, and then walked toward the north end of the building. On the way I glanced into a few of the class rooms. Bored looking kids watching video-taped lectures. Bored looking grown-ups watching bored looking kids. I couldn't quite decide if the adults in the room were there as teachers or security guards.

We walked through the food court, which had been converted into a playground. There was something weird about seeing swing sets indoors. A couple of seniors were hanging out on the merry-go-round, chatting. A white boy with green hair was flirting with a black girl with no hair and rings in her scalp, who was in turn leaning on some Asian kid who could have been either a boy or a girl but had lots of tattoos, who was talking to some white boy who looked pretty normal. Well, the same normal as me, anyway.

We got to the north end of the building, and I saw another one of those big triangular kiosks with a map and a directory on it. I stopped to check our bearing, and had just found the "you are here" arrow, when Summer suddenly shoved me up against the thing.

"Hey! What's the big idea?"

"Shh!" Summer hissed. She was pressed up against the directory next to me. Slowly, she leaned her head out to peek around the edge of the kiosk with one eye, then jerked back quickly. "They're here."

I leaned out to take a look around the other side. Sure enough, twenty meters down the hall there was a big guy in a dark suit standing in front of an open door. Tim had been right. Classic MIBS.

Anyway, the guy was holding the door for somebody, and as I watched a kid about my age came out of the office. A white kid, short, with brown curly hair. The MIBS said something to him, then they shook hands and the kid went off.

Summer tapped me on the shoulder. I pulled my head back behind the directory to talk to her.

"Look familiar?" she asked.

"Yeah," I said. "They do look like the guys in spy movies."

"No, I mean the kid."

I thought about it. "No. I don't think I know him."

Summer rolled her eyes and gave me the "boy are you being stupid" look.

"Cut that out," I said. "I get that look enough from my mom."

"Benji, have you ever looked in a mirror?"

"Oh." I stuck my head back round the directory, trying to get another look at the kid, but he was walking away.

"Oh come on," I said. "He doesn't look a thing like me. I'm much taller than that."

She raised one eyebrow.

"Well I am."

I looked back around the corner again to verify the fact. The kid was almost of sight now, but another one was walking toward us. Another short, white kid. With curly brown hair. And big ears. And...well, let's face it: acne for days.

"This is getting weird."

Summer came over to my side of the directory and stuck her head out to see what I was talking about.

"Wow. Another one. Did somebody clone you or something?"

"Oh yeah. Like somebody is going to clone me. Trust me, if they're going to spend that kind of money, they're going to pick somebody taller. With better eyesight. And better skin, too."

"Oh, I don't know," said Summer. "I think it might be fun to have a couple more of you. My own little pack of Benji clones. I could start a collection."

"Should I be flattered or frightened by that comment?"

"That depends on how you'd feel about being a member of a harem."

The comment went by so fast that I almost didn't register it.

"Now let's see," she continued. "I could have a Benji to do the yard work, and a Benji to do the housework, and a Benji to be my personal Masseur. Then once a week I could take you all out to the arcade and crush you at Slip Stream."

"You seem confident about that."

"I notice that you didn't say 'over-confident'."

"Hey, you only beat me once."

"Hm. And that's out of how many times that we've played against each other?"

"Well, when this is all over you can defend your title, 'Space Knight'."

"Wait a minute," she said. "No."

"What, afraid of a rematch?"

She shook her head, "Dream on lizard boy. I meant, 'No, he's not a clone.' Look at his face. Sort of the same. But not yours."

I took another look, and I could see what she meant. A lot like me, but not me. As we watched, the MIBS came back out of the office and waved the kid in.

"So what the heck is going on here?" I wondered out loud.

"Well, if you were all a foot taller, blond, and buff, I'd think they were having a model search."

I glared at her.

"Not that I don't like you just the way you are, Benji."

Boy, she really knows how to make a guy feel special. I turned and took a good look at the map we were hiding behind.

"Hm. According to this, that's not the principal's office they're going into."

"No?"

"It's the infirmary."

"The infirmary? What could they be doing in there? Researching a cure for acne?"

I glared at her again. "You know, it's ok when I do it to myself, but..."

"Oh Benji," she said, and then punched me in the arm. I had been aiming for a hug with that comment. Remind me not to try the sympathy ploy on her again.

"Well," I continued, rubbing my arm. She hits hard. "Aside from making further jokes at my expense, what are we going to do now?"

"Tell you what. You wait right here. I'm going to go into the infirmary and see what they're up to."

"What?!"

"Well, you can't go in. They'll recognize you."

"And just what are you going to do? Waltz in and say 'Excuse me, but I've noticed that you're building up an army of short fourteen year old boys with bad skin and big ears, would you care to reveal your nefarious plan to me?'"

"Oh come on, you're skin isn't *that* bad, Benji. You know, I'll bet there's a charm that would clear that right up. Maybe something with..."

"You're dodging the question."

"No I'm not. I'm just going to go in there and see what they're up to. They probably won't even notice me. There are always five or six kids hanging around a nurse's office for one reason or another."

"And if they do ask why you're there?"

Summer bent over and grabbed her stomach with both arms.

"Oh gee. Ow. I like, have a really bad stomach ache. Could you give me an alka seltzer or something? Maybe..."

"Wait," I interrupted. "You're going to go in there faking a stomach ache?"

"Yeah," she said, straightening up, "what's wrong with that?"

"No, no, no, no, no! Haven't you ever cut a class before? You *never* tell a nurse you have a stomach ache. Ever since that kid died of appendicitis during a math test two years back, all the school nurses have gotten real jumpy about stomach aches. You go in there claiming one of those and they'll ship you off to an emergency room so fast it will make your head spin."

"Really?"

"Trust me, I know what I'm talking about. I see my school nurse so often that she's got a cot with my name on it. Go with a sprained ankle."

"A sprained ankle?"

"Yeah, nurses like sprained ankles. It's a nice, reassuring injury. They know what to do for it, and there's no chance you're going to die from it. They'll put some ice on it, hold your hand for awhile, and then send you back to class."

"Great!" Summer said, handing me her backpack. "I'll be in and out in five minutes. I'll let you know what I find out." Then she went walking off to the infirmary, leaving me alone. At least she remembered to limp.

I stood behind the directory and waited. I hate being left out of things. It's just not fair. I mean, this is my conspiracy, right? They're after me. So how come I'm the one who winds up doing all the waiting while Summer gets to go and do all the cool counter-espionage stuff?

I called up the time on her notebook, and watched the seconds tick by. I made up my mind that I was going to give her exactly five minutes before I went charging in there. I had the whole scene worked out in my head. I would do a diving roll through the door, and drop the first MIBS with a punch to the solar plexus. Then I'd go into a spinning sidekick and clobber the one next to him. And finally, as the third one was drawing a gun, I would take him out from across the room by throwing a paper weight at him. Yep, that would show Summer. I had the whole thing visualized, every detail of how I was going to come to her rescue.

If I had happened to know karate.

And was about a foot taller.

With another seventy pounds of muscle mass.

And a better complexion.

I came back from fantasy land and checked the time. Six minutes. She'd said she would be back in five. I watched the digits continue to roll by. Seven minutes. Eight.

Nine.

Ten.

Eleven. Where was she? I couldn't just stand here waiting forever. She might really be in trouble. I came out from behind the directory and started walking toward the infirmary. I was so scared that my feet felt like lead and I thought my legs were going to freeze up, but I kept moving forward. I was thinking that I would just walk past and glance in on my way by, but as I got to the infirmary's door it opened suddenly, and a MIBS stepped out, right in front of me.

I almost walked into him. He looked at me curiously.

"Uh......" my mind went blank. I knew I needed to turn around and run away, but I couldn't get my legs to work. Besides, he was so close he would have just grabbed me.

"Oh, hi," he said. He reached into his jacket and I was expecting him to pull out a gun, but he just got out one of those little palm notebooks and read something off it. "You're Thomas St. Germain?"

I had no idea who this Thomas kid was, but he couldn't possibly be in as much trouble as I was in. "Uh...yeah. Thomas. That's me."

The MIBS made a note in his palmbook.

"We're not quite ready for you yet, Thomas. If you'll just take a seat while we finish with the other boy."

He motioned to an empty chair inside the door. I went in and sat down.

Then he closed the door behind me.

## Chapter 33: The Gumshoe

I grab a coke out of Daniel's refrigerator, and walk back to the big main room of his apartment. He's over on the bed, giggling underneath some dark-haired Italian kid who's chewing on his neck. I watch them for a little while, sipping my coke, until Daniel finally realizes I'm there.

"Oh hey Drew!" he says, trying to sit up. That doesn't work, so he switches tactics, and rolls over on top of the Italian kid. He gives him a kiss, and then turns to me. "This is Vincent, my new boyfriend. Vince, this is Drew."

I look Vincent over. Dark hair and the same unnatural green eyes that all the disco-clones have. There's a tattoo, some sort of Celtic pattern, on his left shoulder. He's wearing a saint's medallion and boxers. Marvin the Martian boxers. Probably a gift from Daniel. I nod my head, by way of a hello.

Vince looks me over in return.

"Hey old man."

They go back to kissing. I feel my gut tighten, but I remind myself that I am not the jealous type, and that it is a good thing that Daniel has stopped mooning over me and found someone his own age.

But that doesn't make it any easier.

I turn away from them. I don't know why this should bother me. I had always known it will end this way.

And that seems strange to me, and I stop and think about it. Because somehow, I know that all this hasn't happened yet. But it all will. Right down to the details, a boy named Vince, green contact lenses, and a gift of Marvin the Martian boxers.

I finish my coke, and go to the refrigerator for another one. There's a body in there now. Some old woman with white hair, and a tattoo of a raven on her right breast. From the incisions, it looks like the ME has already done the autopsy: opened her stomach to check the contents, drained the bladder to analyze her urine for drugs. There's a series of specimen bottles next to her. Blood. Urine. Spinal fluid. Daniel's out of coke, so I grab a bottle of iced mocha and close the door.

I step back out of the kitchen nook and into the main room. Daniel and Vincent have moved out to the couch now, where they are eating a pizza and watching TV. And giggling. Vincent looks up at me with his strange green eyes.

"What? You're still here? Why?"

He's right, of course. I have no business here. It will end this way, and there is nothing I can do to change it.

I walk out the front door of Daniel's apartment and into the hallway. Secretaries and technicians crowd past me. A blinking sign on the wall counts down the seconds till air time. I push my way through the crowd and make it to the elevator. The doors open and I step on board.

As the doors start to close, a tyrannosaurus in an Atlanta Cubs t-shirt forces his way in. He lets out a low grumble, which I take for an apology. The other occupants of the car ignore him, but seem angry with me. The teddy bear scowls in my direction, while the cat arches its back and hisses at me.

"Don't mind them," says the snake in the feathered boa. Her delicate tail is wrapped around a long cigarette holder. She takes a puff, and blows a smoke ring at the teddy bear. "They're just jealous."

The elevator stops, the doors open, and I step out onto the roof. The snake follows me. I hear it slithering along on the gravel behind me, and then the sound changes, and I hear footsteps. I turn around and see a woman in a feather boa and a green dress, puffing on a cigarette in a long holder.

Whatever.

I continue walking, until I finally find my car. Some bozo has stuck a flyer on the windshield.

"A Final Tribute to the Work of Alicia St. Cloud. One showing only, Friday the 13th."

I unlock my door, throw the flyer into the pile of trash in my backseat that I've been meaning to clean out, and climb in. The snake lady is sitting in the passenger seat, looking as if she owns the place. Well, actually, looking as if she owns a much better place and just happens to be slumming it in my car.

"Hit the road, mouse breath," I tell her. "No hitchhikers."

She takes a long drag on her cigarette, and blows a smoke ring. It takes the shape of a snake biting its own tail, then dissolves. Cute trick.

"Silly boy," she says. "I'm not a passenger, I'm a navigator. Now drive along. I have another appointment to keep and we don't have much time."

I'm not in a mood to argue, and I don't have anything she'd want to steal, anyway. What's she gonna do? Hijack this tin bucket? So I start the car, and drive off the edge of the building.

We plummet down, the wind whistling past the missing passenger side window. I do need to get that fixed, one of these days. Beneath us, there's a plaza filled with people, and a mound of flowers.

"Speaking of navigation," the snake lady says, "you might want to do something about that nasty impact looming up ahead of us."

Good point. I signal a left, and then turn the car away from the ground. For a dizzying moment, up and down and left trade places, and then it's all OK and I'm driving along the side of the building, glass from the windows crunching under my tires.

I realize that I'm not sure where I'm driving to.

"Well, if you are the navigator," I ask, "where are we going?"

She takes another long drag on her cigarette, and blows another smoke ring. This one was a circle of words. "One Nation Under God." I've got to find out how she does that.

"Well, I'm afraid that *we're* not going anywhere, Kimosabe." she says. "No time. I have my appointment to keep, and you have business of your own to attend to. I just wanted to drop in and wish you luck. And get you pointed in the right direction."

She points ahead with her cigarette holder.

"Speaking of which," she says, "you might want to avoid those window cleaners."

I had taken my eyes off the road, and I have to swerve to avoid a window cleaning crew in a gondola. My tiles squeal and more glass breaks underneath them. In the rearview mirror, I can see the crew yelling and giving me the finger. Well, hopefully none of them got my license plate.

I make another left, and we start back up the side of the building. A hoard of demons is hogging the road, but I honk and they grudgingly let us pass.

"Hey Mack!" one of them yells as I drive past. He's wearing a T-shirt with a pink triangle on it and carrying a picket sign. "You got the time?"

I glance at the clock in my dash board.

"Midnight." I yell back.

We continue up the building. Somewhere near the top, there's a fire, sending a dark column of smoke into the sky. I drive through the flames, and then the sound of breaking glass stops, and I realize that we're driving up the trail of smoke. In the rearview mirror, I see Atlanta below us. There are fires burning all over town.

"Just keep your eyes on the road," the snake lady says, "and listen. First rule: Don't go talk to a psychologist. He'll try to lock you up."

"Huh?"

"Trust me, the thought will occur to you. Don't act on it." She takes another drag on her cigarette. "And by the way, watch out for the moon, it's fragile."

I look back at the road just in time to see the moon looming up ahead of us. At least, I think's the moon. Just not for a long time, yet. The parts in the crescent of light are green, and blue, and red, with clouds like earth. And the parts in the shadow twinkle with the lights of cities. It's beautiful.

And it's also too darned close to miss. I try to brake, but we smash right through it and it shatters into a thousand tiny pieces, raining back down to earth as shooting stars.

The snake lady raises an eyebrow. "And they haven't taken your license away yet? OK. Second big piece of advice: Don't make it easy on people who come to you asking for guidance. Make it as difficult as possible for them to get in and see you, and when they do, couch all your advice in riddles and metaphors. People always figure that they get what they pay for. If you make 'em work for your advice, they'll think it's worth more."

Something bright catches my attention, and I look out the left window to see the sunrise. We must have driven so far that we're climbing into sunlight. I signal a right, and pull the car onto a sunbeam.

"Um, excuse me lady," I say, "but am I supposed to understand any of this?"

She takes another long drag, then flicks the ash out the window. The embers burn in the breeze like little fire flies on our tail.

"Not yet. But you will. Oh, and one last thing. You're going to get really irritated with Laughing Bear in about a week. Give him time. He'll grow on you."

And with that, she unbuckles her seatbelt and opens the passenger side door.

"Wait a minute," I say. "That's it? None of that makes any sense. And what the Hell is this laughing bear all about?"

She turns and takes my face in her hands. "Ah, if only we had more time for this. But my appointment waits." She stubs out her cigarette in my cup holder, extinguishing it with an air of finality. "But don't worry. You will find your own way. And if there's anything else you need to know, your totem can tell you."

"Wait!" I shout. "Who the Hell is my totem?"

But she's gone, stepped out on the breeze and blown away.

## Chapter 34:  The Chosen
## Wednesday the 11th, 2:30 PM

I took my seat and looked around the infirmary.  The MIBS who had let me in was still standing by the door.  Another MIBS was at the back of the room, drawing some blood from one of my almost-clones.  Across from me, Summer was sitting on a cot with one of those blue bags of chem ice strapped to her ankle.  She was arguing with a nurse about why her records weren't on the school's computer yet.  She risked a quick glance in my direction, and shrugged.  Best laid plans.

The MIBS who had let me in handed me a notebook with some sort of form on it.

"Tell you what, Thomas.  If you could fill this out while we finish up with the boy ahead of you, it will speed things up."

I glanced at the form.  Mostly standard medical stuff. Height.  Weight.  Handedness.  Bloodtype.  Natural eye color. Natural hair color.

"Uh...my teacher didn't explain what you needed me for."

"Oh, that's OK." said the MIBS with a big smile that was supposed to be friendly but instead gave me the creeps.  "You see, the Center for Disease Control has just identified a gene that indicates an increased propensity for developing certain skin cancers. The gene is most common among males of your ancestry with pale skin and blue eyes.  If you test positive for the gene, we'll give you a pamphlet detailing steps that you can take to reduce your risks, but there's really nothing to worry about.  OK?"

He was still giving me that creepy smile.  I forced the corners of my mouth into what I hoped was a grin and nodded back at him.  The whole story sounded completely reasonable and sensible.  Except for the fact that he had told a completely different tale to Tim a few hours ago.  And that these guys didn't look like doctoring types to me.  Not unless they'd both gone to med school on football scholarships.

The other MIBS finished taking the blood sample from my twin and popped the full cartridge into some gizmo that I didn't recognize. I glanced over at Summer, who was still arguing with the nurse.

"I still can't find your name in the records."

"Well maybe they misspelled it when they typed it in.  Nobody every spells my name right.  Try  D E Z E R T S K I, sometimes people try to spell it that way."

I looked back at my twin. The MIBS was putting a bandaid on the kid's arm and getting him ready to go. He patted the kid on the back and promised to let him know when the test results came in.

"OK son, we're ready for you now," said the one who'd let me in. I almost jumped out of my skin. I had a feeling something bad was going to happen, and that I ought to try and make a break for it. But the MIBS was right on top of me. He put a hand on my shoulder and led me over to his partner. His partner told me to sit on the cot, and I did. He told me to roll up my sleeve, and I did. He took the notebook out of my other hand and looked at it.

"You haven't filled this out yet?"

I shook my head "no", worried that if I spoke my voice would crack from fear.

"Well you can finish it afterwards," said the MIBS, uncapping a fresh needle.

Well, maybe this wouldn't be too bad. Maybe I was getting all worked up over nothing. Maybe they'd just draw some blood and let me go. I glanced over at Summer, who was still having the nurse check alternate spellings of Dezertski. Then I saw the door open, and another one of my almost clones walked in. With a sinking feeling, I realized who he must be.

"Hi," the new kid said. "I'm Thomas St. Germain. My teacher said you wanted to see me?"

The MIBS in front of me looked confused. I was fighting to come up with an explanation, but my brain had frozen. Out of the corner of my eye, I saw Summer slip down off her cot.

"Wait a minute," said the MIBS by the door, "If you're St. Germain, who are you..." he never had a chance to finish the sentence. As he turned around to face me, Summer did a sort of karate kick and nailed him with her bandaged foot right in the...well, in a place that nice young ladies aren't supposed to kick men. Not that I was going to complain about her upbringing. I only hoped that the chem ice pack had cushioned the blow a little.

The one in front of me heard his partner shriek, and as he spun around toward the sound I saw his right hand reaching into his jacket. I didn't know what he was going to pull out, but I had a feeling that whatever it was I didn't want to see him use it on Summer. There was only one hard object within reach, so I grabbed the gizmo they'd been putting the blood samples into off the bed and banged it against the guy's head as hard as I could.

I felt the thud. In the movies, guys just fall down and stop moving when you hit them like that. This one grabbed the back of his head and knelt down. I could see the blood welling up from between his fingers. I looked down at the gizmo I was holding. There was blood and a little skin and hair on it.

I dropped it without thinking. I hadn't meant to hurt the guy. Well, I mean I had meant to hurt the guy, to stop him from doing something to Summer, but I hadn't meant to *really* hurt him. Just stun him or knock him out or something like that.

Summer grabbed my arm.

"Come on!"

"He's hurt!"

"Well he picked a good place for it. The nurse will take care of him. Now come on!"

She shoved the Thomas kid out of the way (he was just standing there like an idiot), and then ran out the door, with me right behind her. The MIBS she'd kicked in the crotch made a grab for me on my way past, but I ducked and he missed me. Out in the hall we sprinted past the directory, then through the playground and up two escalators. From there it was a long straight run down a hallway toward the doors we came in. I could see the metal detector, and the security guard talking into a phone. And when we were about 20 yards off, I saw him pulling out a taser.

"Wrong way!" I shouted. We turned and took off in the opposite direction, back down the hall. At the first intersection I risked a glance behind us. The security guard was chasing us, but he was way overweight, and we were outdistancing him easily. But there was only so far we could run in this place.

I hung a right and Summer followed me. About 20 yards down this hall was another directory. I stopped to check our position.

"Benji, what are you doing?! They're right behind us!"

"And for all we know, they could be right in front of us too. We gotta figure a way out of here. Otherwise they'll just keep chasing us till we're cornered."

I scanned the map while Summer nervously kept look out.

"Sometime today we would be nice, Benji."

"I'm looking."

"Look faster."

"Ouch. We've got a problem."

"Tell me something I don't know."

"According to this, they've sealed up most of the old mall entrances. I guess for security or something. There are only two regular exits: the one we just came from, and one at the other end of the mall."

"Well let's go then!"

"No good. They'll just phone the guard at that one to keep an eye out for us. I mean," I gestured to the security camera looking down at us, "it's not like they don't know where we are."

"Benji!"

Summer grabbed my arm, and turned me around. The overweight security guard had finally rounded the corner. We took off down the hall away from him.

"Look," Summer said, panting "There has got to be another way out of this place."

"I'm open to suggestions."

We sprinted down to the end of the hall, then took the escalator a level down and started running back the other direction. A hundred yards ahead, I saw another guard come out into the hall. This one looked to be in better shape. I turned around. The obese guard had just made it down the escalator. We were surrounded.

Then my eyes noticed a red box on the wall. It took me a few seconds to realize what it was.

"Got it!"

I ran over, ripped the cover off, and stuck my thumb up against the reader. When this was all over, the school would be able to ID me from the thumb print, but I figured a charge of falsely setting off a fire alarm was the least of my problems right now.

The buzzer sounded, and a few seconds later the hallway was full of kids, with a few teachers vainly trying to keep them all in order. Summer and I blended into a class coming out of some history lecture, and followed them out through an emergency exit and into the sunshine.

## Chapter 35: The Chosen
## Wednesday the 11th, 2:45 PM

Of course, being out in the school's parking lot didn't mean that we were out of the woods. There were still those two MIBS and a bunch of security guards looking for us. I had also noticed several teachers answering their phones, and suspected that they were being told to keep a look out for us. So at the first opportunity Summer and I slipped away from our class and took cover among the cars.

The parking lot was only about half full, which left us with the problem of how to get across the remaining empty blacktop without being spotted. Fortunately, I spotted a drainage grate and Summer and I managed to pry it off.

"You're sure this is safe?" she asked.

"Oh sure," I said, letting myself down into the shaft first. "Tim and I used to go crawling around in the drainage pipes under my school all the time. We mapped them out and even had a secret hideout at one of the intersections. It's where I got the idea for that cool underground base that Zero has."

The shaft was only about five feet deep. I put my hands on Summer's hips to help her in, and she brushed up against me in all sorts of pleasant places on the way down. (And I don't think it was purely by accident, either.) Once we were both inside, we pulled the grate back over, only bruising a couple of fingers in the process.

From there it was just a straight crawl for a few hundred feet, till we came out in a drainage ditch on the other side of the parking lot. I'd ripped a new hole in the leg of my jeans. Summer came out right behind me, and I noticed that her hands were pretty scraped up.

"Oops, should have warned you about that." I said.

"Ah, don't sweat it, I heal fast."

"OK," I said, "But next time we go spy chasing, remind me to bring along some gloves."

Summer stood up and dusted herself off, then climbed up the side of the ditch to take a look back at the school.

"Wow. We crawled that far? Boy do I need a bath."

"Yeah, me too." That's the problem with tunnel crawling. You wind up feeling like you have little bits of concrete working their way into every inch of your skin.

She climbed back down, and we walked along the bottom of the ditch till we hit the next major road. We climbed out there, and found ourselves facing a little strip mall with a Rush-In. Summer suggested that we grab a bite to eat, and I heartily agreed. She got a cup of borscht and I got a cabbage roll.

"By the way," she said, once our hunger was sated enough to talk. "That was a good idea with the fire alarm. You get another bonus point for that."

"You know, you still haven't told me what I get to trade those in on."

"Trust me, it's worth the wait. You want a sip of this?"

"Nah, I don't like beets. You think we should call Tim and tell him what happened?"

"Yeah, good idea."

Summer punched up Tim's number, then leaned over to me so that we could both put our ears up to the receiver.

"Hello?"

"Hey Tim, it's Summer."

"Who? Just a second."

There was an odd popping noise on the receiver.

"Tim?"

"It's OK now, I'm scrambling the signal on this end. Dude, where have you guys been? I've been trying to get through to you for half an hour. I thought the MIBS had grabbed you."

"They almost did." Summer said. "We had to hide out in some drainage tunnels. The phone signals probably couldn't reach us down there."

"What happened?"

"It's a long story," I said, "see, we went to…"

"You'll have to tell me later," Tim interrupted. "Right now you need to get off this line."

"Huh? Why the big panic?" Summer asked.

"Listen fast, cause we don't have much time. Scott's mom got to his notebook before he had a chance to delete his address book."

"So?" Summer asked.

"*So* she gave it to the MIBS. *So* Summer's name and e-mail address are in there. *So* they almost certainly know who you are by now."

"Ick." I said.

"Ick?" Summer turned to me. "The CIA is going to come break down the front door of my house and tell my mother that I kicked one of them in the nuts, and all you can say is 'Ick'?"

"It was an understatement," I admitted.

"Guys?" Tim yelled. "Hello? Listen to me. By now they've got her phone number, too. And they can use that to track you.

You've got to turn off your phone. Turn off the modem in your computer. Turn off everything that uses radio communications. See, as long as those things are on, they constantly send a signal to the cellular network, so that it can tell which of its transmitters you're closest to, and route your calls correctly. So if the MIBS know your phone number they can put a trace on the system and figure out which relay station you're closest to..."

"I get the picture," Summer said, "They'll know exactly where we are."

"Well, not exactly, but within a a quarter mile or so. Close enough to start looking for you at any rate. So shut all that stuff down and get out of there."

"Wait," I jumped in. "There's are some things we need your help with. How do we get in touch with you?"

"Get to a safe place, then call me on a landline or someone else's phone or...no wait. Don't call me at all. Leave me a message at sneakyTim@Ubermensch.com with a number I can reach you back at."

"OK. We've got a lot to tell you."

"Fine. But right now turn off all that stuff and hit the road. They could be closing in on you even as we speak. Bye."

Tim hung up. I looked at Summer. She shrugged and opened her backpack. We went through it, turning off everything that might give away our position. Then she gulped down the rest of her borscht and I picked up the rest of my cabbage roll, and we started the walk back to the MARTA station.

"You got any ideas on where we should go?" I asked.

"Yeah," Summer said. "I've got a friend named Gerald that might be able to help us out. He's a cyber-mage."

"Cyber-mage?" The term had a cool sound to it. "You sure he can help?"

"I hope so," Summer said. "But it depends on whether or not his mom still has him grounded."

## Chapter 36: The Reverend-Senator
## Wednesday the 11th, 2:56 PM

Berta came in with the glass of milk I'd asked for. I took it from her, and then shooed her back out of the office. I was in no mood to try to be pleasant today. I hadn't been able to sleep at all last night. I'd just lain awake, thinking about what could happen. About how easily everything could slip away.

I tried to drink the milk, but even that made me queasy. I hadn't been able to eat anything but a banana all day. My stomach was one big knot. I thought about calling Reggie again and asking how the sweep was going, but there was no point. They'd let me know when they found him.

I looked over the results of the DNA scan on the hair again, still unable to believe what I was looking at. This boy could not exist. It was impossible. There was no way. Not even if Satan himself had suckled him. And yet the boy was here. And he could destroy me, and everything I had built.

I tried to get control of my fear. I was not, after all, unarmed or unbefriended. If the Devil thought me an easy target, then he had miscalculated. I had allies and I had weapons. And though he sends a host of demons against me, I will grind them into the earth.

And that made me think of the Painting. I walked over to look at it, the picture of myself standing alone against the hosts of Hell. Defending the light, but not standing in it. Alicia had understood me all too well. She knew. That the very act of struggling with evil slowly moves one out from the light, slowly burns away the innocence and purity in yourself that you are trying to protect in others. I kept the painting here to remind me of that. That, and of the cost of even the slightest mistake, the slightest weakening of my guard.

I felt a tear roll down my cheek. Maybe it was for Alicia, who understood me. Better than my wife. Better than my parents. Better than I understand myself. And who loved me anyway. Or maybe I'm crying for myself, for the things I have given up to fight this war.

I tried to drink some more of the milk, while I waited for the phone to ring, waited for Reggie to call and say that they had found the boy, that he could no longer harm us. I managed to swallow the milk, but it sat in my stomach like a cold rock. Mercifully, my eye lids closed, and I was finally on the verge of getting some sleep when the phone rang.

"Yes, Reggie?"

"No sir, it's Berta."

"Oh." I had to get a grip on myself. I sounded edgy and nervous. I tried to make my voice sound calm and in control.

"Oh. Yes Berta. What is it?"

"Well, Justin Weir is here to see you again, sir, and..."

"I told you, no visitors!" I said, then realized that I was shouting. "I'm very busy right now, and I..."

"Yes, but he's very insistent sir, in fact...Hey, wait. You can't go in there!"

The doors to my office opened and Justin Weir strode in. He seemed to have misplaced the lost puppy demeanor he'd come in sporting the day before. In fact, today he was looking downright cocky.

"Hello Justin." I said. "Goodbye Justin. Come back when you've made an appointment."

He smiled, and sat down on the corner of my desk. He was rapidly moving from cocky to impertinent.

"Now Reverend, it seems to me we have some business to discuss, and I don't know that it will keep for another day or two."

That was it. I was not in the mood to deal with spoiled children today. I picked up the phone and told Berta to get me security.

"I wouldn't do that," said Weir. Then he leaned over to me and lowered his voice to a whisper. "You see. *I know about the paintin'.*"

My whole body went icy numb. On the other end of the phone, security had picked up. I mumbled "nevermind" into the receiver and hung up. Weir was only a few inches away, looking into my eyes. I could feel the color draining away from my face, but there was nothing I could do to conceal it. I was paralyzed.

He kept looking at me, smiling. The bastard was watching me squirm. Too late, I tried to cover.

"You know what about the painting?" My voice came out hoarse and cracked. I fought to control it, but I couldn't.

He stood up, and picked up a picture of my wife that I keep on my desk.

"Well, to be entirely correct, I should say that I know about the painter. And you. I know what happened."

I felt my chest tighten, and I could see my hands shaking. I tried to hide them beneath the desk, but I couldn't seem to move my arms.

He knew.

"And," he said, "I've got the proof."

Proof? And that's when I realized. He was the one behind it all. He's the one who had found the boy. Images filled my head. A trial. Me being lead to prison in one of those orange jump suits. Everything falling apart, everything slipping away.

He turned to look at the painting. "Nice work." His voice was condescending. As if he'd already won. "It was mistake to keep it though. You…"

He never finished the sentence. There was a pot on the edge of my desk, with some little flowering plant in it that Berta had brought back from her vacation to Israel. I picked it up in both hands and brought it down on the back of his head as hard as I could. The planter shattered into a million pieces beneath my hands, and Justin crumpled over, putting his hands on the back of his head, as blood rushed out between his fingers.

And suddenly my limbs weren't frozen anymore. Suddenly I wasn't the weak and helpless one. My arms and legs sprang into action, as if they were thinking faster than I could. I moved around the desk.

Justin was stumbling, bent over. I grabbed him by the hair, and drove my fist into his face. It was so satisfying.

"You bastard!" I yelled. "You think you can pull this kind of crap with me?!"

I smashed my fist into his face again. My hand stung from the impact, but I liked the pain. Because it was a connection, a little taste of what I was inflicting on him. A way I could feel what I was doing to him.

Still confused, he struck out at me, wildly. The blow landed on my chest, but I barely noticed it. I struck him again, and my hand came back red. Blood was spurting out of his nose and down his face. I could feel my own face burning hot with anger.

He brought his arms up to protect his head, so I hit him in the gut, hard. My fist connected with a satisfying smack, like a water balloon breaking. I heard the wind go out of him, and he collapsed to the floor, struggling for breath.

I kicked him in the face. His neck snapped back like one of those old Pez dispensers, and a spray of blood flew across the room. Then I kicked him in the gut. He gasped and curled up into a ball, trying to protect his stomach, so I stepped over him and kicked him in the small of the back.

"You lousy punk! You want to take *me* down?"

I kicked him again. Two, maybe three times. The last time there was a crunching sound, and he rolled over to protect his back.

Then I was down on top of him, with my hands around his throat. And somehow, he was still fighting me off. Trying to pull my hands away from his neck. Blood all over his face, and a couple of broken ribs, and he was still fighting back. Kicking at me, grabbing at my hands, trying to push me off of him. But I managed to pin his arms down with my knees, and then I got my hands around something he was wearing on a chain around his neck. I pulled the chain tight with both hands. I felt strong. Impossibly strong. But the chain didn't break. And Weir's face turned red. Then purple. Then blue. And he stopped fighting.

I was still kneeling on his arms. I let go of the chain, and rolled off of him. I lay there, next to him, shaking uncontrollably, my body tingling with unspeakable power. The hot clarity of anger slowly fading, and the fear coming back.

As it always does.

## Chapter 37: The Police
## Wednesday the 11th, 3:42 PM

The pictures on the conference table were starting to get fuzzy, and I was trying to fight back a yawn. I'd been popping perk-ups for the last couple of days instead of sleeping, and it was starting to catch up with me. I realized that the ME was still talking and I had no idea what he had been saying for the past couple minutes.

"I'm sorry," I interrupted him. "I got distracted by something up here for a second. Could you repeat what you just said?"

"Sure. Where do you want me to start from?"

I fought to concentrate and bring back the last piece of the conversation that I could remember.

"You were talking about the tox screen."

"Yeah. Well, she tested positive for rohypnol, which is a pretty potent sedative. It's the same stuff we found in the coffee that the guards at the clinic drank. In addition to finding it in the victim's body, we also found it in the blood in the jar on the floor, and in the scrapings we took from the wall paintings, so it's a pretty good bet that she was drugged before they started. She would have at least been immobilized and numb. Hard to tell if she was unconscious or not. "

"Do we know how the drug was introduced?"

"Well, there are no needle marks on the body, which means it could have been absorbed through the skin in a DMSO mixture, or it could have been ingested. Ingestion seems the better bet. We're testing samples from the dishes in her sink. Should have something back for you in half an hour or so."

"Allright. What else?"

"We have a few stray fibers that Shard is examining. One possible match to a human hair found at the clinic crime scene, another linen fiber that matches to the graveyard. And of course there's the mutilation to the body."

I glanced down at the picture of Raven's body on the conference table. Little numbers were blinking next to her mouth, next to the needle sticking into her arm, next to her hair, next to the upside down cross that had been cut into her belly.

"Anything beyond the obvious?"

"Quite a bit. These guys did some really weird mutilation of the body. It looks like they did it after most of her blood was drained off, which is why there wasn't more bleeding around the wounds and on the bed clothes. The tongue was cut out. Oh, and that cross incision on her abdomen turned out to be interesting."

"How so?"

"Well, the wounds are actually more substantial than they look. As near as I can figure they must have peeled back the flaps to do some major surgery, and then folded them back into position when they were done. This woman's uterus was cut out."

"Her uterus?"

"Yeah. By somebody who knew what he was doing, too. I noticed there was no mention of you guys finding a spare organ at the crime scene. I don't suppose that was an oversight?"

"No."

"Then whoever did this must have taken it with them."

"Why?" I thought about it for a few seconds. "Would a uterus have any value to anyone?"

"You mean, besides the person it was originally attached to? Well, not that I can think of. If it were a kidney or a liver or a heart that was missing, I could imagine them wanting it for a transplant. But even if you could transplant a uterus, who would want to? I mean, even if a woman didn't have a working one, she could always rent artificial womb time or something."

I thought about it. In a sick sort of way, this all made sense. They had stolen an aborted fetus from the clinic. Now they were stealing a womb. Even if it wasn't logical, it did fit a pattern.

"What about the needle?" I asked. "Did we get anywhere tracking down the supplier on that?"

"Oh yeah. We gave the serial numbers to data services, and they tracked it down to a lot that was sold to the Peachtree Family Planning Clinic. Guess our perps helped themselves to it while they were there."

"Damn. I'd been hoping for a break with that. What about latent prints?"

"None on the body, so they must have been using gloves when they handled her. As for the rest of the house, Bernie says he lifted a lot of good prints, but he's still working on screening out the innocuous background stuff. So far he's weeded out the victim's own prints and those of a couple of her neighbors who had visited the house recently. That leaves another 14 sets that he hasn't IDed yet."

"OK, have him give me a call when he finds something." I said, and hung up.

I yawned and stretched, and tried to make my eyes focus on the next evidence file, but my concentration was shot. I looked across the room. K'yon was speaking into her headset at ten miles a minute, using some verbal short hand she'd worked out with her agent program. On the table in front of her, documents and pictures flashed by so quickly that I could barely tell what they were. I saw a part of the donor list come up, the people who had been given rings matching the one whose print had been on the body, and then a page from the psych profile that the FBI had put together.

Next to her, Ellise was looking at a chart showing the progress of our canvassing efforts. A map of the neighborhood around the victim's house showed the outlines of all dwellings within a half mile of the crime scene, with the names of the occupants inside. Most of them were green now, with only a few red stragglers indicating people that we had not been able to find and talk to yet. Next to Ellise, another data tech was coordinating the data from our interviews with the victim's known associates. And next to him, another tech was screening the random tips that were coming in from the phone bank. Everything seemed to be humming along smoothly.

Thus assured that the world wouldn't fall apart if I took five minutes to get a cup of coffee and a quick sanity recharge, I put my headset on the conference table and went into the lounge. A couple of guys from the phone pool were in there, taking a late lunch and watching the Cherry Chang show. I hadn't meant to get sucked in by the idiot box, but as I was pouring my coffee I heard one of Cherry's guests talking about how she'd been lured to Satanic orgies by some friends in a diesel rock band. Well, you can't just walk away from a story like that.

I sat down and sipped my coffee while the guest, who had enormous bleached blond hair—Why do the women on these shows always have big hair?—went on to describe the rituals they would enact. She explained how the first couple of times she just got drunk and high and had sex with all the guys in the band. But then things began to change. They started chanting hymns to Satan, and making her drink blood during the orgies. And once they had had her addicted to the drugs, they forced her first into prostitution, and then into luring virgin boys back to the band's apartment where they would be hacked apart with knives as a sacrifice to Satan.

The camera then cut to some stock footage of some diesel band wearing demonic looking costumes and shooting milk out over an audience of screaming teenagers using a giant mechanical penis. When the camera came back to Cherry, it was to interview the fake blond psychiatrist, a self-proclaimed specialist in treating victims of Satanic Abuse. The guy made a lot of scientific-sounding assertions, like stating that 90% of all missing children who aren't found have been the victims of kidnap and sacrifice by Satanic cults. I was waiting for Cherry to ask him the obvious question: if you never found the kids, how do you know what happened to them?

But I guess it didn't occur to her. Just like it didn't probably didn't occur to her to confirm the fake blond's story by comparing it with the missing persons reports for the small town in Ohio that she claimed all this human sacrificing took place in. Like ten or eleven teenage boys are going to go missing, and nobody notices?

Someone touched me on the shoulder and I nearly jumped out of my skin.

"Sorry," K'yon said, catching my eye in a meaningful way.

"No problem," I said, and turned back to the TV. The satanic "expert" was giving a list of warning signs for parents who thought that their children might have become involved in the occult. I kept one eye on the idiot box, but I kept the other one on K'yon, as she walked across the lounge and into the ladies room. After a couple of minutes I got up and followed her in.

K'yon was standing in front of a mirror, combing her hair, which is no small task for her, since it goes down to her waist. I walked up behind her and she saw my reflection.

"I checked the stalls," she said, "we're alone."

"What have you found out?"

"Well, for starters, you were right to be suspicious. I ran your conversation with the Watch Commander through a voice stress analyzer. As soon as you mentioned a connection to Stonewall, his stress level goes off the charts."

"Yeah, I thought there was something weird about his voice."

"An imprecise observation, but correct. And I found something even more interesting. I wanted to know what the Commander did right after your conversation, so I checked the APIN logs. Want to know what he was up to?"

"Do we have to play twenty questions, K'yon? Cut to the chase."

"Nothing."

"K'yon, I was hoping for something a little more..."

"No. Think about it. Nothing. There's a ten minute gap after your conversation when he's logging no APIN activities. No data retrieval, no phone calls, no dictation. No nothing."

"Well, he could have had someone in his office that he was talking to."

"Maybe, but it seemed suspicious to me, so I checked the usage records on his personal cell phone."

"You did what!? How the Hell did you get into those without a warrant?"

K'yon looked at me slyly.

"Don't ask and I won't have to lie to you. Anyway, it turns out the Commander made an eight and a half minute call to a number at Liberty Media. Which means..."

"Stonewall. Any idea what they talked about?"

"Idea, yes. Proof, no."

"Well, if it were legitimate business he would have done it over his office phone."

"Of course."

"OK," I said. "So they were doing something under the table. The question is: Was the Commander doing Stonewall a favor, by tipping him off to out investigation, or was he calling in a favor, and getting Stonewall to spill some information?"

K'yon shrugged. "That, I don't know."

"OK. What about the background check? Did you find any evidence that Stonewall might have acted as a patron for the Commander? Used his influence to get him promotions?"

"Hard to tell. Davison has an interesting history. He climbed the ranks fast, but he also cracked a couple of big cases, and always had good reviews from his superiors. Maybe the guy had some help, somebody pulling strings to get him good assignments, but there's no hard evidence that I could find."

"Any other connections?"

"Just a lot of dead ends. They don't belong to any of the same clubs. They don't subscribe to any of the same newsites. Didn't go to the same school. Nada."

"All right." I said, then ran some cold water in the sink and splashed it on my face. "We've got to be careful. If you find any other connections between this case and Stonewall, keep them under your hat until you can run them by me."

"Will do."

"Good." I dried my face with a paper towel. "And if you should happen to notice any more calls between the Commander and Stonewall, let me know."

I let K'yon leave first, waited a minute, and then went out myself. Back in the lounge, I retrieved the cup of coffee I'd poured earlier. A couple more people had come in to watch TV. I noticed that the Cherry Chang show had been replaced by a news bulletin. Some blond reporter was interviewing a Wiccan girl who'd been attacked by a gang of boys yesterday, allegedly for religious reasons. They'd called her a witch, held her down and lit her hair on fire. The girl described the whole thing in gruesome detail. Then the story switched to some Baptist boy, lying in a hospital bed with a couple of cracked ribs, and a bunch of bruises. Apparently he happened to fit the description of one of the guys involved in burning the girl's hair. Great.

The reporter went on to describe "the growing panic in Atlanta, as we approach what many fear will be an eventful Friday the 13th." The shot switched to a gun store, with signs posted saying that they had temporarily sold out of most types of ammo.

I shook my head. We needed to get this thing wrapped up soon.

I went back into the conference room and put my headset back on. A couple of the data techs looked up as I came in.

"Anything happen while I was out?"

One of the women shrugged. One of the men pointed to a dozen more blinking control numbers on the diagram of Raven's body. No rest for the weary.

I sat down at the table and called up a summary list of all the messages demanding my attention. It had grown to over fifty. OK. Time for some bureaucratic triage. I scanned down the list, separating out the things that had to be dealt with now from the things that could sit for awhile. About halfway down I noticed a call from Tony, updating me on the manhunt. I decided to kill a few birds with one stone, and call him back rather than reading the report. After the usual unnecessary pleasantries, I managed to coax Mindy into dialing his number.

"Hey, Browning here."

Tony has a way of saying 'here' so that it takes up two syllables. Sort of, "he-ah".

"Hey Tony, it's Megan. What's up?"

"Just wanted to let you know I finished interviewin' the victim's family. The report's in the casefile."

"Can you give me the highlights?"

"Well, I don't know how much of it you'll find interesting. The gist of it is that our vic came home to live with her parents for a couple months after she quit her job with Liberty Media. They got the impression that something on the job had upset her, but she wouldn't talk about it. She had a falling out with the family over some religious issues—apparently she'd stopped going to church, and her parents didn't like that—and moved back to Atlanta. There were a couple of attempts at reconciliation over the next few years, but they fell through, and the family had not been in communication with her for 11 years."

"Actually," I said, "I find that very interesting. I just wish I knew what it meant."

"Yes ma'am. Let me know when you do."

"How's the manhunt coming?"

"Nothing yet. I've got Banders' parole officer questioning his known associates about where he is. I figure he's the one person who can ask questions without tippin' our hand. Even if word gets back to Banders, he'll figure it's just a routine check up. I've also got plain clothes watchin' his known hangouts. Mostly stuff up in Buckhead. A strip club. A couple bars. A Brazilian restaurant. Just a matter of waitin' for him to turn up."

"Good. Let me know when you get a nibble."

I paused. I had been wanting to talk to Tony about Stonewall, but I wasn't sure that I wanted to do it on APIN channel, where everything was being recorded for the casefile. I wouldn't put it past the Commander to do a search for any conversations mentioning Stonewall's name. On the other hand, I had good reason to be wondering about Stonewall at this point, and it would look even more suspicious if I avoided the topic.

"Uh, Tony, there was one more thing I wanted to talk to you about."

"Shoot."

"Stonewall."

"Yeah, I was wonderin' when we'd get back to that subject."

"How well do you know him?"

"I watch his news show. Vote the party ticket. Shook his hand once at a fundraiser."

"Well, his name keeps turning up in connection with the case. The ring print from the corpse in the cemetery is from one of his fund raiser give-aways. And all the bodies we've found so far belong to former employees of his. I have to wonder what's up with that."

"You really think Stonewall is tangled up in this?"

"I have to consider the possibility," I admitted. "But it doesn't seem to take me anywhere. The only motive I can think of would be if this were all some sort of publicity stunt."

"You mean, to scare people and improve his political chances?"

"Yeah," I said, "but that doesn't fit the facts. If that's all he was up to, why draw attention to himself by cutting up two of his former employees? I mean, he could have used anyone."

"Agreed," Tony said. "And the timing's not right."

"What timing?"

"Election cycles. The Reverend's not up for re-election to his senate seat for five years. And even if he's planning a run for the Presidency, that election is still more than a year away. By the time the vote rolls around, all of this will be old news."

"I see you've been thinking about this possibility."

"I look at every suspect, Megan. You know that. And trust me on this one: the Reverend is one cagey old fox. If he were behind this, it would have been timed for August of next year, just in time to swing the election."

"Good point."

"And on top of all that, it's a huge risk. Why take it?"

"Allright then, we're in agreement. Stonewall is probably a dead end, at least as a suspect."

"Fine, Megan. I'll call you back as soon as we have a lead on Banders, 'til then…"

"Actually," I interrupted, "there's one more thing, Tony. There was something strange in the ME's report about the murder victim."

"Can't say that I'm surprised, the way this case has been going. What is it?"

"The perps removed her uterus. It wasn't found at the scene, so they must have taken it with them."

"Well, it does fit in with the symbolism we've seen so far. Maybe they're trying to use it to incubate some sort of demon."

"Yeah, I thought of that, but there's one other thing that bothers me about it…"

"Just one? I can think of at least a half dozen things that bother me about somebody ripping a woman's womb out of her…"

"No, I don't mean bother like that. I mean that it seems familiar. Have you ever heard of any cases where a murderer cut out someone's uterus? Particularly one where he removed it from the scene?"

"Huh. Now that you mention it, that does sound familiar. I think there was something like that on the newsites, back around the time I joined the Fourth. Must be fifteen, sixteen years ago now. Some crazy artist hacked up his wife. I remember the stories all made a big deal about how he'd cut out her uterus and genitalia. I don't think they ever did find it."

"You think there's a connection?" I asked.

"Well, seems pretty unlikely to me. That was a straight domestic dispute. No weird black magic mumbo-jumbo."

"OK. Well thanks for clearing that up for me. It was gonna keep nagging at me all day."

"No problem. I'll call back when we get a nibble from our little fish."

He hung up.

Down on the table, two more blinking numbers popped up. I looked over at K'yon, who was dictating in that weird verbal shorthand of hers. I managed to catch her eye, and she stopped what she was doing.

"There was a case about 15 years ago," I said, "some artist killed his wife and cut out her womb. Could you find out…"

"Oh. The Calerant Case. You want newstories or the casefile?"

I raised an eyebrow.

"Did you know," I asked, "that there's a rumor going around that you have a crystal memory chip for a brain?"

"I can't imagine how such stories get started," she said, tapping on some icons on the table top. "Anyway, I've downloaded a short newstory and the full casefile to your agent. Just ask for the Calerant material. Anything else?"

"No..." I was going to add a thank you, but she was already back to her dictation before I had a chance to say anything.

Another blinking number lit up next to Raven's left foot. Well, it would be there in a few minutes. I had Mindy call up the Calerant stories on a blank stretch of the conference table, and sat down to read them.

## Chapter 38: The Gumshoe

I was walking through a cemetery, with all sorts of weird stone carvings of demons and gargoyles and stuff. Their eyes all followed me as I passed. It figured.

I had ditched the car a long time ago, back at the dawn. Driving conditions in this funhouse were just too damned weird, and I didn't need any more points on my license. But at least I had finally found the friggin' turtle.

It was about six feet across, sitting on top of a large spherical rock that was half buried in the dirt. I recognized the outlines of Australia and South America carved into it.

"Yes," the turtle said, slowly turning its head to look at me. "I am the great turtle Acabacnamadecereateneacablerad. I've been expecting you."

It spoke very slowly.

"Great," I said, "Now if you could just tell me..."

"Hmph!" interrupted the tortoise, rolling its eyes in slow frustration. "As I was saying, I've been expecting you. Armed with the arrows of wisdom you come. Armed with the bow of truth you come. Armed with the spear of vision you come. But still you have far to go on your quest."

I groaned, audibly. The tortoise looked annoyed. Well, at least it started to look annoyed. It took him about ten seconds to finish forming the full facial expression.

"AS I WAS SAYING," he roared, for emphasis, "you still have far to go on your quest. First, you must find a ship, to take you across the sea of ignorance, to the kingdom of fear. There you will find an entrance to the underworld. The path there is all in darkness, and you must walk it alone for seven days and seven nights, surrounded by impenetrable murk, until you come at last to the land of the dead, where you must face the hideous..."

I grabbed the damn thing by his leathery neck.

"How dare you!" he roared. Well, roared slowly. "I am the great turtle Acabacna..."

"brick-a-brack whatever. Frankly I don't care if you're the pope." I pulled his head close to my face. "Look bub, first I met the rabbit, who told me that I needed to crawl my way through the brambles of vexation to get the stupid arrows and talk to the fox. Then the fox told me I had to go to the forest of illusions to get the stupid bow and talk to the Hawk. The Hawk told me I had to climb the mountains of despair to get the stupid spear, and then come find you. And now you're telling me there's *even more to this test*? Thanks, but I think I'm ready for my merit badge now. So just tell me where I can find my friggin' totem."

"I told you," the turtle said, pulling back with surprising force. "First you have to find a ship to take you across the sea of ignorance, to the kingdom of fear. There you will find an entrance to the underworld..."

He won out in the battle of strength. My hands slipped off his neck and he pulled his head back into his shell. The voice continued on, echoing from inside. "...The path there is all in darkness, and you must walk it for seven days and seven..."

In frustration I gave the turtle's shell a kick, and he tottered a little on top of his rock. That gave me an idea. I put my shoulder under one corner of it and lifted with all my strength. The shell wobbled for a moment, and then slipped off the rock and landed on its back.

Abracadabra, or whatever his name was, seemed too surprised to quite understand what had happened to him. He stuck a foot out tentatively, trying to find the ground. Then he stuck another foot out. Then its head. A panicked expression came over its tortoise face. Slowly, of course. It put out all four legs and began flailing them in slow motion.

"What? You can't do this to the great turtle Acabacnama-decereateneacablerad! Turn me over this instant!"

I put a foot down on its belly. "Look," I said. "I'm going to put this in language you can understand. I have been having a really bad week. A *really* bad week. And I'm about at the end of my rope. And if you don't tell me what I want to know, then I'm likely to just stack some wood and kindling up under you, pour some water in your shell, and heat me up some turtle soup. Comprende?"

It looked worried.

"But I've told you how to find your totem!" The turtle insisted. "First you have to find a ship to take you across..."

I started breaking branches off a nearby bush and arranging them around its shell.

"What are you doing?" The tortoise asked, trying to bend its head around to see. "I'm telling you the truth! Really! There are rules to these things. Haven't you ever read Campbell? You know, *The Hero of a Thousand Faces*? Really, it's all in there. You have to travel over water, and make a journey to the underworld, where you..."

I continued stacking branches under his shell. "Let's say I don't have time for the whole book." I said, as I got some leaves for kindling. "What's the Cliffs Notes version?"

"What?"

I got out my lighter.

"A short cut?" I asked.

The tortoise took a second to think. I started to light the brambles.

"OK! OK! Go straight on a hundred feet, make a right at the fountain of blood, then a left at the wailing bog. It will be the third door on your right."

"That's it?" I asked. "You're sure?"

"Yeah, Yeah! Just don't blame me if this takes all the fun out of it. Now how about flipping me over, huh?"

I stamped out the burning twigs, and with a big shove managed to get the turtle turned right side up. It shot me a nasty look, and then set about climbing back up on its rock.

And Jen says my interpersonal skills need work. Go figure.

I followed the turtle's directions, which took me out of the graveyard, through a formal garden, past the bog, into a Victorian library, and finally through a stone archway and into the third floor of my own office building.

Surprise, surprise. The third door on the left was my own office. Through the glazed glass of the door I could see something moving around inside. Presumably my totem, the guy who could finally tell me what was going on. I just hoped he wasn't something stupid, like a badger or a poodle or a chihuahua or something like that.

I took a deep breath, opened the door slowly, and stepped into my office. Everything was in black and white, and a neon sign flashed light in through the blinds. All of the office furniture seemed out of date.

And he was there, sitting at my desk.

Oh God. This was too corny for words.

## Chapter 39: The Police
## Wednesday the 11th, 4:39 PM

I had Mindy call up the stories on the Calerant murder and I looked them over while I drank my coffee. After a few minutes, it all came back to me. I'd read about the case when it first happened, fifteen years ago. It would have been hard not to, with the way the press had played it up at the time. The story had had all the makings for one of those ultra-big media events, like the OJ trial back in the '90's or the Tori Spelling conviction back in the early teens: Famous painter kills his wife in a jealous rage. Mutilates the body. Parts of the corpse never found. Yep, it could have been a biggie, if it had just dragged on a bit longer. I'll bet more than one reporter broke into tears when she heard that Calerant had taken a plea bargain and there wouldn't be a trial.

It was still an interesting story, but I found myself agreeing with Tony's assessment: it didn't have much bearing on the case we were investigating now. Oh, there were a couple of interesting similarities. The missing uterus, for one thing. And Calerant was a painter, much like our artistically-inclined perps in this case. But the MO was all wrong. Calerant hadn't actually made any artwork out of his wife's body, in marked contrast to our perps. And his crime had been a poorly planned act of passion, not the carefully orchestrated acts of terror we were seeing now. I read a few more news stories on his wife's murder, but decided that it wasn't worth digging around in the old casefile looking for leads.

As it was, I already had more than enough stuff demanding my attention. I closed up the Calerant files, and went back to work on the galaxy of blinking numbers that was slowly filling the conference table. Over the next few hours I managed to work my way through the constellation of reports surrounding the picture of Raven Straylight's body, and even made a fair dent in the long list of miscellaneous items that had been piling up at the end of the table.

There were a few interesting bits in there. The girls at the FBI's Behavioral Sciences Lab had come to the same conclusions I had about our Perps; namely, that we are dealing with sociopaths, rather than psychopaths. Put another way, the intended target of these attacks isn't the person who is actually assaulted, but society as a whole. Also, Data Services had managed to glean a bit of information about the guy who did the paintings at the last crime scene. Judging by the angle he held the brush at, they were extremely confident that the guy was right handed. However, they could only pin his height down to somewhere between 5'10" and 6'2". Not a huge amount of help there. Forensics had worked out a few more details from the footprints in the yard. And our canvassing effort had turned up a neighbor who remembered seeing a white van parked around the corner from the house. Unfortunately, she couldn't give us a license number.

Around 8, Tony came back in to HQ. I took the opportunity to go out and grab a bite to eat, leaving him with instructions to call me if any of his men spotted Banders. When I got back from dinner there had been no major breaks or crises with the case, so I told Tony to hold down the fort for another couple of hours, then went into the back room to grab a little shut-eye while I had the chance.

I should have known better. Every time I try to get some sleep on this case something bad happens.

## Chapter 40: The Chosen
## Wednesday the 11th, 5:20 PM

We found a tree with a low branch, and used it to boost ourselves over the fence. Summer pulled herself over and hit the ground on the other side, and then crawled behind a bush for cover.

"Hurry up, Benji. His mom might see you."

"I'm coming." I grunted. I had pulled myself halfway over the fence, but my shirt had ridden up, and I was getting a belly full of splinters.

"Benji!" she hissed.

I managed to get myself over and came down in a heap on the other side. I joined Summer behind the bush. Up ahead was a tree with a tire swing, then a big open area between us and the back patio. I noticed that the back door had a flap for a dog. A *big* dog.

"So what did this Gerald kid do to get grounded?" I asked.

"Oh, nothing. He just failed computer science."

"Failed Computer? Wait a minute, I thought you said he was some sort of uber-geek?"

"He is. It's just kind of hard to pass a course when you never get around to turning in the final project."

"Oh. Been there."

"Yeah, well I bet you didn't break into the police computer and put out an arrest warrant on your teacher."

"Ouch. Harsh."

"Oh, that was just for openers. After that he sicced a couple of viruses and a jinx on the school's network, which..."

"What's a jinx?"

"A jinx. You know, sort of like a poltergeist. It's one of those annoying little spirits that makes things break down and go wrong. Like when things are supposed to work, and they don't, and there's no good reason for it."

"Yeah, I've run those before."

"Probably, they're pretty common around computers. Anyway, this one rearranged everybody's grades, and kept losing test results, and jacked the thermostat up to 90°, and pretty much made the whole school shut down for a couple of days."

"How'd they catch him?"

"Well, for one thing, Gerald wasn't doing a very good job of hiding his gloating. And for another, the headmaster is one tough warlock. After they cleaned out the virus, he bound the jinx into a diskette, and then forced it to cough up the goods on who had summoned it. Oh, and there was also this black woman from the police who nailed Gerald for breaching their system. All in all, they had him dead to rights. Still, he hadn't really hurt anybody so..."

"Uh, Summer," I interrupted, pointing out the very large doggie that had just come out of the very large doggie flap. He'd come out to make use of the tree with the tire swing, but was now sauntering toward the back of the yard, and us. The beast looked like a cross between a doberman pinscher and a Shwartzkopf tank. I was looking for a way back over the fence, but Summer put a hand on my shoulder.

"Chill," she whispered, then "Ghost? Here Ghost."

The dog perked up its ears, then trotted in our direction. He sniffed at Summer, who reached out and scritched him behind the ears.

"That's a good boy. Such a good boy. You want to pet him Benji?"

Actually, I didn't want to have anything to do with a dog that was bigger than I was, but I wasn't going to look scared in front of Summer. I gave him a cautious rub under the chin, and noticed that there was a little leather bag attached to his collar, sort of like the one that Summer wears around her neck.

"Hey, what's this? Another charm bag?"

"Yeah."

I laughed.

"What?" Summer said. "You think dogs don't need good luck? Here, let me show you." She unhooked the bag from the collar and opened it up. "See these are spearmint leaves, to ward off accidents, like being hit by a car or something. And these are cumin seeds, to keep him mellow and happy."

"What about this?" I asked, pointing to a seed pod.

"Oh, that's eucalyptus. The smell keeps the fleas off him."

Summer put the bag down and went searching through her pockets.

"You got a pen, Benji?"

I pulled one out of my back pocket and gave it to her. She scribbled something down on a small piece of paper, put it in the charm bag, and then tied it up and put it back on Ghost's collar.

"OK Ghost! Remember our trick! GO BUG GERALD!"

The dog perked up his ears, but didn't seem sure what to do.

"Come on Ghost! You remember this trick. GO BUG GERALD! GO BUG GERALD!"

Ghost finally got the message and took off for the house at a run. I saw his tail vanish in through the doggie door.

"Now what?"

"Now we wait."

Summer sat down and settled back against the fence. I sat next to her. After a couple minutes I tried to hold her hand and she let me.

A while later I heard the doggie door flap open and shut, and a few seconds later Ghost had rejoined us, strangely intent on licking Summer's face. Summer managed to undo the charm bag from his collar, and then passed it to me while she tried to fend off the puppy tongue. I opened up the bag, and found a piece of paper inside.

"Will arrange distraction for my mother at precisely 5:40. Back door is unlocked. Come upstairs to my room. Be quiet."

Ghost was on top of Summer now, giving her face a good slobbering. I distracted him by scritching him on the back, and he turned to slobber me. Summer wiped her face off, and I passed her the note.

"OK. You got the time, Benji?"

I pulled out the notebook and showed her the time. It was 5:37.

We put the charm bag back on Ghost, and then counted down the minutes. At exactly 5:40, we sprinted across the back yard. Summer opened the back door a crack and poked her head in, then waved for me to follow. We tiptoed through a big kitchen with copper pots and something cooking on the stove, then down a hallway with an open door leading down to the basement. I had one bad moment when I heard footsteps climbing the stairs up from the basement, but we raced past it, down the hall, and upstairs before whoever it was could spot us. On the second floor, a tall blond kid who was even skinnier than me waved us into his bedroom. He closed the door behind us, and then turned on some music to cover our voices.

Summer gave him an enthusiastic hug.

"Thanks for sneaking us in, Gerald."

"Hey, no problem," the kid said, shrugging, "I've got to do something to keep in practice."

"This is Benji," Summer said, introducing me. Gerald and I did the wave-but-not-actually-shaking-hands thing.

"So how'd you ditch your mom?" I asked.

"Oh, I blew the circuit breaker in the kitchen, so that she'd have to go down to the basement and turn it back on."

"Nice trick." I said, wondering if he'd show me how to do it.

Summer was still hanging on to Gerald, but for some reason I didn't feel threatened by him. I got the impression that Gerald was old news. Besides, he was a fellow geek. And he had a really cool room.

He'd papered the ceiling of his room with a full color picture of a nebula, and he had at least fifteen or sixteen model space-ships hanging from it. A couple of them were of real space stations, the Freedom and the Libertas, but the rest were all from old movies. I recognized the "Avenger" from *Last Chance,* and the Millennium Falcon from *Star Wars*, but there were a bunch that I couldn't place.

"What's this one?" I asked, pointing out a particularly weird looking ship. It looked like someone had stuck a tuning fork into an egg.

"Oh, that's Voyager." Gerald said. "From one of the old Star Trek spinoffs. Pity they canceled it. The last five episodes were actually pretty good, after they finally killed off Janeway and let Seven-of-Nine run the ship. I can show you where to find the episodes if you want to call them..."

"Actually," Summer interrupted, "we're kind of in a bind, Gerald, and we were hoping you could help us out."

"Sure, what do you need?"

"Well, for starters," Summer said, "I need to get a message through to my mom. She's going to be freaking by now."

"So why don't you just call?"

"Because Benji here is wanted by the FBI, and we're on the run."

Gerald seemed surprised by that and took a second look at me. I could tell that I had just gone way up in his estimation. If only being hunted by the FBI were half as much fun as it sounded like.

"So," Summer continued, "we can't use our phones, be-cause they'll pick up on the signal and home in on us. And I can't call my mom from a pay phone, because her line is prob-ably being tapped."

Gerald rubbed his chin.

"OK. So what do you want to do?"

"Well, I was thinking I could send my Mom an e-mail. Some-thing that she would understand, but that would look ordinary to anyone who intercepted it. But it has to come from somewhere besides my account."

"OK." Gerald said, "So you just want to set up a dummy ac-count you can send e-mail from?"

"Yeah, but it can't look suspicious. None of those remailing services in Madagascar or anything like that."

"OK, OK. I can do it. You got a notebook on you?"

"Why?"

Gerald gestured to a large empty space on his desk.

"They took away my computer. Part of my penance."

I passed him the notebook. He got a screwdriver out, and set about removing the back plate.

"What are you doing?" I asked.

"Patching your modem into my phone. That way the call won't go out on your number. You know, since the FBI is tracing it, and all."

While he worked, I browsed through his bookshelves. Gerald had an impressive collection of old comic books, including virtually every issue of *The F.A.R.C.E. Chronicles* and *The Hunting.* Being a guest, I didn't take any of them out of their plastic wrappers. But I was tempted.

"OK. Got it. " Gerald said. He passed the notebook over to Summer, who started composing a message to her mom. That left Gerald and me looking uncomfortably at each other with nothing to talk about, so I asked him about the comic books. That brought him right out. In addition to the stuff on the shelves, he had boxes of them in his closet, including some old ones that I'd never even heard of but that he said were really cool, like *Sandman* and *V for Vendetta.* He was showing me an old graphic novel called *The Watchmen* when Summer announced that she had finished her message.

"All right, I'm done. If my mom understands the message, she'll shake any tails they might have put on her, and then meet us at the gazebo in Piedmont Park."

"You think she can help?" I asked.

"Hey, my mom is one smart habañero. If anybody knows what to do, it's her. Of course, she'll probably still ground me for hiding you in my room and then sneaking out of the house without asking..."

"I appreciate the sacrifice."

Just then there was a knock on the bedroom door. I froze. Gerald gestured frantically at his closet. Summer and I jumped inside and pulled the door shut just as his mom poked her head into the room.

"Your father will be home soon. Do you want to set the table?"

"Do I want to?"

"Let me rephrase that: set the table."

"OK. I'll be down as soon as I finished the chapter I'm reading."

I heard the door close again.

"Coast is clear."

Summer and I emerged from hiding.

"Is there anything else I can do for you guys?" Gerald asked.

"Well," Summer said, "I know you've gotten into the Atlanta Police system. I don't suppose you could break into the FBI computers and find out what they want with Benji. Could you?"

I noticed that she pushed her chest out when she asked this little favor. Fortunately Gerald noticed it to.

"Uh...I can try. It might take me awhile. And I'll need to hang on to your notebook."

"OK" Summer said, handing him back the notebook.

"You might check out the CIA, too." I added, trying to be helpful.

"Sure," Gerald said. "Piece of cake. Anything else you want me to do while I'm at it? Maybe break into the Federal Reserve and transfer a couple of billion to your account?"

"Look Gerald, if you can't do it..." Summer started to say.

"Hey, did I say I couldn't do it? Just don't expect anything quick. Hm. Maybe I can do an augury and get a clue to one of their passwords. Of course, ever since that weirdness with that Coven in San Diego the FBI has gotten a lot more careful about putting mystical wards around their databases. So..."

"Yeah, great," I interrupted. "Let us know when you find something."

Gerald sighed.

"Anything else?"

I thought about it.

"Well, if you could get a message to my mom, just to let her know I'm ok. That would probably be a good idea." I was still pretty mad at her, but there was no sense having her worry.

"Of course, sir," Gerald said. "And will that be all?"

"Well," I added, "a couple sandwiches would be good, too."

## Chapter 41: The Witch
## Wednesday the 12th, 6:38 Pm

"Hello, Stormbringer residence."

"Hi, Crystal?  This is Holly Jacobs."

"Oh, Holly!  Good to hear from you.  How are Alex and the kids?"

"Uh…that's what I was calling you about, actually.  Is Summer over there by any chance?"

"Summer?  No.  Why?  Is something wrong?"

"Probably not," I said, trying to sound calm.  "She's just off with one of her friends and hasn't come home for dinner yet."

"So, why don't you phone her?"

Like I hadn't tried that.

"Well, her phone has been acting up for the last few days." I lied.  I was getting better at it with practice.  "I think the battery is going.  Would you be sure to give me a call if she turns up over there?"

"Sure thing Holly.  And I wouldn't worry.  You know how teenagers are."

"Yeah, I do.  Well I need to get back to cooking dinner."

"OK.  Bye."

I hung up, and drew a line through "Gerald Stormbringer".  It was the last name on my list of Summer's friends.  No one had seen her.

I glanced into the family room, where Winter was dangling a piece of yarn in front of Urvashi.  I had gotten a bit anxious about letting my remaining daughter out of my sight, but I couldn't let myself get crazy.  She'd be OK in the house.

I went out the back door and into the yard.  It was an early summer evening.  Alex was stripped down to his shorts, lying in the grass.  A little bundle of Summer's hair wrapped around his index finger.  His head propped up on his hands.  Looking into a little fire of ash wood that he had built.

I sat down next to him, and rubbed his back as he stared into the fire.  I was anxious to know what he was seeing, but I knew better to interrupt him when he was scrying.  Every so often he would take one of Summer's hairs and throw it into the fire, and it would go up in a brief flash.  The sun slowly sank below the horizon.  The calls of day birds were replaced by the buzz of evening insects.  The fire burned down to its embers.  And still he stared.

Finally, as the last of the twilight faded, he rolled over onto his back, and rubbed his eyes.

"Anything?" I asked.

He looked up at the sky for awhile, thinking. I suppressed my urge to rush him, and waited for him to find the words.

"I don't think she's alone," Alex said, thoughtful. "I see a lot of things. Coils of a snake. A spider web. Hounds chasing a hare. A buck and a doe, but the doe is lame. I'm not sure what to make of it all."

He looked at me and shrugged.

"But she's alive?" I pressed.

"Yes. I feel sure of that. But..." he drifted off again. This time I couldn't wait.

"But what?"

He looked up again trying to find words. "...but someone is going to die. Close to her. Someone near her."

I felt my chest tighten. What had Summer gotten herself into? I helped Alex up, and we walked back toward the house.

"What do we do now?" I asked.

"I think," he said, and then paused for a moment, "...I think that it's time we called the police."

I nodded in agreement. Alex went to pay some attention to Winter, while I made the call.

"Hello, Atlanta Metro Police. How may I direct your call?"

"Missing Persons."

"One moment." There was a click on the line. "Hello, Missing Persons. How can I help you?" The new voice was female, with that neutral British accent that only computers and announcers for the BBC have. I was talking to a program.

"I need to report a missing person."

"All right. What's the name?"

"Summer Jacobs. She's my daughter."

"Nice name. And how long has she been missing?"

"About five hours."

"Oh, she'll probably turn up. We don't start investigating missing persons till they've been gone for 24 hours."

"Yes, but this is different. She's with a boy. Someone you're already looking for."

"He's a missing person?"

"No, I think he's a witness or something. You found some of his hair at a crime scene."

"I'm afraid that I don't understand."

The voice was annoyingly calm and mellow.

"No, you don't." I agreed. "This boy is in trouble, and my daughter is with him."

"You mean that she's in the company of a wanted criminal?"

"No. Well, maybe. I don't know. His name is Benjamin Danvers. Can you check your files or something?"

"I'm afraid that I still don't understand what you want..."

That was it.

"OF COURSE YOU DON'T YOU DUMB ROBOTIC BIMBO! NOW SHUT UP AND GET ME A REAL PERSON ON THE LINE!"

There was a moment of silence.

"Ma'am, I *am* a real person. Officer Rachel Desai. You want my badge number to prove it?"

"Uh...No. That's OK."

"Allright. Why don't you take a deep breath ma'am, and slowly try to explain what it is that you want."

I took her advice.

"OK. My daughter has been missing for five hours. She's not answering her phone. She's with a boy named Benjamin Danvers, that you want to talk to in connection with another case."

"Do you know which one?"

"Uh...his mom wasn't sure, but she thought it was that big black magic case. You know, the graveyard and the clinic."

"Oh. I can see why you would be concerned. Well..." There was a short pause. "Look, ma'am, I'm not supposed to tell you if we're looking for someone. But would it ease your mind if I bent the rules a little, and tell you that we're *not* looking for anyone named Benjamin Danvers?"

Huh?

"You're sure?"

"Entirely, ma'am. Whenever a detective is looking for someone, we put their name in the system, in case they get pulled over for speeding or arrested on another charge or something like that. Not a thing on this Benjamin fellow."

"Uh...Thanks."

"Someone must have got their story mixed up. Don't worry, your daughter will probably be home in a few hours."

"Um. Yeah. I hope so. Thanks," I said, and hung up.

So what the heck was going on?

I had my agent pull up the phone call that I'd had with Mrs. Danvers earlier that day, and replayed it. She seemed pretty sure that the police were looking for her son. So who was lying? Her? Or the police? I listened to the call again. If she was lying, she was one heck of an actress. But why would the police lie? What was going on here?

I went in and pulled Alex away from a game of "I spy" with Winter. I explained what the police had said.

"So what do we do now?" I asked, when I'd finished.

Alex scratched his head and looked up at the ceiling for awhile.

"We wait," he finally said.

"Wait? We can't just wait! We've got to do *something!*"

"And we will. The net is cast. There is nothing to do until something swims in." He stood up. "Do you want me to cook dinner?"

It's obscene that Alex can be so calm at a time like this. But that's his gift. Stillness. And he's right, of course.

"No. I'll cook. It'll give me something to do."

Alex went back into the family room and rejoined his game with Winter, and I tried to pull something together for dinner. But my mind was elsewhere. First I burned the cornbread, and then I let the rice boil over. Eventually I threw all my energy into a cold curried tuna salad and managed to finish that without disaster.

We ate in the family room, and then watched sitcoms. At least, Winter and Alex did. I wasn't in a mood to laugh. I flipped my visor over to one of the news programs. There had been some more violence. Some Christian boys had been beaten up, supposedly in retaliation for setting a Wiccan girl's hair on fire. There had been a drive-by shooting at the Tree of Life Bookstore. No one hurt, just a lot of property damage. Then they started doing another story on Raven's murder, and I just couldn't watch anymore.

I checked my phone to make sure it was working. It was. It was just that no one was calling. I cleaned up the kitchen. Then I cleaned up the family room. Then the bathroom. Still no calls. When I ran out of things to clean, I checked my e-mail.

There was the usual collection of junk mail, which I tossed without reading. Also a letter from my editor, asking if I was over the flu. A letter from the school asking if the girls would be back in tomorrow. And a short note from Urvashi.

That last one caught my attention. It's not often I get e-mail from the family cat. The contents were even more curious.

"Holly,

Just wanted to say that it was great running into you at the gazebo. We really do need to see more of each other. Let's talk again soon!

Urvashi

P.S. Loved the piece on the Manx. Such clever cats. We should all take a lesson from them."

Uh-huh.

I have no old friends named Urvashi, at least no human ones, and I certainly hadn't been writing any pieces about cats lately. I checked the profile on the sender. It claimed the sender was a female lawyer of Bengali descent, who lived in the Greater Atlanta area, and whose hobbies included gourmet cooking, fencing...and Slip Stream.

Summer was trying to get my attention.  But why all the fun and games?  Why didn't she just call?  Something was going on.  But at least the reference to the gazebo wasn't too hard to figure out.

I found Alex in Winter's room, reading her a bed time story, and told him about the letter.  He agreed to be the one to stay home and keep an eye on our youngest.

Which left me free to go collect our other daughter, and get some answers.

## Chapter 42: The Police
## Wednesday the 11th, 10:49 PM

Two blocks away, I could already hear the noise of the crowd. An ominous, rumbling sound like thunder, punctuated by high pitched shouts and shrieks.

Tony took us south along Spring and then made a right onto Biko. He had to stop for a crowd of onlookers that was pouring across the street into Freedom Plaza. He waited about thirty seconds for the road to clear, then gave up and parked the car on the sidewalk.

I popped a couple more Perk-Ups as I got out of the car, and washed them down with the last swallow of coffee from my travel mug. Well, at least this time I'd managed to grab a whole two and a half hours of sleep before something hit the fan. I slipped on my headset and followed Tony into the fray.

The Plaza was a madhouse. At least three or four hundred civilians were already on the scene, with more coming in every minute. There are a lot of nightclubs and late night attractions in this part of the city, and of course there was a steady stream of people pouring out of the Liberty Media Tower, which rises up out of the North West corner of the Plaza. I saw a couple of camera crews trying to fight their way through the crowd. Probably BNN crews: they'd be the first on the scene since it happened on their doorstep. Overhead, two news helicopters were shining search lights down on the whole show.

The uniforms from the Second Precinct were supposed to be maintaining a clear path to the crime scene, but they were clearly outmanned. Tony and I forced our way through the crowd toward the body. It was a strange mix of people. Club kids in day-glow bar wear. People in business suits. I saw two middle-aged women holding each other and sobbing, as if one of their children had just died. Next to them I noticed a guy holding a six foot tall cross outlined with tinsel, angrily shouting that "Satan cannot stand against the Faithful. The wages of sin are death." I made a point of getting his face on my headset feed, because it seemed strange to me that he would happen to be carrying around a six foot cross when he heard about the crime. Although it doesn't really prove anything. For all I know, there are people who drive around with these things in their trunks, just waiting for an excuse to go be offended about something.

Somewhere in the crowd Tony and I got separated. I tried to call him on my headset, but the sound of the crowd was drowning out everything else. Well, he's a big boy. He can find his own way. I finished shoving my way through to the crime scene and flashed my badge to one of the uniforms holding the crowd back.

The boys from the Second had done the best they could with the humanpower they had, forming a square about ten meters on a side around the body. Which was good, because this body was taking up a lot of room. He'd burst when he hit the ground, and blood and bits of flesh had splattered out in all directions. If I'd had a choice, I would have shut down the whole plaza, isolating the entire place so that we could look for things that might have bounced or rolled away. But it was a bit late for that now.

The ranking officer on the scene was a tall blond sergeant, who was barking orders into a bullhorn, telling the crowd to leave the plaza and disperse. She was not getting much cooperation from them. I tapped her on the shoulder, showed her my ID, and asked if she could get some more uniforms down here to help out. The mob was pushing in on her officers from all sides, trying to get a look at the body. She told me she'd already made the request, and additional officers were on the way.

"What's the deal with this, anyway?" I shouted, pointing out toward the crowd.

"The vic is some VIP," she shouted back. "Singer or something. Somebody recognized him, and then all this happened before we even knew what hit us."

I turned away from her to examine the body. I walked around it, being careful not to step in any of the blood or miscellaneous goo surrounding it. It was a nude male, in his late twenties, and covered in some sort of oily looking substance. I didn't need a degree in forensics to tell me that he'd fallen from a considerable height. I looked around to see where he might have come from. The only building within possible jumping distance was the Liberty Media Tower, but it was a bit far off. He would have had to get a good running start before he jumped, and I've never heard of a suicide doing that. Normally they just step off, kind of hesitantly. Alternatively, the body could have been tossed out of a helicopter or a plane.

I knelt down to get a look at his face, which was turned to the side. There was an inverted cross drawn on his forehead, in a dull red substance that might have been blood. A trickle of blood was coming out of his ear and nose. His eyes were open, a deep blue. And...

I got out my penlight and shined it in his eyes. They were bloodshot, indicating that the capillaries had burst. Normally, you get that in strangulation cases. I'd never heard about it occurring in falling deaths, but then, I'd never actually seen one before, either. I'd have to ask the ME about it.

I was just starting to check the neck for signs of strangulation, when Tony finally made it to the crime scene.

"Nice of you to join us," I said.

"Later," he barked at me, "I heard something on my way in. Let me see the face." He knelt down and I passed him my pen-light so that he could take a good look.

"Damn," he said. Tony doesn't use that word often, so I immediately took notice. "It is Weir. Megan, we're going to need at least three squads in here in riot gear pronto."

"We've already got a request in for some more officers," I shouted to him. "How bad do you think it's going to get?"

"You old enough to remember the riots after Madonna was assassinated?"

I let out a long slow whistle. "That bad?"

"Worse. I just got a glimpse of some of the BNN coverage. We are sitting on top of a powder keg. If I were you I'd get a lot of uniforms in here, and I'd have a team standing by with nausea gas and stun sticks."

I glanced out at the crowd. He was right; they were building up to something.

"OK," I said. "You put a call in to the Second, tell 'em to pull in anything they can. Then get through to the First, and see if they can loan us some help. I'll punch up the current watch Commander at SIB, and see what she can send us. And somebody needs to find out where the heck those crime techs are, I want this body wrapped up and moved..."

I stopped as the sound of the crowd shifted abruptly. A fight had broken out somewhere about 10 meters from our front line. It was too late. The violence propagated, like the rings of waves moving out from a rock thrown into a pond. People mad with grief striking out at people mad with anger. And all of them mad at us for not doing something to stop this. The mob surged through our lines, and the fighting overran us and the body. I tried to keep my feet, but I got knocked over by a man trying to make it past me to Weir's body. Tony tried to get through to me, but it was bedlam.

The last I saw of Tony, he was taking a hit to the head with a big white cross made out of 2x4's. I remember seeing the slogan as it came down on him. "One country under God."

## Chapter 43: The Chosen
## Wednesday the 11th, 11:05 PM

I've never realized how many sounds there are in the night. For the last hour I've been making a game of it, trying to count how many distinct sounds I can hear. Frogs. Fish breaking the surface. A couple of drug dealers having an argument down by the playground. A homeless person rummaging through the trash cans. And birds. I've counted at least 14 different bird calls so far.

It's been raining on and off all night. The clouds overhead glow a pale violet, as they reflect Atlanta's light back to her, and the lake glows a dull violet too, as it reflects the clouds. But everything else is silver. The moon is shining out through a break in the clouds right now, a thin sliver of light, but it's still the brightest thing in view. In between the rainstorms, little wisps of fog rise up off the lake, distorting the reflection of the skyscrapers, and making them look like floating towers in some city of glowing clouds. I'll have to remember that image, and see if I can get Scott to draw it for the comic book. Assuming I ever get back to my normal life, that is.

Summer fell asleep about an hour ago, her back propped up against one of the columns of the gazebo. The moonlight shines down on her face, painting half of it silver, leaving half of it a mystery. She looks so sweet and vulnerable, and yet...even sleeping, there's something cat-like about her. I wish I could draw as well as Scott does. I'd sketch her like this, her face half in shadows, with the towers of the cloud city rising up behind her.

We've been waiting for her mother for hours, and still she hasn't shown. I'd have given up on her by now, but what else can we do? We can't go to my house. We can't go to Summer's house. If we try to check into a hotel, they'll run our cash cards and the MIBS will be all over us. And that's assuming that any hotel would to rent a room to a couple minors, anyway.

Summer mumbled something in her sleep, but didn't wake up. I was getting hungry, so I pulled out another one of the vanilla rice bars that Gerald had snuck out of his kitchen for us. I chewed on it, stopping every so often to listen for a particular bird call that I thought might be a new one. Then I saw the rain coming in again.

The gazebo is out on the halfway point of a bridge across the lake, so you can see the rain before it gets to you. I watched the ripple of it moving across the lake, from south to north, and then I heard it on the roof. I listened to it for awhile, munching on the rest of my rice bar. It was a warm night, and we were under cover. Let it rain.

Off to the east, I saw a figure step out of the trees and onto the bridge. I knelt down, and gave Summer a soft shake. She woke up immediately. I put a finger to my lips and drew her into the shadows. We'd already been kicked out of the park once tonight, by a cop who ran us out at sundown.

Whoever this was, they didn't look like a cop. They were wearing some sort of big formless dress or robe, and leaned heavily on this big staff, taller than me, with stuff dangling from the top. And they were moving pretty slowly, like they were having trouble walking. Definitely not a cop. Probably not one of the MIBS. But also not Summer's Mom. So far we'd managed to avoid all the freaks and homeless people who hang out in the park after dark. Maybe our luck would hold. We kept still in the shadows, hoping that whoever it was would go on by.

I heard the slow tapping of the staff as they approached the gazebo, and then the slightly different sound as they climbed the steps up into it. They came in and sat down on the bench. The white moonlight flashed on silver hair, long and braided down her back. It was a woman. An old woman. I wasn't sure if she'd seen us till she spoke.

"I hope you don't mind," she said. She had a voice like a frog. An old frog. With laryngitis. "It's raining out. Can I share your shelter?"

Summer moved out of the shadows. I followed.

"Of course," Summer said.

"Sorry," I added. "We didn't mean to surprise you. We just didn't know who you were."

"Oh don't worry about that" the old woman said. "At my age, not much surprises me anymore."

Now that we were closer, I could see how deeply wrinkled her skin was. I'd never seen skin like this before. I guess she was too poor to afford the usual surgery. But there was something interesting about her eyes, the way the moonlight flashed in them.

She looked out over the water, and started speaking.

"Last night, I woke, and turned to see,
You lying as always, next to me,
And yet, not you, as I have come
to know you.

The curve of your cheek, frosted by moonlight.
One eye silver in the light, the other hidden in shadow,
The familiar curves of your body, alien, and seductive.
Strange that I could ever think of growing bored with you.
And stranger still
that such a simple thing as moonlight could remind me
Of the precious mystery you are."

The old woman finished, and looked back to us.
"That's nice." Summer said.
"Yeah," I added, wanting to say that I had been thinking something just like that, but not wanting to look like a copy cat. "What's it from?"
"Oh," said the old woman with a chuckle, "it's the beginning of a poem that hasn't been written yet." Then she looked at me strangely. "Maybe you will be the one to finish it."

## Chapter 44: The Lunatic
## Wednesday the 11th, 11:50 PM

"Uh...I don't think so," the boy says,. "I'm not really the mushy poetry type."

His fetch, standing behind him, nods its agreement and slaps him on the back. It appears as a tall man in a dark costume, wearing a black domino mask, with the numeral 0 on his chest. A superhero, I guess.

I see the girl elbow him in the ribs for being rude. Her totem is a wolf, with dandelions woven into its mane.

"Oh, don't blame him," I say. "He's just at that age when boys think they have to prove something. Trust me, I know."

"And besides," I go on, "he's right. Most poetry is just mushy sentiment, or worse, academic word games. But not quite all of them. There are a few poems, young man, just a few, that have a spark of magic in them. Poems that let people see themselves in a new way. Poems that help people find meaning in their lives."

I watch the boy's eyes to see if he understands, but he looks at me as if I'm not playing with a full deck.

"Actually," I say in response, "I'm just playing with a few extra cards that aren't in the standard edition of the game."

He doesn't understand that, either. Ah, if only we could have more time together, there are so many things I could explain to him, so many things I have seen. But such is not to be. And he will find out the important things for himself, anyway.

The girl's totem lifts its head and sniffs the air. It senses something familiar. A moment later the girl stands up and looks across the lake.

"My mom's here," she announces.

The boy looks across the lake, through the veil of rain, at the shadows of the distant trees.

"Where?" he asks.

"There," the girl says, and points to an almost invisible figure, walking the path around the lake toward us.

"How can you be sure it's her?" the boy asks.

"I just am. It's her."

Then, the rest is just as it always is in the dream.

Her mother comes around the lake, and then walks out onto the bridge toward the gazebo. She is halfway to us when more figures step out of the darkness behind her. The men who had been following her, whom the children didn't see. The girl shouts a warning, and her mother turns around. But by now the men are running toward us.

The girl and the boy are frozen with fear, unsure what to do. "Go," I whisper, but they are statues. So I bring just enough of the snake into my eyes to make my point, and say again "RUN!" And the instinct of fear takes them over.

The children sprint out of the gazebo, onto the bridge, just as the men reach Summer's mother. The woman tries to slow the men down, but they easily knock her aside into the lake, and continue charging forward.

And the children are running. Running away from the men, across the other side of the bridge, toward the sheltering darkness of the trees. But it is such a long way. And the men are drawing guns.

I stand up, and walk down the steps toward the bridge. The men fire once. Twice. It doesn't matter. The first two bullets were always destined to miss. It is the third that will find its mark in someone.

Which is why I am here, now. Standing on the middle of this bridge. Because for all my talents, for all my power, the greatest gift that I can give the world is to simply be right here, right now. To be in the way, at the critical moment. So that he will grow up and write poetry.

So in the end, it comes to this.
I never was the first nor best.
But hey—
Whoever said that life's a race, anyway?

## Chapter 45: The Police
## Thursday the 12th, 12:39 AM

"We're almost done with him," the nurse said, "you can see him in a minute."

"Thanks," I said, impressed that she'd found a free moment to tell me this. The waiting area was packed with other people, all waiting for a piece of news on friends or family who had been caught in the riots. I'd given up my chair to an older gentleman who'd been told his granddaughter had a broken leg. Well, at least I still had a prime stretch of wall to lean on.

I pulled out my palmbook and went back to watching the Baptist News Network. They'd been on the scene before I had, so I was hoping there would be something in their footage that I hadn't seen yet. So far they'd shown some close up shots of the body that they took before the girls from the Second turned up to shoo them away, and some overhead shots of the crowd as the riot broke out. Right now, they had a panel of experts on the occult analyzing the case. Their leading theory so far: that Weir had been a secret member of the Satanic conspiracy, and had been using witchcraft to fly over the Liberty Media Tower in order to cast some dread curse down upon it and thereby complete Satan's conquest of America. However, because God is more powerful than Satan, witchcraft won't work over consecrated ground, and thus Weir fell to his death. That was the gist of their story, anyway. Oh they dressed it up a bit with some pseudo historical evidence and a few bible passages, but that's what it boiled down to. Personally, I had a few other theories concerning Weir's death that I wanted to look into before I was going to buy into magical flight.

A nurse touched my elbow. "Officer Strand? We're ready to release him now."

I nodded, and she led me down the hallway to a low desk where Tony was signing himself out. His right forearm was in a cast, so he was trying to sign his name left handed.

"Hey cutie," I said.

He looked up at me. He had a fat lip, and a single blond curl hung down endearingly over a long row of staples in his forehead.

"Don't start with me," he said, trying to finish writing his name legibly.

"Oh, I don't know. It's kind of cute. In a 'Frankenstein if he were a surfer boy' sort of way."

"Yeah, well have you seen yourself in a mirror yet?"

"Touché." I responded. I had a black eye that had swollen shut and was in the process of turning a sickening shade of reddish-purple. On the bright side, it would have looked even worse if I'd had a lighter skin tone. I also had a cracked rib, but at least that didn't show; it was just a hairline fracture. They'd given me a dose of bone grower vaccine and told me not to fall down for a month.

Tony finished scribbling something with his left hand that might have been his name or might have been "fuck off" in Latin, and gave them his thumb print.

"So how bad was it?" Tony asked, as an orderly wheeled him out toward the front door. "Do you know yet?"

"Three dead." I said. "So far. 73 injured. 9 in critical."

Tony whistled. We didn't say anything else until the orderly wheeled him out the front door. Tony hopped out of the chair, and we walked across the street to the parking deck. I checked with Mindy to find out where the car I'd asked for had been left, then took the elevator to the fourth level, and unlocked the vehicle with my thumb print. Tony climbed into the passenger side. We sat there is silence for about a minute.

I hadn't checked the bios on the three people who had died in the riots. I would after this was all over. Intellectually, I know it's not my fault. We're working as fast as we can to wrap this case up. But I also know that if we don't crack this case soon, then those three people who died in the riot are going to have a lot of company.

After a couple of minutes of not talking, Tony pulled out a notebook and started going over the new information on the case that had come up while they'd been stapling his forehead back together. I put on a headset and put a call in to Commander Davison. I hadn't talked to him since the riot, though I had to assume he had gotten word by now. He didn't answer, which was a little strange for him. He normally answers on the first ring. I guess he was in a meeting. Or maybe even he needed to sleep once in awhile.

I left him a message, and then put in a call to Forensics.

"Hello, Baxter here."

I'd been expecting Shard to answer, but I'd forgotten the time. Her shift would have ended hours ago.

"Hi Baxter, this is Strand. I haven't had a chance to check in for about an hour. What have you got for me on the Weir killing?"

"Hmm. You know Lieutenant, I don't know if anyone has ever explained this to you before, but it makes it a Hell of a lot easier on us if you actually bring us back a body to work with."

"I'm not in the mood, Baxter. What have you got?"

He picked up on the tone in my voice and stopped kidding around.

"Sorry. Well, I assume they told you that they couldn't find the body after the riots?"

"Yeah. I heard." I'd seen hero worship before, but this was ridiculous. I could only wonder at what someone was doing with the body now. Were they planning on going into business, selling off Weir's teeth and locks of his hair like they were relics? Or were they just going to have him stuffed and propped up in a chair at the kitchen table?

"So have you got anything for me?" I continued.

"Well, since you'd mentioned the bloodshot eyes, I took a look at the feed from your headset. You were right to be suspicious, that sort of petechia is usually found in strangulation cases, not falls. So he *may* have been killed by asphyxiation before he fell. Of course, a lot of weird stuff happens to a body when it takes this hard an impact."

"So you can't be sure?"

"I'm getting there. Turn on your notebook so that I can video-conference you something."

I did, and an image of Weir's body on the pavement filled the screen.

"I put this model together by interpolating all the images of Weir's body from all the headsets that were wandering around that crime scene. Now, since nobody every flipped the victim over, I can't model his back, but otherwise it's pretty good. With a lot of different angles like this, you start to get a pretty detailed model.

"Now, there are a lot of bruises and abrasions on this guy. Looks like he must have bounced and rolled a couple of times when he hit. If the crime scene had been kept intact, we might have been able to work out the trajectory of his fall from the shape and arrangement of the patches of blood..."

"Baxter..."

"Right, but no point crying over spilled milk now. Anyway, you'll notice these marks around the neck." Baxter highlighted a series of bruises so that they stood out. "Those are ligature marks, probably from a wire or a thin chain. That would be consistent with strangling, but I can't see anyway that he could have gotten them from a fall."

"So he was definitely strangled before he fell?"

"You want my opinion—yes. But you're going to have one tough row to hoe trying to prove that in court without a body."

"Well, we need to do something to keep the DA's life interesting. Anything else?"

"Yep. We figured out what the oily stuff was on the vic's skin."

"How'd you manage that without a body?"

"We got lucky on trace evidence. When they swept the scene after the riots they found a piece of skin lodged in a bush about 15 feet away from the body. DNA typing matches it to some hair samples we took from Weir's home. Probably from somewhere on one of his upper arms."

"OK, so what is the stuff?"

"Are you ready for this? Human fat."

"What?"

"Human fat. As in fat from a human. And not Weir's either, wrong DNA. Not even the same blood type. And there were also a couple of herbs mixed in with it. Deadly Nightshade and Verbena."

Just when I think this case can't get any weirder, it does.

"Allright." I said. "Do we at least know whose fat it is?"

"Well, I did a DNA typing. Female. Caucasian. Brown hair. Brown eyes. Right handed  Type AB positive blood. Assuming good nutrition, about 5'4" to 5'6" tall as an adult. Checked the databases, but there's no criminal or military record of her. So I can't give you an exact ID."

"OK. Thanks. Could you see that this detail gets passed along to the FBI? I'm curious  to know what the girls in Behavioral Sciences make of it."

"Can do. I also…" he started to say something, then stopped.

"What is it?"

"Uh, just something I ran across. I thought I'd heard about something like this before, so I did a search in an occult database."

"And?" I pressed.

"And apparently there are old stories of witches using the fat of unbaptized children to make a flying ointment. Thought you might want to know."

Unbaptized children. And we knew the perps had stolen an aborted fetus from the family planning clinic. Boy this was getting gruesome.

"Thanks." I said.

Baxter didn't have anything else for me, so I took a shot that K'yon might still be up. Sure enough, she was still at HQ, chasing down data trails.

"Lieutenant Strand?" she answered. "What can I do for you?"

"I've got a problem that needs your talents."

"Shoot."

"Well, this may be a wild goose chase. We found some human fat smeared on the latest victim, but the DNA pattern isn't on file with the FBI or the military, so we can't ID it directly.

However, we do have a detailed description based on the genetic traits. Any chance you could run it down for us?"

"Hm. Maybe. Do you know anything about the donor besides the genetic profile?"

"Well, for occult reasons, we think she may be an unbaptized child. So you might check the morgues for a kid matching the profile who died in the last day or two, with incisions that would have allowed the perps to peel back the skin and scrape off the fat. I'd also say that there's a good chance that the fat comes from one of the fetuses stolen from the Peachtree Clinic. If that's the case, see if you can find out who the parents are. Maybe they have something to do with the motive for all this. I know there's not a lot to go on, but…"

"Hm. Should be an interesting challenge. I'll get right on it."

"Thanks."

I hung up on K'yon and turned to Tony.

"You up to speed?"

"More or less," he said, putting down the notebook.

I filled him on the rest of the new developments, including the fat smeared on Weir's skin.

"Human fat?" Tony said, scratching his chin with his good hand. It was clear that he was aware of the occult significance of it. "You know what witches use that for?"

"Flying ointments, I heard. And please don't tell me that you're buying into this black magic mumbo-jumbo theory that Weir flew up over the plaza on his own power."

"Oh, I wouldn't say that I'm ready to buy it," Tony said. "But I wouldn't say that I completely discount the possibility, either. Satan's power is very real, Megan. Even if he has convinced most of the world that he doesn't exist."

There was an awkward pause.

"Of course," he went on, breaking into a smile, "that doesn't mean that I don't have a few questions I'd like to ask about this little incident."

"Good," I said. "I've got a few of my own."

"So what's the plan?"

"Well, I've already assigned some people to backtrack Weir's whereabouts for the last couple of days. Fortunately, a guy like that can't move around without attracting some attention to himself. So far I know that he went into the Liberty Media Tower at around two in the afternoon, and wound up splattered on the ground in front of it eight hours later. I'm hoping we can find a few people to help us fill in the missing time."

## Chapter 46: The Gumshoe

He was sitting in my chair, with his big hairy feet up on my desk, drinking a shot of something dark. He saw me come in and made an odd sort of hand gesture.

"Hey kid, I was wonderin' when you'd finally make it here."

I looked at him in horror.

"My Totem is...Monkey Marlowe? Oh, come on. How corny can you get?!"

He stood up.

"Hey Mac, it's your own damn fault. You're the one who watched every single episode of *Gumshoe Gorilla* as a teenager. You think I like being stuck with this face? Me, I would have chosen to look like Tom Cruise. Maybe that DiCaprio guy."

"Hey," I said, "it could have been worse. What if I'd watched a few more of those Columbo reruns? You could have wound up looking like Peter Falk."

"Ouch. Point taken. Besides, it's not like I need to win any beauty contests."

He opened his desk and pulled out a banana, and stuck it in his mouth like a cigar.

"Well," I said, recovering from the initial shock. "I'm told you're the guy with all the right answers."

He leaned back in my chair and folded his hands behind his head.

"Maybe," he said, "if you've got the right questions."

The desk was covered with loose papers. I moved a few of them aside and sat down on it.

"OK. Let's start off with the basics. Who are you?"

He took the banana out of his mouth and pointed it at me.

"Nope. Wrong question."

He was about to put the banana back in his mouth, but I snatched it out of his hand.

"OK," I said, "what's the right question?"

"The right question," he said, taking the banana back, "is who are *you.*"

"I flunked philosophy." I said, "Can you spell it out for me?"

"You never took philosophy. I know 'cause I was there." He took a bottle of grape juice out of his desk and poured himself another shot. "OK. Let's put it this way. Who are you talking to, when you're asking yourself a question? And who do you think answers it? Oh, and speaking of which."

He leaned over to the filing cabinet, took out a thick folder, and tossed it on the desk in front of me. I read the title.

"Cute men / Flirtation Notes"

I opened it. The fist page was a dossier on Jim-or-Joe-or-John. Turned out his name was Jake.

I closed the file, and my eyes strayed to the papers on the monkey's desk. They were mostly photographs. Pictures from a murder scene, a woman who'd been hacked up pretty bad. Looked like a good chunk of her midsection had been cut out. The other photographs were all of paintings.

"Taking an art class?" I asked.

"In a sense," he said. "I thought I might try and get some work done on the case while you were off chasing wild geese with Stonewall and the Christian Militia. Figured at least one of us should be on the job."

I looked at the photographs of the paintings. They seemed familiar. After a minute, I realized that they all reminded me of that weird painting that I'd downloaded off Jen's system.

There was a magnifying glass on the corner of the desk. I picked it up and examined the signatures. They were all the same. Alicia St. Cloud.

"Good boy," my totem said, as he watched me conduct the examination, "there may be hope for you yet."

"Thanks." I said. "Now maybe you can help me with my next question. Namely, how do I get out of this funhouse and back to the real world?"

The gorilla let out a loud sigh. "Then again, maybe you are as dumb as you look." He gestured around. "This *is* the real world, kid. It's just that most saps are asleep, so they only see a small part of it."

"Fine," I said, "But one of those saps happens to be my client. So is there any way for me to rejoin the sleeping world long enough to get my job done?"

"Oh, is that all you want?" Marlowe said, surprised. "Sure, there's a way." He looked around him, then put a finger to his lips, as if to say, "the walls have ears." He motioned for me to lean close, which I did.

Leaving my jaw wide open for the uppercut he hit me with.

## Chapter 47:  The Police
## Thursday the 12th, 3:51 AM

"So you do remember him coming in?" I pressed.

The man on the other end of the link yawned.  He was wearing a terry cloth bathrobe with a picture of a tiger on it.

"Yeah, like I said.  It's not everyday I meet Justin Weir.  He even said hello to me."

"Great, and do you remember the time?"

The security guard scratched his ear.

"Not really.  Had to be sometime between two and three.  I'm sure it's on the sign in list."

"I'll check on that," I said.  Actually, I had already seen the list, and it had Weir entering the building at 2:38 pm.  I just wanted to see how accurate this guy's memories were.

"And he left?" I prompted.

"Oh, I didn't see him leave."

"No?"

"No.  But I wasn't at the front door for the whole shift."

"Why?"

"Oh, some foul up with my time cards.  My supervisor called me up to his office to straighten things out.  Turned out to be some stupid computer glitch."

"Yeah, I know how those are," I said.  "I remember one week when our computer decided that I'd worked negative seventeen hours and *deducted* money from my cash account rather than depositing it."

"Really?"

"Honest Injun.  So how long did it take to clear up your problem?"

"Just under an hour."

"And that would be from…?"

"Hm.  Let me think.  About three thirty to four thirty?"

He sounded unsure of the time.

"OK, who covered the door for you?"

"Oh, some new kid."

"Well, I should probably talk to him just to be thorough.  You know his name?"

The guy in the Tiger robe wrinkled up his forehead.

"Sorry, I'm not good with names.  Usually have to meet a person a couple of times before I remember it."

"So you hadn't seen him before?"

"Like I said, he's new."

I picked up a tablet and pretended I was looking over a list of names.

"Was it Jones, the tall blond guy?"

"Nah. This guy was tall, but a carrot top. Startin' to go bald, too."

"Well, thanks for your help, and sorry to get you out of bed, Mr. Carter."

"No problem. Not like I was gonna get any sleep after a day like this, anyway."

I hung up, and then had Mindy do a quick search of the driver's license photos for all the security guards employed at the Liberty Media tower. It came back negative. There were no balding red heads that worked there. So either this guy dyed his hair, or he wasn't a real security guard.

I noticed that Tony had turned off his headset and was taking a stretch.

"How's it going?" I asked.

"Strangely," he said. "You ready to compare notes?"

"Let's. What did you find out from the secretary?"

"She remembers Weir coming in to see the Senator. She puts the time at about a quarter till three. She says she doesn't remember him leaving, but she was called away from her desk for a few minutes around 3:30, so she assumes he left while she was out of the office."

"Interesting. I just had a similar conversation with the guard who works the front door. He remembers Weir coming in, but never saw him leave. He also got called away from his post around 3:30. A replacement guard signed Weir out at 3:42, but now nobody can seem to remember the guy's name."

Tony frowned. "That is a bit of a coincidence, isn't it."

"It gets better," I said. "I've got the boys in the phone pool calling up everybody who works in that building..."

"Megan, there have got to be a thousand people who work there!"

"Actually, 1,789, including temps and cleaning crew. And I plan on waking every single one of them up to tell me if they saw Weir leaving the building. People like Weir don't walk around without being noticed. Somebody should remember sharing an elevator down with him, somebody should remember seeing him crossing the lobby, somebody should remember running into him on the sidewalk out front."

"And I take it no one has?"

"So far we are 0 for 1,027." I said, glancing down at the number in front of me on the conference table. Even as I said it, the number rolled over to 1,028.

Tony cocked his head to the side and closed his eyes. It's a little thing he does when he's getting upset and doesn't want to show it. I knew he didn't like where the trail was going. But I also knew that he was too good a cop to ignore hard evidence. I gave him a few seconds to take it in, and then continued, "Which means..."

"Which means that Weir never left Liberty Media." Tony interrupted. "It means that someone in the building strangled him, then stored the body until after dark. The perpetrator then stripped him, painted him with Satanic symbols, and tossed him off the side of the building.

"Probably at least two someones," I corrected him. "The body was a good distance from the building, so he must have been thrown with some force."

"All right. " Tony said. "You think Stonewall's involved, don't you?"

I was glad we were having this conversation face to face rather than over APIN.

"I don't see any other conclusion," I said. "At the minimum, he's the one who ordered the cover up. Several different people could have arranged the computer glitch that pulled the guard off the front door, but..."

"...But Stonewall is the one who sent his secretary off on that errand at 3:30. He asked her personally, I checked. But Megan, it just doesn't make any sense."

"Has anything about this case made any sense?"

"No, I mean think about it. Stonewall's been around for awhile. If he was stupid, he wouldn't have gotten this far. And you're going to sit there and tell me that Weir makes an appointment with him, walks into his office, and then Stonewall wacks him *there*? In his own office? While he's there? I mean, really. If Stonewall wanted to kill the guy, he would have had it done in some way that couldn't be traced back to him. And why would Stonewall want to kill one of his big assets, anyway? Weir's made him a ton of money over the last few years."

"Everything you're saying sounds reasonable," I said, "but the facts disagree with you. All I can figure is that Stonewall figured he could pull some political strings in the department to keep the investigation from going anywhere."

In fact, I had been nervously waiting for the Commander to call and try and talk me out of pursuing this lead. Fortunately, that hadn't happened. Yet.

Tony was scrunching up his eyes, making an unhappy face.

"Well, you got some other way of looking at this?" I asked.

"I don't know. I can't figure this out. I mean, *if* Stonewall is behind Weir's murder, then what does that tell us about the other crimes?"

"I'm not sure," I admitted. "This one wasn't nearly as well planned out as the others. Some of the symbolism is the same, but anyone could copy that off the news..."

Just then K'yon walked into the lounge.

"Sorry to interrupt," she said, "but you did ask to be notified when I obtained an ID on the fat donor."

"You've got it?" I asked. I didn't mean to sound so surprised.

"That is what I said, Lieutenant."

"Great! Who was she?" I was hoping for a connection I could use.

K'yon smiled. "First, wouldn't you like to hear all about the contorted trail of logic I had to go through to track her down? The leaps of imagination? The bursts of intuition? The..."

"Dazzle me later." I said. "Who is she, and how did she die."

"Her name is Carmen Fitzpatrick. And she didn't."

"Huh?" Tony interjected.

"She didn't die." K'yon went on. "No. Still alive and kicking. Works as a night accountant at the embassy suites downtown. Has a little boy, age 5, who likes basketball. Husband works on an oil rig in the Antarctic..."

"Excuse me," I interrupted. "Could we get back to the 'not being dead' part? If she's not dead, how did fat from her body end up on our corpse?"

"Well, I asked myself the same question," K'yon said, "when I couldn't find any matches to her genotype among the records of the recently deceased. Then I thought of another source. Of course, there are now several plastic surgeons who are a bit annoyed with me for hauling them out of bed at 4 in the morning to answer questions. They seemed to be under the impression that having an unlisted number would buy them some privacy. Obviously, they've never..."

"Plastic surgeons?" Tony asked.

K'yon put a finger on her nose and nodded. "A doctor Clarence St. James. The operation was performed this morning. The patient was home resting when I called her. Says she's buying a new swimsuit to show off the results."

"Thanks, K'yon." I said. She nodded, put her headset back on, and went back into the conference room.

I turned to Tony. "Correct me if I'm wrong, but I assume there are no black magic rituals involving liposuction?"

Tony shrugged.

"I'll take that as a no." I took a breath and collected my thoughts. "OK. How are things coming with the manhunt for Banders?"

"No nibbles yet," Tony said. "He must have gone to ground."

"All right. Then turn it over to McCormick. Right now I want you to find out how that fat made its way from the operating table and onto our victim. Go question the surgeon, question his nurse, check out the operating room, find out who does their bio-disposal. But find out how the perps on this crime got their hands on the stuff. Maybe it will give us some hard evidence against them. In the meantime, I'll figure out how to get around this political minefield we're about to go tromping through."

"Sounds like you get the fun job. Be careful."

Tony picked up his headset and went off to grab a car, while I prepared myself for a difficult phone call. It was time for me to have a little chat with Commander Davison about his relationship with Senator Stonewall. Not something I was looking forward to. I had to very careful about how I played this hand. I had Mindy put me through, and was almost relieved when I got the Commander's voicemail.

Which reminded me: I had left him a message almost four hours ago that he hadn't returned. I'd just been so caught up in running down leads that I hadn't had a chance to think about it. I guess he could have been asleep. Still, he would want to wake up for this. I had Mindy punch in his priority code.

And still got no answer. That was not like the Commander.

"Mindy, where's Commander Davison right now?"

"I'm afraid I don't know, sugah. "

"You don't know? Clarify?"

"Commander Davison is not currently on APIN. There are no meetin's on his schedule."

"Well, is he in the building?"

"Signed out at 12:07."

OK. He might have gone home. Or he might have gone out on business relating to the case.

"Did he take a car from the pool?" Police cruisers all have transponders built in, so that we always know where they are.

"Sorry darlin', no."

"Did he take a headset with him?"

"You betcha."

"Well where is that, right now?"

"Like I told you darlin, he's not signed on right now, so I don't have a location on him."

"OK," I said. "Then can you at least tell me how long he has been offline?"

"Three hours, seven minutes."

"All right," I took a deep breath and reminded  myself that there was no point in yelling at a program. "Give me a map, with a plot of his location for the last 20 minutes before he logged off.

"No problem. By the way, sweetie, you might want to lay off the coffee. I can tell you're getting' just a mite jumpy…"

I switched off the audio feed, and picked up my palmbook. There was a map of Atlanta, centered on HQ. A series of time-indexed points stretched out from our parking lot, north up Peachtree, and then east along Ponce de Leon. It stopped at the intersection of Ponce and Highland. I switched my headset back on long enough to have Mindy check the Commander's home address; it was in the south end of town. So wherever he'd gone, it hadn't been home to bed.

I walked back into the conference room and waved at K'yon. She looked up.

"Hold down the fort here. I'm going to go check on something."

"Of course."

I walked around the table, and leaned in close to whisper in her ear. She took the hint and switched off her headset for a second.

"And if you get a chance, find out if the Commander got any calls on his personal cell phone around midnight. He went off somewhere in a hurry, and I'd be curious to know whom he was going to meet."

K'yon nodded, and then went back to dictating some search parameters. I left the room and headed downstairs. On the way, I had Mindy give me a list of all the available officers we had in the building. Konig was just coming back in from a canvassing detail, so I had Mindy put me through to her.

"Konig here?"

"Hey, it's Megan. How much longer you on duty?"

"How much longer you want me for?"

"Good answer. Pull your car around to the front of the building. I'll meet you there."

I beat her there by about 30 seconds. She came around the corner, popped the door for me, and I climbed in. She never did come to a full stop.

"So what's the story?" she asked, as we drove North along Peachtree.

"My Commander's been off-line for four hours, and he's not answering a priority call. We're gonna go check on him."

I checked the magazine for my pistol.

"We're expecting trouble?"

"I always expect trouble."

Konig turned the car onto Ponce, while I had Mindy pull a description of the Commander's personal use car. A midnight blue Kronos, with those retro fins that are coming back into fashion. Should be easy to spot.

Five minutes later, we hit the corner of Highland, the last recorded position of the Commander's headset. I had Wendy slow down, so that I could look at the cars in the nearby parking lots. There's a lot of stuff in that neighborhood that's open late: the Majestic Diner, an old-style movie theater, a drug store. But none of them had a blue Kronos out front.

I had Konig circle the adjacent blocks, in case the commander had parked on one of the side streets. She was the one who finally spotted his car, tucked into an alley behind the Ponce de Leon Branch of the Atlanta Public Library. I told her to keep driving and park around the corner, so that we could approach the scene quietly on foot. As we got out of the car, I unsnapped the cover on my holster. Konig noticed the action, and did the same.

We came at the alley from the south, crossing the parking lot of the library. It had been raining earlier in the night, and the pavement was wet and gleaming. The dark windows of the empty building framed cartoon characters holding books, dimly lit by the corner streetlight.

We reached the entrance to the alley and stopped to get the lay of the land. The Commander's car, parked near the back. A dumpster, closer to us. A faint yellow glow coming from behind it. No sign of movement.

I drew my gun and motioned for Konig to follow me. We moved into the alley slowly, while I made a mental catalog of all the places that someone could pop out at us from. The dumpster. The car. Maybe the roof.

I eliminated the dumpster first, moving quietly up to it, and then turning the corner quickly. There was nothing there but the cinderblock wall at the back of the library, and a metal door, slightly ajar, with light leaking out around the frame. I motioned for Konig to take a look at the car, while I kept any eye on the door. She moved up to to the Kronos carefully, glanced in quickly once, and then took a more careful look with her flashlight. She gave me the all clear sign and then moved up to the door with me.

"OK." I whispered. "I'll open the door, and we'll go in on three."

The door was designed to open outward, toward us, so I took the handle side. Konig took the hinge side, and I had to motion her to move back so that she wouldn't get hit by the door if it opened quickly. I'd made that mistake once when I was a rookie. Nothing more embarrassing than being smacked in the face by your own partner as he flings a door open.

This time I was trying to be quiet. I gave the doorhandle a soft tug, to start it swinging open, and then pulled my hand away. Hopefully, if someone was inside watching, they might think it had just been blown open by a breeze. Maybe.

It had occurred to me that I might be acting a bit paranoid about all this, expecting boogie men at every turn. But the Commander wasn't answering a priority call, and that couldn't mean anything good. And I'd rather be paranoid than dead.

The door continued its lazy swing open, and Konig caught it on the far side to stop it from banging into the wall. I listened for movement from inside the building, and didn't hear anything. So I took a quick glance around the corner, and pulled my head back fast. It took my brain a couple seconds to realize what I had seen.

Good God.

Konig must have seen the look on my face. In the dim light, I saw her raise an eyebrow. I shook my head to indicate I was OK. Then I switched on the video feed for my headset. This had just become a crime scene. As softly as I could, I whispered into the microphone for Mindy to alert the current Watch Commander to send backup and a forensics team.

I waved to Konig and pointed to the wall, then moved my hands apart to indicate that the room on the other side was a wide one. I gestured for her to come in high, and I would come in low. I crouched down, and held up three fingers.

Two.

One.

I went into the doorway kneeling and covering the right side of the room, Konig went in standing and covering the left. I scanned my half of the room for any movement, ignoring the blood on the walls. When I was sure there were no hostiles, I glanced over at Konig's half.

She had her weapon out, but she wasn't scanning the room like she should have been. Her eyes were fixed on the wooden cross that had been constructed against the far wall, and the nude body hanging upside-down from it, pierced by nails and wearing a barbed-wire crown. The body had been smeared with mud or something like it, but there was no doubt as to who it was. I waved a hand in front of her face to snap her out of it. There were two doors out of the room. I gestured for her to take one, while I took the other.

It took us three minutes to work our way through the building. After we'd established that there was no one else inside, we went out and did a circuit of the outside, just in case they were still lurking in the area. Our backup got there a few minutes later, and I sent a couple of them out to record the license plates of all the cars in the area. The perps were probably long gone, but maybe someone else had seen them.

Then I went back inside to take a closer look at what they'd done to Davison, and waited for the crime techs to arrive.

## Chapter 48: The Police
## Thursday the 12th, 5:23 am

"Lieutenant?"

My eyes were fixed on the pavement. I realized that I must have zoned out, watching the light rain come down on the parking lot. I looked up. The sky was overcast, and there was no sign of dawn on the horizon. The man talking to me was one of the uniforms who'd responded to the call for back up.

"Yes. What is it?"

"Uh...the techs are about done. They were wondering if you'd give them the OK to bag up the body."

"Yeah," I sighed. "I'll be right in."

I turned and walked back into the library. I'd stepped outside to clear my head while the crime techs did their job. But the only thing that had become clear was that I needed some sleep.

I went back to the library's staff room, where we'd found Davison. He was still there, nailed to the upside-down cross. The mud the perps had smeared on his body had dried now. So had the blood around the nails. The techs were packing up their evidence kits. Shard noticed me come in.

"You OK?"

"Yeah," I said, "just tired. Give me the basics and then you can bag him."

"All right." she said. "For starters it looks like he put up one Hell of a fight." She pointed to a series of bruises and protruding bones, "Three broken ribs. A dislocated shoulder. Shattered elbow. Numerous abrasions to the head and upper body. Final cause of death was asphyxiation, caused by a blow to the neck that collapsed his trachea. I'll know more after I've x-rayed him, but based on the angle of the final blow, I think he was still alive when they crucified him. That's supported by the tearing around the nails in the hands, here, and here." she said, pointing them out. "It looks like he was trying to pull himself free toward the end."

I knew this should be bothering me more than it was. But it didn't seem real. I just had to keep going through the motions.

"Time of death?" I asked.

"Based on liver temperature, around 3 in the morning. Give or take about half an hour."

OK. He'd signed off APIN at about one in the morning. So they'd spent about two hours doing this, before they finished him off.

"What about the mud?"

"Well, I can tell you more when I get it back to the lab. But it's not native. Everything around here is red clay. That stuff is humus. Probably potting soil."

"Prints?"

"Nothing on the body. They must have used gloves. Plenty of latents in the room. We've got people out printing the library staff for comparison, but..."

"...but you're not hopeful. Great. Anything else I should know about?"

"Hmm...Nothing that can't wait till the lab work's done."

"All right. Go ahead and bag him. I'll read the rest in your report."

Shard motioned to a couple of her techs, and they started cutting the Commander down, using saws to remove the chunks of the cross he was nailed to. I went outside, and caught a ride back to HQ with some other techs ferrying back evidence kits.

We parked, I took the elevator up to the fourth floor, and walked back into the conference room. Some of the faces had changed, as people came on and off duty, but the buzz of activity was the same. Another schematic up on the table, of another body. Another constellation of blinking red numbers covering it. The last few days were starting to run together.

It took me awhile to notice that K'yon was trying to make eye contact. I nodded back to her, and then went out to the lounge to pour myself a cup of coffee. She joined me, and held out a cup for me to fill.

"Just thought you'd want to know," she whispered, "I ran that check on the Commander's personal cell phone. He received a call seven minutes before he signed out."

"Who from?"

"A number in Iraq. It's a known redialing service."

"Any way to backtrace the call from there?"

"Not unless you want to invade the whole frigging country. Again."

"Don't tempt me. At this point I might just try it."

K'yon took her cup and went back into the conference room. I looked down at the black liquid in mine. Even coffee wasn't looking good to me anymore. I wasn't going to be of any use to anyone in this state. I went back into the conference room and deputized a kid named Andropov to hold down the fort till Tony got back. Then I went to the back room, grabbed a cot, and told Mindy to wake me up in four hours.

If I had time for any dreams, I don't remember them. All I remember is waking up to the sound of fighting.

## Chapter 49: The Chosen
## Thursday the 12th, 7:48 AM

I swatted away another mosquito that was trying to find its breakfast on my arm. He and his brethren had kept me up pretty much all night. Every time I would start to drift off, a fly would land on my face, or a bug would run across my arm, or something—and I don't want to think about what—would stir in the newspapers underneath us. Summer, on the other hand, was out like a light. She was cuddled up next to me, with her head on my chest. Every so often she would let out a little snore. It was adorable.

I lifted my head to look down at her leg. She'd tripped on a root when we were running out of the park last night. The blood had dried, and the cut had scabbed over, but her knee had swollen up like a soccer ball.

Oh well. I guess we were lucky to at least have the alley to ourselves. Several homeless people had come by, looking through the trash, but none of them had bothered us. Thank God for small favors. I still had no idea what we were going to do next, or how we were going to get out of this mess. I'd given up thinking about it. For the last few hours I'd let my mind go blank, as I watched the sky slowly turn from black, to pink, to blue.

Summer finally sat up, stretched and yawned.

"Sweet dreams?" I asked.

She leaned over and kissed me on the forehead. Which was probably a good choice, since I hadn't seen a toothbrush or mouthwash in almost 24 hours now.

"How's your knee?"

She tried to bend it, and let out a yelp.

"I'll take that as a 'not good,'" I said. "Do you think you can walk on it?"

"I don't know. Where are we going?"

That was the question. Well, when in doubt...

"How about some breakfast?" I asked. "You want something to eat?"

"Good idea, I'm starving."

We'd eaten the last of the rice bars last night, but I still had a fifty dollar bill that Gerald had given us. He didn't say where he'd gotten it, and I didn't ask. I helped Summer up, and she experimented with putting some weight on her knee. It was still pretty tender, so I put an arm around her waist and had her lean on me for support.

We'd crashed in an alley behind the Dreamakers Playhouse, about a block from the park. Working together, we managed to limp our way out to Fourteenth St., and then up the hill toward Peachtree. There's a diner on the corner. We walked in together, like rejects from some three-legged race, and I got Summer up on one of the stools. Then I sat down on the one next to her, and set about trying to get the waitress's attention. I'd never actually paid for anything with cash before, so I wasn't sure how this was going to work. I wound up propping the fifty up in the slot for cash cards, figuring the waitress would see it and know we were ready to order.

Sure enough, she came by a few seconds later. She took a look at the fifty, then at my dirty clothes, then at Summer's black and blue leg.

"Don't ask," I said. "I'll have two eggs, corned beef hash, and a coke."

Summer ordered some cereal and juice and a fruit salad. The waitress took our order along with the fifty, then vanished back into the kitchen with a "Don't Ask, Don't Tell" attitude.

While we waited for the food, I fished the ice out of my water glass, wrapped it up in a napkin, and held it against Summer's knee.

"I think this is supposed to help with the swelling."

"Thanks," she said, taking the ice pack from me and holding it herself.

The food came quickly, along with our change, and we ate in silence for a few minutes.

"So," Summer finally said, "what are we gonna do now?"

I took another bite of the hash to give me a few seconds to think before I answered.

"Well, we can't run forever. And we still don't know why they're chasing us."

I took another bite of food, hoping that Summer would jump in with an idea. But she was unusually quiet.

"OK," I finally said, trying to sound confident, "it seems to me that the first thing we should do is get in touch with Gerald, and see if he's been able to find out what the Hell is going on. Then we'll just...take it from there."

"Yeah." Summer said, seeming to perk up a bit. I think she was just feeling a little lost without a plan of action. Like I was. "That sounds like a good idea. I think I saw a pay phone on the way in."

She started to get up, but I put a hand on her shoulder to stop her.

"Are you nuts? You don't need to put any more mileage on that knee till it's healed. I'll make the call. You sit here and finish breakfast. Oh, and order me some more toast."

I grabbed a couple of the dollar coins that had come back in change, and went outside to make the call. It was shaping up to be a hot day. I was just punching in Gerald's number when I heard a voice behind me.

"Is this going to be a long call?"

I turned around. It was a guy in a black leather jacket He was kind of looking me over in a funny way, but then, I was in Midtown, and you know what that means.

"Maybe five minutes," I said, and turned away quickly. I figured that if I didn't look at him, he wouldn't think I was interested.

It was at that point that I became aware of something hard poking me in the back. Given the way my week had been going, I didn't have to ask if it was a gun.

## Chapter 50: The Police
## Thursday the 12th, 9:55 AM

I heard shouting nearby, then a shattering sound. Then a solid thud, as something hit the wall, hard.

Huh? For a moment I thought that I was dreaming it all. It took me a minute to realize that there really was a fight going on in the next room. I pulled myself up off the cot, and staggered to the door. I opened it, blinking back the bright light and struggling to see what was going on.

Out in the lounge, two of my fellow officers were in the process of trying to beat each other senseless. It looked like they'd both taken a couple of solid blows to the face, but so far the only real casualties were the furniture and the coffee pot. Across the way I could see Tony and a couple of data techs standing in the entrance to the conference room, watching the fight.

I cocked a sleepy eyebrow at Tony. He shrugged, and held up his cast. I thought about trying to handle it on my own, but walking into the middle of a fight between two idiots is not my idea of a healthy way to start the day. I looked at Tony and tapped my ear. He nodded, and tapped his headset with his good hand, indicating that it was already taken care of.

It took about a minute for the uniforms that Tony had called to arrive and break everything up with stun sticks. By then the fight had already been winding down on its own, as the combatants had pretty much beaten each other to a pulp. After they were subdued, I grabbed the one who looked to be in the better shape by his collar.

"What the Hell is going on here?"

The guy had a fat lip, there was blood coming out of his mouth, and it looked like he'd lost a tooth or two in the scuffle. Suffice it to say that his diction was *not* crystal clear. However, after a couple of minutes of listening to his lisping and gurgling, I managed to get the gist of the story out of him: Apparently, the two officers had been watching television, when a news report came on about the investigation into Justin Weir's death, and some of the stranger occult accusations that were floating around about him. One of the officers, who was a Mormon, had made a rather unpleasant comment about Weir, and about how the whole Baptist organization had been riddled with Satanic agents for years. The other officer, being both a Baptist and a die-hard Weir fan, had gotten a bit emotional, and voiced his objections to said comment in a forceful manner. And from there things had rapidly gotten out of hand.

Jesus. And these are the people who are supposed to be keeping the peace?

By the time I had gotten the whole story out of the guy, and compared it with the one from his fellow gladiator, the medics had arrived and were starting to patch the two up. The uniforms who had subdued them seemed unsure about what to do. Ordinarily, we would have reported this to the Watch Commander, but...well, he was currently in the morgue. I didn't even know if they'd gotten around to appointing a replacement for him yet. One of the uniforms looked at me.

"So what do you want us to do with them, Lieutenant?"

Great. Like I needed this to deal with. I ran a hand through my hair. These guys were really asking for it, but if I threw the book at them I'd be making enemies out of them and all their friends in the department. And besides, where would I be now if somebody had nailed me to the wall every time I had screwed up?

"Take them down stairs to holding. Put them in the same cell. Give 'em an hour. If they apologize to each other, and give me their personal word that this will never happen again, I'll let them off with a reprimand in their files. If they decide they'd rather beat each other to a pulp again, then break 'em up and file assault and battery charges."

The uniforms dragged our miscreants away, and about then Mindy chimed in to remind me that it was time to wake up. Gee. Thanks.

I went over to the vending machine. At least they hadn't broken that. I grabbed a vanilla protein shake  and some dried fruit. Tony came over and punched up a coke and some sweet potato chips.

"So how'd you sleep?" he asked.

"Oh great. Nothing like waking up to the sound of mayhem in the morning."

"Hm."

He munched his chips in silence for a few seconds.

"I hate to bring this up," he went on, "first thing in your day and all, but you might want to take a look at the newsites."

I raised an eyebrow.

"What's happened now?"

Tony swallowed a mouthful of coke.

"They're broadcasting pictures of Davison's body. You know, up on the cross and everything."

"What!? How the Hell did they get their hands on those? Who leaked..."

"Easy, Megan. Nobody leaked anything from our end. As near as we can figure, the perps must have taken their own pictures and e-mailed them to the press a few hours ago."

Jesus.

"So how's the public taking it?"

"Pretty much the way you'd expect." Tony said. "They're scared. If a police commander can get butchered like that, then nobody's safe. It's gettin' ugly out there."

"How ugly?"

"Well," Tony said, taking a sip of his coke, "There were already a few more vigilante acts last night, even before the news of this hit. A couple of Wiccan girls were 'arrested' by some Baptist civilians for being up in the north end of town, and 'deported' back to Decatur. Not hurt, but real scared. A boy in Sandy Springs wasn't so lucky. He got tied to a telephone pole and doused with kerosene. Third degree burns over most of his body, but there's a good chance he'll live. We think he may have been targeted because of a book he was carrying, called *The Satanic Verses*. Also, somebody shot up a new-age herbalist shop over in Decatur. Nobody hurt, just property damage. A couple hours later, someone broke the windows of a Christian bookstore and started a fire. Probably in retaliation."

I put a hand over my face. It was starting.

"It gets worse." he continued. "This morning, the Christian Militia mobilized, movin' units into Marietta and the north end of town. They released a statement to the press, sayin' that if the police couldn't protect their families, the militia would. The Nation of Islam has followed suit, puttin' armed guards on the corners of the black Muslim neighborhoods down in the south end of town. And the Mormons up in Sandy Springs have mobilized some guard units of their own. They're a bit more polite than the other two groups, but they're just as heavily armed."

I rubbed my head. I should have seen this coming. I'd read about it in that book on rumor panics. The conservative religious factions, with their belief in an absolute evil, are always the first to succumb to the panic. And the most likely to shoot someone in the name of God.

"Any confrontations?" I asked.

"Not yet. The three big militias are all stayin' put in their own neighborhoods, so they're not likely to run in to each other. There have been a couple of odd run-ins between them and some precinct cops, but so far none of them has actually opened fire on an officer."

"Good," I said. "Maybe there's still a chance to wrap this thing up before everything hits the fan. What progress did you make while I was off in dreamland?"

## Chapter 51: Summer
## Thursday the 12th, 10:05 AM

I thanked Petrov for the use of his phone, and punched in the numbers. Tim answered on the second ring.

"Hey?" he said.

"Tim, it's Summer, you got a minute?"

"Summer? Uh...my mom told me not to talk to you again. Bye." He said, and hung up.

Ten second's later, Petrov's phone rang. He motioned for me to return it, but I explained that it was just my friend calling back.

"Hello?"

"Summer? It's me. We're on a scrambled line now, and I've got a couple minutes between class. What's going on?"

"They just grabbed Benji."

"Holy Shit! How'd they find you guys?"

"I don't know. He went to make a call at a pay phone and someone nabbed him."

"MIBS?"

"I don't know, this guy looked different. Leather jacket. Kept his right hand in his pocket. I think he had gun there."

"Man. Poor Benji. I wonder what they want with him?"

"I don't know," I said. "But I think it's about time we found out. I managed to grab a cab and follow them to a house in Midtown. I'm watching it from down the block right now. There are two cars in the driveway. Can you cut class and get down here with a couple of those trackers of yours? If they move Benji, I want to know where they take him."

"Uh...yeah sure. It's not like I was going to pass that history test, anyway. I'll grab Scott and some of my listening gear and hop a train south. Where exactly are you?"

I asked Petrov if he knew the name of the street we were on. He smiled and told me. Petrov was being a real sport about all this. I'd explained the situation to him, and he agreed to help out. Apparently, I was the same age as his daughter back in Ukraine. He'd only charged me for the ride over, not all the time we'd been sitting here watching the house. Which was good, 'cause all I had was a twenty dollar bill that had been left over from breakfast.

"Corner of Gore St. and 8th," I told Tim. "Get here as soon as you can."

## Chapter 52: The Witch
## Thursday the 12th, 12:12 PM

I had spent the whole night talking to cops, and my opinion of their conversational skills had been revised significantly downwards.

At first, they thought I was a lunatic. And not that I can really blame them for that. I mean, I come running out of the park, soaking wet, flag down a squad car, and then start babbling some nonsense about my daughter having run a way with some boy who is slated to be the main event at a human sacrifice, and that some guys in business suits are shooting at them. What are the cops supposed to think?

Anyway, after they administer a drunk test, and a drug test, and call my husband to verify that I'm not mentally ill, I finally get them to go search the park. Turns out there's no sign of my daughter, but the police do find a dead woman dressed up in Cherokee ceremonial gear. Or so it seemed. Apparently when they got her down to the morgue she turned out to be a man, dressed like a woman, dressed up in Cherokee ceremonial gear. All of which meant that I got to go down to the station house and tell my story all over again to an entirely new set of cops.

Then things got really interesting. They managed to identify the corpse as Ice-in-Summer, the Cherokee Holy Woman (or thereabouts) who had been stabbed back on Monday. Which meant that the case was no longer a simple shooting, but a high profile political assassination. So suddenly the SIB came into the picture, and decided that it was really *their* case. Which meant that I got to tell them the whole story all over again, to *their* detectives. Pity that the tale didn't become any clearer with repetition.

They finally decided that they were done with me just after noon. Well, at least they were looking for Summer now, if only because they thought she might be a witness to the shooting. On the way out of the station I ran into a small band of Cherokee who were making life miserable for a desk Sergeant. They were all dressed up in traditional garb and war paint, and one of them was wearing a bear head as a sort of helmet. I didn't even stop to ask.

I walked back to the park, picked my car up from a nearby lot, and started the drive back to Decatur. On the way, I tried to figure out how to handle this mess. Somehow my daughter had gotten mixed up with black magicians, a dead Cherokee cross-dresser, and a couple of guys who go around shooting at people before they even know who you are. I don't think Dr. Spock covered this situation.

I got home around 12:30. The remainder of my family was in the kitchen, finishing off lunch. Winter had Urvashi up on the table and was letting her eat off her plate, which they both know she's not supposed to do. Alex was staring absently into his noodle soup. He had that faraway look he gets when he's been scrying too long.

I explained what had happened at the police station, and he nodded.

"Has she tried to get in touch with us again?" I asked.

"No," he said, looking back down into his soup. I wondered if he was seeing something in it or just playing with his food.

"Will she?"

He stirred his soup, and looked up.

"Yes. "

Thank the Goddess. Then they hadn't caught her or killed her yet.

"When?"

Alex stretched his neck, twisting his head from side to side for a few moments. He looked like he was still half off somewhere else.

"Tonight," he said. "Just after moonrise."

Alex isn't normally so precise. But then, our daughter's life isn't normally on the line. I went to check the calendar. Moon rise was at 11:08 tonight. I would need to be ready for it.

I picked up the phone, and put out a call for the coven.

## Chapter 53: The Police
## Thursday the 12th, 2:15 PM

Tony walked back into the conference room.

"You want tuna fish, or roast beef?" he asked.

"Uh...tuna fish."

He tossed me a box from the vending machine. Gourmet cuisine.

"So how's it comin'?"

I rubbed my eyes. "Slowly. I feel like I'm so lost in the details that I can't see the whole picture anymore. There has to be something that links these crimes together, some reason the perps are choosing the people and places they are."

Tony chewed on his sandwich.

"You know, Megan, it could be some sort of geometry thing. What if we plotted each of the crimes out on a map..."

"Been there, done that. They don't make any kind of shape. I also had an expert check the names of the victims for any sort of funky anagrams and the addresses and phone numbers for any psycho math games. Nada. She couldn't come up with a thing."

Tony munched some more of his sandwich. I picked up mine, and forced myself to eat it. But my mind wasn't on food. I knew that I was missing something.

"Any new trouble in the world outside?" I asked.

"Do you really want to know?"

I thought about it.

"No. I don't need the distraction right now."

We ate in silence for another five minutes. Tony smiled at me for no good reason. How he can smile at a time like this is beyond me, but it was a welcome sight. Before we'd finished our sandwiches, K'yon came back in and relieved Fuentes.

I opened the package of moist towlettes that comes bundled with the sandwich, and wiped my hands clean.

"Back to the salt mines?" Tony asked.

"Yeah, back to the salt mines." I said. "How about you recheck the forensic evidence, and go over the witness statements. See if there's anything we missed, or anybody you want to reinterview."

"Sure thing."

Tony dutifully put on his headset, and started calling up old reports and diagrams on his little section of the conference table.

I sat back in my chair and tried to find a different way to wrap my brain around the facts.

I jotted down a list of the victims and what had been done to them:

Commander Davison: crucified
Justin Weir:  thrown off a building
Raven Straylight: exsanguinated
Delilah Collins:  drugged, stripped, and used in ceremony
Carl Phillips: mutilated posthumously

I looked over the list, trying to think about what these people had in common.

Well, there was one obvious thing. Aside from Delilah Collins, the guard from the clinic, they were all dead.

I thought about that for a minute. Maybe Collins wasn't really a victim. Or rather, maybe the perps didn't *think* of Collins as one of their victims. As far as they were concerned, she'd probably been more of a prop. They'd used because she on hand, convenient to use. But they hadn't killed her. They hadn't raped her. So it's not like they had some score to settle with her personally.

I looked at her name again, and then crossed it off the list. That left me with four names. And they all had one thing in common: Senator Zachariah T. Stonewall. Davison had been connected with him politically. Weir sang for his record company. Straylight had been his personal secretary. And Phillips had been his bodyguard.

It was way too much to be a coincidence, but what did it mean? If Stonewall was cleaning house, killing off everyone who knew something about him, then why mutilate someone who was already dead? Or on the other hand, if Stonewall was doing the whole thing as a publicity scam to scare people into voting for him, then why call attention to himself by killing people connected to him? It didn't make any sense. There had to be another connection.

I looked over the list again, trying to think of something they all could have had in common. My eyes stopped on Weir's name. There were still some things that bothered me about his killing. The MO didn't quite match the others. The planning seemed more haphazard. And I just couldn't see our perps engaging in that whole clumsy stunt of stealing human fat from a plastic surgeon. If they were going to use fat, they would have just taken it from one of their earlier victims, or the late term fetus they'd stolen from the clinic. The more I thought about it, the more Weir's killing looked like the work of a copy cat.

I crossed his name off the list as well.

Three names left. So what tied these three together? I put on my headset, and started setting up database searches, trying to find a common link. And there wasn't one. They didn't belong to any of the same organizations. They didn't have any relatives in common. They didn't go to the same high school or college. They didn't grow up in the same town. They had never all worked for the same company. There was no record of any financial transactions between any of them, and as far as the phone records were concerned, they had never even called each other.

There had to be something. I moved on to less likely connections. I checked the attendance records for the school Straylight taught. Neither the Commander nor Phillips had children who went there. I checked the sales records from Phillip's store. Neither Davison nor Straylight had bought a gun from him. I checked Phillips and Straylight for criminal records, thinking maybe they'd been arrested by Davison. Nope. Straylight had no record. Phillips had been arrested once on a concealed weapons charge, but not by Davison. Finally I had Mindy do a massive search of any file, anywhere in APIN's memory, that mentioned all three of their names. Nothing.

Then I remembered that Straylight had changed her name, and did the search again under her old name, Roberta Stevens.

And I got a hit.

Exactly one hit.

I opened it up, and it was the casefile on the old Calerant murder. You know, the guy who cut out his wife's womb?

Have I mentioned before that I don't believe in coincidence?

I'd read a couple of the news stories on the case the day before, and hadn't run across the Commander's name. Small wonder. It turns out that he wasn't the primary detective. But he was on the team doing background interviews, talking with everyone who had been in contact with the victim in the last few days before her death. In that capacity, Davison had talked with Roberta Stevens and Carl Phillips. *And* the newly-elected Senator Zachariah Stonewall. It turned out that Calerant's wife, Alicia St. Cloud, had been working on a portrait of the Senator for the several weeks before she was killed, and had seen the Senator the day before her death.

I decided to read through the whole casefile. Normally, that would take days. Fortunately, the Calerant investigation had been a short one. The evidence against him had been strong, and led to his arrest fairly quickly: Two days before the murder, a restaurant full of people had heard Calerant accuse his wife of having an affair. She was killed in their home, and there were no signs of forced entry, indicating that the assailant either had a key or had been let in by the victim.

She had been killed and then mutilated with a carving knife from her own kitchen, and the only prints on the blade belonged to Calerant and his wife. Calerant's alibi, that he had been at his studio alone all night, was unconfirmable. If it hadn't been such a high profile case, they would never even have gotten around to doing the background interviews. But with the whole world watching, the lead investigator had decided to cover all the bases.

It took me hours, but I went through every document, every piece of forensic evidence associated with that case. And didn't find much. But there was one thing that jumped out at me. The date. The one at the top of the casefile. It read June 11, 2009. The murder had taken place exactly one week before Rebecca Stevens quit her job with Senator Stonewall. Coincidence?

I finished reading, but still didn't feel any closer to an understanding of my current problem. The only other thing in the casefile was the raw headset footage from all the officers who had worked on the case. Literally thousands of hours of it. I got up and grabbed a yogurt from the vending machine, and then looked over my options. I decided that the raw footage of Davison's interview with Stonewall might be worth taking a look at. I'd already read his summary of it, but he might have missed something.

I brought up the video on one of the few remaining blank areas on the conference table, and called the audio up on my headset. The interview had taken place in Stonewall's office at Liberty Media. The Senator looked nervous, but that was to be expected. Politico types are always anxious about being associated with a scandal. Even just knowing the victim was a lot closer than they wanted to be to a murder case. Davison asked him the usual questions about the victim's mood, if she said anything to indicate that she thought she was in danger, so on. There was nothing unusual about the interview, and nothing interesting.

Except for the time gap.

It came in the middle of the interview. Davison's headset fritzed out for about ten minutes, and didn't broadcast. When the picture came back, Stonewall looked a little red in the face, and seemed to be sweating. He asked Davison if that was all the information he needed. Davison said that it was, thanked the Senator for his cooperation, and left. By this time, Calerant was already in custody, and the DA was cementing her case against him.

Ten minutes. It wasn't a smoking gun. It could have just been a dead battery or a loose wire. Or, it could have been something more interesting. I checked into Davison's records. A month after that peculiar malfunction, Davison was transferred to S.I.B. Three months later, he was made the lead investigator on a high profile case involving the murder of a principal who had set up a drug dealing network at his high school. It's unusual for so junior a detective to be assigned to such a major case, but Davison had cracked it, garnering a reputation in the media as a wunderkind. Several more high profile cases followed in rapid succession, the sort that can make a detective's career, but that usually make the careers of detectives who have been on the job a lot longer.

I was beginning to see a pattern. Davison had known something about that case, and used it to have Stonewall pull some strings to advance his career. Rebecca Stevens had known it, too. Maybe she couldn't prove it, or maybe she didn't want to come forward with it, but she knew it. And because of it she had quit her job with Senator Stonewall, and eventually quit his faith as well. And Phillips knew about it, too, which explains why Stonewall gave him such a cushy retirement deal.

Of course, that left one big question: what was "it"? I hated to fall back on stereotypes, but the first thing that comes to mind with a televangelist is a sex scandal. The media had never found out who Alicia Calerant-St. Cloud had been having her extra-marital affair with, and had concluded that Calerant had been mistaken, that he had killed his wife in a jealous rage over a lover who didn't exist. But what if they were wrong? What if portrait painting had developed into something more intimate?

OK, as theories go, this one didn't have a lot going for it. There were a lot of assumptions behind it, and precious little evidence. But it did fit the few facts as I knew them, which was a far sight better than anything else I'd come up with.

So. Let's say that Stonewall was having an affair with Calerant's wife. A sex scandal would be bad enough for his career. But a sex scandal that led to a murder? He would never live it down. So Davison found out about it, and forced him to pull some strings to get him good cases. Rebecca Stevens found out about it, and lost faith in him. Phillips finds out about, and just considers it another secret he keeps as part of his job. It fits. But then why does someone start killing them after all these years?

There were two possibilities. Stonewall could be cleaning house, killing off everyone who knows his dirty secret. But that brought me back to the problem of Phillips; why dig up a guy who's already dead? No, the second possibility made more sense. Calerant, having killed his wife, was now after her lover, and everyone who had protected him.

I took a deep breath. Up at this level of supposition the air was getting pretty thin. Still, I couldn't see any other trails to follow. I did a check on Calerant. He'd been released from prison two years ago, and had been meeting regularly with his parole officer every Friday. And he was still living in Atlanta.

A thought hit me. I got K'yon's attention.

"Can you drop what you're doing for a second and run a search for me?"

"Of course, Lieutenant. What do you want to know?"

"Get in to the state prison records. See if there was ever any contact between our man Banders and a prisoner named James Calerant. See if they were ever at the same prison, or…"

"Got it," she said, before I could finish the question. "They were cellmates from 2018 to 2021 at the Clayton State Correctional Fac…"

"That's it!" I shouted. I grabbed Tony. "Drop everything. Round up some men and send them to the home of James Calerant. If you can find him, hold onto him till I can get an arrest warrant. K'yon, give him an address."

"128, Wimbledon Place." she said, having already looked it up. I swear, one of these days I'm going to scratch her just to see whether she bleeds or sparks.

"Uh…Yes ma,am." Tony said. "You want to let me in on what's going on?"

"I'll be happy to," I said, "as soon as I figure out how I'm going to explain this to a judge and get him to swear out a warrant. For the moment, just accept that Calerant is our man and go get him."

Tony looked confused.

"NOW!"

"Yes ma'am!"

I turned back to K'yon.

"Is there a point in me telling you to put a data trap out for any activity by Calerant, or have you already done it?"

"Traps have been set to catch any use of his bank accounts, cell phone, or known web accounts."

"That's what I thought. Also find out who he's been hanging out with since he got out of prison. If he's not at home, maybe we can find someone who knows where he is."

K'yon set to work compiling the list. At least now we had a good guess as to who was behind this, and why. I had zippo on evidence against him so far, but I might get lucky when we brought him in, and get a positive fiber or shoe print match linking him to one of the scenes. Heck, maybe he'd even be carrying a weapon. Either way, I needed to get this crazy off the streets, before the city freaked out completely.

## Chapter 54: Jen
## Thusday the Twelfth, 3:09 PM

As soon as I heard the door lock again, I picked the blanket up off the floor and threw it back over to the bed. I'd been using it to hide the the thaumaturgic triangle that I'd drawn on the carpet a couple of days ago. It really should have been done in chalk or salt, but the only thing I'd had available was some packages of soy sauce that they'd brought in with my dinner one night—take out Egg Fu Yung. Well, at least the goons were feeding me well.

I knelt down in the middle of the circle and got to work. Ordinarily, I would have stripped down before trying magick like this, since clothing tends to create a barrier between one's personal energy and the universe's, but it was just too darn hard to undress with handcuffs on. I focused my mind, and tuned my body to the ambient flow of magickal energy that permeates the universe. Somewhere, far beyond these basement walls and the steel door, was the open sky, and the power of the stars. Somewhere, beneath the carpeting and the concrete floor, was the mother earth, with her limitless strength. Between them I knelt, repeating the charm of sending, building up the power of a spell within my circle, and focusing on the image I wanted to broadcast.

I had been trying to get out a sending ever since they grabbed me on Sunday afternoon. I could only hope that I was getting through to someone in the coven. Maybe one of the seers, Raven or Alex. My best chance had probably been on Sunday, when the coven was gathered for the new moon ceremony. Still, I had to keep trying. I was the only one who had an inkling of what Calerant was up to, and I had to get out a warning.

My concentration was broken by the sound of the heavy deadbolt being slid back on the door. I jumped up and threw the blanket back over the design on the floor. I had to be careful. Most folks wouldn't even recognize a thaumaturgic triangle, but these guys were into some serious black magic. If they saw the triangle and the circle, they might realize what I was up to.

The door opened, and two of the thugs came in with some teenage kid they had all bundled up. I still hadn't heard the goons use any names, so I was calling these two Bruiser and Bashful. So far I had seen a total of four thugs in Calerant's employ. I still wasn't sure what he was up to, but you don't hire that kind of manpower unless you're going to use it for something.

They took the hood off the kid. A boy of fourteen. Blue eyes. Brown curly hair. Small Roman nose. I didn't need to ask his bloodtype and whether or not he was left handed to know who he was. But I still didn't know why Calerant wanted him so bad. Or what he had planned for the boy.

They unhandcuffed the kid, and he stepped back from them, rubbing his wrists. I held out mine.

Bashful looked at my handcuffs and laughed.

"I don't think so," he said.

"Ah, come on." I said, making eye contact. If I'd known they were coming, I would have had a glamour ready, but they'd caught me unprepared. "I'm getting itches in all sorts of places that are hard to scratch in these things."

"You should have thought of that before you threw my buddy into the wall." said Bashful. Bruiser was motioning like he thought they should leave.

I shrugged. "Can't blame a girl for trying."

I took a step toward Bashful, slowly. He let me. I had decided that Bashful was the weak link in the bunch. I was clearly his type, and I got the impression that he liked a women who could throw him around a little.

I slowly raised my hands, and then let them rest lightly on his chest.

"Your buddy just got careless. I'd be happy to show you that throw, sometime, if you'd like?"

Bashful laughed then stepped back carefully. But not before I'd gotten what I was really after: a stray hair that had lodged on the front of his shirt. I gripped it in my right hand. Later, I could try and use it to work some sort of sympathetic magick on him. Assuming I didn't get a chance to break one of their arms first, and make a run for it. I'd been waiting for one of them to make the mistake of coming in alone again.

Bruiser smiled at me and wagged a finger, and then they both walked out through the door, backwards. Darn. They were too smart to turn their backs on me a second time. The door closed, and I heard the heavy metal deadbolt being slid back into place. I had already checked my room thoroughly for a physical weakness and found none. Concrete walls, steel door. If was going to get out of here, I would have to exploit a human weakness.

I turned to the kid. The one that Calerant had been keeping such careful track of. Maybe he had some answers.

"Hi," I said, sticking out both hands to shake. "I'm Jen. And you're...?"

"Benji," he said. He seemed confused.

"Welcome to my little paradise Benji. The maid service is a bit lacking, and there's only one monitor, but we have a well-stocked print library, and the food is surprisingly good. There's a little bit of shrimp curry left over from lunch, if you like." I motioned to the takeout container. He shook his head.

"Who are these guys, anyway." he asked. "FBI, CIA?"

"Huh?" The guys that I'd seen so far were clearly hired muscle, not government pros. But I wouldn't expect a kid to tell the difference.

"Do you know why they brought you here?" I asked.

He shrugged. "I was hoping you could tell me. I've been on the run from these guys for a couple days."

"Really?" I prompted. Then the kid started to spin me some crazy story about a bunch of Men in Black Suits who'd turned up asking his friends where to find him, and how he'd put a tracer on one of them and followed them to a school where they were taking blood from an army of clones and tried to get him, but he slipped out and got away until they started shooting at him in a park and he slept with his girlfriend in an alley and then some guy in a leather jacket grabbed him while he was using a payphone...or something like that. He was talking fast, and I couldn't follow it all.

The kid was obviously too scared to be thinking straight. I wish that I had news that would calm him down. But the things I knew fell into the "good cause for panic" category.

I still hadn't figured out why Calerant was so interested in this kid. There had been oceans of material about him on Calerant's hard drive. Birth records, adoption records, a genetic profile, a couple highschool photos. I'd figured that maybe he was Calerant's son, so I'd downloaded the genetic profile—along with some of the creepier occult stuff I'd found. But no dice. The kid's bloodtype and Calerant's were all wrong, among other things.

"So what are you in for?" he asked.

I thought for a moment, weighing how much I wanted to tell him. But the kid was probably in so deep that nothing I could say would put him in more danger.

"Ah, I was working a case and Calerant's name came up." I watched his face, to see if he knew the name. His interest level did perk up suddenly.

"You're a cop?"

"Uh...no. I'm a PI."

"Oh. Well that's still pretty cool. So who is this Calerant guy?"

"You've never heard of him?"

The kid thought for a minute.

"No."

"Hm. Well, he's an artist."

"You got captured by an *artist*?" The kid asked.

"Yeah, well so did you." I reminded him. The kid did have a point though. If I hadn't gotten sloppy, I wouldn't be in this fix now. I'd made some fast guesses about a connection between Calerant and Stonewall. I figured as an artist, he might keep a journal, so I broke in and downloaded some stuff from his hard drive.

And boy did I hit the mother lode. All sorts of creepy occult stuff. Copies of Stonewall's speeches. And all this data on the kid. Still, I should have known that it was a mistake to go back to his apartment for a second look around. But how was I supposed to know that a painter would have his own hired muscle?

Well, at least one of those had a few years of bad luck to look forward too. He was probably still picking bits of that mirror out of his face.

I watched the kid. He'd changed his mind about the curried shrimp, and had picked one up with his fingers to nibble on. OK. He said he didn't know who Calerant was. But maybe he knew something about what the painter was up to.

"So Benji, you been following the news?"

"Um..." he chewed and swallowed. "Not for a couple days. I've been on the run."

I gestured to the TV in the corner of our little cell.

"Myself, I haven't had much else to do lately. You heard about the weird occult stuff going on?"

There was no noticeable flash of recognition. He chewed on another shrimp and said, "Oh, you mean that stuff at the graveyard and the abortion clinic? Yeah, we studied that in school."

He continued eating, but now he was losing interest in the food, and was starting to look around our cell. His eyes landed on the toilet, which had no privacy screen. He wrinkled his forehead. Boys worry about the silliest things.

"Uh Benji. I need to ask you something, and I need you to think hard, 'cause it's important. OK?"

He looked up at me, with big trusting eyes. "Sure. If it'll help us get out of here."

"Do you know anything about those occult crimes? Anything out of the ordinary, anything that other people might not know."

"No, not that I can think of. But my girlfriend's a witch, though. She might know something. Why, is this same artist guy tied in with all that?"

I decided to level with the kid. We were in a fix, and he was probably in even more trouble than I was. And my intuition said I could trust him.

"Yeah, Benji. I found plans for the rituals on the hard drive at his apartment. And I've had a couple of odd conversations with him over the last five days. He's behind it all right."

"Why?" the kid asked. "What's he trying to do?"

"I don't know." I admitted. "I asked him, but he said something that I didn't understand. Any chance that you'll know what it means?"

"I don't know. Try me."

"What he said was, 'Sometimes you can only save a thing by destroying it.'"

## Chapter 55: The Witch
## Thursday the 12th, 6:30 PM

The coven hears my call, and they come. Throughout the afternoon they filter in by ones and twos, gathering in my kitchen. I serve a light meal, for we will need our strength for the night's work ahead. By five o'clock there are eight of us. By five thirty we are ten. And just before six Shard arrives, making our number complete. Or as complete as it can be.

We finish our meal, and then we each light candles and go out to the backyard. Eleven of us, no longer thirteen. Raven dead, and Jen...who can say what has become of Jen? Shard has brought the athame, the sacred blade, and she lays it carefully on the stone which will serve as our altar. Then she and the others form a circle, leaving me standing by the knife. There had been no discussion of this, of which of us would take on Raven's role. But the others seem to have made a decision.

I pick up the blade, cold and heavy in my hands, and walk out to the edge of the circle. I raise it aloft, and begin to trace the boundary between the worlds. As I reach Shard, she catches my eye, and gives me a little nod. And then she steps forward and calls to the guardians of the East for the powers of Storm and Intellect. And I can feel it. The old familiar sensation of electricity in the air, of building power. It is working. Margaret calls to the South for the fire of Inspiration. Alex, to the West, for the waters and the deep mysteries. And finally Ivan, to the North, for Earth and the Life Force. With each call, the power grows and changes, and the magic draws closer. Then I reach the point where I began.

"The circle is complete," I intone. "We are between the worlds."

And I can feel the magic. Coursing between the members, like a circuit that's just been closed. We are in the place between, where dreams brush against the waking world, and the possible kisses the infinite. And I am so thankful. For I had not been sure that it would work for me.

We begin the magic. Spells to save my daughter, and Jennifer, and Benjamin. Spells of protection, to keep them safe from harm. Spells of scrying, to find them. Spells of hindering, to slow their enemies.

For hour after hour after hour we work our enchantments, the power within the circle growing and growing, till the boundary between the worlds shimmers with the energy we are shaping. We chant. And when our voices begin to falter, we dance. And when our limbs begin to tire, we make dolls and charms, and work sympathetic magic.

At moonrise we raise a cone of power, and Shard steps toward me, holding a piece of charcoal.

"This is the ash of an oak." She says, drawing on my face. "An old oak, that was struck by lighting. But the oak is strong. And the lighting did not kill it. Take its strength with you." Then more softly, in my ear. "And take mine with you, too." She finished her drawing, then pricks her thumb with the athame and puts a drop of her blood on my cheek. Then she kisses me lightly.

We open the circle, and I leave to go find my daughter, while the others re-form the circle to work still more spells of protection. I see Shard pick up the athame and begin to trace the boundary as I go inside.

I grab my notebook and check my messages. Nothing on voicemail, but there is another e-mail note from another old friend that I'd never heard of. This one mentions lunch at Czech-Out. Smart kid. There are a couple dozen of those in Atlanta. But there is only one that Summer and I eat at regularly. The one over on Peachtree, next to the High Art Museum.

I grab my keys and head for the door. On the way, I catch sight of my face in the hall mirror, and see what Shard had drawn. My eyes stare out from behind a wolf mask.

"Good," I think, as I open the door. "Let it be a warning to them."

## Chapter 56: The Gumshoe
## Thursday the Twelfth, 8:40 PM

I sat up suddenly, my head hurting. I was in a small dark place, but I could hear the sound of crickets and frogs. And there was someone nearby.

"Shh," said a voice I didn't know. "Don't be alarmed. You're safe."

A moment later he turned on a flashlight. And I almost jumped out of my skin. His face was a bizarre collection of blue and white streaks. For a second I though I was looking at a mutant zombie or something, and then I realized that it was just some guy in warpaint. Although the big blue smile painted on his face seemed more like something a clown would wear than a warrior.

We were in a tent. There was a first aid kit open nearby, along with some clay bowls full of...well, I'm not really sure what was in them, but it seemed to be a collection of dried plant leaves and roots. There was a deerskin blanket over me. I pulled it off, and discovered that I was still wearing those Bugs Bunny boxers I'd borrowed from Daniel.

I looked back at the guy in the warpaint, trying to judge if he was dangerous.

He saw me measuring him up.

"My name is Laughing Bear." he said. He was wearing jeans and a quill breastplate. "We've met before."

I looked at him, trying to imagine what his face would look like without all the paint. It was his arms that I finally recognized.

"Yeah," I finally said, "at the coffee shop. You were with Ice-in-Summer?"

"Yes."

I tried to stand up, but my legs weren't quite with the program yet. Laughing Bear caught me.

"Take it easy," he said. "You've been out for two days. I managed to feed you some soup, and keep you hydrated, but your body is still pretty weak."

"Two days?"

"Yeah."

"Figures, you wouldn't believe the crazy dreams I was..."

I stopped there, because just then Tigger poked his head out from behind Laughing Bear and made a face at me. You know,

Tigger. From the Winnie the Pooh cartoons. I rubbed my eyes, but when I stopped he was still there, bouncing around the tent on his tail and laughing.

This was going to take some getting used to.

"Where are we?" I asked.

"In a holy place," Laughing Bear said, "up in the mountains. Ice-in-Summer asked me to bring you up here and look after you."

"OK. Where is she? We really need to have a talk." Boy was that the understatement of the century.

"Dead," Laughing Bear said. He smiled as he said it, an odd smile. "Oh, and before she left, she asked me to pass along another sad message. By now your employer is dead as well. She regrets that she couldn't warn you about it in time to stop it, but it was his path and could not be changed."

For once, I didn't even think about the possibility that I was being lied to. No. Weir was dead allright. But Jen wasn't. And now I knew how to find the guy who was holding her.

"Where's my communications gear?" I asked.

Laughing Bear opened up a backpack and got out my throat mike, my earphones, and my palm display.

"Thanks."

I got on line with Sherwin, and had him run a search of all the commercial web sights in Atlanta, looking for the one that mentioned the name Alicia St. Cloud the most often. He came back a second later with the answer.

I turned back to Laughing Bear

"How far are we from Atlanta?"

"Counting the hike back to the car, a bit more than three hours."

"Good. I'll need a lift back to town."

I tried to stand up again, taking it slower, and actually made it this time.

"Oh, and I could use some clothes, too."

"Of course," Laughing Bear said. He opened up a backpack and pulled out a long buckskin dress, with beaded ornaments.

Oh this week just gets better and better.

## Chapter 57:  The Reverend Senator
## Thursday the 12th, 11:25 PM

It was almost midnight.  I was sitting in my office with the lights off.
The glow of the city seeped in through the windows, painting everything a greenish-blue.  In the distance, I could see the bright flashes
of police helicopters as they shone their search lights down on trouble
spots.  My desk was tuned to the news, droning on through a list of
tragedies and crises.  Riots in South Atlanta, where the police had
tried to arrest a Nation of Islam Guard for shooting some vampire
girl.  A fire fight involving some Libertarians over in Stone Mountain.
A clash between police and the Christian Militia up in Marietta.

I should have been paying more attention.  Rallying my troops,
or something.  But I was consumed with my own problems.  Weir,
for one.  I still had no idea just how much the police knew about his
death.  I had plenty of contacts in the precincts, but the case had
been bumped over to the Special Investigations Bureau.  Davison
had been my eyes and ears there, but now he was dead.  Which left
me deaf and blind, waiting for the police to show their cards.

Then there was the boy.  The boy who could take apart everything I'd built.  I was still waiting to hear back from my men who
were looking for him, but I was no longer hopeful.  They'd spotted
him once, the night before.  They'd had him in their sights,  but
they'd let him slip away.  It's been 24 hours now since they'ed last
seen him.  He could be anywhere.  I'd sent my agents to search
Weir's home, on the odd chance that he might have been keeping
the boy there, but no luck.

I leaned back in my chair and looked out the window.  So
many unknowns.  But at least I did have one advantage.  I'd figured out who was behind all this.  The one who had told Weir
about the boy and put him up to blackmailing me.  It hadn't been
that hard.  I'd simply made a list of everyone who ever knew
about the boy.  Davison.  Stevens.  Alicia.  A couple of others who
have died over the years.  They were all dead now, except for me
and one other.  And I imagine he'll be coming for me soon.

I watch a police helicopter as it approaches from the distance.
It hovers about fifty yards from my window, and shines its search-
light down on the plaza.  People have been coming there all day.
Some of them lay flowers on the sight where Justin impacted, like
he was some sort of martyr.  Others—I don't know who, I never

gave the order—came to denounce him as a witch and a satanist. The two groups had been getting into fights all afternoon, until the police finally closed off the whole area. That was almost twelve hours ago. And still there were people trying to sneak in, trying to touch the spot where he died.

If I made it though this, I was going to have figure out what to do about Weir. It was nauseatingly ironic. In death, he was splitting my church in a way he'd never managed to in life. I'd seen the demographics. Among the faithfull, every age group over thirty-five was buying the cover story, that Weir was using Satanic magic to fly, and had fallen when he tried to cross holy ground. But the twenty-five to thirty-five-year-olds were split, and the twenty-five and unders were behaving like he was some sort of saint.

How easily it all falls apart. You make one little mistake. Then you have to commit a larger sin to hide the smaller one. Then a still larger sin to cover that one. And so on, until that one stupid mistake is dragging down your whole life, forever forcing you to more and more desperate acts.

My desk rang. I'd told Berta to hold everything but a few critical calls. I studied the blinking words on my desk. One said "ANSWER", the other "IGNORE". I let it ring twice more, then turned off the news and touched the spot that said "ANSWER".

"Stonewall here."

"Yes Reverend," said Berta. "Sorry to disturb you, but we've had a rather odd video call come in for you from someone who would only give their initials as J.C. And you did ask to be notified if we heard from them again."

"Put him through."

"Of course."

My desk lit up with a painting of a woman. She was wearing a virtual reality visor and headphones, and holding up a set of scales. I looked at it in puzzlement, and then the painting's expression shifted, and her lips moved.

"Reverend Senator Stonewall. I must say you're looking a bit harried this evening."

He was using a mask program, translating his facial expressions onto another image.

"Hello Calerant. Still hiding behind your art, I see."

The painting of the woman laughed.

"Not one of mine. My wife's actually. I would have thought you'd recognize her style. But then, I guess you didn't have long to know her."

The painting morphed into a photograph of Alicia. She smiled at me and went on.

"But I am pleased that you do at least recognize my handiwork. I was worried that you wouldn't have figured it out by now."

"It took awhile. But you left enough hints lying around."

"Yes, well any good performance piece has to have a certain amount of prelude, to build suspense before the climax. Wouldn't you agree?"

"I'm not a critic."

"Really? How strange. I spent a lot of time in prison listening to your program—the warden was so pleased that I showed an interest in religion—and it seems to me that you're critical of just about everyone. Artists, gays, new-agers, rock musicians, Methodists..."

"Cut to the chase, Calerant. What do you want?"

"What do *I* want? So many things, actually. My wife back. My life back. But I don't suppose that I'm going to get either of those. So why don't we talk about something more practical. Like what you want."

The picture of Alicia reached out and pulled a scared looking boy in front of the camera with her. He was about fourteen, with curly brown hair and blue eyes, like mine. I didn't have to ask who he was.

"I don't believe that you two have had the pleasure of meeting yet. Senator Stonewall, this is your son, Benjamin. Benjamin, this is your father, the right good Reverend Senator Zachariah Stonewall. I would introduce you to your mother as well, but she died some years ago in a misunderstanding."

The kid looked at me, his eyes full of fear and wonder. I looked at him. But I wouldn't give Calerant the satisfaction of seeing me crack.

"What?" The picture asked. "You don't see the resemblance? Well, I admit that he certainly didn't get your chin Senator, but wouldn't you say that there's something about the cheek bones, the eyebrows? Hm? Well, no matter, a simple DNA test will clear it all up. Just a few fibers of Benji's hair, compared to your DNA pattern. Which now that I think of it, will be on file, won't it? They do that with elected officials, in case there's ever a question of someone trying to impersonate you. I believe they instituted the practice after that poor soul tried to pass for Senator Stallone using cosmetic surgery and a fake thumb print. Pity. He might actually have gotten away with it if he could have gotten the speech impediment down.

"Anyway, like I said, your DNA will be on file. And of course, my wife's pattern will still be on file with the police, since she was a murder victim. Hm, it really does work out very nicely. I would think even a reporter could wrap this one up."

The picture of Alicia smirked at me.

"OK Calerant. So why are we talking? If you're planning on going to the press, then why haven't you done it yet?"

The picture morphed again, into another picture of Alicia. But in this one her mouth was drawn out in a grin, and the color had drained from her face, except for a dark bruise over her left eye. I didn't want to show weakness, but I had to look away. The death mask of Alicia spoke.

"What? You think that all I want is your job? We are talking, Senator, because I want so much more from you. We are talking, because I want to be able to watch you as the realization sinks in that everything you have built, everything that matters to you in your life is about to crumble away. We are talking because I want to hold you close while you die, because I want to look into your eyes and watch as the hope drains out of them, as all your dreams come to a bitter end, as you die knowing that history will brand you a hypocrite and a monster."

I forced myself to look at the picture of Alicia, her eyes open but vacant, like a doll's.

"It's a simple deal," the picture of her corpse went on. "I'm waiting for you at the High Museum of Art. It shouldn't take you more than ten minutes to get here. But I'll be generous, and give you fifteen. Come alone and unarmed. We'll face each other, armed only with our rage, and end this the only way it can end, with one of us ripping the other's heart out. If you win, you can leave with your son."

I stared into Alicia's dead blue eyes, trying to find some trace of Calerant, who was hiding on the other side of them. I knew where he was now. I could send the police. Let them deal with him. But I couldn't afford to have them anywhere near that kid.

"As I recall, you're ten years younger than I am, Calerant. It's not a fair fight."

"Then don't come, and I'll take Benji here to one of the news services. You have fifteen minutes to decide." He paused. "Oh, and not that I don't trust you Zach, but I will be having men standing by. They won't interfere in our fight, unless you try to cheat and bring a gun or something, in which case they'll shoot you. Which would be rather anti-climactic, don't you think? So do be a good boy and play fair."

The connection ended, and the picture faded from my desk top. I checked the time. 11:43. The High Museum was a straight shot down Peachtree from here. He was right, it would take me about ten minutes to get there.

But that still left me five minutes to arrange some surprises for the bastard. I started making calls. He had no idea who he was messing with.

## Chapter 58: The Police
## Thursday the 12th, 11:31 PM

I should have known it was a bad idea to go into the lounge. CNN was playing on the television. I found myself sitting down, watching the bad news trickle in, bit by bit.

Down in the south end of town, a teenage girl, dressed in black and on her way out to party at one of the vampire clubs, had been stopped by a Nation of Islam patrol. When one of the guards asked why she was dressed up that way, she made a rude gesture that one of them interpreted as a spell. She was now in critical condition, and would probably lose the arm.

Up in the north end of town, members of the Christian Militia had surrounded the house of one of the few Wiccan residents of the area, and built a bonfire in his front yard—with the clear implication that they weren't there to toast marshmallows. One of the man's neighbors had tried to help him, and had been shot in the leg for her trouble. Officers from the Fourth eventually turned up and rescued both of them, but three people died in the resulting shoot out. We were lucky that only one of them was a cop. When it comes down to service revolvers against automatic rifles, the results are usually a lot worse.

The Mormons, at least, hadn't shot anyone. Yet. But they had set up road blocks, stopping cars that tried to come into their neighborhoods. It was only a matter of time until they stopped the wrong person and something got out of hand.

Then there was all the random mayhem that nobody had claimed responsibility for. Someone had shot up a gay club in Midtown with an automatic rifle. Someone had burned down a Unitarian church. Oh yeah, and my personal favorite: Someone had decided that a coffee shop in Little Five Points was a hub of Satanic activity. They'd lobbed a pipe bomb in during the early evening rush. The news was running footage of a girl in a renaissance ball gown trying to pull herself out of the wreckage. There was blood streaming down her face, and as she lifted an arm to pull herself forward, I could see that her hand had been blown off.

The governor had mobilized the national guard to try and calm things down, but I don't know what he was planning on doing with them. It was just too late. No matter what happened with the case now, we would be dealing with the consequences of tonight for years to come. The public had lost faith in us. And the cycle of retribution would go on for years.

And all because I hadn't made the connection to Calerant sooner.

I turned off CNN, and went back into the conference room with my coffee. No point in sulking when I had a job to do.

"Any word?" I asked K'yon.

"Still no sightings of Calerant or Banders, I'm afraid. Browning is on his way back from the apartment. He left two men to watch it, but the evidence suggests that Calerant hasn't been there in about a week."

"Great. I don't suppose we got lucky with the data trap?"

"Not yet. And, I don't think we will either. I checked his bank records; last Friday, Calerant transferred $400,000 to an account in the Cayman Islands."

"Whew. So much for the starving artist image."

"Yes. At any rate, since then he's been a ghost. No uses of a cash card in his name. No bank activity in his name. No uses of a cell phone in his name. No uses of an internet account in his name. The guy has made himself invisible."

"No one's invisible," I said, wishing that I had something with which to back up that assertion.

I sat down and re-read the psych profile on Calerant that the prison psychologist had done. It was remarkably unhelpful, full of terms like "intelligent", "perceptive", and even "charming". The psychiatrist's recommendation to Calerant's parole committee stated that the subject had been a model prisoner, had remorse for his crime, and was probably the victim of a sudden loss of control, not likely to be repeated.

"In short, it is my opinion that Mr. Calerant does not pose a threat to society."

Not a threat to society. Boy, had Calerant snowed that guy.

I reread the other accounts of Calerant's life since the murder of his wife. In addition to the prison psychiatrist, there were several articles from art journals. Apparently, Calerant had managed to continue painting throughout his prison term and since his release. I took a look at some of his pictures, just to see if I could get inside his head. His old stuff was kind of interesting, but I had to say that I didn't care for his new stuff at all. The painting of the Virgin Mary being vivisected by Freud should have been enough by itself to convince the parole board that he was not a well man.

By the time I finished reading, Tony had come back in.

"Anything new?" he asked.

I shook my head.

"Maybe we need to try coming at this from the other way round," I suggested. "If we can't find Calerant, then maybe we should try finding his next victim."

"And you think you know who that is?"

"Don't you?"

"Stonewall, I guess."

"It's the only thing that makes sense," I said. "If this is about revenge, then sooner or later Calerant will have to go after the man who slept with his wife and drove him to murder."

"*If* we've got this whole thing right." Tony corrected me. "We still don't have any proof to back up this theory of yours. Still, it is worth a shot. You want me to put a couple men on Stonewall?"

I paused for a second. One does not casually order surveillance on a U.S. Senator if one values one's job. But this situation went well beyond career concerns. I took a deep breath, and said, "Yes. But keep it subtle. I don't want to scare off Calerant before we can nail him. Does the Senator's car have an anti-theft transponder?"

Tony said a few phrases into his headset, and listened to the answer.

"Yeah. He's got two cars registered in his name, and one registered as a corporate vehicle through Liberty Media. All of them with anti-theft protection."

"Good, we can use the transponders to keep track of him. Get a couple of officers tailing each of those cars, hanging back out of visual range. The Senator is probably most vulnerable while he's in transit. If Calerant makes a move on him, I want to have some manpower close enough to respond."

"All right. But what if Stonewall uses his helicopter?"

"Oh yeah, the helicopter." I thought for a moment. "Don't worry about it. The only way Calerant could take that out would be with a surface to air missile or something like that. And while I wouldn't put it past the bastard to get his hands on one, I don't think he'd resort to blowing Stonewall out of the air. Based on what we've seen, I think Calerant will want a somewhat more...*personal* experience with Stonewall."

"Yeah, I think you're right about that."

Tony put in a call for some more manpower to set up the surveillance on Stonewall. We were getting stretched pretty thin, with all the stuff that was going on, but I was betting they could spare me another three cars and six plainclothes.

In the meantime, I called up the location of Stonewall's cars on a map. The only question was which one the Senator was using right now. One was at his home in Marietta. Another was at the Liberty Media Tower. And one...was parked in an alley just a few blocks away from us.

"K'yon, take a look at this." I blew up the map around the third car, his roadster. "What do you think he's doing in our part of town this late at night?"

"Huh." She leaned across the table to look at the map. "Let see what's around there." She spoke quickly into her headset, and a list came up on the table. "Hm. The Alliance Theater. He might be taking in a show. There's a diner a few blocks south of there that's open late. A couple of apartment buildings. Public Library Branch. The High Museum of Art. A dentist's office. A Czech fast food place..."

"Wait a minute. The High?"

"Yeah, it's about three buildings over from where he's parked."

An art museum. And Calerant did have a flair for the dramatic.

"What's going on there?"

K'yon called up a listing.

"Nothing, this hour of the night. During the day they're exhibiting a show of modern masters. Vandermeer. Karov. Al-Absin...and Alicia Calerant-St.Cloud."

K'yon looked up, and our eyes met. I'd give you the bit about not believing in coincidence, but you're probably getting sick of hearing it by now.

"Get some backup to the High Museum," I told her. "But make sure it's quiet. No sirens, no lights. And *nobody* goes in until I give the OK."

K'yon nodded, and set about making it happen. I grabbed Tony by the arm.

"Come on."

"Come on where? I was just setting up the surveillance you asked..."

"Forget it. We've found him."

## Chapter 59: The Artist
### Thursday the 12th, 11:50 PM

A clock on the wall was ticking down the seconds to midnight. It was the only thing in the room that wasn't part of the sculpture. A Vandermeer, one of his ponderous installation pieces. He'd put monitors along the wall, endlessly playing gunfight scenes from old Hollywood Westerns, while in the center there were three glass columns, where the bodies of real gunshot victims floated in formalin. I never did find out how he got their families to agree to this. Probably told them he was doing some important piece of art that would protest the violence of the media, save the lives of others, that sort of rubbish.

The whole piece was rather obvious, but there were some parts of it I liked. One of the columns had a little girl in it, no more than five. There was a hole in her little chest, and the incisions from the autopsy were clearly visible. Her long blond hair floated in the formaldehyde. The whole scene would have been moving, if Vandermeer hadn't overshot the mark by putting a teddy bear in there with her. It turned the whole thing from horror to schmaltz. Tisk. He should have known better.

Still, while it might be cheap and sentimental, the piece did have its uses. I had reset the monitors to receive the newscasts from several different services. Scenes of police firing nausea gas. A young black man being knocked down by one of those big rubber rings the police use as riot bullets. Men in Christian Militia uniforms firing rifles from behind a barricade. A riot somewhere in Midtown that the police were trying to break up by spraying foam. Video from the aftermath of a bombing at a coffee shop. Quite the collection of carnage.

Well, I reminded myself, it's not like I caused this. They've all been stacking up the kindling for years. I just provided the match.

Ralph came by, still dressed in his security guard uniform, and assured me that the building was secure. He had turned off the remaining parts of the alarm system, and the other guard—the one who was not in my employ—had been quietly sedated without incident.

"And the security cameras?" I asked.

"Jack is working on those now. A couple more protocols that he has to bypass, then he can patch into them. Five minutes, tops."

"Good." I said. I needed the cameras working. I still had some contacts in the press, and I had told them to be waiting for a special broadcast around midnight. After all, one can't have a performance without an audience.

"And the rest of the preparations?" I asked.

"Wu is downstairs watching the front door, ready to escort your guest up when he arrives. Mikael is in the basement placing the charges to cover our escape. Cynthia and Rupert are seeing to it that the doors and elevators in the building are set up precisely as you requested. And Lucien is seeing to the lighting in the gallery."

"Excellent." The gallery was where the final confrontation would take place, and I wanted to make sure that the event was suitably cinematic. Regretfully, Lucien lacked any formal theatrical lighting experience, but he seemed to have an intuitive feel for the aesthetic components of the craft, and his experience in hot-wiring security systems gave him a good grounding in the electronic requirements. It is so nice to have good help. And prison had been such a good place to find it. You would think more people would do their recruiting there.

I thanked Ralph for his efficiency, and asked him to go fetch Benjamin and bring him to me. I was hoping to spend a few minutes with my wife's son, before this all came to an end.

While I waited for Ralph to bring him, I watched the scenes of violence roll on, and the seconds tick by on the clock. Another shooting. Another riot. Another bombing. A little taste of the war they have all been so busy preparing for. We have had too much peace, and people have forgotten what this is like.

Ralph finally escorted Benjamin into the room, and then at a nod from me went outside to wait until he was called. I looked over Benjamin's clothes. They were ill fitting, and the style would have been more appropriate for someone three years younger than he was. I guessed that his adoptive mother was dressing him. There's a certain style that women resort to when they don't want to admit that their sons are getting old enough to know about sex.

That fit with what I knew of his adoptive mother. I had not liked the idea of placing him with such a rigidly fundamentalist family, but it had to be. If he had grown up Wiccan, or Unitarian, or atheist, then it would have been too easy for Zachary to de-humanize him. Benjamin would have been one of the others, the evil menace that Zachary preaches against. No, for this to work, there had to be no doubt in Zachary's mind that he was killing an innocent.

While I was evaluating him, Benjamin looked around the room. His gaze finally landed on the bodies in the glass chambers, and his eyes went wide with fear.

"Relax," I said smiling, "I'm not planning on throwing you in there with them. Certainly not after all the money I've spent to get you here."

He continued staring, his gaze fixed on the same blond girl that I'd been looking at earlier. Well, at least the boy had taste. Almost certainly from his mother's side.

"If you don't mind my saying so," I went on, "it was awfully inconsiderate of you to choose to run away from home during the one week when I happened to have need of you. Singularly bad timing, my boy. And dangerous, I might add. If Stonewall had found you before I did, things might have turned out...awkwardly. Luckily, I happen to have contacts among the underworld, courtesy of my extended stay with the Georgia Correctional System. I dare say that with the size of the bounty I was offering, I must have had half the underworld in Atlanta out looking for you."

Benjamin didn't speak. His eyes moved from the bodies floating in formaldehyde to the monitors. He had a slightly shellshocked look about him. Not that I can blame him, given the sort of day he's been having. Finding out that he was adopted, a bastard, and the son of Zachariah Stonewall and a murdered woman. Well, that's a lot of new information to absorb, all at once. And he still doesn't know the worst of it. The full story of his conception reads like something out of a Greek tragedy. Sophocles would have staged it an amphitheater with a chorus. I'll have to settle for an art museum, and a handful of hired thugs. Let's hope history approves of the results.

Benjamin continued to stare at the monitors, his eyes moving from images of riots to shootings to graphic pictures of the wounded.

"It's not a new phenomenon," I said. "In 1190, someone in the British city of York started a rumor that the Jews were kidnapping gentile children for human sacrifice. There was of course, no truth to the story, but it got repeated so often by so many people that the gentiles came to believe it was true. In an orgy of fear, they murdered the entire Jewish population of the city in a single day and a single night. Later..."

I had planned to go on and describe the fate of the Knights Templar, the Cathar Heretics of France, and several more recent groups, but I noticed that Benjamin was staring intently at the monitors and giving no indication that he was hearing a word I said. Well, I should have known that a history lecture could not compete with television for a teenager's attention.

I watched the news with him for a moment. An anchor was reading a statement, while in the background the station played slow motion footage of a young man's head exploding as it was hit by a bullet.

"Your mother saw this coming," I said. Even fifteen years ago, she had seen the seeds of it. The great blessing, and the great curse of the information age: that you can always find something that agrees with you. The movie that shows you the world as you believe it to be. News programs that demonize your enemies and affirm your virtues. Friends who will tell you that you're right in everything you believe. And isn't that what people really want? Oh, a few of them may claim that they want to be challenged by new ideas. But in the end, most people just like to be told that they're right.

The trouble is, when everyone is right, it means that none of the people who really should be talking to each other are a part of the conversation. How was it that Alicia used to put it?

"When a culture has no common art, it has no common language."

Benjamin was looking up at me. The reference to his mother had pulled his attention away from the televisions for a moment.

"Would you like to meet your mother?" I asked.

The boy suddenly tensed up, and I could read his panicked expression.

"No, she's not in one of those," I said, gesturing to the tanks of formaldehyde. "But she is in the building. Come, I'll introduce you to her."

I offered him my hand, but he didn't take it—no big surprise there. I turned and walked out of the room. Benjamin followed me, and Ralph trailed along behind us in case the boy tried to make a break for it. We took the elevator up to the third floor, and walked to the gallery where all of this would be concluded.

Lucien was just finishing with the lights. He'd done a nice job; most of the gallery was dim now, except for the small lights shining on the individual paintings, and a large puddle of illumination at the center of the room. Just the right setting for a murder. Lucien nodded to me, and then left to attend to the rest of the set up.

"Here she is," I said to Benjamin, spreading out my arms.

He looked around the room, tentatively. Then curiosity won out over fear, and he began to walk around the gallery, examining his mother's paintings. I followed him at a few paces distance, while Ralph waited by the entrance in case there was trouble.

"Most of these are from your mother's portrait series." I explained. "She spent the last two years of her life traveling the country, interviewing people from different subcultures. Talking to them, trying to understand them. And trying to get that understanding into a picture."

Benji walked past painting after painting. Elijah Shabaz, spokesman for the Nation of Islam. Jack Corkland, head of the Aryan Nation reserve in Wyoming. Rebbe Schwartz, of the Hassidim. Bishop Gonzales, the controversial head of the Florida diocese.

"Your mother thought that she could help people to understand each other," I explained as we walked. "She thought that art could change the world. I know it sounds naive now, but there was a time when she and I both believed it."

I did not add that I still did. Only now I knew how hard it is to get people's attention, how hard it is to crack through the walls that have grown up between the subcultures. In the end, the one thing that everyone understands is fear. If you want their attention, scare them.

Benjamin stopped in front of a picture of Jeffrey St. George, the gay congressman. Like all of Alicia's portraits, it wasn't quite what you'd would expect. She hadn't painted him leading a rally, or arguing on the floor of the House, or even fighting with Stonewall. No, Alicia had painted him having dinner with his lover. They are at a restaurant somewhere. The two men are leaning across the table, talking to each other, holding hands, smiling. And yet...there's something about the eyes. They don't sparkle with love. No, they're trying to conceal something. Doubt. Worry.

"I remember when your mother painted this one," I said. "She told me that she was trying to capture the moment. The exact moment when they both knew that it was over." And she had done it, too. I have seen people look at this painting and then begin to cry.

I looked at Benjamin's face, as he examined the painting. I was looking for bits of Alicia. He did have her eyes, a bit of her chin. And while I know that it's naive, I would like to hope that he has a little of her gift as well. It would be nice to think that it has not gone out of the world altogether.

I turned back to the painting, and we stood there together for awhile. Looking at the work of his mother, my wife, aware of the strange connection between us. Then my phone beeped.

"Yes?" I answered.

"It's Wu. Our guest has arrived."

## Chapter 60:  Friday the 13th
## Midnight
## The Artist

"Thank you, Wu."

So it had begun, the final movement of this bloody concert.

"Take our guest to the lounge, and strip search him.  Then have him change into the new set of clothes laid out for him.  Don't let him keep anything large enough to conceal a weapon.  Oh, but do see that he keeps his ID.  No sense in giving the police unnecessary trouble in identifying the body."

"Of course," Wu said, then hung up.

I turned back to Benjamin.  I wished that we could have had more time together.

"Your father is here," I told him.

Benjamin looked up at me.  There was no longer any fear in his eyes.  Whether that meant he was brave or just numb I couldn't tell.

"And you're really going to kill him?"

I almost laughed.  If only it were that simple. If that was all that the situation required, I would have just done it years ago and gotten it over with.  But the debt I owed to Stonewall demanded so much more than just blood.  How do you begin to repay a man for taking away your wife, your freedom, and your life's work, all in one blow?  The best work I ever did, I did with Alicia, and when she died, all the soul went out of my art.

And besides, the debt is not just mine.  He did not just take Alicia away from me, but from the world.  All the paintings she would have done, all the people who would have been changed by them.  How would you judge a man for taking Michelangelo's work away  from the world, or DaVinci's?  What payment could possibly make up for that crime?

I looked back at Benji.  There was so much to explain, and so little time to do it in.

"Come," I said to him, and motioned for Ralph to follow us.  "There is one last bit of preparation to attend to before we meet the Reverend Senator.  And I have a favor to ask of you, Benjamin."

The boy laughed.  It was a strange sound, filling the empty places of the museum.

"You want *me* to do *you* a favor?"

"Yes," I said.  "I realize that my kidnapping you and plotting the murder of your father might not put you in the most receptive frame of mind just now. But do at least listen to my request. You may feel differently about it by the time this all over."

## The Witch

I turn into the Czech-Out's parking lot and take the first available space. Inside the restaurant the lights are still on, and a few late diners are sitting down to their meals.

I step out of the car, and into the warm night air. I feel odd. My feet strangely light on the pavement. My senses strangely sharp. I turn, to see if anyone has followed me this time, and catch sight of my reflection in the driver's side window. Strange eyes stare out at me from behind the painted wolf's mask.

I walk over to the Czech-Out, but don't go inside. I stare in through the windows, studying the building's occupants. Summer is not among the diners. I move away from the building, and circle it, sticking to the shadows. A lazy breeze brings me the smells of the city: men and cars and garbage, and the rich green smell of leaves in late summer. But not her smell.

The restaurants windows spill fluorescent light out onto the parking lot, but it seems weak and colorless. Stronger, and closer, are the colors of the night, colors I had never noticed before. Deep blues and purples that I had always thought were black. Overhead, I can see the fluttering wings of bats, flickering silver in the weak light of the young moon. And in the bushes...

Yes. There's someone there. Watching me. I make another circle of the parking lot, and meander casually, on a path that will take me within a few feet of his hiding place. So close I can hear his breathing. Then, when it's too late for him to flee, I step through the bushes to confront him.

"Who are you?" I ask, as I grab him.

"Uh...I'm Tim. I...uh...are you Summer's Mom?"

"Where is she?"

"Um...she's watching the museum, see Benji's in there, and she hurt her leg, so we figured I should come and..."

"Show me," I growl.

## Jen

I was sitting in the thaumaturgic triangle, trying another sending. Focusing on Benji, trying to warn the coven that he was in danger, that he was going to be the next victim.

They'd come to the cell about an hour ago and taken him. I'd tried to stop them, but handcuffed and three against one, I never had a chance. There were a lot of nasty images running through my head of what they could be doing with the kid right now. I'd seen the news reports on Calerant's other victims, and I'd seen the diagrams from his hard drive. Benji had given me a lock of his hair, and I tied it in a knot of protection. But that was a pretty sorry defense against big time black magic like this. The only real hope was to get a message through to the coven.

I chanted the charm of sending and over, until midnight, when the monitor in the room suddenly came on. I tried to ignore it and concentrating on the spell, but then I realized that it was talking to me.

"Ms. Gray."

I looked up. It was a painting, like some old Dutch master or something. A girl, sitting backwards in her chair, talking to me. She smiled and went on.

"I suppose you know who this is, so I won't trouble you with the introduction."

"Yeah, I know Caler..."

The painting just went on talking without waiting for my response. A prerecorded message.

"I wanted to take this chance to apologize for keeping you confined here for the last week, and I am particularly sorry if the accommodations were anything less than comfortable. I'm afraid I had not planned on having guests, and the arrangements had to be made at the last minute. Unfortunately, I simply couldn't have you poking around in my affairs at this particular time. However, now that the my business here is nearly completed, there is no longer a need to keep you confined. The door to your cell will open automatically at the conclusion of this message.

"I would like to compensate you for your time, and for the business you undoubtably lost while in my care. Among the various books in your cell is a copy of Milton's *Paradise Lost*. If you will remove the bookmark from it, you will find a series of numbers. These are the control codes for an account with Credite Suisse. In exactly one week, $40,000 U.S. dollars will be deposited to that account, to be used in any manner you wish. I know, it's not a large sum to compensate you for a week's imprisonment, but I have other expenses and a number of employees who are expecting bonuses at the end of this messy business.

"And in answer to your next question, yes, there is a catch. If at anytime during the next week you mention my name in any way, the money will not be forwarded. This includes both my involvement in your disappearance, and my interest in the occult.

After the week is up, you can collect the money and say anything you please. And if you still wish to go to the police or the press, that will be your choice. But by then you may see the situation somewhat differently.

"Goodbye Ms. Gray, and I wish that we could have met under better circumstances."

The monitor shut off, and I heard the lock on the door click open.

I walked over to it cautiously. There was no one on the other side. I was looking out into the basement of a private home. There was an envelope with my name on it taped to the wall. I opened it, and found the keys to my handcuffs.

I grabbed the copy of *Paradise Lost* then went upstairs, carefully, expecting trouble, but the house was deserted. I took a look around the place, but there was nothing interesting left—no documents, no data storage devices, no clothes. The place looked like a hotel room after the guests had packed up and gone. Whatever Calerant was up to, he wasn't coming back here.

I tried the phone, but it was disconnected. Figures.

## The Witch

The walk takes about five minutes, the boy babbling at me all the way. A long complicated story about Summer and Benjamin being chased by mysterious secret agents. The ravings of a mad conspiracy buff. I wouldn't believe a word of it. That is, if I hadn't seen it for myself.

Tim goes on explaining his own involvement in the story, finally getting to the end. "...and that's it. And uh...well, I should also tell you that Scott and I had to cut school and break curfew to help out Summer. So, I was kind of wondering if you could talk to our moms when this is all over, you know, kind of explain everything?"

"Yeah," I think, "If I ever understand it all myself."

We draw close to the High. We stop talking, and move slower, more quietly. Past the parking deck, and then down an alley that runs behind the museum. A single light is on, over a steel door. Tim motions me forward, and we sneak over to a dumpster near the door. In the shadows, behind it, we meet another boy I don't recognize, and my daughter.

"Mom?" For a strange moment she seems frightened of me. But I grab her, so anxious just to have my hands on her again, and after a second she hugs me back. And when she finally pulls away, it is with the familiar annoyance of a teenager trying to look cool in front of her friends.

"So Mom," she says, casually, as if she hadn't disappeared for two days and a night. "What's with the radical facial?"

I look her over.

"You OK?"

"Sure," she says, "Banged up my knee a little, but nothing that won't heal. Hope the same is true of Benji."

The boy. In the excitement of seeing Summer again I'd almost forgotten him.

"Are you sure he's still inside?"

"Pretty sure," says the other boy, who I guess must be Scott. "We saw them load Benji into a van back at the house. Then it stopped here, and we caught up with it. About half an hour ago, a guy came out that door and drove the van away, but Benji wasn't with him."

"And," Summer added, "We keep hearing voices and people moving around in there." She picks up something and holds it up into the light where I can see it. A rifle mike, one of those listening devices they use in corporate espionage. "I've listened to a couple different conversations, but I can't figure out what's going on. I thought I heard Benji a few minutes ago, but I can't be sure."

I look at the rifle mike, and wonder which one of them owns it, and why. My daughter certainly does keep some interesting friends. We would have to talk about this later. For now I gave her another hug, and whispered in her ear.

"By the way, I hope you realize that grounding will not begin to cover this one."

"Yeah Mom, we can talk punishment later. Right now what are we going to do about Benji?"

I suppose I should be thankful. Thankful that my daughter still thinks I can fix anything. I wish I had the same faith.

Logically, I should take my daughter and get her to safety. Call the police, and wait for them to deal with it. But I've promised the boy's mother that I would try to get him back to her. And if I'm right, the people who are holding him are the same bastards who killed Raven.

The police aren't prepared to deal with serious black magic like this. But I am. I walk with the full power of the coven behind me, with the power of the horned man within me, with my prey clearly before me.

"All of you, go back to the restaurant. Boys, call your Mothers and tell them you're all right. They're probably worried sick about you. Summer, call your father. *I* will look after Benjamin."

The children hesitated, but I gave them a look that indicated I meant business, and they started to walk back down the alley. Summer limping, the boys supporting her from either side.

Good. With her safe, that leaves me free to do what needs to be done. I move quietly to the metal door, and pull on the handle. It opens easily.

### The Reverend Senator

The oriental thug watched me as I undressed, keeping a pistol aimed at my midsection. I should have known that bastard Calerant would pull something like this. The thug watched me strip naked, a smug grin on his face. I comforted myself with the thought that he would be dead in a few minutes.

By now, my men would be surrounding the building, waiting for my signal to move in. But that didn't change the fact that for the moment I was alone in here, defenseless. Or close to it. I risked a quick glance at the pen and the watch, sitting on top of my clothes. The pen was an executive toy, a tear gas shooter. It wouldn't kill anybody, but it might buy me a little time. The watch was what I really needed. I'd been wearing it for years, but had never used it before. It contained a homing beacon, so that if I was ever kid-napped I could alert my security to come find me. Tonight, I would use it to signal the attack, once I knew where our objective was. As soon as I was in the same room with the boy, I would turn it on, and my men would come in, save me from this maniac, and capture this child who could destroy everything. We would have to be careful what we did with him. We couldn't afford to have traces of his DNA turning up later. Maybe cremation would do the trick.

The whole thing was a dangerous game. But Calerant was right—I had no choice. As long as he had the boy, he had my life in his hands.

The thug handed me a set of boxers. My usual brand; Calerant had done his homework. When this was all over, I would have to find out who among my household staff had leaked the information to him. The thug turned and handed me the pants. Then the shirt. He was beginning to relax his guard. When he turned to pick up the socks and shoes, I grabbed the watch and slipped it into my pocket. I was quick, and he never noticed. I put on the socks and shoes, smiling to myself. The game was half over, and the poor bastard didn't even realize it.

### The Gumshoe

Laughing Bear made an elaborate show of holding the door for me as we went in. I would have belted him for it, but we were creating enough of a scene as it was. Him in the warpaint and the quill breastplate and me...well, you know. I really needed to get back to my apartment and get some of my clothes, but there wasn't time for that just now. Oh, well. At least the other people in the restaurant didn't see the bouncing tiger who came in with us.

Linda was sitting in the back of the Czech-Out, toying with a cup of coffee. She watched us walk over without getting up.

"You OK?" I asked, sitting down at her table.

She looked back at me, and as she did so her alter ego stepped out from behind her, a woman in a black leather body suit with whiskers and a whip.

"Am I OK?" she said, as the catwoman cracked her whip for emphasis. "You've got some nerve asking that question. You disappear for two days without so much as a phone call. Not even when the story about Justin hit the news. Hell, I was getting ready to plan your funeral too. I mean, hey, as long as I'm in practice. Then I get a phone call from out of the blue saying you're coming back to Atlanta and you need some help, and...and...and, who the Hell is Tonto here, anyway?"

Laughing Bear was about to say something inappropriate, so I elbowed him in the ribs hard enough to take the wind out of him.

"That's kind of a long story," I said.

"I'll bet." She took a sip of her coffee. "By the way, those shoes don't go with that dress."

I turned a slightly deeper shade of red.

"Look," I finally said, "I don't have time to explain everything, but I do have a lead on the guys who kidnapped Jen and murdered Justin. I could use some backup, and I figured you'd want a piece of this. But if you're not..."

"Oh, you figured right. So where are they?"

"Just down the road," I said. "Come on."

We all left the diner, and walked down the street toward the High Museum of Art. Overhead I could see white strands, silver and ethereal in the moonlight, converging on the museum. A couple of them were shaking violently.

I guess the web had already caught a few flies.


## The Reverend Senator

The Oriental thug led me back to an elevator, and pressed the button for the third floor. I steeled my nerves for what was coming. Once I knew the boy was here, I would give the signal. From that point it would take my men somewhere between three and five minutes to enter the building and reach me.

But that was still three to five minutes that I would have to last against Calerant. If I was lucky, he would be in a talking mood. Maybe I could goad him into gloating for awhile. If not, I would actually have to fight the man. I fingered the watch in my pocket. If only I had been able to keep the pen as well.

One way or another, this would be over in a few minutes, and Calerant would be dead. I thought about what it would be like to watch him die. And maybe that could finally be the end of the whole thing. Calerant had thoughtfully disposed of everyone else who knew about my old sins. Once he was gone, there would be no one left who could accuse me.

Except myself, of course. But I had made my choice long ago, and there was no going back. I am sorry, Alicia. But one's woman's life is nothing compared to the salvation of a country.

## The Witch

I step through the door, and find myself in a large room. The lights are off, but there's a steady glow coming from the vending machines. My eyes adjust quickly. I can see tables, chairs. It looks like an employees' lounge. I stand perfectly still, listening for the sound of someone else in the room. Movement, breathing. But there is only the low hum from the Coke machine.

I move across the room quietly, sticking to the walls so that I can hide if someone enters suddenly. I reach the other door and listen. Footsteps. Close. But getting further away.

I crack the door open, and take a look. The lights are off in the hall too, but I can see a figure walking away from me, carrying a flashlight. For a moment I think he might be a security guard. But guards wear uniforms, not jeans and a t-shirt.

When he rounds a corner, I emerge from the lounge and take off down the hall after him, my feet hitting the floor softly and silently.

Come my little mouse. Show me where your friends are.

## The Gumshoe

"This?" Linda asks, looking at the Museum. "This is where we're gonna find the guy who killed Justin?"

"Uh…Yeah. It looks that way. " The white strands of the web converge on the museum, running through the walls to some point inside. That's where all the answers will be.

"You want to tell me how you know this?" she asks.

"Not really," I say.

The cat woman pops her claws.

"OK. Can you at least let me in on the plan for how we're going to get into that place?"

"Oh sure," I say. "We're going to follow those three guys."

"What three guys?" Linda asks, losing patience. I can't say that I blame her.

"The three guys over there in the shadows, the ones who are breaking in through the side door." I say pointing. I can't really see them, but I can see their totems. A Knight on a warhorse, a banner with a cross flying from his lance. A fat little Cherubim with a shotgun and a cigar, naked except for a camo cap. And Glinda the Good Witch of the North.

I wonder about the last guy.

We sneak over quietly, until we're close enough to see what they're doing. It's not hard; they're pretty intent on the door. There are three of them in military gear with rifles. They put a thermite charge on the lock, and then stand back as it melts the thing into goo. Whoever they are, they're not getting points for subtlety. Then two of them go in while the third stands guard outside.

I motion to Laughing Bear to circle around and approach the guard from the other side. He gives me the OK sign. I give him a couple of minutes to get into position, and then I say in a loud whisper.

"Oh, come on Francine, just drop the whole nice girl act."

Linda picks it up from there, going off on some whole diatribe about how she is not "that kind of girl" and how she only thought that she was into transvestites, and how if I didn't remove my hand from her breast I will soon be removing it from my lower intestine—I'd sure hate to be a guy who got out of line on a date with her. Anyway, sometime between "pathetic male need to keep score" and "small dicked cross-dresser", Laughing Bear comes back to say that he has cold cocked the guard and we can drop the act.

### The Artist

Wu brought Zachary into the gallery. He looked older and fatter in real life than he did on TV.

"So nice of you to come, Zachary," I said. "I do apologize for the inconvenience about the clothes, but after all the trouble I've gone to in order to arrange this little encounter, I didn't want to have you spoil everything by pulling out a concealed gun or something like that."

I smiled at him. I could afford to smile, now.

"I trust the new clothes are to your liking? I tried to get the style right, based on what I've seen you wear on television. Conservative, but expensive, with just the right color accents for that sense of power. I had to guess a bit on the measurements, though. Hm. Looks like I may have left a little too much room in the seat. Well, I did try to get it right. I wouldn't want you wearing something that you wouldn't be caught dead in. Not tonight."

Zachary stuck his hands in his pockets and scowled.

"Where's the boy, Calerant?"

"Oh, yes, forgive me for not making introductions. You probably are eager to meet your son."

I motioned for Ralph to bring Benjamin into the room. Zachary's eyes lit up as soon as he saw him, and the color drained out of his face.

"How...?" Stonewall stuttered. "How can he exist?" For the first time I saw a glimmer of fear come into his eyes. I moved closer, to enjoy it better.

"Oh, you still don't know? I would have thought you would have worked that out by now. Maybe you're not as clever as I thought."

I moved closer still. Close enough to look at him eye to eye. To watch the sweat dripping off his forehead. To drink in the smell of his fear.

"I'm almost tempted not to tell you. But then you wouldn't be able to appreciate the irony of the situation."

"The irony?"

"Oh yes, the irony. You see Zachary, the funny thing about all this—the supremely, tragically, horribly funny thing—is that you did it all for nothing."

I moved closer still. We stood, only a few inches apart.

"When my wife died, she was no longer carrying Benjamin. We had reconciled, and decided to keep the child. But my wife had a mild health problem that made it difficult to carry children to term. So we had transferred him to an artificial womb, at the Peachtree Family Planning Clinic."

Finally, a look of recognition in his eyes. About time, I'd left him an obvious enough clue.

"I can see how you might have gotten the wrong impression, though. What exactly did my wife say to you, on that afternoon when she came to your office to break it off. Did she tell you that she was pregnant with your child? Carelessly inexact of her."

"I can't help wondering how it all played out, there in your office. Did she tell you about the child before or after she broke off the affair? Did you quarrel? Did you think she was going to use the child against you? That she would end your political career?"

The fear burned in his eyes now, sweat poured from his

forehead. I continued smiling.

"Is that why you went to her that evening? Is that why you and your man killed her? Oh, and that clumsy affair with cutting out her uterus—not very subtle. But I suppose you had to take the evidence with you."

His chin quivered. I could see moisture in his eyes. Good grief. Was the man actually going to cry? Now that would be theatrical. I moved around to whisper in his ear.

"And you did it all to save your career. Silly Senator. How could you have loved her, and not known her better than that? Alicia would have ever told anyone. The child would have been raised as our own. And no one would ever have known that you are only human."

## The Witch

I've been following him for a few minutes now. Always just around a corner from him, always in a shadow, always just out of sight. I am hoping that he will lead me to the others, but his movements puzzle me.

We've been up and down several hallways now. I watch what he does, but I don't understand it. He has a small wand, which he's using to lock and unlock doors. I assume it must have someone's fake print on the end of it. But there is no rhyme or reason to what he does with it. On one hallway, he will lock all the doors to all the offices. On another, he will lock all the doors but one, which he takes great care to leave slightly ajar.

He uses his flashlight, never turning on the overheads. Maybe he worries that they would be seen from the street. He steps through a door at the end of a hallway, and I quietly follow. This one, like the other, has been carefully left open.

I step through it, and emerge into a long gallery. Narrow spotlights shine down on bizarre sculptures. My quarry is up ahead of me. He walks down a long row of sculptures, and I follow him, darting from shadow to shadow. Finally, he goes through another door. I run up to it, silent as fog. But this is one is locked, and I can follow him no further.

## The Reverend Senator

He circled me. Watching me. Gloating. Smiling. That's it, Calerant. Go on talking. Just a few more minutes and my men will be here to wipe that smile off your face for good.

He paused, and watched me in silence for a moment. Had he come to the end of his little story? I had to play him out just a little longer.

"Just one question, Calerant. Why? If you knew all this fourteen years ago, why didn't you say something about it then? Why wait till now?"

He smiled even broader, as if delighted to have the chance to expound on the subject.

"What could I have done to you back then, Zachary? Oh, I suppose that I could have used Benjamin to prove that you had an affair with my wife, but there was no way to prove that you killed her. No, your frame of me was much to thorough. And of course, it quickly became obvious that you had someone within the police force working to manufacture more evidence against me. Discovering who it was took a little more time. But then, time was something I had plenty of."

"And besides, some things are best savored over time. I mean, after all, what did you really have to lose fourteen years ago? 'Junior Senator falls from grace over sex scandal'. Wouldn't have been much of a story, now would it? No, I had to wait for you to build a life. I had to wait until you had something worth taking away."

"The only real question was exactly how to do it, how to make you pay. For the longest time I couldn't imagine anything adequate. When you killed my wife, you took my love, my art, and my freedom, all in one blow. But more than that, you took her work away from the world. All the paintings she would have done. All the minds and souls she would have changed forever. Think about it. What would you do to the man who deprived the world of Michelangelo, or Shakespeare, or Mozart?"

"It took me a long time to dream of something that would satisfy the demands of justice."

## The Police

I offered to drive, but Tony insisted that he was up to it. I shot a look at the cast on his right arm and raised an eyebrow, but I could tell that this was going to be one of those macho pride things. So, I shut up and let him do it.

And he did manage to get us to the museum in one piece. I had him pull around the block and park behind the public library, so that we could sneak up to it on foot. We grabbed a pair of night vision binoculars out of the trunk, and then jogged back up to the street, finally crouching behind some bushes with a view of the museum.

"Anything?" Tony asked, while I checked out the building with the binoculars.

"Yeah," I said, after a minute. "There's a guy with a rifle loitering by the front door."

I passed the binoculars to Tony.

"Where?"

"To the left of the statue," I said, pointing his head in the right direction. "Back in the shadows."

"I see him," Tony said. "He's got a headset on, but it's not one of ours. Looks like a military model."

"Could he be National Guard?" I asked. "The governor called them in a few hours ago."

"Nah, I don't think so," Tony answered. "Not without a uniform."

"Well, if he's got communications gear on, then he must be talking to someone. How about we take a look around and see who his friends are. I'll work my way around the museum to the right. You go left. I'll meet you in back and we'll compare notes."

"Got it."

## The Gumshoe

We moved quietly down the dark hallway. Laughing Bear had his tomahawk out. Linda, being more practical, had drawn a pistol.

At the end of the hall, there was a stairway. The door to it was locked, but the mechanism was a cheap indoor affair that I popped with my cash card in five seconds.

"Do you actually know where you're going?" Linda asked me in a whisper, "Or are you just making this up as you go along?"

"Shush." I said, as I opened the door. I wasn't about to explain that we were following the strands of a spider web, one that seemed to converge a few floors above us.

## The Reverend Senator

He stopped talking, and just stared at me for a few seconds. I tried to ask another question, anything to keep him talking, but he put a finger to my lips. Then he stepped back, and took off his jacket, handing it to one of the thugs who was watching us.

He unbuttoned the sleeves of his shirt, and rolled them up. An utterly evil light came into his eyes.

"And now, Zachary, let's finish this the way it was meant to be finished." He feinted a punch, and I jumped back.

"Oh, come now Zachary. Don't disappoint me. Not after all the time I spent planning this. Surely you have some fire in there? Some rage left? Or is it only unsuspecting women that you can kill?"

He took another step toward me.

I tried to find my anger, something that would let me fight back. I'd beaten Weir, after all. And he'd been even younger and stronger than Calerant. But I'd been angry then, and now all I could find was fear.

Where were my men? Why weren't they here yet? Please God, I know this is not your plan for my life. I am your instrument, sent to lead the nation back to you. You can't let me die like this!

And He heard me. All my life, I've been waiting for the sure sign that God is listening, watching over me, that He cares what happens to me. And finally it comes.

In a shower of sparks, all the lights in the room short out, and we are plunged into darkness.


## The Witch

Locked. OK, Holly, think. The High Museum is big, but I've been in here before. The Picasso exhibit, last summer. Where would they be? Think.

They're trying to do a ritual. They'll need space for that. Where is there a big open area in the museum? Some place where they could lay out a circle and...

The lobby. It's huge. And it has that black marble floor. It would be the perfect place for a ritual.

I make an educated guess as to where I am, and then start working my way toward where I think the lobby should be. It takes awhile. There are some locked doors in the way, and I have to climb up two floors before I can find a way through. I come out on the third story balcony, looking over the vast empty space of the lobby. Weak moonlight filters in from the skylight, two stories above. It passes through the giant mobile, throwing bizarre shadows around the room.

I look down into the lobby, but there is no one there. No candles. No circle. No black magicians. I have guessed wrong.

I continue staring down into the dark pit of the lobby, as I try to think it through again. Where else? Maybe one of the galleries. But there are so many. I'll just have to start looking, and hope I find them in time.

I am turning to begin my search, when the faint sound of breaking glass calls me back to the railing. Down in the lobby, three
men come through the front doors, the dark shapes of rifles in
their hands.

It appears that I am no longer hunting alone.

## The Police

I worked my way around, trying to stay in the shadows. I spotted
three more gunmen, each watching one of the entrances to the museum. But it was strange; they were all facing *toward* the doors. As
if they were watching for people trying to get out, rather than in.

Tony was the one who found the gunman by the south entrance, lying behind some bushes, out cold. He called me over
the headsets. By the time I caught up with him, Tony had already
checked the guy's ID. He handed me the driver's license.

"Chase Smith," I read. "Mean anything to you?"

"Nah," Tony said, "But this does." He held up the guy's hand,
which had a ring on it. A ring with a silver cross surrounded by a
circle of gold. It was too dark for me to make out the words
engraved on it, but I had a pretty good idea what they said. "One
Nation Under God."

"One of Stonewall's?" I asked.

Tony nodded. "Yeah. Maybe a body guard. Or Christian
Militia. This model of assault rifle is standard issue for them."

"OK," I said. "But if he's guarding Stonewall, shouldn't the
old man be around here some place?"

Tony shrugged. I took a look at the kid. Blond. About 6'1.
180 lbs. Probably about 20. He had a nasty welt on the back of
his head. Maybe a concussion. I was about to call in for an ambulance, when a burst of automatic weapons fire went off inside
the museum.

Tony and I hit the dirt and drew our pistols. Well, I drew my
pistol. Tony had to fumble around for a few seconds to get his
out. It's not easy to draw a gun with your left hand out of a right-
handed shoulder holster.

While we were lying on the ground, I had Mindy put a call
through to K'yon.

"Yes, Lieutenant?"

"Hey, we've got shots fired here. Where's that back up I told
you to have in the area?"

"Uh...I'm afraid they're still about three minutes away,
Lieutenant."

I relayed the information to Tony.

Tony cocked an eye at the door. "Do we wait?"

"Do you want to be the one to explain that we waited outside for backup while a U.S. Senator was being shot or crucified or something worse?"

Tony shook his head.

"I didn't think so."

We crawled over, and took up positions on either side of the door.

"On three." I said.

I just hoped that Tony was a better left-handed marksman than he was a left-handed driver.


## The Reverend Senator

I hear men bumping into each other in the darkness, and shouting. Then far off, gunshots. My men are finally here. All I have to do is survive a few minutes longer. Then the tables will be turned, and I can be the one to gloat over Calerant, as the life drains out of him.

I stumble my way to the wall, and feel around for a door. I know there was one here somewhere.

Ah! I find it and pull it open. The lights in the hall are out as well, but an exit sign provides enough illumination to see. I run toward it, grateful for an escape. But the door beneath the exit sign is locked.

I try the door next to it. Locked too. And the one next to it. Down the hall, I can see someone turn on a flashlight and begin to pan it around. I try another door.

Open. Thank you God.

I step into another hall, and shut the door behind me. I run along, trying to find another unlocked door I can get through. An office. A closet. Anyplace I can hide until this is all over. But every one I try is locked. Then I get to the other end of the hall, and finally find a way out. A door that someone left ajar. I push it open, and step out into one of the galleries.

Ahead of me stretch row upon row of sculptures, eerily lit by dim spotlights. Strange modern things. Twisted pieces of wood and stone and metal, like the after effects of a tornado hitting a trailer park.

I hear another burst of gunfire, but it's still far off. I strain to hear more, listening for any sign that my men are closer, that they'll get to me before Calerant and his goon squad. But what I hear isn't gunfire. It's footsteps. In the hallway behind me. Slow. Casual. Unconcerned. Only one man could be mad enough to stay calm in this asylum.

I run. I can still hear his footsteps, loud in my ears. I glance over my shoulder. I should be able to see him by now, but he's not there. But I can hear him. Coming for me.

If I can just stay away from him for a few more minutes. I reach the other end of the gallery. It makes an L turn into another display area, but I stop for a moment. Something on the sculpture in front of me gleamed in the light as I approached it, and I've just realized what it is.

A knife. A long, copper knife, some sort of antique, but still usable. It's been driven into the side of a piece of drift wood balanced on a piece of rock. I grab the handle and pull. It's stuck. But I pull harder and finally it comes loose. I have never wanted anything so badly as I wanted that knife.

I whirl around, expecting Calerant to be on top of me by now. So you want to fight, you bastard? Why don't you try it now? But I still can't see him. Is he hiding in the darkness somewhere? Maybe behind one of the sculptures? Where is he?

I'm torn by the desire to run after him and rip his guts out, and the desire to run away and save my life. But I can't see him. I know he's there, I can hear his breathing, but I can't see him. I whirl around again, thinking he's snuck up behind me, but he's not there.

Then I turn and run, fleeing into the next gallery.

### The Police

Tony and I burst through the door, and into an empty storage room. Boxes of cards, stationery, stuff for the gift shop. We opened the next door, and moved into a back hallway, but it was empty too. I heard another burst of automatic weapons fire, and a few pistol shots from further inside the building, but I couldn't decide which direction they were coming from. While Tony and I worked our way cautiously down the hall, I asked K'yon for directions.

"Come on." I insisted. "They've got to have a map of this place on file with someone."

"Presumably, Lieutenant. It's just a matter of finding...got it. It's coming up on your display now."

I pulled out my palmbook and took a look at the map. Good grief, this place was huge. And it was a warren of interlocking galleries and back hallways. I put the display back in my pocket. That was no help. Calerant and the Senator could be anywhere in here, and I didn't have time to search the whole building.

Then a thought occurred to me.

"K'yon, can you find out what gallery the Alicia St. Cloud exhibit is in?"

"Of course...The Rousseau gallery. Third floor. Take the door at the end of the hall and turn left; then the second door on your right will lead you to a staircase."

I relayed the information to Tony, and we made our way down the hall, per K'yon's instructions. But the door was locked.

"K'yon..."

"It's OK." she said. "I've got the museum's emergency override codes. Try it now."

Tony tried the door again, and it opened.

"All right," I said softly, "Let's finally get to the bottom of this mess."

### The Gumshoe

Linda heard the gunshots and pricked up her ears.

"Assault weapons," she said. Sounds like it came from below us. Maybe the ground floor."

We were in a long gallery now, filled with bizarre sculptures, eerily lit. The threads of the web converged just ahead of us, around a corner. Finally, the answer.

I kept walking.

"Uh...aren't we gonna do something about that?" Linda asked, gripping her pistol.

"Why?" I asked, "Do you really want to go up against assault rifles with that pea shooter?"

"No...but."

I kept walking. She grabbed me by the back of the dress and stopped me. "OK, that's about it!" she hissed in a low whisper. "Someone is going to start doing some explaining *real* quick, because I have had it up to here with..."

Laughing Bear chose that particular moment to open his mouth.

"Excuse me," he said, interrupting Linda, "but have you actually tried Prozac? It might help..."

Linda let go of me and turned her attention to Laughing Bear.

"Look, Tonto," she said. "I will cut you a certain amount of slack because you have a nice body and you're not wearing a shirt. But don't push it."

"Oh. You just seem kind of tense..."

I started walking again, and followed the strands of the web around the corner and into the next gallery. And finally there it was. The center of this whole web of intrigue and lies. The big answer.

I looked at it. Then I looked at it again. Then I blinked, rubbed my eyes, and looked at it one more time. Then I walked over to the wall and started beating my head against it. Why? Why can't anything ever make sense?

The center of the web had a tear in it. Half the web was anchored to a piece of sculpture. The other half to an unobtrusive beige metal door in the wall. Not exactly the answer I'd been looking for.

I examined the statue. It was some abstract hunk of metal, with all sorts of crazy projections. It looked like someone had put a giant slinky through a giant garbage disposal. The door was similarly uninteresting. Beige and metal, probably leading to offices or something. I tried to pull it open, in case it led to something significant, but the damn thing was locked.

So. This was it. I had been shot at, roughed up, and chased across most of Atlanta. And all to find a bad piece of sculpture and a locked door. It was enough to drive me crazy, if I hadn't already been there.

Linda and Laughing Bear finally caught up with me, having finished their argument.

"Well?" Linda said, getting exasperated.

"Well," I said.

"Well, well," said Laughing Bear.

"If you'll excuse me for a moment," I said, and then I went over to the door and banged my head into it really hard. And for once, that approach to a problem actually worked.

As my head exploded with pain, everything came into focus. For a single instant, I could see the whole tapestry of the world, how everything fit together. And I saw how much depended on me doing the correct thing, the important thing, right now. A thing that would defeat an unspeakable evil, and set the world on a different course. I had a moment of complete and total clarity.

And now I understand why most people choose to go through life in a confused stupor. Because clarity is a real bitch. To actually see how every tiny decision affects the universe? Good grief. I would probably spend the next week worrying about the cosmic ramifications of whether I leave the toilet seat up or down.

But at least now I knew what to do.

"Come on," I said.

I walked over to the sculpture, and grabbed one of the metal bars, and pulled.

"I could use a little help with this," I added.

Laughing Bear cheerfully came over and added his muscles to the effort. Linda looked at me like I was out of my mind. Which was a pretty accurate assessment.

"You really have lost it. You know that, don't you Drew?"

"Actually," I said, straining. "The problem is that I've found it. Which is even worse. Now are you going to help?"

She looked disgusted, but she came over and gave us a hand, and we were finally able to break off the metal protrusion from the rest of the statue.

"Now what?" she asked.

By way of an answer I took my shirt off and wiped our fingerprints off the bar—As a former cop, my prints were on file, and there was no way was I going to try and explain my role in this little caper. Then I walked over to the door and wedged the bar in place, bracing it closed.

"OK." Linda said, still looking confused. "Now what?"

"Now we go." I said, and started leading the way out.

She grabbed my arm.

"What? Why?"

"Because that was it. That was the reason we were here."

"Wait. You told me we were here to catch Justin's killer."

"We just did. Among other things."

"Huh?"

"Come on, Jen will be waiting for us back at the office."

"What? This is crazy!"

"Yes," I said, "But that's the way it is."

We got to the end of the gallery, and I took them through another small metal door that someone had thoughtfully left propped open.

"Come on," I said, "he left an escape route for his men. They've opened a hole into the storm drains underneath the place. We can use that to get out of here without talking to the police. Which, believe me, is in all of our interests."

## The Police

"OK," K'yon said. "Now take the first door on your right." As we walked toward it, I heard the lock click open. I pushed the door open, cautiously. We kept hearing gunfire, but we hadn't seen any of the combatants yet. It was like being in the middle of a fight between ghosts.

"OK," K'yon said when I told her that we were through the door. "You're almost there. The door at the end of this hallway will open onto a gallery that connects to the one housing the Alicia St. Cloud exhibit. After you go through it, just turn right and follow the chain of galleries until they end in a large rectangular room. That's where the St. Cloud Exhibit is being shown."

Tony and I jogged quietly to the end of the hall and reached the door. I turned the handle slowly and gave it a gentle push, hoping to open it quietly. But it was stuck. I tried pushing harder, but it still wouldn't give.

"K'yon, have you unlocked this door yet?"

"Of course Lieutenant."

"You're sure?"

"Yes. According to my display it's unlocked."

"Great," I said. "It must be jammed."

Tony and I went to work on it together, but it was no use.

"It's no good," I told K'yon. "It's braced by something solid on the other side. Can you plot us a way around it?"

"Working..." came the response. "...Yes, but it's going to take another five minutes or so. You're going to have to go back down a floor, cross under the galleries, and then try to come in from the other side."

There was another burst of automatic fire.

"By they way, where is that backup I asked for?"

"Apologies," K'yon said, "they're taking longer than expected to arrive. ETA about two minutes."

"Fine. Now just give me the new directions to that gallery."


## The Reverend Senator

I run through the second gallery, another long hallway. Another set of sculptures, another set of spotlights. They seem to fly past me in slow motion as I run down the hall. The details strangely sharp. A tiny skull, maybe a cat's, stares back at me from atop a mound of bones. A hologram of a woman being hit in the head with an axe, blood and brain flying everywhere. A wax statue of two men doing unspeakable things, while one strangles the other with a rope.

I reach the end of the gallery, and take the opening to my right, into the next. I run into the middle of a square room—and stop. It's the end of the line.

It's her. She's here. She's everywhere. No matter where I look, every wall is covered with one of the paintings. I don't need to check the signatures to know. It's her. Everywhere. Overpowering.

And there is no way out. It's a dead end. Except for a door. Another one of those little access doors, like the one I came out of. But it's locked. I know because the boy is trying to open it and can't.

The boy. I focus on him, and it pulls me away from the paintings. My son.

He turns to look at me as I run into the room, but he doesn't stop his work. Pulling on the handle. Kicking at the door. Desperate to open it.

I walk over to him, slowly. He sees me coming and puts his back to the door, his eyes wide with fear.

"I'm sorry," I say.

"You killed my mother," he says, but his voice is weak. I can't tell if that was an accusation or a question.

"I'm sorry," I say again, trying to make my voice sound comforting. "I am so sorry for that." There is no point in denying it now. But perhaps I can keep him distracted with the details. "There was so much at stake. I was so frightened. She could have brought down everything."

I take another step toward him. He's still too scared to move. Good. Once he's gone, there will be no evidence against me. My men will find Calerant. And we'll put the bodies somewhere where no one will ever find them.

I take another step toward the boy, slowly. His eyes go down to the knife in my hand. But he still doesn't move. It's like rabbits. If you walk at them very slowly, they never quite work up the nerve to sprint away. Not till it's too late. A few more steps, and it will be over. Stab him once in the belly, qiuckly, to make sure he can't run away. Then hold him down and slit his throat. We'll have to do something about the stain in the carpet. Maybe bleach, or something like that to scramble his DNA. But there will be time to worry about such things later. Once I'm safe. Another two steps, and...

Then someone grabs me from behind. Calerant. How could that bastard get behind me so quietly? Just a minute ago his footsteps had been loud enough to wake the dead.

He has me in a bear hug, but I have the knife. I struggle to bring it up, and cut deep into his forearm. He lets go. I spin around and face him.

"You wanted me angry, you bastard?! You wanted fire?! Well you've got it!"

I can feel the anger flowing through me, the power. I slash at him, but the devil is quick. He steps forward and catches my hand with the knife. I bring my other hand up on the hilt and try to drive it into him, but he is strong. So strong. We stand there with the knife between us. I put all my might into it, trying to drive it into his chest.

He turns his head toward the boy and says "Run!" The boy listens, and sprints past us, back out the way I'd come in. He's escaping, and it's all slipping away again. I have to finish this now.

I focus all my strength on the knife and push. Calerant looks back at me, still holding me off, both hands on the knife. And we stand there for a moment, fighting over the blade. Then he gives me this queer little smile, and suddenly lets go. The knife shoots forward, and before I've even realized what's happened, I've buried it in his chest up to the hilt.

He falls backwards, hitting the ground with a thud, his arms out to his side. Blood is shooting out of his chest and gurgling out of his mouth. But he's still smiling. I pull the knife out, and more blood sprays up, covering my shirt and face. And it feels so... good. So good to see the demon dying. And why shouldn't it? Why shouldn't it bring me pleasure to kill the enemies of God?

I look down at his face, wanting to see his defeat. Wanting to see in his eyes that he knows I won. But the bastard is smiling at me, as if I were the one whose life was leaking out onto the floor and he was the one on top gloating. I pull the knife out of his chest and drive it into him again, but he just keeps smiling. I stab him again and again and again. And finally, he shudders and stops breathing, and his eyes glaze over.

The monster is dead.

But the boy is still out there, and he can still hurt me. My men are closing in, but I can't take the chance that he'll slip away somehow. I sprint after him, blood dripping from the knife, my shoes leaving bloody prints on the carpet.

## The Witch

The sound of gunfire is everywhere now. Not steady. But in bursts here and there. As if the warring parties are searching for each other in the darkness, only making intermittent contact.

Perhaps I should be afraid, but I'm not. If anything, I feel safe in the darkness. The night is my ally. Let them be afraid of me.

I'm moving toward the galleries on the third floor, thinking I will check them out first. Everywhere the overhead lights are out, but individual spotlights shine on the paintings and the statues. That seems strange to me. I can't imagine that the museum leaves these on all night. I also can't imagine why anyone else would bother to turn them on. I've just entered the fourth gallery when I hear the sound of running feet. I try to go back out the way I came, but I had let the door close behind me, and now it's locked. I press myself up against the wall, in a puddle of shadow between two sculptures, and watch.

A moment later I see a short figure running down the gallery toward me. Instinctively I know who it is. Finally, the boy. Then behind him, another figure. Larger. Darker. The light glinting off something in its hand. And I don't need to be a seer to feel the monstrous evil of it.

The boy reaches the door I just tried to leave by, and realizes that its locked. The larger figure slows down, like a wolf that has cornered it's prey, and is studying the best way to take it down.

So this is it.

I step out of the shadows.


## Benjamin

I'm trying to work the door, but it's locked. There's gunfire going off all around me, but that doesn't matter because I know that *he's* right behind me. And if I can't get through this door in the next few seconds then I'm going to die. But the door is locked, and I know that I can't open it. And I can hear his heavy footsteps running down the hall behind me, getting closer. And I pull with all my panicked strength. I hit it and kick it and scream at it, but it won't budge.

Then the footsteps slow down. And I turn around. He's here. And there's no where to run. And I realize that I'm going to die, and there's nothing I can do about it. He walks toward me, slowly. A dark silhouette, the dim light glinting off the knife in his hand.

Then suddenly I feel something new. Something even scarier. Something old, and frightening, like a half remembered nightmare from my childhood. Like all the reasons I used to be afraid of the dark.

And it steps out of the shadows next to me, its face like a wolf, wearing the darkness like a shroud, its eyes inhuman. Cold and alien. And I think I'm going to cry, because I'm so scared and there is nothing to do.

Then, miraculously, it turns away from me. And moves toward my father. And I realize with a burst of relief that it hasn't come for me. And it seems smaller now. Not a werewolf, just a woman. But dark and frightening, in a way that only a woman could be.

And he stops, because he can see her too, and he can *feel* her too. And he tries to circle around her, to get at me, but she won't let him. Then he yells, and charges at her, slashing with his knife. I see the blade connect with her arm, and blood flash through the air. Then they fall upon each other like animals.

And I can only watch. My mind too scared to think anymore, to realize that I should try and run past them, get away from both of them. I can only stand with my back to the door, and watch them wrestling on the floor, growling out sounds that I didn't know humans could make.

Then suddenly there's another person in the hall, though I never even saw her come in. A black woman, holding a pistol.

## The Police

"Freeze!" I shouted to the two figures wrestling on the floor. "I mean it!"

The woman rolled away from the Senator, and looked up at me. For a split second, I thought she was wearing a wolf mask, but then I realized that it was just some sort of crazy occult design painted on her face. I noticed that the Senator had a knife, and that the woman had a matching cut on her arm. Maybe the old boy was better at taking care of himself than I'd given him credit for.

"OK. I'm Lieutenant Megan Strand of the Atlanta Metropolitan Police Department. Senator, are you all right?"

Stonewall just stared at me, his eyes wide with fear. The poor guy was obviously too terrified to think straight. Can't say that I blame him, given a look at the woman who'd been attacking him. I moved between them, to make sure that the woman couldn't lunge at him. I kept my gun level at her, not sure what sort of wacked-out state of mind she might be in.

"OK, sister, the game's up. Where's Calerant?"

She didn't say anything. It was hard to read her expression behind the funky make up, but I thought she looked puzzled.

"Look sister," I said, "we can do this the easy way, or..."

"Look out!" she shouted, looking over my shoulder.

"Yeah, right" I said, "Like I'm going to fall for that..."

I was cut short by a hand reaching over my shoulder. Before I could sidestep, it had grabbed my chin and jerked my head back. I saw the flash of the knife coming down...

...and then I heard the shot.

Something red and wet sprayed over my shoulder. The knife clattered down to the floor in front of me.

I ripped the other hand away from my chin, and spun around to level my gun on Stonewall, who had a surprised expression on his face. He sank to his knees, making gurgling sounds and clutching his right shoulder.

Beyond him, I saw Tony with his pistol out. This was not what I had been expecting when I told him to cover me.

"What...?" I started to say, and then realized that I had turned my back on the woman. I turned to the side, and started backing up, so that I could keep both her and Stonewall in my field of vision. Not that Stonewall looked like he was going anywhere but the ER.

I took another step backward, and was about to put in the call for a medic when I stepped on something that whimpered. I spun around and found a scared looking kid, hunkered down in the shadows near the wall. I was standing on his foot.

I carefuly moved to the side, trying to find an angle from which I could watch him and the woman and the Senator.

"Can someone please tell me what is going on here?" I muttered under my breath.

"Perhaps I can help," chimed in a voice on my headset. "Sorry for the slow response, lieutenant. I was distracted by something that came up on the newsites…"

"K'yon, there's been a shooting, we need…"

"…medical attention. Of course, it's already on its way. And your backup has surrounded the building and is moving in. Now might I suggest that before you say anything else, you have a look at your palm display?"

I kept my gun ready, and pulled out the display with my free hand. K'yon had patched in a video feed. It was something shot with a wide-angle lens, of a room with five people in it. Two of them had guns out. It took me a second to realize that one of the figures was myself. I also noticed the Microsoft News Network logo in the corner.

"What the Hell?"

"Uh…it would be prudent to watch your choice of language, lieutenant. The museum's security cameras have audio pickups as well."

I lowered the volume of my voice.

"How…?"

"I don't know yet, but they're not the only ones. By my count, twenty other networks are broadcasting you live right now. Oops, make that 21."

21 networks? I looked up and spotted the security camera. Great. I'd never gotten stagefright while making an arrest before.

"How long have they been watching us?"

"You, not long. The Senator…looks like about five minutes. I'm still catching up on all the footage myself. But if you'll keep your display out for just a second, I'll call up a little scene that took place at the St. Cloud exhibit a few minutes ago. And I think it will answer some of your questions.

"Oh, and try to look like you know what's going on. I think you and Browning just became heroes."

## Chapter 61: The Police
## Monday the Sixteenth, 2:11 PM

I took a moment to collect myself before I went in. I knew that I was tired and I wasn't thinking as clearly as I should. I'd popped another Perk-Up on the way over, but I couldn't feel it kicking in yet. I must be building up a tolerance.

I had been naively hoping that I would be able to catch up on my sleep after we finally caught the guy responsible for all this occult weirdness. Of course, I hadn't counted on catching a U.S. Senator. On camera. In front of a few million live viewers. Yeah, like I was really going to be able to quietly slip away for a vacation after *that*. I'd been on the go non-stop for the last two days; filing reports, handling press conferences, getting all our evidence in order for the DA. We couldn't afford a screw up on this one. Everything had to be perfect.

I yawned.

"OK." I thought to myself. "Just focus and get through this. One more thing to do, and then you can go home and get some sleep." Finally. I'll take a week off work and not leave bed the whole time.

I opened the door. The DA's secretary, a young red-headed guy, was taking a phone call. I let him finish, then introduced myself and mentioned that I had an appointment. He smiled and lead me into Ms. Biko's office, closing the door behind me.

Inside, the DA's office was a study in minimalism, all straight lines and gleaming black—much like her hair. I wondered if she'd gotten the coif to go with the furniture, or the other way around. The room was devoid of any personal touches. No pictures of family. No photographs of her with politicians. No clutter to hint at a religious or a political leaning. The only thing that interrupted the smooth black surface of her desk was a small bonsai tree, sitting on the corner.

She stood up as I came in. She was wearing a smart dark business suit. No jewelry or accessories, of course.

"Lieutenant Strand," she said, offering me her hand. "I'm District Attorney Seraphim Biko. I appreciate you making the trip downtown." She gestured to a seat, a single thin sheet of black metal bent into the approximate shape of a chair. It didn't look like it could possibly hold my weight.

"No problem," I said, risking the chair and finding it surprisingly sturdy. "Was there something you didn't want to discuss over the phone?"

"Oh, no," she said, a little too casually. Something about her tone put me on my guard. "It's just that sometimes it's nice to do business face to face for a change, don't you think?"

"Of course," I said. "And I am eager to wrap up my end of this case, and pass it off to your office." Yeah, let the lawyers deal with this mess.

"Yes, it is an *interesting* case," Ms. Biko said, and then paused for a moment. "I did have a couple of questions, though..."

"Oh?" I asked, trying to sound surprised. "Was there something my people left out of the reports?"

"Oh, nothing like that." Ms. Biko assured me. "Almost the opposite in fact. I'm afraid that the sheer volume of evidence in this case is a bit daunting. I'm having trouble interpreting it all. Would you mind giving me an overview? Just so that I can make sure that I'm drawing the right conclusions."

"Of course," I said, endeavoring to sound pleasant while I tried to get my tired brain to focus. I wasn't buying her poor-little-me-couldn't-possibly-understand-all-those-files act for one second. "Where would you like me to begin?"

"Well, let's start with our strongest case. The murder of James Calerant. How conclusive would you say the evidence is against Senator Stonewall?"

"Irrefutable," I said. "The murder was recorded by one of the museum's security cameras. Our data recovery experts examined the footage and authenticated it, by comparing the strings of characters woven into each frame with the Museum's security codes. They confirm that the pictures have not been tampered with in any way. Furthermore, the physical evidence is consistent with the version of events shown in the footage: The pattern of blood stains on Stonewall's clothes matches that in the footage. The knife in his possession when we arrived is an exact match to the murder weapon. And traces of blood from the blade and Stonewall's clothes have been DNA matched to Calerant."

"Hm...yes, the physical evidence does seem compelling." She paused. "I noticed that you didn't mention a material witness. Wasn't the boy present?"

"Benjamin Danvers. Yes, well..." I focused on keeping my poker face. "...he appears to be suffering from hysterical amnesia."

"Amnesia? Really?" She raised an eyebrow. I could tell that she didn't believe the kid's story anymore than I did.

"Yes," I said. "It seems that he can't remember a thing between the time he was kidnapped from a pay phone on Peachtree street until we recovered him."

"Hm," Ms. Biko said. "How unfortunate."

"Yes," I agreed.

"Any chance that he'll recover before the trial?"

"You would have to ask his doctor." I said, trying not to sound too skeptical. Personally, I just wanted to know why the kid was lying. I mean, who was he protecting? Stonewall? The guy was his father, but he had also murdered the kid's mother, and tried to kill the kid himself. Somehow, I couldn't see the boy going out of his way to protect him. But who did that leave? Calerant?

"Hm. Well, it probably won't matter at trial. Not with the video footage. We are, at least, clear on Stonewall's motive for this and the other crimes, I hope?"

"Yes," I said. "I think we've put it all together. But, it is a bit complicated..." I looked at her for a reaction, and she gestured for me to continue. Great. I swallowed hard and launched into it.

"It appears that the whole story began fifteen years ago, when Benjamin Danvers was conceived. Genetic testing proves that he is the child of Senator Stonewall and the artist Alicia Calerant-St. Cloud. This suggests that the two had an adulterous affair, almost certainly during the period when she was painting his portrait. Based on the Senator's on-camera confession, we now believe that he became aware of her pregnancy, and either murdered or ordered the murder of Ms. St. Cloud, and had her uterus removed to destroy forensic evidence of their affair—namely, the fetus. Apparently, Senator Stonewall did not know that the fetus had already been moved into an artificial womb at the Peachtree Family planning clinic, due to a health condition of Ms. St. Cloud's.

"We are not sure how, but it appears that he recently discovered his mistake, and set about correcting it, while at the same time planting evidence of satanic rituals to cover his moves and possibly advance his political career. The vandalism incident in the cemetery was just the prelude, an event to create public panic, and to make sure that his later actions would appear to fall into an occult pattern. The second incident, the attack on the Family Planning Clinic, was orchestrated to allow the destruction of the clinic's database. Since Benjamin Danvers had been incubated in one of its artificial wombs, the database contained a record of Stonewall's genome—a record that could come back to haunt the Senator later. After that, Stonewall eliminated the only two living people who knew of his crime: Raven Straylight, formerly Roberta Stevens, who had been his personal secretary, and SIB Watch Commander Dean Davison—although in fairness to the Commander, he may only have known about the affair, not the murder.

"The other murder, that of Justin Weir, is a bit strange, in that it does not appear to fit the pattern of the coverup. However, we have testimonies from witnesses at BNN that there was a well known feud going on between the Senator and Mr. Weir. Most likely, Stonewall simply took the opportunity to eliminate an enemy under the cover of the ongoing pattern of occult crimes.

"We are still not sure exactly how Stonewall located Benjamin Danvers, although we have run across some interesting clues. Several of his employees have admitted to visiting high schools and taking genetic samples from 14 year old boys of Danver's general description. Incidentally, this probably explains some of the odd calls we received from concerned parents over the last few days about secret government genetic experiments. So we can be pretty sure that Stonewall was conducting an extensive search for him, and by Danvers' presence at the museum, we can infer that Stonewall found him.

"The incident at the High Museum of Art was intended to be a cover for the disposal of Benjamin Danvers, and was probably supposed to be the last in the series. Among other evidence at the scene, we found a discarded notebook, with its hard drive wiped. Fortunately, our data recovery team was able to reconstruct most of the files, which included diagrams for an occult ritual site to be constructed in the museum's lobby. It appears that Stonewall was planning to use a pottery kiln in the basement of the building to reduce Danvers' body to ashes, thereby denaturing his proteins and making a genetic identification impossible. The ashes would then have been used in drawing a pentagram."

I paused. "Calerant, it appears, simply got in the way. As near as we can tell, the boy was trying to escape, and was being pursued by the Senator. Calerant tried to protect him and...well, you saw what happened."

"Yes." Biko said, her poker face staring back at mine. "I did. Although I must say, I am rather anxious to know why Calerant was in the building."

"I was too," I admitted. "Shortly after the arrest, I conducted an interview with the museum's curator. He informed me that Mr. Calerant had been asked to do an installation piece for them, and had been given permission to stay in the museum after hours and work late. It appears to simply be a bizarre *coincidence*." I tried not to grit my teeth on the last word.

"Yes," Biko said, folding her hands together and examining me. "A very strange coincidence in deed. Still, such things do happen."

She leaned back in her chair.

"I understand you arrived on the scene just after the killing?"

"Yes," I said, trying not to sound nervous.

"In fact, I believe there was something about it in the report." She touched her desk and tapped on a few icons until she found the document she wanted. "Ah yes, you were delayed for a few minutes by a door that was jammed shut. I see the time indices here. It looks like you would have reached the gallery in time to prevent Calerant's murder if you hadn't been forced to take that detour. Interesting. That wouldn't be the same door that was found wedged closed with a piece of sculpture, now would it?"

"Yes, Ms. Biko. I believe it was."

"Hm. Another funny coincidence that. Who do you suppose put it there?"

Oh, I had a pretty good idea who put it there. Calerant or one of his men. To make sure that we didn't arrive before the murder took place. The whole evening had been as carefully choreographed as a Broadway Musical. I just couldn't figure out how he'd known that we were coming, and that we would need to use that particular door. The security cameras weren't working in that hallway. Like about 80% of the other  cameras in the building, they had been shut down before we arrived.

"I...I have no idea." I said.

She stared at me for another moment or two.

"Well," she said, "it's probably not important. What matters is that we have a solid case, and this whole messy business can go to trial. The public can rest easy." She paused again, looking me straight in the eye. "By the way, there isn't any doubt, any doubt at all, that Stonewall was the one behind all of the phony occult crimes, is there?"

"None whatsoever." I said. "The shoes that Stonewall was wearing when we brought him into custody have a distinct cut in the right sole. It matches footprints found at the cemetery and outside Raven Straylight's house exactly. Furthermore, the depth of the prints and the compression of the soil are consistent with his weight. Fibers from his shirt and jacket were found at three of the crime scenes, and a hair from Raven Straylight was found lodged under the collar of his shirt. Also there were small droplets of blood that had lodged in his shoe laces. Some have been DNA matched to Commander Davison, while others are a match for the rooster that was sacrificed in the graveyard. And the knife that he used to attack me and murder Calerant is made of an unusual copper alloy, that matches particles taken from cuts in the mutilated corpse at the graveyard, the rooster, and Raven Straylight."

"Hm. That sounds pretty definitive."

"Yes, Ma'am."

"Still, it is a pity we don't have any actual witnesses."

"Yes," I agreed.

"Any chances of finding his accomplices? Getting them to testify against him?"

"Unfortunately, we weren't able to capture all of his accomplices when we surrounded the museum," I explained. "We caught several members of his personal guard, but an unknown number of persons eluded us and escaped through a tunnel in the basement that linked up with the storm sewers. Apparently, they had brought a sonic sledgehammer with them. It's a device that breaks up concrete using..."

"Yes, I am familiar with the tool. Go on."

"Anyway, the ones we've captured either don't know anything about the other crimes, or won't talk. And there's no forensic evidence directly linking any of them to the earlier scenes."

"So it's possible that some of the guilty parties are still at large?"

"Yes."

"And your chances of finding them?"

"Well, we have identified one of them as Jack Banders. He has a rap sheet as hired muscle, and was probably working freelance for Stonewall. We might get lucky and pick him up at a later date. We also have a partial index finger print on another perp, but we haven't been able to identify it yet. I'm afraid we don't have many other leads, so I'd have to say that our chances of finding the remaining accomplices aren't good."

"Hm." Biko seemed to meditate on that for a minute. "Well, we have the ringleader, and I suppose that's what matters."

"I suppose."

She drummed her perfectly manicured fingers on the desk for a moment.

"I must commend you on your work Lieutenant. I can't think of a case where I've had such overwhelming physical evidence to work with. I'm afraid it won't be much of a challenge to prosecute. It is such a neat little package."

"Yes," I said, "yes it is."

Then we stopped talking, and just sat there, sizing each other up, trying to decide how much the other one really knew. We'd both read the reports. We both knew that this had all been much too easy. And we're both wondering about some of those weird little coincidences. And I could tell, she was dying to know what really happened.

I wish I did, too. In my gut, I know that Calerant set this all up somehow. And I would give my right eye for five minutes alone with him, to find out how the Hell he pulled it off, and just what was going on in his head. I mean, I understand the revenge thing. But Calerant wasn't just playing with Stonewall, he was playing with all of us. There was a larger game, that I haven't quite figured out.

Calerant went out of his way to create the panic. Then he went out of his way to destroy it. After Stonewall was arrested on television and the word got out that he had faked the whole Satanic menace, the riots died down and everyone went home. And now everybody is kind of embarrassed by how easily they were all deceived, and how easily things got out of control. Now the newsites are all busy writing touching little editorials about how much we all learned from the experience. The Mayor's called a town meeting to try and get the subcultures talking to each other. And there are even a few interesting speeches coming out from some of the religious leaders, ideas like "let's try to convert people by example rather than firepower". I don't know, maybe it's the start of something. But let's see if they still remember it all when the next news cycle rolls around.

Anyway, like I said, things are quiet again, and it's all because Stonewall has been caught, all because the case against him is so pat, all because nobody has any doubts that he was the one behind all of it, and there is nothing more to it. I'm sure as Hell not going to open up that can of worms again. And I'm getting the impression that Biko, sitting across her desk from me, doesn't want to, either. And what would be the point anyway? I mean, even if we could prove what really happened? Calerant would still be dead, and Stonewall would still be going away for life in prison. Just with a slightly shorter set of names under his list of murder convictions.

"By the way," I ask, "are you going to do anything about the old Alicia St. Cloud murder?"

"I'd been thinking about that," Biko says. "There really isn't a point in going after Stonewall for it. His on-air confession could be subject to interpretation, and he's had fifteen years to cover his tracks. It would be a very hard case to win. And it's not like he's going to be getting out of jail anytime in this millennium. I will try to have Calerant's conviction overturned, though, as a public gesture."

"I think that would have meant a lot to him," I say.

"Yes. By the way, I was wondering..." Biko starts to ask something, then pauses, and thinks better of it.

"Is there anything else?" I finally ask.

"No," District Attorney Biko says. "That's all I really needed to know."

She stands up and shakes my hand, and then I leave. To drive home, and finally get some sleep. Still, I can't help thinking about the case as I cross town. And I wonder if I'll ever know what really happened, and if it would matter if I did.

As far as the world knows, Calerant died a hero, saving the life of a child, and cleared of the accusation that he killed his wife. And Stonewall, he'll go down in history as a monster. And I'm content to leave it at that. Because the real story is probably pretty damn messy, anyway.

I'll let the philosophers debate truth, and I'll settle for order. Keep people from killing each other today, and we'll let tomorrow sort itself out.

## Afterword:  Benji
## Friday, September 4, 9 PM

Dad walked ahead of us, keeping his eyes forward.  I think he was trying to give Summer and I a little privacy.  Not much, but a little. I guess he figured he owed us, given the whole couch incident after dinner.  (We'd all gone in to the family room to watch TV, and Mom had deliberately taken the middle of the sofa, to make sure that Summer and I had to sit to either side of her.)

We got to the car, and Dad climbed in.  I got Summer's door for her, and then jogged around to hop in the back seat from the other side.  Resting on the seat between us, someone had left a Bible and a pamphlet called "True Love Waits." Subtle, Mom.  Real subtle. Summer reached across and took my hand, letting it rest on the Bible.

The car still smelled all warm and bakey, from the peach muffins that Summer had brought with her to dinner at my house.  She leaned in close to me and whispered.  "Your dad seems to like me."

"Yeah, well you scored big points with the peach muffins.  Do I even want to guess how you knew about my dad's secret weakness?"

She looked at me coyly.

"Why Benjamin, I don't know what you're referring to."

She glanced up, and caught my dad looking at us in the rear-view mirror.  He looked away quickly.

I was pretty sure that Summer had used some sort of spell to find out about my dad's passion for peach muffins.  I was tempted to ask if she'd also put some of those "peace and tranquility" herbs into the batter, but I figured I'd better keep plausible deniability on that score.

I was about to ask her how she thought the whole thing went, but just then my dad cleared his throat, his tactful way of indicating that Summer and I were leaning too close together.  We sat back in our seats, but continued exchanging looks.  I still could not believe that my parents had invited her over for dinner.  Maybe it was the fact that Summer's mom had saved my life—on national television, no less.  Or maybe it was just their sneaky way of trying to stay in control of the situation.  After they heard the whole story  about our week on the run, they must have realized that I would find some way to see her no matter what they did.  Heck, if the two of us can outwit trained mercenaries, how tough can it be to slip away from my parents for a few hours?  So they might as well let us get together somewhere that they can chaperone.

Or maybe my parents were just reacting to the new order of things. Everything has been really strange in the weeks since that Friday the 13th. Like the world had been shaken up, and settled down into a new pattern. The video that came out on the news that morning had hit everyone pretty hard. Stonewall confessing to the murder of my birth mother, then trying to kill me, then stabbing Calerant to death, and finally being wrestled to the ground by a witch. And as if that wasn't enough, a few hours later the DA announced that the Senator was also the one behind all those satanic murders and vandalism and what not. He'd faked the whole thing. People have been trying to get their minds around all that.

And they've been acting differently. It's hard to say exactly how, but you can't help but notice it. Like a couple days ago, in civics class, Mrs. Bradley gave us a whole lecture on how to lead by example and win converts among the infidels. Yeah, really. She was actually encouraging us to go out and *make friends* with unbelievers, as a way of bringing them to Jesus. Go figure. And I don't think that we're the only kids being told to do things like that. Last week, at Lost World, there were a couple of Mormon kids who came up and asked us to play SkyLord with them—and this with Tim wearing a dangly crucifix earing, and Scott in his Last Supper t-shirt (the Calerant one, remember?) and all. Like I said, everything had changed.

Me included, I guess, though I'm still sure exactly how. I know a lot more about what really happened than most folks, and I suppose I could put a monkey wrench in the official version of events if I wanted to. I've had a lot to think about these last few weeks. I've started writing some of my thoughts down, as a way of figuring things out. I've got pages and pages of notes and ideas. Maybe I'll use them for another comic book someday. But it will be a whole lot different than Zero.

I still don't know what to make of Calerant. I'm not sure how much of everything he had planned out, and I don't know how to judge the things he did. But I have decided to honor his last request, and not tell anyone that he kidnapped me. In a weird sort of way, him taking me as a hostage probably saved my life. And it's not like I owe Stonewall any big favors. Although I will say this for the bastard: he's made me appreciate Mom and Dad. Maybe they're adoptive, maybe they're uptight, but at least they aren't knife wielding maniacs. I've promised myself that I'm going to cut them more slack in the future.

Anyway, I told the police that I couldn't remember anything about my kidnapping. They aren't real happy with my sudden attack of forgetfulness, but there's not a lot  they can do about it.

I've stuck with the story, and they've pretty much given up asking me questions about it.

Now, if only the press would give up so easily. Ever since the 13th, they've been all over me: trying to get interviews, wanting to take my picture, all that. They camped out on our front lawn, followed me to school, bugged my house, and even tapped my phone a few times. (Tim found out about that, and started scrambling my calls.) But it's been three weeks now, and they finally seem to be losing interest. Still, the whole thing has taught me a lesson: this being famous thing isn't nearly as much fun as it's supposed to be. I've decided that when I grow up and become a writer, I'm going to do it the same way I do the comic book—anonymously. Let the press hound somebody else.

Summer gave my hand a squeeze and smiled at me. One of these days, we would have to sit down and talk about everything that had happened, try and make sense of it all out. But that would have to wait for a day when I wasn't still looking over my shoulder expecting to see a reporter with a rifle mike.

Dad pulled the car up outside Summer's house. We got out, and I walked her to the gate.

"Well," she said, "it has been an interesting evening."

"Yeah," I agreed. "You want to try it again next Friday?"

"Oh sure. I've faced down scarier things than your parents."

"Great," I said. I decided not to mention that my Mom was taking a course at church on how to lead Pagans to Jesus.

"Oh...and there's one more thing," I said. "I wanted to give you this."

I handed her the piece of paper.

"What is it?"

"Um...a poem actually." I said, feeling suddenly stupid. "I was thinking about you, and some of the stuff that crazy Indian lady said to us in the park, and some of the things that we went through, and...well, you've made me realize some things about myself."

Summer looked at me funny. "Wow. Poetic too. That's another bonus point, Ben."

Then she kissed me. Then I kissed her. Then we kissed.

Dad can give me grief over it later.

# KEITH HARTMAN BIO

Keith Hartman grew up in Huntsville, Alabama, which in addition to being "Rocket City USA" also has the distinction of being one of the few cities in America ever captured by a Russian general. (Or so the story goes, a lot of weird things happened during the Civil War.) He graduated from Princeton University, then went on to study at the London School of Economics, then started a PH in Finance at Duke University. Sometime around his third year of the program, he realized that he really didn't want to spend the rest of his life teaching MBA's how to screw each other, and ran away to become a writer.

His first book was *Congregations in Conflict*, an examination of nine different churches and how they dealt with the issue of homosexuality, sometimes in surprising ways—like the Southern Baptist Church which voted to marry two gay men, the whole order of celibate monks who came out of the closet, and the Black Catholic church which expelled its gay organization in order to be more "inclusive".

Keith currently lives in Atlanta with his cat, Urvashi, named after a Hindu Goddess known principally for lounging around and letting the world admire her beauty. His hobbies include RPG's, juggling, acting, and falling down in interesting ways.